Moonglimmer

Michael Kott

Moonglimmer

For my Friends worldwide.

If you know me and you are reading this, you are one of them.

Moonglimmer and Ceellia

CHAPTER 1

St Michaels, Maryland

"But this is what spies wear." Moonglimmer looked to Ceellia, who was perched next to her on the top of the passenger-side front seat. "Tell her, Ceel. What was the name of that last show we watched?"

"Holy Flammerian, how many times are we going to have this conversation?" Sheila Wells said. "You two are so exasperating. We need to be at the airport by the time his plane lands, and you know how traffic is going up Maryland's Eastern Shore this time of day. Especially crossing the bridge." Sheila glanced at the clock on the old Corvair's dashboard. "We'll barely make it now."

The two Distans remained quiet.

"Okay," she said in an annoyed voice. "We don't have time for this. I give on the clothes, but you're not taking part in the airport surveillance."

"That's bullcrap," Moonglimmer pointed out. "Why do you continually question our choices? You know we Distans are fully capable of dressing ourselves. We're sixteen years old!" Moonglimmer shook out her head of fiery red hair as she stared at Sheila.

"Sixteen and still incapable of following orders. I told you what clothes to wear. Why do you two have to question everything?" Sheila said through gritted teeth.

"Clothes, schmoes," Ceellia said. "We're just eight inches tall. Who's gonna notice the clothes we wear? If they see us at all, they'll be flabbergasted by our size. Besides, I thought it was our mission to intercept him at the airport."

"Have your bit of rule bending, but there's no mission for you two at the airport. Floressa will take your place. She knows what the correct attire is for a mission like this."

"Can't we at least tag along then, and see what she does?" Ceellia whined, brushing a yellow curl of hair from her forehead.

"I still don't see what's wrong with jean shorts and a tank top," Moonglimmer wailed. You are so mean, Sheila."

"Sorry, Ceellia. I can't hide three of you, that's why it was either you on your first mission or Floressa, who is experienced in this. She and I will handle the airport . . . *meeting*," Sheila replied. "You two will wait in the car. That's final, no wiggle room. Understand? And you, Glim—to answer your question, I've told you a million times, no shorts or tanks on missions. If they see you wearing jeans and a top that covers your fur, they'll think you move because you're animatronic Barbies. Barbies don't have fur on their arms and legs. Explanation enough?"

"My mom gets to have all the fun," Moonglimmer muttered, looking sullenly at her mother, who was seated on Sheila's shoulder.

"I told you two to follow the rules if you want to get your chance," Floressa said to Moonglimmer with a stern look.

Ceellia, seven inches tall with bright yellow eyes and a slender body covered, except for strategic places, with a thin coat of light yellow fur, put on her pouty look and flew over to the dash. Her long, yellow hair was a contrast to Moonglimmer's red hair, fur and eyes, but otherwise they looked very similar.

"But I did my hair special," Ceellia moped. "And now I learn he won't see us at the airport?"

"You two are so exasperating," Sheila replied. "You must learn to follow instructions. The whole idea of the mission was he wouldn't see anybody. He won't see Floressa, either," Sheila said. "She'll be undercover like we discussed, plus she listened to the dress code at our meeting last night. You two always do your own thing. However, I'll let you follow him after he leaves the airport. But you can't be seen. He doesn't know Distans exist, so let me handle introductions at the right time. Hopefully, I'll get him over to the house later tonight. Maybe then, oksey dokesy?"

With a defeated look, Glimmer nodded.

"I'm cold," Ceellia moaned.

"You think about that. Was shorts a good choice?" Sheila said.

As Sheila put the car in gear and drove on, Glimmer and Ceellia stuck their tongues out at the back of her head.

Baltimore-Washington Airport, Baltimore, Maryland

Better get it over with, Jake Foley thought, as he headed for the airport exit and reached inside a pocket for his phone. As he slowed and looked for a more private place to make the call, he was bumped from behind.

"Oh, I'm terribly sorry. You kind of stopped short," said Sheila's soft female voice. "Airports are busy places."

He turned around as a very attractive young woman pushed reddish brown hair from her green eyes. She was small, maybe five feet tall, he reasoned.

"My fault, ma'am," he chuckled. "I didn't know someone was that close behind. Guess I need eyes in back of my head."

"Wouldn't that be nice?" Sheila smiled. "And, for the record, my name is Sheila, not ma'am, and I'm four foot ten and a half." With that, she briskly walked away.

Sheila? What a coincidence. That's the name of the girl Dad wanted me to look up in St Michaels.

And how did she know what he was thinking?

* * *

As Sheila strode toward the airport exits without looking back, two tiny eyes, hidden in the back of her thick hair, watched Jake.

"Did you tweak him, Floressa?" Sheila thought the words.

"Yes. Instead of Laura, he'll call Dan. You remember that friend of his from school?" The words, in answer to her question, formed in Sheila's mind.

"That Romeo? I certainly do," she mentally replied as she pushed through a door to the short-term parking area.

* * *

After watching Sheila until she was out of sight, Jake found a comfortable spot at an unused departure gate. It was fairly deserted when he sat down and pulled up Dan's number. He had originally intended to call Laura, but Dan had popped into his head. Who better to get advice from? After all, Jake had shared the better times of his life with Dan.

And, coincidentally, the worst.

Hopefully, after he saw Dan he could try to patch things up with Laura and then skedaddle back home. If there was time, and that was a big if, he'd make a little detour to St Michaels and satisfy Mack's request that he look up that Sheila girl. Or maybe he'd just tell Mack a little white one, say that she didn't answer his call.

He wasn't really sure what had possessed him to come back here. Mack thought it was his powers of persuasion, but after initially rejecting his Dad's plea, Jake had felt compelled to return for other reasons. Reasons he did not understand himself. Now, he was about to do what he swore he would never do—go back into his past.

It was with mixed emotions that Jake called Dan. As much as he looked forward to seeing him again, just the thought of being back in this long departed area conjured up visions of his stupidity, and he knew it would force him to relive memories he had firmly relegated to bygone times. Unfortunately, leaving Annapolis completely behind ten years ago had forced him to leave Dan, Brian and–

"Security, Northrop Grumman," a young female voice announced over the phone. "Mr. Burch's office. This is Maggie, can I help you?"

"Is Dan in?" Jake asked.

"Who should I say is calling, sir?"

He hesitated. Was this the right thing to do? Here was his chance to back out. If Dan asked, Jake just didn't know how to tell him why, after ten years, he was back.

"Sir? Are you there?"

"Sorry, uh, Maggie. Please tell him it's Jake." The opportunity to talk to his long lost friend was too much to pass up. It was partly why he had given into his dad and agreed to come here in the first place.

After a very short pause, he heard, "Jake! Is that really you? Jake Foley?"

"Hi, Dan. Yeah, it's the pariah."

"You're no damn pariah, Jake. How have you been, buddy? Where are you?"

"Times have been better, Dan. I'm at BWI." How easily he felt swept back up into their lives of a dozen years ago. It was as if time had stood still.

"BWI? You're here? In Baltimore? Did you get on the wrong plane?"

Jake wished he knew what had possessed him. Why was he here? His reasoning now seemed a bit fuzzy to him. "No, a friend of Mack's passed away. I'm supposed to head down to St Michaels to pay respects on his behalf." Jake hated to start out with a little fib. The funeral had

5

already taken place. It had taken his dad a week to talk him into coming and expressing condolences.

Jake immediately felt maybe the call had been a mistake. "Maybe I shouldn't be bothering you."

"Bothering me? Are you freakin' nuts? Do you know how long I've waited to hear you've come back? Screw the phone, though. I want you to meet me. Here in Annapolis. How about our old hangout? The Dragon Pub on West Street."

Jake's mind screamed, *No, don't do it!* But his voice said, "When?"

"You'll come? Great. How about six p.m.?"

Jake looked to his watch that still showed Chicago time. He had three hours. "Okay."

"One more thing, Jake. You know Brian is in charge of admissions at the boat school right now. Should I invite him too? Can you handle both of us?"

Jake hesitated. His original thought was to involve just Dan. The three had been roommates, best friends, until they had parted ways when they graduated almost twenty years ago. Years later, when they came back together, things had changed, but they were still the best of buds. Then . . .

"Okay, sure, why not? I'll meet you both at six."

Jake turned his phone off and immediately thought—*what the hell did you just do?* However, while the die was cast, he began to think maybe he should just not show up. While he wanted to see them badly, Jake had the unwanted feeling that he was headed toward another collision of the multiple threads of his life. St Michaels and Annapolis had always been kept separate by more than just the Chesapeake Bay.

What possessed you to come back here, anyway? he wondered.

In the end, he suspended the mental war of choices, got up, collected his carry-on bag and headed for the car rental.

* * *

Jake had always loved the location of BWI, which was south of Baltimore. He took the airport exit road to I-97 and cruised south toward Annapolis. As he drove, he became conscious of a small, white Chevrolet Corvair that had gotten on his six when he left the airport. It seemed to follow him, but Jake finally decided they were just on the same course. Any intrigue had to be his imagination. Who would be following him? The car never got close enough for him to see the driver. He only noticed the old 1960s rear-engine car because it was a classic and a personal favorite. He had always wished he was back in the late 1950s or early 1960s, when all the cool cars prevailed.

In no time at all, he found himself on Highway 50 headed east. Memories of this drive swirled around inside him, as he had probably driven this beautiful stretch of highway hundreds of times. After exiting on Highway 70, Rowe Boulevard, he drove down to the dock area of downtown Annapolis. As usual, the parking was horrendous, but perseverance paid off.

He walked over to Pip's, an old favorite from the past, and picked up a sandwich. He'd had nothing to eat on the plane but crackers and peanuts. After finishing most of the sandwich, he walked over to the boat docks and tossed the remaining bread to the ducks that swam among the anchored boats. As he waited to cross Randall Street, he looked up the street and could almost make out the main gate of the Naval Academy. His old school.

He then saw the white Corvair make a right turn from King George Street, in front of the main gate, onto Randall. Seconds later, it drove past him. Jake was sure it was the same car that seemed to tail him from the BWI airport. However, he quickly dismissed it as coincidence because, seeing a head of curly reddish-brown hair, it was plain the driver was a young woman. Why would she be following him?

Wait. Had he seen her somewhere before?

Inside the White Corvair

"Floressa, did he see me?" Sheila frantically checked the Corvair's rearview mirror as she sent out the mental question.

"Yes, but I whirled the remembrance of the airport incident in his head with his past. He now just thinks you looked familiar. I pushed his mind toward recollection of old memories of when he lived here and tweaked that historical side of him that I remembered. That should occupy him for a while. I didn't think you wanted me to really mess with his memory," Floressa mentally replied.

Jake on the Streets of Annapolis

Distracted by the sight of the classic white car, Jake stumbled on the edge of a cobblestone. Thoughts of the girl in the white car were suddenly replaced by the remembrance of the construction back in the mid-nineties, when they redid the downtown area streets to mimic the old colonial days. The change to cobblestones had caused a headache, because they'd decided to do it right at Naval Academy graduation time. It was hard enough already to park anywhere around Annapolis, let alone with the downtown in disarray. Jake had been a company officer at the boat school back then, advisor to about one hundred and twenty midshipmen, and he'd heard no end to the litany of complaints from visitors and family members who struggled to cope with the town's ill-conceived timing.

Now, why had he thought of that?

He glanced to his right, at what they called Market Place, and specifically at Middleton Tavern, a fixture since 1750. As it had been to George Washington, Thomas Jefferson, Benjamin Franklin and members of the Continental Congress, it was a familiar hangout from Jake's days here, both as a Naval Academy midshipman and later as a company officer. World history, especially the American Revolution, had interested Jake since his days here in Annapolis. As he looked around, he mentally kicked himself. Ten years, he thought, was too long to be away from this place he loved, the cradle of the American Revolution. He recalled that after the Treaty of Paris, which ended the war, was ratified down the street at the State House in 1784, the colonists celebrated the war's end right there at Middleton Tavern.

Unseen by Jake, off to his left, the white Corvair exited the nearby traffic circle and headed out of sight.

Reluctantly, Jake turned the corner on Main Street, walked past another hangout, Buddy's Crabs and Ribs, and saw an older gentleman a short distance ahead. His white hair stuck out from under a baseball cap, reminding Jake that George Washington had walked this same path up to the Maryland State House when, after having led the fight for freedom from England, he resigned his commission. Everyone, especially the King of England, thought General Washington would set himself up as ruler of the colonies but, Jake recalled, all George wanted to do was go back to being a farmer.

Why was all this historical trivia suddenly clogging his head?

In between Middleton Tavern and Buddy's, Jake walked past small coffee and specialty food shops, interspaced with a mix of fashion boutiques and touristy gift shops. As his fixation on history faded away, he smiled. Having had a plethora of girlfriends in his six-plus years here, at one time or another he'd probably been in all of these places. It was like coming home.

He checked his watch and saw it was getting toward time to meet Dan and Brian.

As he traversed the Circle and headed up Main Street, he failed to notice the small white Corvair pass him once again, this time on the opposite side of the street.

Inside the White Corvair

After once again negotiating the circle by the dock, Sheila drove back down Main Street, passing Jake once again as he stared in a store window.

"Oh, he's so cute!" Moonglimmer said as she flitted away from the side window of the car. Sheila's quick turn caused the ends of Glim's long red hair to swish across Sheila's nose.

"Glim!" Sheila mock-swatted at the small shock of crimson hair as she looked over from behind the steering wheel. "You're sixteen, and he's like twenty years older than that. Besides, he's six feet tall and you're six inches. And a Distan."

"So? I'm not gonna mate with him! I'm just gonna spy on him like you asked. And I'm seven inches tall, not six. It just helps that he's cute. Right, Ceel?"

"Actually," Ceellia said from her position perched on the rear of the car's back seat, "I'd say he's dreamy."

"Don't you think so, Mother?" Glimmer turned to Floressa, who shook out long, aqua colored hair. "Wouldn't he be perfect for our guardian here?"

Floressa buzzed in close to Sheila, alighting on her shoulder. "You know that's impossible here on Earth," Floressa replied. "And of course I think he's cute. Always did, even when I was your age. But what have I constantly told you about bothering Sheila while she's driving?"

Ceellia's soft yellow wings unfolded and she flew over by Sheila, where Moonglimmer joined her, hovering. "I can't believe you have such a gorgeous brother, Sheila, and we've never met him." Ceellia's long yellow hair draped between her fast-beating wings.

"Come on, both of you young ones," Sheila said as she followed Church Circle and exited onto West Street, then pulled over and parked. "You know the story. I recall we shared a crib when we were newborns, but he doesn't know I'm his twin sister. He doesn't accept

Flammeria, our home world. He prefers Earth. That's why he was in their Navy. I hope he didn't notice us following him."

"Well, wasn't he born here?" Ceellia asked. "Doesn't that make him an Earthman?"

"I was born here too," Sheila replied. "To Flammerian parents, just like Jake. In my book that makes us Flammerian. We just happen to live on Earth."

Sheila lowered the window about five inches. "Okay, down to business. You two know what to do. Don't let anyone see you. I wish you wouldn't have dressed like tourists in those shorts and tank tops. I should have my head examined for not checking you out at the Keep."

"No, I should have inspected them," Floressa said. "I told you, Glim, to dress appropriately."

"We did." Glimmer smiled. "We're dressed to spy."

"It can't be helped," Sheila said. "Floressa and I will wait for you where I showed you, on State Circle. And, I've told you numerous times, you're not going to be spying on him, just facilitating my communications."

Ceellia looked at Glimmer, and the two broke into teenage-like giggles. "Yeah. Right. We're spying!"

CHAPTER 2

Dragon Pub, Annapolis, Maryland

Jake was seated in the Dragon Pub, the place where he had spent so much time with Brian and Dan so many years ago. He took a deep breath and tried to calm his nerves, but having just walked through the familiar streets of Annapolis had stirred up all kinds of recollections. Memories he'd spent the last ten years trying to suppress.

"Hi, Sweetie! I'm Ellie. What'll you have?" asked a perky, petite, blond server who had pushed her way through the crowds to get to his booth.

Jake noticed her short blonde hair and clean-cut look. No tattoos, no jewelry. "Wait a minute," he said. "Are you a mid?"

"Shhh," she said. "I'm a firstie and I need the money."

"Okay, Ellie, your secret's safe with me. Sam Adams draft, Gorgeous. Keep me full." Jake knew it was against the rules for midshipmen to work, but he never supported any rules that had to do with regulating their free time. After all, he had flouted them. Especially in that last year when, as a firstie, he had gained all those privileges, forbidden for the prior three years, but had no money to take advantage of them.

"Yes, sir," she said, and gave him a huge smile and a mock salute. Seconds later, she was back up at the bar. Jake glanced around. The place had changed little in the ten years he'd been absent from the scene. The walls were still as he had remembered them, covered in a strange mixture of paintings of crab fishing in the bay over the years, and Navy photos from around the world sent in by Annapolis grads. And it was just as crowded.

Jake studied first the pictures above his booth, then the worn wood of the table he sat at while he waited. Not only had Dan, Brian and he shared this very table many times but—

"Hello, Jake," a soft female voice whispered at him from off to his left.

He froze at hearing that voice from the past.

Jake had been looking down at the floor, so the first thing he saw was her sandaled feet, toenails painted in a very familiar shade of very dark blue, almost black, polish. It was a shade from his past that he knew well, *Russian Navy*. Jake looked up to a hand, fingernails done in the same shade, extending a draft out to him. Finally, he glanced up to her face as she stood next to him, still holding out the beer.

Framed by gold highlighted, brown hair, the one brown eye and one blue eye of Rachel Anne Paney stared back at him. Her mixed eye coloring was the result of an inherited condition called complete heterochromia. Whatever the reason, Jake thought the result was stunning. Rachel was one of three women that Jake considered the most beautiful women he had ever met, and one that could give him orders.

Rachel and Jake had been a thing back when all hell broke loose and he ended up abandoning the Atlantic Seaboard. He had left her, and her trademark nail polish, behind. Now, ten years later, he saw she had hardly changed at all. Jake didn't know if she was there to shoot him or just scream at him. She did neither. After placing the beer on the table in front of him, she said, "Move over."

He did.

Rachel swept a slim, but curvy, five-foot-five lithe frame in next to him and proceeded to put her hands around his neck.

Here it is, he thought, *she's gonna choke me.* And after what he had done to her, he wasn't about to stop her. But Rachel was not performing according to Jake's script for jilted women. Instead, she pulled his startled face down to hers and planted full pink lips on his, delivering a fervid kiss that he remembered from the past. He was dumbfounded by her passion, but enjoyed every second of it. She finished by lightly brushing her lips across his.

"Whoa, Jake, you still can kiss."

"Hello, Rachel Anne," he managed to get the words out, even while wondering if she would follow this up by sticking a knife into him.

"Surprised to see me?" she murmured sexily.

At that point, reality began to catch up to him. A lot of questions started slugging his brain. *What* is she doing here? *How* did she know I was here? *Why* didn't she slit my throat? Before he could ask a single one, she answered them all.

"Dan told me you were in town, and I got out of him that you were meeting here at six. For me, he said he'd be a little late if I promised not to bring a weapon."

It figured. Dan never could turn down a favor to Rachel. Jake didn't think there was a man alive who could say no to the smile which seldom graced her gorgeous face. "How did—"

"I work for N-G too, but in Ocean Engineering. Everyone thinks all we build is airplanes, but we've got our hands in other pies too."

"Yeah, I can remember when Northrup and Grumman were separate companies."

"They merged in 1994. There were other acquisitions along the way, including Ingalls Shipbuilding. My area of expertise. But let's cut the company politics bullshit. Wondering why I didn't just kill you right here?" She grinned wickedly.

"Yeah, that thought had occurred to me." Still dumbfounded, Jake's head was going up and down like a bobblehead. "You were an innocent party to the events in my life back then. You didn't deserve to be treated like shit by me."

"That was my original thought." She smiled briefly, but then her look changed to one of dead seriousness. "When Dan told me you called, I said to him, 'Tell that S.O.B. I hope he rots in hell.' Then I said, 'No wait. I want to tell him myself. Show him what he'd been missing.' So consider yourself told and shown." When she finished, she slapped him hard across the face, her eyes sparkling in triumph of having told him where to go. "My goodbye present, jerk."

As she got up to leave, he grabbed her wrist. "Wait, Rachel Anne. Please. I deserved that, but there are things I wanted to tell you. It's part of the reason I came back."

"Is that why you called DAN and not me? Look, Foley," she said, as she shook his hand off, but sat back down. "I was in love with you back then, but you up and left without a word. Not a single word." Tears glistened in her eyes. "That was ten damn years ago. YEARS, you asshole. Not a peep from you in ten years. Why should I listen to you now?"

"Because I've spent ten years brooding over my mistake, wondering how I could make it up to you. Coming back here, to Annapolis, was the first step. Talking to you was to be step two, but . . . I was afraid to call you." He stopped when she got up. Jake thought he'd lost.

For a few long moments, those heterochromatic eyes gazed deep into his blue- grays. She then slipped the napkin out from under his beer and dried her eyes. "I promised Dan I wouldn't interfere with your reunion if he let me meet you first," she said with a sniffle. "So I'm gonna split. Here's my address. If you still want to lay some bullshit on me after your get-together, come and see me. Ought to be good for a laugh." She snuffled and struggled with her emotions. "I've got to get outta here before I cry, you son of a bitch."

"When?" he asked.

"Whenever," she said, taking a deep breath and standing. After stuffing the slip of paper in his shirt pocket, she took a long swig of his Sam Adams and was gone.

* * *

Rachel Anne and Jake had met when she was a youngster and he was a first class at the Naval Academy. That is, she was in her second year and he was in his fourth, ready to graduate. Jake played second-string basketball, and she was a cheerleader. The guys, Jake included, privately called Rachel the Ice Princess because she never gave any of the males the time of day. One evening, in a game where Navy was far enough ahead that Jake had gotten a rare chance to play, he chased a loose ball in the hopes of impressing the coach. Only instead, he ended up tumbling over the foul line and knocking Rachel off her feet. Literally. He knocked her shapely legs right out from under her and wound up lying on his back. Rachel had fallen right on top of him, and he found himself looking up at her sitting on his stomach, facing him, with an astonished look on her face. They both stared at each other in shock for what seemed like minutes, but it was more like a few seconds.

Amy Porter, Jake's classmate, former love interest, and the cheerleading captain, broke the silence by kneeling at the side of his head and saying loudly, "Hey, Foley. If you wanted to meet Rachel, you just had to ask me. This is a little extreme, even for you."

Rachel, Jake, and everyone within ten feet broke out in howls. After the game, he left Alumni Hall, only to find a suddenly shy Rachel waiting for him at the door.

"So . . . did you really want to meet me?" she asked.

"Who wouldn't?" he answered, even though he was actually dating another classmate, Alexandra Allen.

That evening they walked along the breakwater and talked, and Jake's ego was satisfied when he finally got her to admit she was kind of attracted to him. At the time, he was flattered, mesmerized by this girl's beautiful eyes and her heart-breaking smile . . . but he stayed loyal to Alex. After that night, Rachel and Jake would simply grin and nod when they saw each other around The Yard.

Five months later, Jake graduated. He ran into Rachel the day he left, and they promised to stay in touch, but that was easier said than done in the Navy. Jake, together with Alex, went up to Newport, Rhode Island, for Surface Warfare Officers School, while Rachel remained at the Yard for her last two years. Seven months later, Alex and Jake broke up when she left to catch her first ship out of Mayport, Florida, while Jake went down to Norfolk, Virginia, for his.

* * *

A slap on the back pulled Jake from the chronology of the past, and he looked up to see Dan.

Jake was one of those guys who didn't maintain a line of friendships back to birth. Some guys had friends from growing up, grade school, high school, old neighbors, and so on. Except for Dan and Brian, Jake had only the immediate friends from his current situation. That was it. In many cases, like the present, it meant he had no one. Except . . . he could always count on his old Academy roommates.

After the two enthusiastically fist-bumped, then guy-hugged, Dan settled in the booth across from Jake. Dan was still in Navy shape. His hair was as thick and inky black as ever, and, like Jake, he still boasted an athletic build.

"Sorry I'm late—" Dan started.

"I know. Rachel preceded you."

"Hey, I'm sorry about that . . ."

He trailed off when he saw Jake's hand signal to stop. "Not a problem, Dan. I was actually glad to see her. I hear you work together."

Dan was visibly relieved to be off the hook. "Well, not together. She's a field consultant. I'm just a security dick." Dan took a swig of the beer that Ellie had silently plopped in front of him, and looked Jake in the eye. "I think every single guy and half the married ones at work have hit on her only to be rebuffed. Of all the girls you dated, and the number was legion, Rachel was simply the best. That girl stuck by you through thick and thin. I lost count of the number of times you dated others on the sly, before going back to her. She didn't deserve what you did to her."

"I know. She could still give Miss America contestants a run for their money," Jake nodded.

"Forget her looks," Dan continued. "Although I know it's difficult for you to see past them. That girl was always nuts about you, Jake. If you know anything about loyalty, you know its face is Rachel. What she ever saw in you is beyond me."

"I know. I was a shit to leave her. She was an innocent victim."

"She knew, you know."

"She knew what?"

"About you. Going out behind her back. I was always amazed that she would forgive you so easily."

"Well, I know neither you nor Brian would tell her, so there was only one way she could have known. Kyra?"

Dan nodded. Kyra had been Rachel's roommate at the boat school and, through Rachel and Jake, met Dan. Even now, after a wild courtship, a legendary Academy wedding and two kids later, Dan and Kyra were just as much in love as the day they met.

"You should know," Dan pointed out. "Kyra told me the moment she met you, she recognized you for who you were, roaming eyes. She tried to convince Rachel to dump your sorry ass for a year. Until finally . . ."

"I won Kyra over with my charm."

"You asshole. Yeah, now she's one of your biggest supporters. Heaven only knows why. What can I say? My gorgeous wife is flawed."

"Look, I really do need to apologize to you for not staying closer in touch."

"No problem, Jake. We made that pact the day you left. Just keep Brian and me in the loop. You've done that. You still with your dad?"

"Yeah. Sometimes I wonder who needs watching more, Mack or me."

"So what brings you here?"

"I told you. Mack asked me to attend the funeral for an old pal of his in St Michaels. Well, that isn't altogether correct. I also really wanted to see Rachel—"

"Rachel, or that April?"

"Rachel. Let's not get into April, okay, Dan?"

Dan nodded. Jake's heart raced at the thought of April. Part of the agreement that he and April had was that they not stay in touch, so he had no idea where she was anyway. Ten years was a long time in the Navy; she could have changed addresses five times or more. Or . . . she could have gotten out. She could be married with five kids. Heck, did she even graduate? If she did, did she make it through flight school?

"Jake Foley!" The loud yell had come from off to his left.

Jake looked up to a Naval Officer in whites. "Brian!"

Brian pushed his way through the crowd and the three of them embraced. Jake felt terrible at that moment for having abandoned his two best friends those ten years ago. They had kept in touch electronically, but he knew it was a cheap substitute for face-to-face time.

Brian threw his cover on the table, and Jake saw the 'scrambled eggs' on the cap's bill. It was a sign he had achieved the rank of full Commander.

"Look at the freakin' ribbons on you," Jake joked. "Did you win some war single-handed?"

"Shit, Jake. Nowadays they give you a medal just for not screwing up."

"Well then, you shouldn't have any!" yelled Dan good-naturedly.

The little blond server was back again when she saw Brian. "What'll you have, Commander Hurst?" she asked.

"Keep the Sam Adams coming, Ellie. In pitchers."

Unseen by Dan or Brian, she brushed a shapely bare leg against Jake, winked at him and left. As she walked slowly away, Jake couldn't help running his fingers down the back of her shapely thigh. That got him a head turn and a big smile. *That's how I always get in trouble,* he thought. People were always saying he looked younger than his actual late thirties, and sometimes even acted like it.

After Jake and Dan kidded Brian about *his* friendliness with *Ellie,* they once again reviewed notes on where they'd been in the past ten years. The last time they were physically together had been when Jake bolted the area. Brian, who had married a year before Jake left, had a son about that time. He had added another son and a daughter since. Dan had married a month before Jake split; he now had a daughter and son. When they looked to Jake, he held up an empty finger.

No ring, no wife, no kids.

CHAPTER 3
DECISIONS

While the three of them drank and celebrated their reunion, Jake felt a little out of place for having abandoned his friends years ago. Dan and Brian were nothing if not forgiving, though, urging him to forget past bad times and celebrate the new good ones. Cajoled by Dan, Jake agreed to a barbecue at Brian's on Saturday. While he went along with their plans, he silently presumed he'd probably be gone by then.

When they finally broke up, Jake stumbled down West Street toward the City Dock and his rental car. Strangely, that little Corvair passed him as he was abreast of Buddy's, then turned right at the Main Street Circle and continued on past the Dock. How was it possible, he thought, that whoever owned that car seemed to be following the same schedule as he was?

When he reached the rental car, he slipped into the back seat and planned to doze for a good thirty minutes. It was a trick he'd learned. A quick, half-hour catnap would sober him up enough to drive safely. Only tonight he found he couldn't sleep. Seeing Rachel had disturbed him more than he realized. Now he began to question his past choices.

Ten years ago, at the time of the big fight with Laura, he had still been an officer in the Navy—the Earth one, not some Interplanetary Star Fleet Academy—so his allegiance was pulled in both directions. Right after he refused to get involved with the mission of the undersea station, operated by Flammeria, his planet of loyalty, he left the area, letting his Earth friends think it was a personal problem that was responsible for the abrupt departure. After all, they had no idea he was not who he seemed. In the end, he had resigned his US Navy commission and left both threads of his two lives behind.

Unfortunately, he also gave up Rachel, the girl of his dreams, a girl every bit as beautiful as his sister, but from Virginia, on Earth. He had finally decided that he couldn't continue that relationship without her knowing his ancestors were from somewhere far, far away.

That would surely be a deal-breaker.

* * *

The idea of going to Rachel's rose in Jake's mind, but he still felt a little unsettled on how to explain his past disappearance. Before he'd left Chicago, he had promised Mack to go to the Wellses, so now he considered going there. Just to say he did. However, while they wouldn't have minded his Annapolis side trip, they might not appreciate his showing up late in the evening and three sheets to the wind.

Vexed by his choices, he pulled his cell phone out, saw it was around 9:30, east coast time, and that he had several text messages. The times indicated they had come while he was in the pub. It had been so noisy in there he had not heard them. They were from Gert, the Wellses' housekeeper, who had repeatedly texted 'When are you coming?'

While he was keying in a reply that he'd wait until morning to drive to St Michaels, the phone buzzed in his hand. Shocked by the coincidence, he looked down to a text message from the Wellses' daughter, Sheila, who he had never met. At least not since they were a year old. That's when Jake's family moved to Illinois.

Sheila's message simply said, "You will come now. We're waiting. Don't you dare delay till morning!"

He felt powerless to resist as he started the car and backed out of his parking space.

St Michaels, Maryland

Very carefully, Jake drove back to 50 East, and in moments was driving across the Severn River Bridge. Following the directions Mack had given him, he soon found himself through Easton and on St Michaels Road. The road meandered a lot, but thanks to his Dad's explicit routing and his cell phone, he made it to the right street despite being bleary-eyed and dog-tired. He finally pulled into the driveway and parked by the house. This was working out perfect, he thought. He'd get this out of the way, stop and see Rachel, and maybe even get to call Laura tomorrow. Then catch a flight back to Chicago.

Stepping out of the car, he was greeted by the sound of crickets chirping and . . . something else. Like the sirens in the Odyssey, several female voices called out to him. However, the voices appeared to be only in his head. The moon was full and bright, and he could see past the flower gardens that dotted the entire property down towards a pool of blackness he knew must be some branch of the Miles River. The gardens were slightly elevated above a perfectly maintained lawn. Small ponds of various sizes were interspersed throughout. His first impression was he was in Monet's gardens. But he was in St Michaels, Maryland, not Giverny, France.

The cerebral voices continued, telling him that he should proceed toward the river and find . . . what? In answer to the mental urgings of unknown temptresses, he turned and went off into the gardens. As he walked, he noted the land ran level for a hundred feet or so, and then was cleverly terraced so it gradually sloped down to what seemed to be a channel of the river. When he got closer to the water, he was able to make out a huge expanse of the dark river on his far left while closer to him, framed by the blackness, a group of large rocks huddled under a grove of yellow-flowering ornamental trees. Tree branches drooped gracefully over a large, still pond almost covered with water lilies. Big enough to fit a small house within its banks, it was probably the biggest pool he had seen so far. Behind it, grass continued to slope gently down toward the channel. Here the channel was so narrow, he thought, that like George Washington, he could probably throw a silver dollar across to the other side. Where the large pool ended, continuing on to the right, was another expansive flower garden backed with a stand of bamboo that towered twenty feet or more.

However, Jake was drawn to what seemed to be the source of those seductive voices—the group of boulders, sheltered under a large tree's mass of yellow flowers. As he drew near, what appeared to be several enormous dragonflies shot away from the area and headed for more distant flower gardens. He had never seen any that big. Could the dragonflies have made those human-like sounds? No, he thought. Besides, the voices seemed to be of actual human women. And—they were not audible, just in his head.

A sudden breeze rustled the branches, and he could now see a girl, sitting on one of the large stones and looking away from him in the direction of the river. She was barefoot and wore a clingy aqua dress, with yellow blossoms from the tree woven into her reddish-brown hair.

He instantly knew it had to be Sheila. Though she appeared no older than eighteen, he knew she had to be his age—thirty-eight. It was her Flammerian genes that, like him, kept her so young.

He stopped behind her when they were maybe a foot apart. Elevated by her perch on the boulder, her head was even with his. To get her attention, Jake cleared his throat.

"I know it's you, Jake." She let out an audible sigh. "My wish has finally been answered. You're here."

After a few quiet seconds, she turned around and he saw her face. Jake was absolutely astounded. As her emerald eyes flicked over him, he took in what appeared to be a slightly smaller version of Laura. Her hair was a different shade of red—reddish-brown instead of auburn—but there was no mistaking her ancestry, like his, was not of Earth.

Abruptly, she wrinkled her nose at him and then said, "It's about time you showed up."

His mind suddenly cleared and he said, "That was you at the airport."

She gave him a wink. "Have fun in Annapolis?" she smirked.

"You seem to be attuned to my thoughts," Jake finally said. "Why were you there? Why the mystery? Are you angry about something?"

She turned away and was silent.

And how could she know anything about Annapolis?

While he waited for an explanation, his mind went back to a visit he'd had from Laura a few months before their big blowup ten years ago. They had met for dinner in Norfolk and she gave him a little figurine.

"I call her Moonglimmer," Laura had told him.

He recalled staring at the figurine, a young girl dressed in a frilly red dress with fiery red hair that cascaded down her back. Perched on a white, daisy-like flower, she had soft pink flowers wreathed in her hair, with matching blooms at her arms, wrists, and ankles. A look of calm graced her face as she happily waved bare feet in the air. On her back were translucent rose-colored wings.

"This is a fairy," he had told her. "I don't understand. Why are you giving me a fairy statue?"

"Actually, it's the likeness of a Distan, Jake."

"What's a Distan?"

"Find the girl with the face of this sculpture," she said. "She'll tell you, because you'll have found the lost woman in your life."

He recalled smiling and shaking his head because, of course, he thought she was talking bullshit.

"I'm serious, Jake. She's out there somewhere; you just have to find her."

He looked again at Sheila, who had suddenly turned around. It was as if a veil that had clouded his mind was suddenly removed. He was looking at and talking to the girl whose face graced the figurine.

He shook the recollection out of his head, momentarily hoping there was some way he could see Laura and make amends for his disgusting behavior the last time he had seen her.

"You're remembering that little statue Laura gave you, aren't you?" Sheila chuckled. She gazed at him with sparkling green eyes. "I guess it was worth posing for after all. You've done well by coming here. The key to unlocking your past is here in this garden, Jake. Not to mention maybe it can provide you with a direction for your future."

"Key to unlocking my past?" he repeated. "I don't understand. I know my past."

"Oh, you do, do you? If that's true, who am I?"

"You're Sheila Wells, daughter of my Dad's late partner. I'm sorry for your loss."

She gave him a slight nod that told him she accepted his condolences, then said, "Do *you* know anything else about me? Think way back, Jake. Hint, hint. We shared that crib."

Why was she playing this game? He recalled she had left messages for him back about the time he had his tiff with Laura. Is that why she had an attitude? "Well, other than yours is the face of that figurine my sister gave me years ago," he said, "My earliest recollection is that you and I did share that crib when we were born."

"Wow. Give the boy a gold star. Let's forget the figurine for now. Just why do you think we shared that crib?"

"Convenience? I don't understand the point of this exercise." Her prolonging this discussion began to irritate him.

"The point is that like any *Earth* male, you need to be hit on the head to see the light. However, I'm going one better. I'm hitting you between the eyes. I'm actually your half-sister, Jake. In fact, we're kind of twins."

"That's not possible." Her words were so unexpected, his voice was tinged with disbelief. "Is it?"

He had thought of Sheila at times, wondering why they were thrown together in that crib, why Laura and his Dad kept mentioning her. But that they were siblings was a scenario he had never considered. Why not?

"Did my dad, or Laura, put you up to this? Who the hell are you?"

"Who the . . . hell . . . am I? I just told you, your sister. For the love of Zeus, can you be that dense?" Then she took a breath and spoke more calmly.

"Look, Jake. You wonder why I seem upset. You think I have an attitude? Well, look at you. You don't appear to take anything seriously. We shared the same mother, so I am a real sister to you. We have different fathers. You should have known all of these things ten years ago. I wanted to tell you then, but you ignored my mental attempt at communication and ran away. This is not your Dad's or Laura's idea, but mine. They'd given up on you. But I thought, as your little sister, I could succeed where they had failed. You were born first, so you're older—and you should be the responsible one."

She paused and perused his face, then took a deep breath and continued. "Laura and I desperately need you. Note it's not Laura or your dad saying it, but me, your till now unknown little sister. So now that you know, what will you do? Run away again? Or, for me, will you stay? Help us? Help Laura, Help . . . Me? Please?" She brushed a reddish curl from her eyes.

Jake shook his head in silence. He had this fleeting image of a crib, and that one of the two babies was him. But that was all. In fact, all of his memories growing up were like still photographs. Why was that? It was something he had just always accepted. He preferred to look ahead.

"Look, I told Dad and I told Laura, I don't do the Save the World thing. I'm just an ordinary guy—"

"Don't say that!" she yelled. "You're not some ordinary guy, you're my brother and I'm not asking you to save the world. I want you to help the Distans. World saving is Laura's job. Will you please help me? I have no one else to turn to."

Jake knew this would suck him into the Flammerian Mission. Why else would Dad have sent him?

"I told you, it was not Laura or your dad's idea to send you. He only did it because I asked. Pleaded actually." For a long moment, Sheila just looked at him, a hopeful, beseeching look on her face.

"Look, Sheila, I'm really not that guy. I—"

"You want to help me, *but* . . . Well, you can stuff that argument."

"Hey," he said, "cool off."

"I will not! I need you. You are not ordinary. You took all that school across the bay threw at you and shrugged it off. You were a decorated Naval officer. I know about the stuff that happened on your ship. How you saved those men. All I'm asking is you now save me, your twin."

"How could you know that? The shipboard incident was never reported in the press . . ." Jake met her gaze, trying to control his annoyance. *First Mom, then Laura, finally Dad . . . and now they've gotten this girl to pretend to be my sister and—*

"I said half-sister!" she said loudly. "Damn, you make me so mad."

"I repeat, cool off..." Jake started, noticing again that she seemed to know what was in his head.

"Go to . . . No, I will not swear. Unlike you, I don't pretend at anything," she continued. "Okay. Now I see it. Laura's wrong. You can't be that guy. Why did I think you'd listen to reason? I think the Flammerian Jake, the guy chosen for this task, was switched at birth with some Earthling." Her tone changed to one of sadness, and she looked down at the still waters of the pond as she shook with silent tears.

Jake was immediately conscious she was the second woman that he had reduced to tears tonight. However, Sheila's stinging words had done their job, and weakened his resolve. Laura had once said some bullshit about them being chosen for their role in all this. That had to be some load of malarkey. "Okay, let's calm down," he said, thus unknowingly sealing his future path. "Say you are my sister. I just don't understand, what is so important that—"

"Please don't say it unless you believe it," she said hopefully as her head came up and she fixed misty eyes on him. "What's so important? Flammeria has a two-fold mission here. Laura hinted at it to you, so don't pretend to not understand. You know that the other planets think our mission is to monitor Earth for another catastrophic flooding event, like the one that devastated civilizations here many years ago."

"Wait," Jake interrupted. "Flooding? I thought prior civilizations were destroyed by a comet breaking up when it got too close to their sun?"

"Which then caused earthquakes and flooding in many areas of Earth. Did you learn only half of history? Then, when the federation appointed Flammeria as Earth's watchdog, our ancestors noticed the planet's atmosphere mix was ideal for the Distans."

"How do I know that Distans even exist? I've never seen one, and you all telling me so doesn't make them real."

"My telling you should be enough." She affixed him with a bright smile. "If your father had told you about a twin sister in St Michaels, would you have believed him?"

31

"Well," he started. "Depending on how Mack said it—"

"Mack?"

"That's my pet name for Dad."

"Okay, I tried reaching out to you. Laura's right. You're an ass."

"Let's calm down," Jake smiled, then frowned. "She said that? Laura called me an ass?"

"She called you a lot more than that, but I'm a lady. However, she also called you a lot of good names too, so I'll give it one more try. Look," Sheila continued, "far more importantly, there's a secret mission to harbor and protect the few remaining Distans at all costs. They are dying out. Human life is everywhere and adaptable, but this world's particular atmosphere mix was ideal for them. This planet is their last hope unless we can find another suitable one. Laura is in charge of the first mission, being Earth's Watchdog. I am in charge of the second, secret one…"

Jake recalled Laura telling him that there were multiple reasons for their presence on Earth.

". . . finding an alternate home for the Distans," Sheila continued. "With the threat of a Zantite exploration party, both missions become vulnerable. I know your father has told you the Zantites harbor a desire to take over this world. So now Flammeria has authorized us a third mission, to convince the Zantites to leave. Peaceably, if possible. Both Laura and I need help with that one. It's beyond our capabilities. However, our past leaders, including your father, foresaw the need for us to one day confront invaders. That's why you were sent to the American Naval Academy, so someone would know how to fight like the Earthlings."

Jake was sure that other planets had far better weapons than Earth. Why must they fight like Earthlings?

"What wasn't expected," Sheila glared at him, "was you would become an Earthling and turn your back on your heritage."

"Hey, I was born on Earth—"

"Of Flammerian parents, you deserter. That makes you and that other traitor Flammerians. Yeah, Laura and I know all about the pact you have with that bitch. Unfortunately, to fight off the Zantites, you two are all we have. However, from what I'm seeing, if we're counting on the two of you, all is lost."

Jake now knew he was dealing with a spitfire. While she obviously believed all she said, he knew there was something else happening here. But, for now, here is where he was supposed to be.

"Okay, but April is not a bitch."

"Point taken—I shouldn't have called her that. But are you committed to help? Laura insists we need you for some third mission. So are you in for the long haul?"

CHAPTER 4
DISTANS

"Uh," Jake started to say, thinking there was no harm in listening. But could he speak for April?

"No hesitation," Sheila interrupted. "Wait. Whatever I tell you, no explanations, sight unseen, you must believe. Agreed?"

For a moment he just stared at her. Something told him she was the real deal. Besides, after ten years, what more could Laura ask of him? "Yes," he said. "I will believe you. Is this about your Distans?"

"Hmm," she mused. "The Distans are only one of our tasks. And what about helping Laura? Discouraging the Zantites?"

Oh, that. Jake looked away, but didn't say no.

"You need to talk to me, Jake, and you need to accept all three. Being wishy-washy doesn't work for Laura, or with me."

"And just when do you spring a fourth mission on me?"

There was a visible intake of breath from Sheila, but her face revealed nothing. "What fourth mission? I don't know anything about any fourth mission. That would be between you and Laura. Tell you what. I'll give you time to decide on the three missions. In the meantime, do you want to meet the Distans?"

"Look, I'd like to start over with you," he found himself saying. "I'll believe whatever you tell me, Sis. And of course I'd like to meet your Distans." For now, he'd play along.

"Whoa, you called me Sis, so we're making progress. Start over, huh?" As she stared at him with a half-smile on her face, it became obvious to Jake that she enjoyed toying with him. Just like Laura.

He also realized that because she looked so much like Laura, she probably was his half-sister, so he had added her to his short list of the most beautiful women in the world. She was now one of four, two of who were his sisters. The third was obviously Rachel, while the other was April, the one he had been involved with when those events years ago caused his ten years of flight.

"Okay, Jake. We can start over. But only if you make me a promise," she said suddenly.

"What?"

"Promise me that once you meet the Distans, you'll not run away again. No, wait on that. I'm a realist, so, if you break that promise and do run away, promise that you'll at least keep their existence a secret. You're a Flammerian, so I know you take an oath very seriously. If you promise, you'll do it. I need your word here."

He looked at her long and hard. Jake had no qualms about keeping the Distans a secret. He'd done secrets all his life. And he had no problem hearing what the Distans had to say. He hadn't flown eight hundred miles to set things straight with his past, and then just say forget it and return.

Finally, he realized she was waiting for an answer. One that he should have given with no hesitation.

"Of course I promise," he said. "What have I got to lose?"

"Just life as you know it," Sheila smiled coyly. "Like me, Distans can be very persuasive." She punctuated that by wiping a finger softly across his cheek. "Okay, do you remember that little figurine Laura gave you?"

"Of course. It looked just like you. You could have modeled for it, except you're not six inches tall, your hair isn't that curly, long or fiery red and you don't have wings," he joked. "You've got the face, body, dress and flowers down right, though."

"You're right. Except for my face, it wasn't actually me. Several females modeled for it, and . . . they really are six—uh, make that seven—inches tall. They have the most gorgeous hair you've ever seen, and do have wings."

"Very funny. I'd like to see that."

"Well then, turn around," a small voice said, coming from right behind him.

He turned, and was face-to-face with a beautiful little creature hovering at eye-level and staring at him. She was about seven inches tall, with a slim female body just like a human girl, except for her height and the rapidly beating little wings that kept her floating in front of him. Like Sheila, she also wore a form-fitting gown that was aqua in color. So was her gorgeous, curly, long hair. Aqua. And her eyes. Aqua.

While the little creature might have been unbelievable to someone who was born on Earth, Jake knew something the normal Earthling did not. The universe was populated by a myriad of lifeforms. He had never seen one so small, though.

"Hi, Jake," she smiled. "My name is Floressa. I'm a Distan."

"It's a pleasure to meet you, Floressa," he mumbled, still astonished by what he was seeing. So this was one of the little creatures he had mistaken for dragonflies. And Laura had not been talking bullshit . . .

"Oh, Jake is so handsome, Sheila. Just like I remem . . . uh . . . too bad for you he's related." She fluttered her eyelashes at him. "Of course, that wouldn't matter, Jake, if you were a Distan. Distans are superior creatures. We have no choice but to practice endogamy. It's not a problem, though, as we have no deleterious alleles."

One thing he had not expected from this little creature was a lecture on genetics. He knew he was staring at her, but he couldn't help it. It wasn't her size, or the wings, or what she said; it was how she said it. So matter of fact, plus . . . she was stunning.

She giggled, a most appealing sound, and looked to Sheila, then back to him. "Have you suddenly lost your vocal cords?"

"Sorry," he said. "I was just astonished by your beauty."

"Oh, he's charming too," she giggled again. "In the past, I've admired you from afar, Jake. Too bad you're not a Distan. We could—"

"Careful, Floressa," Sheila said. "Floran will get jealous."

"Come, Sheila," came a voice from behind Sheila," you know male Distans don't get jealous of full-sized humans." A slightly larger figure popped out on Sheila's right, unmistakably male and dressed in an extra-long, light blue gown. Jake realized he had been behind Sheila all this time.

"Floran is my mate, Jake," Floressa said. "Now don't you get jealous. It just means you and I will have to be careful when we meet . . . clandestinely."

"Floressa, please," Sheila said. "You know how modest Jake is. You'll embarrass him with your outlandish suggestions."

Floran smiled. "I think Jake will soon come to understand that Distan girls' sexual innuendos are merely playful. After all, the rest of us have to listen to them all the time. Come Floressa, now that you two have made your point, I need to get out of this ridiculous gown."

Floressa flew very close to Jake and whispered, a bit loudly, "I know all the secret places to meet in the gardens, Jake. Later I'll fill you in." However, by now he realized she was just teasing.

"I wanted to give Jake a tour," Sheila said. "Have him meet Glim. Is this a good time? Not too late? Maybe I tired her out earlier . . ."

"No, it's a perfect time," Floressa replied. "It's time that lazy daughter of ours realized it's not all fun and games. Just because I told her Jake is very hard to keep up with, she now uses being kept busy for the next few days as a reason to go to sleep early. We'll just go down and make sure she's up and around. Give us a few minutes to tidy up, then meet us in the Keep." With that, they flew off.

"Does their existence shock you?" Sheila asked.

"No, not really," he bluffed. "It's a big universe. Plus, Laura had mentioned Distans to me. But what did she mean by, 'Jake is very hard to keep up with?' And why should she know I'm modest? How do you even know that?"

"Come on, you thought Laura was feeding you bullshit, didn't you? And just a moment ago, you were probably wishing Floressa was five-foot-seven instead of seven inches, weren't you?"

"Uh . . ." Her candidness shocked him.

"I didn't need to read your mind to know that was what *your* reaction would be," she smiled. "You see, Jake, your reputation precedes you. To answer your questions, though, let's just wait till you meet the daughter. All will be made clear in time."

"Is Floressa one of the ones who modeled for the statue?" he asked.

"Yes. The statue was a composite of Floressa's slim body, her daughter's hair, and my face. Her daughter was much younger then, so Floressa substituted. Now, except for physical size, all three of our bodies are close in proportion. I'll take you to the Keep, but first I need for you to take a detour with me through the gardens while I explain a few things. You agree, of course, to forget what I'm about to explain if you decide to abscond after you meet . . . uh . . . our little Moonglimmer, do you not?"

"Moonglimmer?" Jake asked.

"The daughter."

Jake was very in the dark, and it wasn't because of the hour, but he wanted to see where this was all going. "Okay, but let's be honest, though. You know I'm probably staying, but before you start, you brought up another question. What's the Keep?"

"Our Distan colony was moved here from England, where they were initially brought to this planet eons ago. They loved the castles there, so they call their underground city the Keep. Ours here is a copy of the one in England, but built under the center of the gardens, underground." She hopped up. "Now, we can't talk while we walk. I'll tell you when it's safe. So shush."

With that, Sheila put a finger over his lips, grabbed his arm, slid off the rock, and pulled him along through the grass. At the next garden, she walked up to a patch of slightly darker green grass and planted her bare feet on a particular spot. "You can talk now," she said.

"I don't understand the need for silence while we walk," he said.

"The rock where you originally found me is the one I always sit on, because it is not an ordinary one. It contains a scatterer. It's a device that blocks listening devices, which the Zantites might use, by chopping up audible voices and dispersing the sound waves at very low levels in random directions. That's why I get barefoot when I perch up there. My feet contact the surface and engage the device. Neat, huh?"

"So here you're standing on a scatterer now?" he asked.

"Yep," she said, and perched up on her toes to accentuate her bare feet as a colorful Distan flew close to him.

"That's just Roseena," Sheila said. "She's a mite curious."

The little female, dressed in clingy yellow and black, buzzed past his face and dodged down into the flowerbed. She did not come back up.

"You'll have to watch out for Roseena," Sheila said. "She's a huge gossip and a pest. In addition, she's a flirt. Much more so than Floressa, but not near as bad as the young ones."

"The young ones?"

"The teenagers are no different than their full-sized human counterparts, Jake. They love to shock, and they've been waiting for this moment for a long time. They've never interacted with a younger male human. You may be surprised at what they say and do."

CHAPTER 5
EXPLANATIONS

"But we're like night and day in size," Jake said. "How can they—"

"I don't mean they'd want to mate with you! I know you're a skirt chaser, but where is your mind, Jake? You didn't take Floressa's teasing seriously, did you? They just love flirting. In fact, almost all of the Distan females are very sexually frank. They embarrass me sometimes with what they say. Let's just say, you've been warned."

He looked to the ground where her feet contacted the device. "Should I be standing on . . .?"

"When someone activates the scatterer, it covers a range of ten feet. So you need not touch the device also. You must remember to do so if you're alone, because sometimes you may be out here with the Distans, and you must be in contact with a scatterer when you talk to them. There's one at each raised garden, and I will show you where they are, but remember—you must make contact with your bare skin for it to work. I don't know the exact science of this; it has something to do with nerve endings. Anyway, the others are buried throughout the gardens and hidden by a type of grass which allows you to contact them through it. Don't forget, you must be in contact when you talk to the Distans—or even about them. We can't take a chance of some listening device discovering the colony."

"What's the big secret?" he asked. "Who would be listening anyway?"

"All in due time, Jake. I'll point out the other scatterers, then let's go to visit the Keep."

He nodded and followed her. As he trudged along and looked down at the ground, he felt a little used. Just when he had thought all of this baloney was left behind, now he was back and here was a whole new curveball. He was now part of the 'baloney.'

"You okay?" Sheila asked.

He nodded and asked, "How do the Distans come and go between the gardens and the Keep?"

"They have a number of entrances all over the garden," Sheila explained. "In fact, every flowerbed contains at least one, as well as every pond. They flit about the garden during the day, but at night they usually stay in the Keep. We have an entrance tunnel to the Keep hidden in the basement. In case you haven't guessed, they're our gardeners. They love flowers; they're a source of food to them."

"Every pond?"

"Yes. They can swim, and those entrances are very discreet. The profusion of water lilies tends to help hide what's underwater. Much easier to escape from prying eyes. If you check, most of the ponds have a large underwater rock. Beneath it is usually an entrance to a cave which leads to a shaft that they use to return to the Keep."

"They're all so small. How do you fit into their home?" he asked.

"Actually, very easily," Sheila laughed. "There's a large room for interaction between us. You weren't intimating I was big, were you?"

"No," he said, flustered. "Not at all, I—"

"Relax," she said. "I was pulling your chain. Laura's right. You do embarrass easily."

After a hasty tour of the garden scatterer sites, Sheila pulled him through the remainder of the gardens and toward the house.

On their way back, he marveled at the gardens, despite still trying to digest the news of having a half-sister and being once again put in this position of making a decision. When they reached the driveway, the ornate front door swung open and a small, thin woman hurried out.

"Is that you, Mr. Foley? I'm Gertrude."

"Hi, Gertrude," he said. "Please call me Jake."

She nodded. "Pleasure to meet you, Jake. Call me Gert. It's too bad your father couldn't come." Her British accent seemed more pronounced than it had on the phone.

"Well, he's been . . ." Jake stopped talking, because he was unsure if Gert knew of the underlying reasons Mack sent him.

"Gert is aware of all that goes on here," Sheila explained.

"I know it's late, but have you eaten?" Gert stood with hands on hips, a stern look on her face.

"No, I thought—"

Slim fingers gripped his arm in a tight squeeze. "While you're downstairs, I'll get started on something," she insisted. "Coffee?"

"That would be great, Gertrude." Morning or night, coffee was his magic word.

"Gert, please call me Gert." With that, she practically pulled him into the house while Sheila followed with a smirk on her face.

"Please give him a quick tour of this floor, Gert, while I run up and change," Sheila said, and looked at Jake. "I only wore this to give you the full effect of the statue. Likewise did Floressa and her mate. We don't dress like this normally. I'll just throw on something and hurry back." With that, she rounded a corner and was gone.

He had still not gotten over the grounds, so the expansive interior just added to the awe he felt. Gert first pulled him into a huge living area with little furniture. Straight ahead, a hallway seemed to go on forever, but then he realized it was an illusion, for it actually led to a porch with ceiling-to-floor windows. Even from where he stood, he could see the reflection of the back gardens.

Gert then dragged him off to the right, into a small dining area attached to a larger one. From there, he imagined it merged with the kitchen.

"I know you're going to visit the Distans with Sheila," she whispered. "When you come back up here, I'll have something ready. I've also made a fresh pot of coffee."

* * *

Sheila returned in a long, light blue, satin-like robe. He looked at her questioningly, feeling a bit uncomfortable.

"What?" she said as he looked to the side. "I'm going to bed after I give you the tour. Wow, you are shy." She then led him across the kitchen and through a door that opened into the basement. When they got to the lower level, she spoke again.

"The tunnel is behind that phony wall," she said as she pointed.

"Should you be talking?" he asked.

She gestured to the floor. "The entire floor here is a scatterer. But if you're down here alone, remember—bare feet."

With that, she suddenly hopped off the last step and onto the floor, pulling him with her. She lay her head against his chest and put her arms around him. "I can't believe you're finally here," she murmured.

He returned the hug, feeling surprised but not displeased.

"Thank you for finally coming," she said, smiling a little shyly and pulling back.

"Sorry it took so long. Now, are you going to explain where we are?" he replied, embarrassed at his ignorance of all this.

"The tunnel extends out about a hundred and fifty feet into the garden," she began her instructions, tucking a strand of hair behind one ear. "That is, below the garden. It leads to a big room. The very top one foot is honeycombed with entrances from the gardens and ponds. Some, of course, connect before they exit into the Keep. The next top three feet is divided into homes for the Distans. We have one hundred and twenty homes. Room for expansion, you might say. The homes are mostly of the same layout inside. The Distans are not materialistic, fussy, or vain. Well, except for clothes. They are very gregarious, so they spend most of their time in the social area and the gardens."

"Social area?" he asked.

"That's what's actually called the Keep," Sheila said. "It's the large lower room, below their individual homes, where we interact with them. Above that are some expansion homes and the array of tunnels. Come, I'll show you. Be prepared though, you'll be facing what amounts to an inquisition."

"Inquisition?" he questioned, as she stepped forward on bare feet and reached back for his hand.

"Figure of speech." Sheila paused to push curls out of her eyes. "The young females are going to ask you a lot of questions. Many quite personal, if you know what I mean. And… I'm not allowed to interfere, so I can't intercede and save you embarrassment. You'll be on your own."

"How hard can that be?"

"Funny boy. You'll see. Remember, I warned you."

"You know, you talk like any other human I know—" He stopped, noting the look of hurt on her face. "Something I said?"

"You think that because you've lived among other Earth humans all of your life, it gives you the right to think you're more human than me? Damn it, whether you like it or not, I'm your half-sister. Just because our parents come from elsewhere than planet Earth doesn't make them or me less human than those living here. You should know better than to think the human race evolved on this planet."

47

"I know they didn't," he snapped. "Humans develop through evolution. The more advanced colonize planets using spaceships."

"You know, the more advanced also don't like being called human," she reminded him with a stern look.

CHAPTER 6
INTO THE KEEP

Her apparent mood switch told him he had misspoken, so he tried to backpedal. "Look, I didn't mean to slight you, it's just that you look . . . you dress . . . I . . . you talk like a native."

He knew it sounded crazy, but didn't know how to apologize for something he really didn't mean. By the look on her face, he could see any further attempt would probably only make it worse, so he clammed up.

"Nice try for a save, but I do get out and try to fit in here on Earth. But let's get one thing straight," she said, appearing to choose her words carefully. "My only interest in you now, after all these past years of you ignoring me, is getting you to help protect the Distans and foil any plans the Zantites may have. Unfortunately, years ago a mistake was made and—"

"Whoa," he said. "I wasn't ignoring you! I didn't know who you were until—"

"Don't you lie to me!" she said loudly, then took a deep breath. "You remember sharing a crib with me, don't you deny it."

"Well, yeah, but—"

"No buts, Jake. Weren't you curious about who the hell I was? Weren't you at all interested?" She paused, and he knew he should have said he was dying to know. That would have been the truth, but he kept quiet. Because he was also worried about what else he had forgotten—was this why Mack had him come?

"You have a terrible time relating to people," she continued. "Why don't you just face it? How many friends have you made in the ten

49

years since you argued with Laura, *your sister,* then took off?" She spat the 'your sister' out like it was a curse word.

Of course, she was spot-on. He was thirty-eight years old and still single. Laura, Dad, and now this newfound sister were the only family left in his life. He barely had any friends.

"What did you do after you had that argument with Laura?" she asked.

"I left the area."

"Jake, that was ten years ago. That's what I mean. Laura asked you to do something and—"

"I had other personal problems," he said a bit loudly, then quieted down. "I could never tell anyone from Earth who I really was." He took a deep breath. Why was he telling her this? Why didn't he just leave?

"I know, but normal humans, including Flammerians, face their problems. They don't run away from them. What did running away buy you?"

"I just bounced around the country." The words came out in a very low voice.

She bent closer to him and put an arm around his shoulders.

"And?" she asked.

"Three years ago, I attempted to start my life over by settling in New Mexico, far away from all of this. That's when Mom . . ." He looked into her eyes. "Our mom passed away, I left what few casual friends I had in Tucumcari and came back to check on Mack. I've been there, in the south suburbs of Chicago, ever since."

"I was there, at Mom's funeral. In disguise," she admitted. "I so wanted to talk to you then and . . . after all, she was my mom too. I did get to talk to your dad then. Mostly about station business. We were trying to figure a way to bring you into the fold. He thought that years ago the station might have made a mistake."

"What mistake?" he asked.

"You're the mistake, Jake. The station invested its hopes in you and that other one. You know who I mean. In deference to you, I'll try to think better of her. Then you both walked away from us."

"She's only done what I asked her to do. We didn't buy the station grooming us for a military academy without asking us first," Jake replied, "that's all. We should have been given a choice."

"Would it have made a difference?"

"No, we actually liked our professions. However, a choice would have been nice."

"That's your and her problem, and I'm not in the mood right now to explain the reasoning to either of you," she hissed, then removed her arm from his shoulders and pushed him away. "Suffice it to say I agreed with all that was done."

"Yeah, and now I'm left without a world. I don't fit in here, and I wouldn't fit in in Flammeria. Let's just both cool down, then you can lead on," he said.

"Will you stop with the 'cool down'? I am composed. Just because I argue with you doesn't mean I'm angry." She took a deep breath and looked at him in silence for a few seconds. "Well, maybe I'm a little mad." She punched his shoulder.

He couldn't help it; he laughed out loud.

"Are you laughing at me or with me?" she asked.

"With, I hope."

"Okay," she chuckled too. "Just give me a make-up hug and then let's make the grand entrance?"

Glad to be out of her scathing admonishments, he nodded. "Look, I'm sorry that . . ." He stopped talking, put his arms around her and pulled her close. She had the same sweet scent that he recalled from hugging Laura. No other girl had quite the impact on him that his sisters did. There was something different about them.

She hugged him fiercely, trying to make up for many lost years. When they finally parted, she said, "One more thing, however, in way of preparation for what you'll see within the Keep. Distans don't have to constantly flit about, pretending to be dragonflies. They prefer to walk like you and I and keep their wings tucked in. When they talk to you, they'll usually fly up and sit on your shoulder. Pay attention to what I do now, just in case you really stay and help both of your sisters."

He watched as Sheila touched three bricks on the wall of the basement in a particular sequence. The wall in back silently slid open several feet. Beyond it was a slightly narrower, lit tunnel, maybe seven feet high, that angled down and led off in the direction of the garden.

Sheila motioned him into the tunnel and, with bare toes, pushed on what appeared to be a brick at the base. It moved easily and the wall slid back in place. It was quiet as they followed the short length of tunnel and stopped at a door that was obviously the entrance to the Keep.

"Ready?" she asked.

"Let's go for it," he said.

Sheila touched a button on the wall and the doorway slid open. Despite Sheila's mini-education, Jake was ill prepared for the scene. The big room was relatively cool and seemed filled with Distans. He lost count at thirty, and at least twenty-five of them were female. Most were sitting in what looked like a small theater, a TV show playing in the background, but all of them had turned their seats to face the doorway and watch their entrance. A female, dressed in a simple, knee-length pink dress and what appeared to be pink tights, got up and turned the TV off. She flew to the two humans, hovering for several seconds in front of Jake's face, then flitted over and landed on his shoulder. She walked on tiny spiked heels that pinched his skin. He winced a little, which the Distan apparently noticed and quickly sat down.

"Hi, Jake," she began. "I'm Grecenna, the leader of this colony. You are most welcome. It is so nice to have Sheila's twin brother finally among us. All of my sisters are anxious to meet you, so maybe we'll talk sometime in the future." She then looked to a gathered group on one side and said, "He's all yours."

With that at least a dozen little females took to the air and flew around him.

"The teens," Sheila whispered. "Pick one or two to talk to first, Jake. Just make some sort of a sign to them and they'll sit on your shoulder."

"Huh?" was all he could say.

Sheila knew he was embarrassed with the ceremony. "Just pick one, Jake, the ritual is important to them," she said. "Don't be such a coward. It's all in fun."

He took in the dozen or so slim little creatures circling and chuckling around him. Each was prettier than the next. This wasn't so bad, he thought, and decided to get into the spirit of things. One in a fiery red sundress, with very familiar matching hair, kept flitting in close to him.

"The one in red is Floressa's daughter," Sheila whispered. "Recognize the hair?"

Jake caught the little Distan's eye and winked at her, and she landed on his right shoulder. Again he felt the pinpricks of high heels, until she settled herself as close to his ear as she could get.

"Pick Ceellia, too!" she urged him in a low voice, obviously not wanting to upset her other friends by playing favorites. "She's the one with hair the soft shade of yellow."

As the teens continued to circle him, he gradually became aware that they all wore different colored long-sleeved dresses with tights. It seemed no two Distans wore the same color. He glanced back and forth at each fairy-like Distan, and came to realize that the dresses matched the lighter hue of its wearer's skin and complemented her hair. When he looked closer at the one in soft yellow, being careful to not be caught staring, he realized what he thought were tights was actually a thin coat of fur. The gown was not long-sleeved, either—she had fur on her arms too. Skin was only visible on her face, hands, and feet. The remainder of her visible body was covered in a very light coating of soft yellow fur that matched the color of her skin. Out of the corner of his eye, he could make out that the little pixie on his shoulder had very light red feet, but from her ankles on up, he noted a matching shade of red fur. Ditto on her arms. He realized that Grecenna hadn't been wearing tights, but pink fur instead.

"Please pick Ceellia, Mr. Jake?" The pixie on his shoulder had noticed him staring, and now stood to whisper in his ear. When he looked over at her, she batted her red eyelashes at him. The little creature was simply gorgeous. Her long lashes matched her fiery red hair, a mass of curls extending all the way down her back.

When he glanced at Sheila for help, she merely giggled along with Floressa, who had flown up and now sat on her shoulder.

What could he do? He nodded to the teen in soft yellow, who then threw her little arms up in a gesture of triumph and landed on his left shoulder. Ceellia's fur covering highlighted her light yellow skin. Like the one in red, her curly, yellow hair extended all the way down to her waist.

"I'm Moonglimmer," said the one on the right. "Thanks for picking Ceellia. We're best friends and we share everything . . . especially our male conquests."

He had picked the fiery red Moonglimmer not because of what Sheila had said, but because she seemed familiar and, if he were judging a Distan beauty contest, she'd have been the winner.

"Wait a minute. . ." he said after her words had caught up to him. "What male conquests?"

"Come on, Mr. Jake. You had your choice of a dozen or so of the prettiest Distans. You chose me. Conquest!" She winked to Ceellia, who was also holding up her arms in a show of victory.

Jake looked to Sheila, who was still giggling along with Floressa. No help there. "So," he said to Moonglimmer. "I'm just Jake, not Mr. Jake. Can I call you Glim?"

She nodded and assumed a bashful pose, showing him just one eye as her hair swept over the other and she touched a finger to her mouth. "You more than anyone deserve that right, Mr. Jake."

He narrowed his eyes to question that, but Sheila said, "I'll explain that later."

"So, are you a typical Distan teen?" Jake asked Glim.

"Yep," she said. "I'm eighteen and . . . Well, I've been itching to talk to you about your girlfriend."

"My girlfriend?" he said. "I don't have one."

"You don't have one?" She looked wide-eyed at Sheila, who shook her head. "Who did I just—"

"Glim!" Floressa said loudly.

"Uh," Moonglimmer stammered, seemingly confused. "Are you like Sheila? Gay?"

Chapter 7

Moonglimmer and Ceellia

"Moonglimmer!" Floressa yelled. "What did I say about those nasty little assertions? I told you before, Sheila's business is private. She has sacrificed her personal life to care for us, and you know little about Mr. Jake at this time. Apologize to her and Mr. Jake right this minute."

"I'm sorry." Moonglimmer looked to Sheila, her head down. "I thought . . . you said . . ." She then seemed to recover and smiled. "Maybe you and Mr. Jake could get together."

"Jake is my brother, Glim. It's forbidden in human circles to have those kinds of feelings for your sister or brother. At least here on Earth."

"But you told me you loved him," Moonglimmer pointed out.

"Uh . . . like you love your mom and dad," Sheila replied.

"I'm sorry, Mr. Jake, but what happened with your girlfriend?"

"I told you I didn't have one," he replied. "If I did, it would be none of your business, Glim." Wow, he thought, she was a nosy little thing.

"Jake does not have a girlfriend at this time," Sheila further explained.

Moonglimmer still looked perplexed. "Sheila said you've just been bumming around the last ten years, wasting your life. Is that because you lost your girl?"

Jake looked at Sheila with raised eyebrows. "Is my business the only thing you all talk about?"

"Wouldn't you be better off with a woman?" Glim asked innocently. "Like Rachel?"

"How did she . . .?" Jake asked.

"I thought her name was April . . ." Ceellia whispered in the direction of Moonglimmer.

"Sheila isn't the only source of my knowledge," Glim said. "I know about all of your girls and . . . a lot more . . ." She smiled coyly and giggled.

"I know too," Ceellia joined in.

"Glim? Ceellia?" Floressa interrupted. "What did I tell you?"

Moonglimmer stopped speaking and looked from Floressa to Jake to Ceellia. "What?" she asked. "Am I talking too much again?" Ceellia had become quiet.

Floressa crossed her arms and nodded. "Just a wee bit. Mr. Jake doesn't know everything yet. Do you recall Sheila and me prefixing our shared opinions with the words, BETWEEN YOU AND ME?"

Jake gave Sheila a questioning look.

"Later." Sheila mouthed the words. He tried to keep from flinching in pain as the two little pixies seemed to enjoy digging the spikes of their high heels into his shoulders.

Finally, Moonglimmer sat down on his right shoulder just below the ear, while Ceellia fluttered over and grabbed his other earlobe. She then flipped up, using the ear to help propel her upwards. Seconds later she landed on his head, knees first.

"No shoes on his head," Sheila warned.

In answer, two tiny missiles flew just past his eyes, and the pair of Barbie-sized yellow shoes landed on the table. Seconds later, Glim's red shoes joined them.

Glim then flew off his shoulder and momentarily hovered right in front of him. "Sorry. I forgot we shouldn't be wearing the shoes around you, Mr. Jake." She gave him a secretive little smile, like they were co-conspirators, and returned to sitting on his shoulder.

"Do you like my red outfit?" Glim asked. She promptly fluttered around in front of him to make sure he could see all sides of her.

He felt Ceellia's feet leave his head. She had taken off and now hovered next to Glim, posing in her yellow dress. Except for their color difference, they could have been twins.

"You need to settle an argument, Mr. Jake," Glimmer suddenly said. These words were accompanied by the lifting of her dress. "I think I have the nicest . . ."

"What are you two doing?" he asked. "Do Distans practice modesty?"

"Modesty, shmodesty," Glimmer said with a shake of her head.

"Glim, what did I tell you not ten minutes ago?" Floressa asked.

Glimmer looked at her mom and then lowered her eyes. "To take it slow with Mr. Jake because he's probably a prude. But that's the fun of it, Mom." She dropped the hem of her dress and turned to face him. Her little red eyes captured his. "I'm sorry, Mr. Jake. I was only going to show you my legs."

"Uh, we'd better go, Jake," Sheila said.

"Just a minute, Sheila. Did you tell them that?" he asked. "That I was a prude?"

"No," Sheila said. "Not exactly. I didn't say prude."

"I think what you said was he might be offended by our nudity," Ceellia said. "We'd never show him anything, but isn't that what a prude is?"

For the first time since he'd met her, Sheila looked embarrassed.

"No problem," Jake said. "I'm not a prude. I just like to take things slow." As best he could, he glanced from Ceellia to Glim, who were again perched on his shoulders. "It's a pleasure to meet both of you girls," he said to them. "If you were both ten years older and about five feet taller, I'd love to see whatever you wanted to show me under that dress. And my name is Jake, not Mr. Jake."

"Sheila's almost five feet tall, will she do?" Glimmer laughed. She and Ceellia giggled and flew off.

"We need to talk, Sis," he said to Sheila. He gripped one of her small wrists and walked her over to the corner and two chairs. "Sit," he ordered. She did.

"I'm sorry, Jake; it was a poor choice of words. I thought . . ." She stopped when she saw his upraised hand.

"I'm not mad at you. How do they know about Rachel and April? And what else did you tell them about me?"

Her head was downcast.

"Sheila?" he prompted. "Wait. How do you even know about Rachel and me? Not to mention that April and I never did anything together. At least not in public."

How could these little creatures, who hours ago he hadn't even met, know about the women of his past?

"Can I explain all of this to you tomorrow? I need to make a run to the station, but I'll be back later and will tell you all. Besides, I thought you wanted to see Rachel . . . I'm sorry, I did kind of invade your mind earlier, so I knew of those plans, but . . . I . . . I never read any private thoughts of yours. Okay?"

"You know I want to see . . . ?"

"Rachel," she nodded. "That was your plan, wasn't it?"

"Well, yes, I had hoped to have the time to visit her."

"That's fine, do so. Go now. Meet me by the rock tomorrow afternoon? Please, Jake?"

"You'll tell me everything?"

"Everything. Oh, and by the way, it's a lost cause asking them to drop the Mr. Jake. It took years before I got them to stop calling me Miss Sheila. You just can't argue with a Distan. If you have any questions before you leave, you know where to find me."

* * *

After Jake enjoyed a midnight breakfast and his coffee allotment, Gert said she was going to check on Mrs. Wells. Sheila, he noticed, had donned a pair of shorts and a t-shirt and now came to the table.

"I thought you were going to bed," he remarked.

"Sorry to disappoint, but this is what I was wearing under the robe. It's what I wear to bed. Before you go, come with me."

Together, she and Jake walked back down to the river. As he gazed out at the dark water, it dawned on him then that, somehow, he had definitely made a choice. He was staying. At least for a day or so. Hopefully, by then, this would all wrap up and he could return home.

He looked over to where the moon reflected off the still water of a pond, and an odd question occurred to him.

"Is the TV for you or them?" he asked.

"Them. In fact, we'll probably get in an argument when I go down later to sleep and ask them to turn it off. Our little wingers love Earth soap operas and the latest in movies, especially romantic comedies. I bring them DVDs all the time. They can handle them quite nicely. They have seating for a hundred of their size around the screen. It's going constantly, so you'll have to get used to it. They're all little night owls."

She laughed as if in recollection of something very funny. "Sorry. I'm picturing your face when they dug those spike heels into your shoulder. Way to take pain, Jake. In case you wondered about that, watching TV all the time has made the girls much more fashion conscious than their relatives in Europe. They dress extremely well, and they like to wear those high heels. I'm not sure why."

"Moonglimmer said she forgot not to wear them around me. But I've never seen her before."

Sheila squeezed his hand to stop him from talking. "That explanation comes tomorrow."

"What if I don't decide to stay?"

"Then you'll never know," she smiled. "Have I answered all of your other questions?"

For a moment he just looked at her. Had she somehow maneuvered him? But no, except for some feeling that he had been maneuvered here, he still felt in control of himself. "Not quite, just a few more."

"Okay, but as I told you after we visited the Distans, you're free to go to Rachel. Hopefully, now that you're back in Maryland, you'll take the opportunity to mend some fences. In both your Earth life and with family."

"You seem very familiar with my schedule," Jake said suspiciously.

"I sensed all of your plans when you first arrived. Now though, I can guess at one of your questions. You want me to tell you a little about the Distans, right?

"Yes," he nodded.

"They're actually from the planet Distania, which orbits the star Sirius B in the constellation Ursa Major. It's a small planet with an atmosphere mix exactly like Earth's. The Distans lived on the planet in peace, but once they and their abilities were discovered, it became apparent that they would be sought after and enslaved—"

"Whoa. What abilities?"

"Later with that. Just listen. Flammeria might be called the rescue planet, because like they did for Earth when civilizations were destroyed by the comet, a small, secret group traveled to Distania and convinced the Distans to put their trust in them. Knowing Earth's atmosphere suited their very specific needs, it was reasoned that no one would think to look for them on a planet known to be hostile and considered dangerous.

"So a small group of them were secretly brought here to Earth and situated in what is now England. On Earth's calendar, that was around 2000 BC. Wars seemed to constantly take place around Britain, so it was decided to open up a second colony in an area that was sparsely populated at the time. That was in case the first was inadvertently discovered. So, around 750 AD, the Keep was secretly built here in what is now Maryland. After the war they call the American Revolution, the house was added. As you know, the station has been in the Atlantic Ocean off of Virginia since the comet turned things upside down on Earth twelve thousand years ago. Laura said that erratic comet is on a return leg back, and we are thinking of moving the Distans in case there is another event like the last one. At least this colony."

Jake was quiet after this revelation. He thought about how his parents and the countless others who manned the station had given their lives for this planet. Why didn't he feel the same about things?

"This has remained a small colony because we have no control of the land situation here on Earth. A few Distans remain on their home planet, but the major group of them was moved elsewhere about the same time these came here. That location has been kept a closely guarded secret. None of us know where. Or if they even survived."

He nodded again while scanning the gardens, and saw a few Distans winging from flower to flower.

Sheila noticed him watching. "Flying as they do, with their legs together and straight back, they look like large dragonflies from afar. You have to get quite close to notice their human qualities. It helps that many of the flowers picked for the gardens grow up to five feet tall. It gives them added cover."

"Who made that Moonglimmer statue?" he asked.

"Floran. Floressa modeled for your statue, but he used my face and Glim's hair. Floressa thought it wouldn't get your attention unless she was naked, and she actually volunteered to do that, but I talked her out of that and convinced her to wear the gown. It was Laura's idea to call it Moonglimmer because . . . well, she had her reasons."

"They look like the fairies of Earth legends."

"Good catch, Jake. Distans have probably inspired all the fairy legends that abound in England. However, they do not like to be called anything but Distans, or by their given name. And almost no one on Earth knows about them, what they really are. Our parents knew of their existence, and Laura used to play with them when she was a little girl, as did I later, of course.

"But no one else at the station knows, except for the former leader, Mattik. This is important, Jake. You can tell no one of them. No one. They've been in St Michaels, under our protection, for a very long time."

"How many are there?" he asked.

"One hundred and forty-four at the moment, but there are several pregnant females. They are human in all ways, except they have wings and that fur covering. And are only six to eight inches tall, of course.

"Many of their family names are similar, that is their way. Moonglimmer is the exception. For my eighteenth birthday, Floressa's gift to me was to allow me to name her newborn daughter. I really wanted it to be special, and that windy night I was sitting on the rock where you found me. As I stared up into the stars, the wind kept whipping the branches of the tree, causing the moon to appear to glimmer."

Jake nodded. "Moonglimmer. A pretty name."

"I also wished that night for you to come back home. That request took almost twenty years." Sheila wiped at her eyes and he felt like a chump. "Anyway, you'll get the hang of the Distans' methods pretty quickly. I did. Floressa and Floran are not married though; Distans have no such institution, but they normally mate for life."

Jake didn't know what to say. Relationships were always difficult for him. Feeling suddenly uncomfortable and grasping at straws, he asked, "Where do their clothes and shoes come from?"

"Some are secretly made on our home planet and come in on our supply flights. Some are made here. A lot of the doll clothing on Earth fits them, so I'm always on the lookout for that kind of stuff for them. The wingers know how to sew, and I have several Earth ladies who think they're making doll clothes for my many nieces. Anyway, when they walk on your shoulder, I know their little high heels pinch, but please just suck it up and don't complain—about anything for that matter, because they offend easily. The males are shyer and tend to keep to themselves."

He nodded.

"And now, based on that inane question, I assume you're done and we can both do what we have to. Still staying?"

She was so direct, he thought. He still had many unanswered questions about his heritage and the inter-relationship they apparently shared with the Distans. He thought about how he had been manipulated into this situation and . . .

But wait. If there had been some scheme by Laura and Sheila, along with Mack, wouldn't Sheila have acknowledged it? Unlike Laura or Mack, she seemed very open and honest.

Heck, he had taken the time off anyway, and what did he have to go back to?

"Yeah, I'm in your spell," he finally said.

"Good," she smiled. "That's exactly where I want you." With that, she turned around and asked, "Are you coming?"

Together, they walked back to the house.

CHAPTER 8

RACHEL

Jake was a little apprehensive about making the drive back to Annapolis, as he still had gotten no sleep and it was two a.m. when he finally left St Michaels. He hoped that Rachel would not be upset at his coming so late. With all of the revelations from Sheila and his agreement to meet her tomorrow afternoon, he figured it best to try and patch up relations with Rachel when he could, and have his head clear on that matter, at least.

When he found her apartment, he knocked, and then heard the sound of someone moving to the door. When Rachel swung the door open, he was momentarily taken aback. All she had on was a long t-shirt, just barely to her thighs.

She reached out, grabbed his arm and pulled a startled Jake into her apartment.

"What the hell?" she hissed. "Do you realize what time it is?"

"You said whenever and I couldn't wait till tomorrow," he said.

"Oh? But Dan and Brian were still more of an attraction than me?"

"Whoa, whoa," he said. "One question at a time. Dan, Brian, and I were having a reunion. You know how guys are. I would be considered a pussy if I left early. I have no idea what time it is, but I don't recall you saying I should be here before a certain hour. And no, Dan and Brian are not more of an attraction than you. No one is." To simplify things, he had decided not to tell her of his side trip to St Michaels.

Rachel crossed her arms and momentarily stared at him. "You are so full of shit, Jake Foley. It's after three a.m. The bar closes at two. What the hell were you doing for the last hour?"

"I . . . uh . . . napped in my car. I wanted to be sober for you . . ."

"More goddamned bullshit. You haven't changed one bit in the last ten years. Next thing I'll find out is . . . you're . . . you're not married, are you?"

He held out bare fingers and shook his head.

"Girlfriend?" she asked.

"I thought that was you." He could swear she exhaled a sigh of relief. "You're not married, are you?"

"You're pretty presumptuous after ten damn years," she snarled.

Despite her bluster, he knew she had waited. He hoped it was for him.

"And no. I'm not married. If I was I wouldn't be living here alone."

He moved closer, but she pushed him away. "Maybe I should just get a room somewhere and come another time," he offered.

"Don't be an asshole. Stay the night. You can go wherever after breakfast."

He gave her his best humble nod.

"I'll make up the sofa." She disappeared down the hall, then returned with some sheets and a blanket. She quickly made up the sofa, brushing off his offers to help, then sat on the makeshift bed next to him and turned his head so that he was facing her. Conscious she was only wearing a t-shirt and despite his tired condition, he stared over at her and gave her his best hurt-little-boy look.

"That shit is not gonna work on me," she snarled. However, her bi-colored eyes seemed to be inviting him in. A few seconds later, she gripped his face in her hands and surprised him by kissing him hard.

After taking a breath, the t-shirt she wore was on the floor, her lips returned, and she plunged her tongue into his mouth. While continuing to keep her lips pressed to his, she grabbed his hands and put them on her breasts, then alternated trying to get his shirt off and pulling at his pants. She finally gave up both tasks and said, "For God's sake, Jake, get your frickin' clothes off."

He did the best he could, trying not to tumble off the sofa in the process.

Afterward, he lay there exhausted. She had ended up on top of him, with her head buried in his chest, her naked body crushed up against him and her legs wrapped around his. Asleep. He wondered why he had left this treasure behind. Rachel, despite her cool "Ice Princess" demeanor in public, was an absolute tigress in bed. He had missed that.

* * *

Years ago, after their initial meeting at the fateful basketball game and his subsequent graduation, they lost track of one another. She graduated two years after him and went straight to a ship in Norfolk. While she was there, the ship was decommissioned, and the crew, instead of being reassigned, was released from active duty. The Navy was downsizing then, and rather than look for people who wanted to leave, they were arbitrarily letting people go. It didn't matter that someone like Rachel, who had dreamed all of her life of a Navy career and had been a model midshipman at the Academy, wanted to stay in. She was simply let go.

Jake found this all out when he returned to Annapolis for a tour as a Company Officer at the Naval Academy. Each of the thirty companies had an experienced officer assigned as a sort of guidance counselor and advisor.

One sunny day, he was running along the seawall, and there, coming from the opposite direction, was Rachel. She was working as a civilian in the Admissions Office then, while still trying to get back on active duty. They went out on a date and were steady from then until the incidents that caused him to up and leave Annapolis, and life in general, almost a decade ago.

* * *

Now, as she slept, he kissed her everywhere he could reach, hating having abandoned her the last ten years. Jake knew now that his decision to return had been right. His demons were here, in this beautiful place. While he had denied it outwardly, inwardly he had always known that to extinguish them, he needed to return, back to where the Gods of Fate had chosen to crush his life.

Suddenly, Rachel awoke, perked up and moaned softly. "Jake, you son-of-a-bitch, why did you leave me? You rotten bastard." She swiveled her head so that she could stare into his eyes. "No, don't answer that. I'm squashed and uncomfortable on this damn sofa. Come with me."

She grabbed his hand and led him over to her bedroom. "Get in, you asshole, I'm still mad at you."

"Yes, ma'am," he replied softly.

"And don't ma'am me," she sputtered, then shoved him on the bed. Quickly, she curled up with him and once again kissed him passionately.

It was a bit too dark to make out her two different colored eyes, but he wanted to. He so loved and had missed that feature of her.

She unwound her legs from around him and slowly relaxed her body. "I should have gotten a bigger sofa."

He turned into her, but she pushed him back down, then crawled on top of him. He could feel her breasts against his chest. He put his hands on her bare butt, intending to press her closer to him. Instead, she wiggled loose of his grip and sat on his stomach, stretching her legs out in front of her and planting her feet on each side of his head, trapping it between them. Positioned so, she looked down on him and giggled.

"What's so funny?" he asked, running fingertips along the inside of her bare legs.

"This is the position you and I were in when we met. Do you remember the basketball game?" She used her toes to bat at the sides of his head.

"Yeah," he laughed. "But you were wearing clothes then."

"Well, if you want I can put some on." She started to pull her feet back.

He grabbed both of her ankles and, pulling one of her feet to his lips, kissed a *Russian Navy* painted toe. "I see you're still using that same color polish."

She gleefully waved her fingers inches from his face and fanned them so he could see the dark color on them too. "You always loved the color, Jake. It's all I've had of you these last ten years. In fact, you picked it out. Remember?"

"Of course I remember."

* * *

It had been in a small pharmacy up in New England on a weekend trip they took. Rachel had forgotten her shampoo, and while she was choosing some, the colorful racks of nail polish caught his eye. In particular, a shade of midnight blue. He picked it up to read the color. It was called *Russian Navy*.

Rachel had come back and plucked the small bottle right out of his fingers, asking, "Like this shade?"

He had smiled, and she went back and bought it. He had never seen her wear another color since.

Small things like this were swimming back into his memory. Like needles into his brain, they said one thing: He was an idiot to have left her.

* * *

Still astride him, Rachel provocatively dragged her fingernails across his chest. At that moment, he glimpsed something jumping up at the foot of the bed. Turning, in the dim light he found himself looking into the glistening eyes of a cat. Not just any cat. This one was the size of an ocelot, but silver with black spots and huge paws. It quickly padded up to him and put its nose bare inches from his face.

Rachel giggled uncontrollably.

"What the hell kind of cat is this, Rachel? It looks like a goddamn snow leopard." *Ahh, here it is*, he thought. *Her way of getting even. Mauled by her pet wildcat.*

"Close. Her name's Snow," Rachel whispered. "Get a grip, Jake. You should see your face. Snow's bred to look like a snow leopard, but she's really very sweet. She's a California Spangled cat. Harmless, my big, brave hero."

The large feline retreated to Rachel and put its paws up on her bare leg. Rachel scooped her up and planted a kiss on the top of the cat's head.

"Okay," she whispered to the cat. "I think you and I have had enough playtime, Snow. We're scaring the big bad man who . . ." she paused. "Well, at times he can be very sweet. Let's all cuddle up under the covers and get some sleep." Rachel moved from her perch astride him to kneeling beside him. When she reached over to pull the sheets back, the headlights of a car flashed through the window and briefly lit each of her eyes in turn. First her left, blue one, and then her right, brown one. The long-missed sight filled him with remorse. She snuggled her naked body under the sheets and thin blanket, all the while not taking those eyes off Jake.

She'd barely lain down before she asked, "Whatcha thinkin' about?"

"How stupid I was to have left a woman as beautiful as you," he answered, then pulled her close and kissed her.

"Am I supposed to interpret that as you're back?"

"If you'll have me."

"Please don't ever leave me again, Jake." After she said it, he thought she was going to cry. Rolling back on top of him, she held his hands down while they rubbed noses. It had always been her way to follow up on something she was serious about with a playful act to break any awkward moment.

She then lay down next to him, leaned over, and licked the tip of his nose. "We'll get caught up on the last ten years tomorrow. I need some sleep."

Snow, sprawled on Jake's chest, bumped his head with hers. Jake turned and looked, once again, into Snow's eyes. One was green; the other was gold.

CHAPTER 9
RECOLLECTIONS

When Jake awoke very early the next morning, he found his legs hopelessly tangled with Rachel's. Snow, lying on top of her, was staring up at the TV screen. As he contemplated how to unleash himself without waking Rachel, her hand came up and patted his cheek. Looking over, he saw four different colored eyes staring back.

"You're not trying to get away without buying me breakfast, are you, Jake?" Rachel cooed the words with a put-on sexy voice.

He smiled. "Of course not. I was just trying to figure out how I was going . . ." He couldn't tell her about Sheila and St Michaels.

"Busted," Rachel laughed. "There's a nice little homey restaurant just across the street, lover. You owe me big time."

"Who's first in the shower?" he asked, and playfully slapped her bare bottom.

"Don't you want to do things together, Jake?"

He nodded hesitantly.

"Well then, that includes the shower. Especially the shower."

Jake had forgotten how much fun, if it could be called *fun*, Rachel could be. Taking a shower with her was an adventure in terror; she just loved to grab and slap things. In addition to being wild in bed, she was downright crazy in the shower. He complained to her, but it was oh so much fun.

* * *

An hour later, they sat in the Blue Crab Restaurant, and Jake looked across the table at the girl he had left behind. Parts of him ached from their bathing exercise, but thinking of those ten lost years made him want to bang his head on the table. He had slept with his share of women, but Rachel was the only girl he had really enjoyed sex with. With her, it was way more than just the physical. She was unpredictable and passionate, yes, but he could also sense the love. At times he dreamed of the two of them in different places, places they had never been. Wishful thinking, he reasoned. Memories that could have been.

When Rachel picked up her coffee, sipped from it, and fixed that exotic gaze on him, he knew her mental wheels were turning. They started catching each other up on the last ten years, Rachel quickly cutting to the chase. "Look, Jake, I'm not married, never have been, have had no serious boyfriends and have worked for NG for the last ten years. Plus, I'm still madly in love with you. How about you?"

"Ditto," he said. "Life without you has been boring. I've worked a lot of odd jobs . . ."

"What about April?"

She knew, he thought, how to cut through the bullshit. Her sudden question had stunned him to muteness.

"Do you think about April at all, Jake? What happened back then?"

Inwardly, he sighed, looked up at Rachel, and knew. He could dodge the question and the past no longer. His fear had been that seeing Rachel and his buddies would make him slip back into the nightmare of those events, and cause him no end of misery.

On the contrary, however, seeing them, especially Rachel, had lifted his spirits enormously. Little did they really know that his running away had nothing to do with them and more to do with his ancestry. Talking about April Elliott, and facing those horrendous days in their entirety, would have to be the next logical step to restoring the relationship with his friends and full-blooded sister.

After all, despite what his Dad and Sheila might think, his friends and sister, not the politics of Flammeria, were the main reasons he had agreed to return. Since then, he had successfully gotten back in touch with the only friends he had on Earth. He now needed Laura back in his life, and he felt compelled to do almost anything to make it so.

"Do I think about April?" he finally answered her question. "No, I try not to." He knew that was a dirty lie and not the right way to start off. In reality, he thought about April a lot, but if he told Rachel that now, she'd probably just get up and walk away. "We can talk about it though, if you want."

"Really? You know I was always on your side in the whole sordid affair, Jake. Why didn't you stay and fight her accusations instead of vamoosing?"

"I don't know." He shook his head. Inwardly, he was glad she was focusing on that and not on if he was ever in love with April. "I just don't know. The whole thing took me by storm." He mumbled the words, more lies. How was he ever going to set things straight?

The words to *Feels Like Home* suddenly erupted from her cell phone. He recalled it had always been her favorite song. Several singers had made a recording of it, and Rachel had them all, but she especially liked the version by Chantal Kreviazuk.

He remembered how she'd ask him, "Jake, don't you love this song?" And he realized he did. He loved everything about Rachel, including her music.

Now, she glanced at the cell and said, "My boss. I've gotta take this, Jake. Hold that thought."

* * *

As Rachel talked work with her boss, his mind drifted back to April. When he was a Company Officer at the Naval Academy, April had been a plebe, first-year midshipman, in his company. He was advisor to one hundred and twenty mids. April had been as driven as any of them, if not more so. She wanted to be a fighter pilot. Shit, when they came there, everyone wanted to be fighter pilots. The Academy even had a name for it: *The Top Gun Syndrome.*

Over the four years, they all seemed to gravitate to their future niche. A year into the Academy, Jake knew he wanted to drive ships instead.

In contrast, April never wavered in her conviction. Jake tried to pay no more attention to her than he did to any of the guys, or the other girls, in the company. It was hard, though, because she was a beautiful girl. He recalled she had Academy regulation short blonde hair and stood a tiny bit taller than Rachel, but with two eyes of the same color: blue. At the time, he thought Rachel and he were headed toward breakup and their own goals, so he allowed himself to *feel* things for April. Even though he was her superior in rank and age, he knew this girl could order him to do things and he'd not complain.

Back then, she was enamored of his experience and the fact that, as she put it, "You're not some pimply-faced, high school geek," which is where she placed most of the guys in her company. She'd come to his office often, and never lost an opportunity to lay a hand on his, bump him with her foot, or somehow come in physical contact with him. Her body language was clear, but his sense of duty was clearer. Jake resisted the temptation. But it was not easy.

While April was obviously looking for companionship, it did not deter her in pursuit of her goal. More than anything, she wanted to fly. She made that crystal clear in their many conversations.

For that, and the fact that she wouldn't give them the time of day, her classmates despised her. They misunderstood her focus on the future and her seriousness as some type of superiority complex. They wouldn't talk to her, and were always trying to steer her into trouble. This situation was an underlying reason for her frequent visits to his office. He felt sorry for her, because he had come to the Academy the same way. Fixated on what he wanted to do.

However, he carried a secret within: He and his classmates weren't of the same species.

In his Academy days, he had been blessed with two great roommates who broke him out of that head-in-the-sand mold. And though his imprint on the Academy was not stellar, he had enjoyed his 'Four Years by the Bay.' Up until his tour as a company officer, his active duty Navy experience had also been satisfactory, but he was leaning towards getting out when his required five years of service were up, the following year. His heritage lay just off shore of Norfolk Naval Shipyard, the Navy base he was stationed. Each time his ship headed out of port and steamed over the Norfolk Trench, he would be covered in sweat, worried that would be the day it would all come together. If they ever discovered the station, the Navy would have no idea its mission was peaceful. He envisioned they would just see strange craft and probably attack them. Jake thought often of his past, and his people being confronted by the US Navy, including him. Where would his loyalty lie?

For April, who had wanted the dream of the Naval Academy and to fly a jet aircraft more than life itself, the Academy experience was far less than she had expected. Oh, it was clearly partly her own fault, as she refused to overlook the faults of her classmates and accept, in her mind, that she was probably a little bit more mature than they were. Jake constantly advised her to do so, and she tried. She really did. But they'd always come back at her with some stunt or trick that would infuriate her, and she'd return to square one.

* * *

"Jake, I have to get over to Baltimore after breakfast. I've got to do a presentation there." Rachel snapped him back to reality.

"That's fine. I've got to go to St Michaels anyway. Errand for my dad."

"Will you still tell me about April?"

He nodded.

"You're not gonna leave me high and dry again, are you?"

"No, Rachel. My days of running are over. I might have to stay in St Michaels for a few days. Can I come back to you after?"

Her eyes brightened. "You'd better, Jake. Or I'll hunt you down to the ends of the earth."

After they finished breakfast, Rachel came over, kissed him and said, "Snow and I will be waiting for you."

CHAPTER 10
LET'S MAKE A DEAL

After Jake dropped Rachel off at her apartment, he walked back to his car to find Glimmer and Ceellia waiting inside, perched up on the dashboard. They eyeballed him as he slid in.

"What are you two doing here?" he asked.

"We're assigned to you in case Sheila might need to mentally communicate with you," Ceellia recited in what appeared to be a rehearsed answer while Glim merely smiled.

"How did you get here?" he asked.

"That's a silly question," Glim answered. "You drove us."

"You mean you've been with me the whole time?"

"Of course. We were with you at that pub too," Glim said.

"We saw Miss Ellie make a pass at you," Ceellia chuckled. "Are you going to sleep with her?"

"She didn't make a pass at me, she—"

"She gave you the touch and the look, Mr. Jake." Ceellia winked. "We know the touch and the look. We saw where your hand went. Why don't you want to sleep with her? She was willing."

"No, I . . . wait a damn minute. That was before I met you. How could you even know about that?"

"We were there."

"How did you get there?"

"Sheila drove us. We followed you."

Things started to add up for Jake. "Does Sheila drive a little Corvair?" he asked.

Both nodded. "I love that little car," Ceellia said.

So that's how Sheila knew everything he was doing. This was all unbelievable.

"When we come back, we'll go with you again to Miss Rachel's," Ceellia said.

"No, when I come back you're both staying in the car."

"You can't do that," Glim said.

"We're telling Sheila you're not following the rules and you're mean to us," pouted Ceellia.

"Go ahead and tell her, you little snitchers. I have groveling to do at Rachel's and I don't like witnesses."

Both crossed their arms and legs and were quiet. Before he could start the car, Sheila's voice echoed in his head.

"Jake, you promised to do anything I asked. Why are you refusing to take the Distans with you?"

"I—" His verbal answer was cut short by Glim flying up in his face and holding his lips sealed with her tiny hands.

"You just need to think your answer, Mr. Jake. I will transmit it to Sheila," she said. "Verbatim."

"When did I agree to that?" He ignored Glim and said the words out loud.

"Just before you left you said you'd follow all house rules. House rules for you and me include going nowhere without a Distan."

"You are one sneaky little . . ." he said to a grinning Glimmer. But he knew he'd been had. *"Sheila, they want to spy on me."* He thought the words this time.

82

"ANYTHING I asked, Jake. They are to go where you go. It's not spying; they will assist you in any way you, or they, see fit. Forbidding them to do their job is not an option for you. Understood?"

Jake looked over to the smug looks on their little faces.

"Look, Jake. It's up to you to reason with them as to what they tell me and the girls in the Keep. Outside of things that affect them or the station, they are not required to tell me anything; but in the Keep, they are little gabby Gerties. I've already heard a blow by blow about someone called Miss Ellie. Really, Jake? Do you just chase any skirt? Ceellia said she was twenty-two years old. Isn't that a little young for you? Anyway, I'm always able to negotiate with my Distan, Floressa, for her discretion. Learn how. In the meantime, you will take them with you and treat them as you would me. Don't worry, they won't be seen. Understood?"

"Okay," he mumbled.

"Think the word, Mr. Jake," Ceellia chirped happily.

He did, and then both of them took positions on his shoulders.

"What?" he asked.

"You've made a wise decision, Mr. Jake," Glim said. "Now we're ready to negotiate for our silence in the Keep about girls like Miss Ellie that you make passes at, and anything else we witness you do with women."

"You know, I think the two of you actually have something in mind, and I'm stuck with it. Am I right?"

"Very perceptive of you, Mr. Jake," Ceellia said.

"I shouldn't be telling you this," Glimmer said. "But we want to show you we're on your side. You have the option of requesting that some other Distan be assigned to you at any time. We want your promise that you'll not ask to replace us. It would do you no good anyway, we all follow the same rules."

"Okay," he nodded. "That's reasonable. Anything else?"

"Just one more thing," Glim smiled. "Since you're staying to help Sheila and us, we get to be party to all of your adventures. No telling us or Sheila it's too dangerous."

"No," he said. "That's too much."

"Suit yourself, Mr. Jake. So now we're free to blab to anyone," Glim stated. "I'm sure Miss Rachel would love to hear about your affair with Miss Ellie."

"Affair?" he said. "She just . . ."

"The way we saw it, you definitely encouraged her," Ceellia interrupted. "Wow, Glimmer," she continued. "That means we can play tricks on Miss Rachel, too. Now she sees us, now she doesn't."

Both giggled in anticipation of making his life a nightmare. "Let Mr. Jake try to explain us," Ceellia snickered.

"I can't believe my mom's stories were so true," Glimmer said. "We've only been with him one night and he's gone after two women! Mr. Jake is quite the operator. Wait until Miss Rachel hears about where he put his hand on Miss Ellie. I guess we should be careful around him."

"Oh, I don't know," Ceellia replied. "Might be fun. You want to try that touch on me, Mr. Jake?"

"Okay," he said. "We need a truce while I think this through. How about we make a deal? I'll go along with all your demands except the last one . . ."

Both little ones were slowly shaking their heads.

"But . . . wait, there's a but."

"No buts," Ceellia said, and stomped a little high heel into his shoulder.

"Just a minute, Ceel. Let him make his proposition," Glim said. "Go ahead, Mr. Jake. We might accept a but."

"I'll explore the adventure demand with the two of you later. That means we'll discuss it in the near future and come to some kind of agreement. Until then I need your word that what happens tonight, and occurred last night, is between us."

For a moment the two of them stared at one another. Jake could almost feel their mental communications flying back and forth. Finally, Glimmer broke eye contact with Ceellia and looked at him.

"Okay, Mr. Jake. Ceellia wanted to hold out for your total surrender to our demands, but I reminded her I am your Distan and I want you to realize that I can be reasonable. After you see how discreet and helpful we can be, I'm sure we'll come to a satisfactory arrangement. So, in the spirit of friendship, we accept your offer."

CHAPTER 11
BACK TO ST MICHAELS

As they hit the road for St Michaels, Jake tried to reconstruct those last few days ten years ago when he had left the area. He had been so focused on what was going on with Laura that everything that happened outside of that main 'family' event, like his memories of the situation in Annapolis, was foggy. What he did recall was that even back then, Rachel had stuck by him.

Why then, did he leave her?

On the drive back, the lyrics of Lauren Christy's *River of Time* coming out of his cell phone pulled him back to the present. Obviously, Rachel had gotten hold of his phone at some point the previous night or that morning and programmed it in. While he normally abhorred music coming from a phone, she loved it, and her choice of song, another of their favorites, brought a smile to his face. He saw from the caller's number it was Rachel. A glance to the passenger side of the front seat showed both Glimmer and Ceellia curled up together, asleep. They had pulled out a t-shirt from his overnight bag as a blanket.

"I miss you already," Rachel simply said. "Please hurry back." Then she hung up.

When he reached the Wells house, he parked in the drive. The Distans were now awake and sitting primly on the dashboard. As Jake looked over at them, Ceellia pulled her dress up to show more of her shapely little legs. She gave him a wink. He shook his head at her flirtatiousness.

"We're going to get something to eat, Mr. Jake," Glimmer said. "If you need us, we should be back in the garden in half an hour." With that, the two of them left through an open side window.

Once inside, Sheila looked up at him from over a cup of coffee. "Welcome back, loverboy."

"Loverboy?"

"That's the talk of the Keep. We all hardly slept, waiting for updates from Ceellia in the wee hours of the morning. Coffee, Jake?" she asked with a smile. "Are you hungry?"

He shook his head. "Just coffee. Thanks."

She got up, placed a mug in front of him and poured the coffee. He mixed in a few drops of cream.

Before he could sit down, Sheila asked, "Walk with me, Jake?" Without waiting for an answer, she went to the front door, opened it and walked out.

He scooped up his mug and followed her. She was standing in the driveway, staring at the wisteria vine that had claimed the middle of the pavement. Tendrils of the voracious vine, looking for something to grip, stuck out in all directions.

Now, he noticed that the driveway actually curved around the right side of the house. He walked over and looked down the drive—at the Corvair he had seen last night.

"Like my wheels?" Sheila came up behind him and giggled, then turned somber. "Please don't tell any of your friends about me," she asked. "Would you promise me that?"

He couldn't help nodding. What she said and knew no longer surprised him. Strangely, he trusted her.

"We need to go to the . . ." she began to tell him.

"Rock. I know." He gulped some coffee and then set the cup on the steps as she linked her arm in his and practically dragged him to the spot by the flowering trees. After slipping off her shoes and climbing up on the stone, she started.

"I've decided that before I go, I wanted you to understand something. Moonglimmer never heard about Rachel and April from me. Actually, it was quite the opposite."

"How is that possible?" he asked. "Aren't you the only one who can read my mind? Wait, Laura? Did Laura . . ." He stopped talking, because Sheila was shaking her head. "Who?"

"I was going to wait until tomorrow to tell you all of this, but I think it's time I told you something." She paused and looked out over the river. "I never meant to be so mysterious," she finally said. "You need to know the reason why the Distans are so important. And how Moonglimmer knew about Rachel and April."

"I'm waiting," he said.

She licked her lips with a pink tongue and looked at him coyly. "The Distans read and transmit thoughts, from one individual to another. Or sometimes it's just one way. But either way, the Distans can both read minds and relay all of our internal thoughts to each other."

"Wait," he said. "You're saying that a Distan read my mind and . . ."

". . . Transmitted your thoughts mentally to me. Yes. We can be easily trained to communicate by thought, but even that requires a Distan close by. Couldn't you figure that out by Glim and Ceellia coming with you?"

He nodded, but he had suspected that Glim was just the transfer medium, not the—

"When you arrived, I had Floressa read your mind for your agenda. That's how I knew."

While she talked, he stared out over the river and tried to resolve his mind's fluctuations at this revelation. "When was this?" he asked.

"At BWI," she said. "Your dad gave me the flight information, and the Distans and I followed you from the airport. He said you'd come straight to us, but Laura said she thought you'd go to Rachel first. Floressa planted the idea of you calling Dan instead. We followed you, and Moonglimmer and Ceellia then took over at the pub."

"You sneaky—"

"I'm not done." She took a deep breath and shook her head. "There's more. I didn't want to tell you because I didn't want to drive you away, but now that you're committed to me, at least for a few days, you should know the truth. If you wish to reverse your decision to stay or go, I'll understand." She paused and took another deep breath.

"For Pete's sake, Sheila spit it out. Do you think anything can shock me now?"

"This will. At various times in your past, a Distan was assigned to you and followed you around."

She was right. She could still shock him. "Followed me around? How is that possible?"

"They can fly, Jake. Very fast. And they're very adept at hiding. Plus, I gave them a ride to . . . the Naval Academy."

"No!" was all he could say.

She nodded. "Floressa was assigned to you during the years you went to the Academy. She was a teenager at the time. The stories, especially of your dates, she came back with are legend. Also as a teen, Roseena was your Distan during your time there as a Company Officer. She's the source of all the Rachel and April stories. Now, since you returned, you've been assigned to Moonglimmer. And since Ceellia goes with her everywhere, it's like you have both of them."

"Wait a minute," he said. "How is all that possible? At the Academy?" His mind raced with the images of all the crazy stuff Floressa and Roseena could have witnessed.

Sheila's eyes twinkled with excitement as she relayed this. She appeared to actually enjoy seeing him fret. "They have to be within fifty feet of you, so Floressa or Roseena would flit from tree to tree on the Yard, following you. They searched your mind for news, which they would immediately transmit to me. At other times they had a spot on the windowsill outside your room. I had told them to never go into your personal thoughts, except for when they related to the station, but Roseena didn't always listen. She would share things in the Keep she never told me about. That's how Moonglimmer and Ceellia know all about your . . . escapades. I feel terrible telling you all this."

"They searched my mind and sent stuff to you? You were with them?"

"I told you, I drove them. I was usually parked in one of the midshipmen lots. I probably got hit on a million times. It was so much fun and great for my ego. I know a lot of your classmates. In fact, I once went on a date with Dan. He'll probably not recall, as Floressa had to do a little tweaking with his memory. He was very persistent." She actually smiled while telling him of her espionage work. "Will you forgive us for invading your privacy back then?"

He should have been furious with her, but her smile was mesmerizing. All he could do was nod. And by doing so, forgive.

She brightened instantly.

"We should be getting back," she said. "I have to leave soon, and you should get some sleep."

"Okay," he said hesitantly, as she stared down at him. He held a hand out to her to help her down, but she made no attempt to move.

"You're not mad?" she finally asked.

"How can I be mad at my little sister?" he grinned.

She unexpectedly jumped from the rock as if she expected him to catch her. Luckily, he did. She then hugged him tightly and finally gave him a little fluttery kiss on the lips. "Thanks, Jake," she finally said. "You've made your little sister very happy."

As Sheila strolled back with him, she paused at each flower garden and pond, where she proceeded to identify every flower, plant, and creature they saw. He knew she was happy, and was pleased to have been part of that. Distans would initially fly towards her, but then they seemed to sense their need for privacy and changed course, never getting closer than a hundred feet or so. They flew very fast and Jake never could get a good look at any one of them, just brief swatches of color.

"In case you haven't noticed, I really have had the Distans stop reading your personal thoughts," she said when they stopped on a scatterer. "I understand your need for solitude. Sometimes, I think I misuse my . . . gifts. I'm afraid I sometimes don't respect people's need for privacy. Through Floressa—by the way, she's my Distan—I end up knowing what they're thinking." She looked up at him sharply. "I know now it annoys you. Plus in your case, it's plain wrong."

"I appreciate that," he said.

"Can I ask you for one more favor?" she said.

"I guess," he said warily.

"Just promise me you'll continue to do anything I ask?"

For a moment their eyes were locked together. When in this position once before, he had split, and what had it gotten him? A wasted ten years. "Okay, I promise. I won't desert you, Sheila." At least not for a few days, he thought.

"I'm not asking you to do any kind of station mission. At least not yet." She gave him a smile when she said that, and he knew she was playing him, but didn't care. "For now, let's just say you'll obey house rules," she continued. She poked a small finger into his chest. "Without question. This is important, Jake. I need to trust you. With absolutely no possibility of you failing me. The Distans' very existence may depend on you."

He still couldn't believe this girl was not only a relation, but practically his twin. "Anything." He finally gave in and said it, but wondered why he agreed to such a vague statement. However, since there was no mission involved, what could she possibly ask him to do between now and tomorrow afternoon? After that, he reasoned, all bets would be off.

"I knew I could count on you," she whispered. "Okay, I've got to leave, and you need to get some sleep." They walked back in silence and, after she went up two steps toward the house, she turned around, looking even more diminutive next to the stairs.

"You are a little one," he said.

"Good things come in small packages," she winked. "Aren't you glad we're not monozygotic?"

CHAPTER 12
USOS

Jake awoke two hours later to Gert knocking at his door.

"Come on in," he called out, and propped himself up in bed.

"Sorry to bother you, Jake. I have a message from Sheila. She had a problem with the boat down around Norfolk. She'll try to be back here tomorrow around noon. Said she'd contact you this evening."

He nodded. Better late than never, he thought.

"Jake?"

He looked up. Gert was clearly nervous about something.

"Sheila sounded troubled. I sensed all was not right. I'm worried about her."

Jake frowned. "Well, there's not much we can do until we hear from her. The shoreline along the southern bay area is enormous. We don't know exactly where she is."

Gert nodded, but she looked even more troubled. "I'd better look in on Mrs. Wells. Are you staying here tonight, Jake?"

Until she asked, he didn't realize he was now free tonight. "Will you be okay if I go back to Annapolis?"

She gave him a knowing smile. "Of course."

"Thanks. I'll be back around noon tomorrow."

He knew it would be useless to try to leave without the two little pixies, so after cleaning up and getting dressed, he went to the garden and strolled among the flowers. He hoped to convince them to let him go it alone. In no time at all, Glimmer and Ceellia were buzzing around him. He found a patch of the strange grass that marked the location of a scatterer, slipped off his sandals, and made contact.

Before he could say anything, Glimmer blurted out, "Mr. Jake, we've been thinking we need to renegotiate our deal now. What we heard . . ." She said those last three words slowly, as if they were shocked by his actions. Would he never live down his initial attraction to Ellie?

"Okay, okay," he said. "Let's not waste time, you little blackmailers. Any adventure I go on, you can come too. But you're on your own."

Ceellia snickered.

"What?" he said.

"Mr. Jake, you can't even take care of yourself. You need us."

"Don't worry, Mr. Jake, we'll still protect you," Glim added.

"Whatever," he said. "I'll agree to your original deal, is that what you had in mind? Right now, I'm going back to Annapolis. Can I ask you to remain here?"

"Uh, there's something I guess you don't quite understand, Mr. Jake," Glimmer said, with a little smile. "We are not allowed to let you leave at any time without at least one of us with you. It's required of us. If we let you go alone, we're in a world of trouble."

That was annoying. "Just why do I need you little flying Barbies with me?"

"Mr. Jake," Ceellia pouted. "We have names. Ceellia, that's me, not Ceel or Ceely, and Moonglimmer, which you can shorten to Glimmer, Glim, or whatever, that's her choice. But definitely do not call me by any of your smart little names. Please?"

"Okay, okay," he nodded. "Would you, *Ceellia*, tell me why . . .?"

"We must be with you," Glimmer interrupted, "because we facilitate thought transmission among Flammerians to make it difficult for the Zantites to intercept messages of any other type. Sheila will only communicate that way. As long as you're engaged in Flammerian communication, we must be with you."

"But doesn't me standing on a scatterer here do that? Besides, there are none away from this house, so what's the use?"

"The Zantites' spying methods are very poor, except at this location. Scatterers can overcome their more advanced methods here. Using mental communication away from the house, you are safe, because we Distans know how to defeat their more primitive techniques, if necessary," Glimmer informed him.

While he listened, Ceellia's facial expression had turned into a sad grimace, eyes droopy and mouth turned down. He thought she was going to cry.

"Don't you like us, Mr. Jake?" she sniffled. "Are we really bothering you that much?"

Now he was furious with himself. Of course, these cute little angels had been perfectly pleasant, and he really did enjoy their company on all these long drives. "I'm sorry, Ceellia, Glimmer. I've been a terrible companion, and of course I'd like the two of you to come with me. Just be careful at Rachel's house. She has a cat, and . . ."

"We get along fine with cats, Mr. Jake," Glimmer interrupted. "We've already communicated with Snow. We had to, otherwise she'd have made vocal noises to Rachel, trying to alert her that we were in her apartment."

"You were in her apartment? You talked to the cat?"

"Cats are superior creatures, Mr. Jake. Yes, we speak their language. And yes, we told you we were with you that first night."

"You were in the pub, and then I thought you went to the car . . ."

"We were with you everywhere," Ceellia squealed. "I want to meet Rachel as soon as possible, Mr. Jake."

So this wasn't about Ellie, but Rachel and him. "What is the big deal about meeting Rachel?"

"When she knows I exist, I might get to be her Distan," Ceellia explained. "If so, she'll be the first non-Flammerian a Distan gets to work with. And, since she's your mate, Glim and I will get to work and live together.

"She's not my mate," he replied.

"Not yet," Glimmer chuckled. Both began to giggle.

"Get in the car," he said.

Jake started to follow them as they zipped toward the car, but he was intercepted just short of the driveway by an even smaller Distan who wore an orange gown that the wind tried to blow up over her knees. She was finally able to grip her gown between her little orange-furred ankles.

"Hi, Mr. Jake," she said in a small voice, pushing lush, orange hair from her eyes. "I'm Reena."

"Hi Reena," he replied. "What are you doing over here? I thought you all just hung out by the gardens."

"Normally, we do. But I saw you here and just wanted to buzz around you. Are you going away? Will you visit us again soon?"

"First chance I get," he smiled.

"Maybe we can become friends after you get back," she said, and flew off.

The wind picked up speed around him. How had she known he was going away? Then he remembered his two little gossip girls.

* * *

This time, when she came to the door, Rachel was dressed. It was good to know she didn't greet everyone packaged in just a t-shirt and panties.

"Jake!" She threw her arms around him. "I thought . . ."

"Change of plan, but I might not be able to come up tomorrow night. My host in St Michaels is stuck in Norfolk until then."

"Anything to do with the USO reports?"

"USO reports?"

"Yeah, there have been consistent reports down there of USOs, and you know the Navy takes them seriously."

"USOs. We're talking underwater submerged objects, right? Like UFOs, but in water?"

"Yeah. You were in the Navy, Jake. You've seen the reports of them all the time. Just outside and around the entrance to the Bay is a hotbed for them." He'd seen the reports, but knew what they were. Flammerian ships, operating underwater.

"Come on, Sexy, let's eat," he murmured. "Food first, then we can talk current affairs." As he went out the door, Snow was staring up at the TV screen again, wagging her furry tail. He thought he caught a glimpse of reddish hair and flash of yellow, just on top of the wall-mounted TV.

Ten minutes later, they were sitting back in a corner of the Blue Crab. Once again, he marveled at this girl he had rediscovered.

Rachel looked up from the menu and asked, "Okay, do you remember what we were talking about this morning? Or should I say who?"

He nodded. "April Elliott."

"Look, I know I said I wanted the story, but now I'm not so sure. The important thing is you came back. You wasted ten years, but you came back. I know you didn't exactly come back for me, but . . . Wait a minute. You didn't come back for her, did you?"

"Are we still talking about April?"

"Who else? Didn't Brian tell you she's down in Oceana?"

While that news rocked him, he covered it up. "No, he didn't, and no, I didn't come back here for her. I went to St Michaels on family business, Rache. I drove up here, to Annapolis, in a weak moment." In actuality, he couldn't tell her the truth, because he still didn't know for sure why he had come back.

At his spoken comment, she looked a little downcast and her head drooped.

With two fingers under her chin, he gently lifted her face to look back at him and exclaimed, "Hey! It turns out it's the smartest thing I've done in a long time."

She immediately smiled. "In that case, maybe I don't want to know about April after all." She sipped her wine and pursed her lips at him. "What kind of family business brought you to this neck of the woods?"

"Hey, enough talk about me and my business. That's an endless bore. What have you been doing the last ten years? Why haven't you gotten married?"

"I can't answer that, as I'm still working on the guy of my dreams. I lost him for a few years and now he's back. To stay, I hope. What have I been doing? Ocean engineering consulting, working for NG. Now talk about boring . . ."

He was still stuck on her phrase about the guy of her dreams. She was obviously referring to him; he wasn't a complete waste of space. He could not understand for the life of him how he had treated their relationship so flippantly. How could he explain it all to Rachel? He no longer wanted to keep secrets from her, but that he might not even be the same species was a whopper. And where could he begin to explain?

". . . I know you came for the funeral of your dad's friend, but what prompted you to come here, and want to see me, after ten years? I'm not complaining, just curious."

"Could you trust me again, Rache? I know it's asking a lot, but it's very complicated. I promise to tell you eventually."

"Woo, sounds like a mystery, Jake."

"As a matter of fact, it is, Rachel Anne, and I'm still trying to unravel it all."

At that point their dinners arrived, and he switched to asking questions about Rachel's job. When he pressed her on dating, he couldn't believe she had been just waiting for him to return. He couldn't conceive of loyalty to that extent. This girl could have the pick of the litter, and she'd waited for him?

After dinner, they returned to her apartment and hit the king-sized bed. They were both pretty beat from the long day. Of course, a completely naked Rachel Anne Paney was not exactly a tonic for sleeping. Once in private, the girl would shed her clothes like a duck does water, and that was a sight he'd never tire of. Rachel simply enjoyed being naked, and he never saw reason to argue with that.

That night, though, he was really beat and desperately needed rest. He had thought it was from all the driving and no sleep, but he was also worried about Sheila. As Rachel tried to tempt him by running *Russian Navy*-painted fingernails up and down his leg, he groaned and thrashed around, loving her attention, but also wishing she'd just let him sleep. Finally, she playfully slapped his butt.

"You're such a stud, Jake. Your stamina is like zero. Do you mind if I catch the news?"

He knew she was disappointed, but all he could do was grunt into the pillow.

The TV came on and Snow crawled up next to him. He thought it was in sympathy, but when he looked at her, she was staring intently in the TV's direction while her tail rhythmically swished back and forth, brushing his nose. A car commercial for an Annapolis dealer played across the screen.

He shut his eyes and tried hard to sleep, but was beset with worry because Sheila had not called tonight as Gert had said she would. He couldn't help wondering what was happening to her. Seeing Rachel and the guys had brought back his life of ten years ago, but he couldn't shake there was some other reason. Dad surely hadn't encouraged him to return just to reconnect with Rachel and his friends.

However, as long as he was here, he could use the time to make peace with Laura and face his heritage.

CHAPTER 13

ON THE ROAD

"Talk to me, Jake," Rachel said as she sat next to him on the bed. She had turned down the TV, and he felt the surge of a little more energy after having finally had a brief nap.

Should he tell her about Sheila and his dad? He regretted not having trusted her about April years ago.

"Have you ever heard of Flammeria?" he asked her.

Rachel got up, padded over to her world globe and searched it diligently. Finally, she sighed and went over to her computer. After hammering away at the keys for several minutes, she stopped, looked over, and pouted. "Spell it for me, Jake."

"F L A M M E R I A," he said slowly. He considered stopping her, but liked watching her move around naked.

"That's what I thought, but all I get is apparently a restaurant in Germany."

"Okay, I should have told you that searching the internet or the globe for the country named Flammeria was useless. You need to search a map of the star system Alpha Centauri B, or you'll never find it."

"Alpha Centauri?" She walked over to the bed and flopped down next to him again. "You're such an asshole playing around with me. You know how gullible I am."

"ACB is part of a three-star system in the southern constellation, Centaurus. It is also the closest system to Earth's solar system, and though it's not general knowledge on Earth, it's just one of thousands of worlds out there that support human and non-human life."

She laughed out loud. "Like *Men in Black*?"

"No, *Men in Black* was fiction, but there actually are beings from other planets living there and . . . here."

"I'm not that gullible. If what you're joking about was true, why would they pick Earth?"

"I'm not joking. Flammerians are here to monitor Earth. They were first called in about twelve thousand years ago when a comet passed close to Earth and devastated the Lumerian and Atlantean civilizations. Flammerians aided in the rescue of survivors and gave some of them a place to call home. Earth is a volatile world, so the Planetary Alliance—"

"What Planetary Alliance? You talking *Star Trek* shit now? What happened to *Men in Black*?"

"No, listen. There really is such a thing. They assigned Flammeria the task of monitoring Earth for similar occurrences. I know, I'm—"

"You are so full of shit!" She playfully used her foot to push him.

"—one of them." Jake said those last few words almost silently, to himself. It was hopeless.

"Tonight off the coast of Virginia, in the area east of Cape Henry, the Navy is searching for a strange object reportedly seen entering the water early this morning. According to eyewitnesses, the craft seemed to first hover near a cabin cruiser in the area . . ."

At that, Jake sat up and listened to the report coming from the TV.

"Okay, did you find some energy?" Her head popped up and she shimmied over. Smooth *Russian Navy* nails brushed his cheek.

"Shhh," he groused.

"... then appeared to enter the ocean, without making a splash, and disappear. Onlookers said the cabin cruiser then sped away at high speed toward the waters of the bay. The Navy has refused to comment on reports that strange craft have been tracked in the area for months."

Her smooth fingers slipped across the skin on his leg. "I'm stark naked, and you feed me this space crap then get up for some news story? I thought you were tired. I was letting you sleep."

"I am." His mind raced. *Cabin cruiser*. Sheila had said she was detained down around Norfolk. Was there a connection?

"In a related story, the Coast Guard is reportedly searching for a cabin cruiser described as old and about seventy-five to eighty feet long. The Coast Guard refused comment when asked if it was related to the Cape Henry sightings and the Navy's search."

Rachel hopped up and went into the bathroom.

A nanosecond later, Glim was in front of Jake's face. "Mr. Jake, Sheila uses that boat to visit the station. Ceellia and I are afraid something has happened to her. I'll try to contact her for you." Glim then resumed her spot by the TV with Ceellia.

His mind went into what-can-I-do-to-help mode.

"Jake, what's wrong?" Rachel said as she returned. "You look like you've seen a . . . wait a minute . . . is this about the USO on TV? You got interested in that awfully fast. Have you seen one? That a part of your space opera?"

"Actually, I've seen a lot of them, I—"

Suddenly, Sheila's voice came into his head. *"Thanks for having Glim contact me. I hate to do this to you, Jake, but I think I need your help."*

The shock of hearing Sheila's voice in Rachel's bedroom caused him to stiffen.

"Jake?" That was from Rachel. She had gripped his arms and shaken him. "What's wrong?"

He grabbed her and pulled her close. "Shh!" he urged.

She pulled his head down until it touched hers. "Ouch!" she exclaimed. "You're pinching my shoulder."

Out of the corner of his eye, he saw Ceellia with a 'Yikes' expression on her face, hovering above Rachel's bare shoulder and slipping off her little heels.

"I know you're with Rachel, Jake. That's why this is so awkward. Glim said you just saw the news, so that's why I'm interrupting you. What the news didn't say is they have my general description. It's from a vague photo really, taken by a satellite when I was momentarily stupid. I need your help to get out of here. Can you, will you, come for me?"

"Yes," he thought, knowing that Glim would transmit the message. *"Anything, remember?"*

"Do you know where Plum Tree Island National Wildlife Refuge is?"

"Yes, I do, but it's closed to the public," he thought. He saw Rachel looking at him strangely, so he tried to wrap up the conversation.

"I know, that's why I picked it. I managed to evade them and put the boat in a hidden cove on Cow Island. I'm afraid that when daylight hits, they'll surely locate it. I need to get far away."

"I'll be there as quick as I can, Sheila." Then, her mental voice was gone.

"What the heck was that all about?" Rachel asked. "Are we talking about the boat we just heard them describing on TV? Who's the girl, Jake?"

"What girl?" Had she heard that? He suddenly realized why Ceellia had apparently landed on Rachel's shoulder and then hovered so close to her.

"The one that was talking in our heads. What's going on, Jake? Are you some kind of spy? Is that what this is all about?"

"You said you'd trust me, remember? The girl is . . . Look, I promised her complete secrecy, so it's up to her to tell me when I can share with you what's going on. Yes, that's her boat. I know this all sounds strange but—"

"I know what she said. I could hear her voice in my head, too. Is there a microphone or something planted in your head? Did I hear because I was so close to you? How does she do that?"

He took a quick glance up above the TV screen and saw a smiling Ceellia. Obviously she had been beaming Sheila's thoughts into Rachel. But why? "I can't explain thought communication to you, Rache." He didn't understand it himself.

"Thought communication? Are you trying to tell me you can instantly message someone by thinking it?"

"Again, I'm under oath to be silent. I know it's a lot to ask, you trusting me after all that just happened, but will you? For me?" Why had Ceellia allowed her to hear that? It made things so complicated. He glared up at where Ceellia had been, but she had apparently returned to her hiding place.

"Okay, you bozo, I'm going to trust you, but you've got just twenty-four hours to explain things to me. Now, where is Plum Tree Island Refuge, Jake? I'm going where you're going." Rachel was already up out of bed and throwing on a blue sundress.

Jake stopped searching for his clothes long enough to look at her. "What do you mean you're going? I can't take you into something that may be dangerous."

"You're sure as hell not leaving me behind. You're going to help a *girl*. If it's not too dangerous for *her*, it's surely not too dangerous for *me*. I went to the Academy. I'm a trained warrior, remember? I lost you once; I'm not going to lose you again."

"This is nuts, Rachel. I can't drag you into a family problem—"

"This is your family problem?" She looked at him with eyes the size of saucers. "The whole goddamn United States Navy and Coast Guard are after that boat."

He took a deep breath. She was right, as usual. In addition to being gorgeous and intelligent, Rachel had always relished a challenge, and her help might be needed. Besides, hadn't Sheila already included her by having Ceellia communicate her words? "Okay, I'll explain what I know as we drive. Come on, Nancy Drew."

"Nancy Drew? Really? If you wanted to be funny, you could have at least made me someone more grown-up and up to date, like that PI from the novels about Baltimore. You know, Tess Monaghan."

"Are you still reading Laura Lippman?"

"Yep, read everything she's ever written."

"Are you coming or talking, Tess?"

"Wait. I need underwear."

* * *

Twenty minutes later, they were cruising west on Highway 50. Jake brought Rachel up to date on some of the family mystery, leaving out his dad fighting the War of the Worlds back home. Also, in deference to Sheila's wishes, he did not mention their alien heritage or his two little communication specialists that, out of the corner of his eye, were visible in the rearview mirror, hiding behind his ball cap on the rear ledge. He guessed he hadn't told her much; mainly that the USOs were a secret, exploratory craft. She didn't ask, so he never mentioned they were not from this world. If she wondered why the Navy was chasing something of their own that was secret, she never let on. To her numerous questions of who the hell was Sheila, and why did he have to pick her up, he asked her to simply trust him. Sheila would explain it all at the right time.

"And who is Glim?" she asked. "Sheila mentioned someone named Glim had contacted her. Is Glim male or female?"

"Female," he said, with a check in the rearview mirror. Glimmer and Ceellia were both leaning forward in a sexy pose with puckered lips. "Most definitely female."

She grew quiet. He deep-sixed the idea of going back to his attempt to explain Flammeria to her. Let her think it's a joke. He thought she assumed he was loony and wished he'd never returned to her life. But again, he had misjudged her. Amazingly, she agreed. She trusted him.

"After we pick up Sheila, and I find out what the hell this is all about, I think we should go down and take the bridge-tunnel to the Eastern Shore," she said as they merged onto Interstate 95 heading south. "If they should locate her boat, Interstate 95 would be their first target for an escape route."

"Eastern Shore roads will put us closer to St Michaels, too. Good thinking, Rachel Anne. What I don't understand is why you're doing this. Putting yourself in this mess. I have nothing to lose; I was already drummed out of the Navy. You've made something of yourself."

"Two reasons, Jake. First of all, you know I *joined* the goddamn Navy, and they felt I was unnecessary. I spent four years at Canoe U, got my commission and did a great job. Then one day they decided to downsize and just said, 'We don't need you.' I was drummed out too, so the hell with 'em. This is like spittin' in their eye. God, I feel like a pirate." She punched him in the arm. Hard. "Besides, you know I love adventure. This is so right up my alley."

He grimaced and rubbed his sore arm. He recalled she was unpredictable.

"You can be such a pansy," she mocked him. "I hardly touched you."

In a flash of headlights from a truck headed north, he could see the sparkle in her brown and blue eyes. He smiled over at his little buccaneer. "You said there were two reasons. What's the second?"

"Why, I love you, Jake. Always have, always will." He didn't deserve her, but for some reason the gods had smiled on him.

He reached over and gripped her hand. Her eyes glistened in the moonlight and he knew she was close to tears. He leaned over to kiss her, but she pushed him away.

"Eyes on the road, mystery boy. Sheila needs us, remember?"

* * *

Around Rachel's hometown of Richmond, they picked up Interstate 64 and continued to race east.

At that point, Sheila again beamed a message into his head. *"Take 171 until it ends at Messick Point. I'll contact you and Rachel then."*

"I heard," said Rachel. "How does she do that? And how did she know I was in the car?"

"I don't know, but it sure saves time. I don't know how she knew you were with me," he lied.

"It's like she has a little spy camera in the car," Rachel said.

He could swear he heard a giggle from the back seat, and Rachel even turned around, but she saw no one. Mentally, he tried to send a caution message to Glimmer, but there was no answer. Was he doing it right or was she ignoring him?

Rachel rested her head on his shoulder and reached up with one hand to lay fingertips on his cheek. "What do Sheila and Glim look like? Are they pretty?"

He just nodded, not knowing how to tell Rachel about the little figurine of Moonglimmer and what Laura had told him. He had left that part out of the explanation of the events swirling around them. When Laura gave him that figurine, he assumed she meant for him to discover Sheila, or even Moonglimmer, but had her reference to the woman of his dreams been for them? He didn't want the woman of his dreams to be his sister or even the Distan. That phraseology ought to have romantic meaning. Those words should be meant for Rachel.

"Prettier than me?" Rachel asked.

He looked over at her. "No one is prettier than you." And he meant it.

In answer, she kissed his cheek. "You say the nicest things, Foley. That'll get you in my panties every time."

CHAPTER 14
SHEILA'S REVELATION

Forty-five minutes later, they turned onto Highway 171. Rachel dozed in the seat next to Jake, and Glimmer was perched on his shoulder. The clock on the dash read 2:34 a.m. He covered the last few miles slowly, knowing that just to the south was Langley Air Force Base.

Shortly after crossing Wythe Creek Road, Sheila's *"Stop"* registered in his head. He did, and Rachel popped instantly awake. In that split second, Glimmer was gone.

Outside it was completely silent, and only wisps of fog punctuated the black night. Suddenly, from out of the scrub at the side of the road, a figure appeared. Sheila did a little wave to them and Rachel reached back to open the rear door. Sheila ignored that and instead opened the front passenger door. After getting a good eyeful of Jake's sister, Rachel slid in closer to him while Sheila noiselessly planted her small body next to her.

"Rachel's plan to take the eastern roads is a good one," Sheila said. She then embraced Rachel and kissed her. "Thank you for helping. I've looked forward to meeting you."

Seeing the look in Rachel's eyes, Jake realized that she had not been adequately prepared for Sheila. Her reddish locks swept past Rachel's face, and he knew it was going to be a job convincing her that Sheila's status was solely kind of family. Even worse, he imagined, Rachel might dredge up his attraction to April, and he would be forced to admit he was a weak son of a bitch when it came to a pretty face on top of a well-shaped body. His only hope here was for Sheila to admit to Rachel that they were related.

"How did you know I was with Jake?"

Did he detect jealousy in Rachel's question? Maybe it was because she stared at him after asking it.

"That's complicated, but I will tell you later, once we're out of danger," Sheila said, while her eyes scanned the back seat for Glimmer and Ceellia. She knew they were hidden, but just wanted to acknowledge them.

"Exactly what kind of danger did I drag Rachel into?" Jake asked.

"That, too, in due time." Apparently convinced they had so far made it away cleanly, Sheila looked over at Jake. "We must clear the Bay Bridge-Tunnel first, before they close it."

"How do you know they'll go that far?" he asked. By this time, they had already rejoined I-64 and continued east towards the Hampton Roads Bridge-Tunnel.

Sheila just looked from Rachel to Jake and said, "I picked up their radio traffic. They feel they have the proof they need if they can apprehend the driver of the boat."

"What proof? Of what?" Rachel asked.

Sheila was silent.

"Jake, did you drag me into anything illegal? Are you smugglers?"

"No to both," he said. "Just be patient."

"What about your boat?" Rachel kept asking questions. He was glad she was still talking. While he should have been concentrating on getting them out of this situation, instead he was occupied with the hope Rachel didn't think there was anything romantic between Sheila and him.

"It's no longer needed," Sheila said. "They'll find it belongs to my mother and eventually return it to her. Mother is safe; they'll know she couldn't have possibly been the driver of the boat. Eventually, they'll come to the conclusion that the boat had been stolen and abandoned."

"But wouldn't they naturally suspect you?" Rachel asked.

Sheila shook her head. "Besides Jake, my mother, our hired help, Gert, and a few close uh . . . co-workers, and now you, no one knows I exist."

The last revelation from Sheila had shut even Rachel's inquiring nature down. Jake could just imagine what was going through Rachel's mind. He didn't know how she kept from screaming, "I want answers!" The three were quiet as they roared through the Hampton Roads Bridge-Tunnel. When they emerged from the tunnel, Jake followed Route 60, Ocean View Avenue, the shortest route he knew to the Chesapeake Bay Bridge-Tunnel.

"Did Jake tell you about me?" Rachel asked Sheila.

"In a way, but not much," Sheila answered. "I have other sources."

"I promised Rachel some answers," Jake interjected. Up ahead he could see a flashing overhead sign. He had a good idea of what that meant.

Sheila looked to Rachel, who wore a downcast expression.

"It is not what you think," Sheila said to her.

They finally approached the flashing light. TUNNEL CLOSED. USE ALTERNATE ROUTE blinked down.

"Turn around, Jake, and let's take the long way up I-95; they can't stop every car," Rachel advised.

"Too late," Sheila said. "I'm sure they've closed the other tunnels. They'll be looking for me either on 95 or in this area."

"There aren't enough cops and military to cover every street," Jake said.

"But where can we go?" Rachel lamented.

Jake's mind went into overtime. Having spent four years on ships home-ported in Norfolk, he knew the area well. Taking a chance they wouldn't assign priority to the road they were on, Route 60, he stayed on it past the tunnel exit. He knew it swung past Fort Story and then headed south. But then he recalled the newscast . . . *Off Cape Henry.* Cape Henry was located on Fort Story.

Sheila suddenly spoke to what he'd just remembered. "Get off this road, Jake. Going close to Fort Story is far too dangerous."

When he saw the Highway 279 exit on the right, he practically slid across the road and almost sideswiped a pickup, whose driver blared his horn at them. "Sorry," he mumbled.

"Watch your speed, Jake. Last thing we need is a traffic stop," Rachel pointed out. He exited, slowed to the limit and kept going south on 279.

Rachel looked to him as they crept down the road. "You have a plan, Jake, or are you making this up as we go along?"

"You wanted adventure," he replied. "This enough excitement?"

"Just what did I get myself into?" Rachel asked, then looked to Sheila. "Are you sure you're not some kind of wanted criminal?"

"No," Sheila smiled. "I am not a criminal and in no way am I romantically involved with Jake. Quite the opposite. I will tell you everything later, is that okay?"

Rachel just smiled, then looked to Jake and then back to Sheila, who was wearing a red sundress that closely matched Rachel's blue one. "That dress really complements your gorgeous hair," Rachel observed. "Looks like we dress alike, but aren't you a little cold? I sure am. I grabbed the first thing I saw. Didn't think this would be an all night thing."

Sheila shook her head, red curls bouncing every which way. "I'm okay; my internal body temp has always been a little high." She gave Jake a glance when she said that.

Rachel scooted closer to Jake, opened his shirt and planted cold hands on his bare chest. He yelped and turned the car's heater on.

"You're lucky it's not my feet, Jake. They're like ice cubes. When we stop, you're warming them up. By the way, where are we headed?"

"The Outer Banks. In fact, I thought we'd go all the way down to Rodanthe. I have a buddy down there who has a boat." He hoped he was still there.

"Actually," said Rachel, "we don't have to go that far. My uncle has a fishing boat in Oregon Inlet. I can call him. We'll look like any charter boat party."

"That's great, but they might stop any charter trying to get into the bay," he pointed out.

"That's true," Sheila added. "However, there's an alternate way for me to get back to St Michaels if we can get close to the ocean. I have some friends who'll pick me up."

"Uncle Rick will be glad to take you out on his boat," Rachel beamed, then frowned. "Crap, I hope he doesn't have a charter scheduled. What time is it?"

They all glanced at the car's clock. It read 3:35 a.m. "Wait to call him. Let's see . . ." Jake mentally calculated the time down to the barrier islands and Oregon Inlet. This early, he knew the roads would be relatively empty. "I'd say we should get there about five-thirty, give or take."

He had wanted to talk to Sheila on the trip down, but assumed she didn't want to take a chance on Rachel hearing something prematurely. She'd start the ball rolling with an explanation, for Rachel, when she was ready to do so. Sheila, for real or for cover, went to sleep once they were on the road leading to the Outer Banks.

When Rachel closed her eyes and her head lolled against his right side, he felt the small feet of Glim on his left shoulder and her voice in his head. *"My mother is now with us. Ceellia and I are available, but Sheila asked us to stay out of sight unless she tells us otherwise. We found a way into the trunk of the car, so we'll hide in there. Think our names if*

117

you need us." Then she was gone. Floressa had been with Sheila on the boat. He couldn't believe that with five others in the car, he still felt virtually alone.

* * *

Rachel, who had been catnapping, perked up as they rolled across the Highway 12 Bridge to the Outer Banks. "Jake, I'm hungry." *Russian Navy* fingertips caressed his cheek. "Are there any restaurants open?"

"I could eat something too," Sheila announced as she awoke also. "I'm sure we're out of danger now."

The dashboard clock now read 5:02. "Let's keep our eyes open for someplace to eat," he replied.

Shortly after they entered the town of Nags Head, Sheila pointed. "There!"

He was surprised to see an all-night diner. He hadn't remembered any restaurants open this early on previous trips. But the Outer Banks were constantly changing, and someone obviously thought there was enough business at this early hour, from fishermen and people like them, headed to Oregon Inlet or further down to the towns south along the barrier islands, to make a living. Jake pulled up to the restaurant, pleased that there were no other cars.

He looked at the two girls, in sundresses as if it was ninety-five friggin' degrees. In actuality, outside it was probably closer to sixty. To top it off, Sheila was barefoot. It occurred to him that he had seldom seen shoes on his newfound sister's feet.

"I don't like shoes," Sheila smiled. "Don't worry, Jake. No one will notice how we're dressed." Had she read his mind? At that thought, Floressa peeked out and smiled at him from behind Sheila's hair. He should have known.

"What?" he replied. "You gonna use *the force* on them?"

She merely smiled. When Rachel wasn't looking, Floressa darted toward the back seat to rejoin Glim and Ceellia.

Inside, it looked like a one-man operation. A short guy with a neat beard and curly hair that stuck out from under a cook's hat came out from behind the counter as they sat in one of the booths. The air inside the little restaurant was tinged with the smell of fresh-brewed coffee and recently fried bacon.

"Mornin' folks. Welcome to Nags Head and the Dolphin Diner. I'm Bud, owner, cook, dish washer and waiter. Can I get you all some coffee?" Jake expected some comment on how the girls were dressed, but Bud just smiled pleasantly.

Jake looked across to Sheila, who smirked back at him. Could she control some kind of force? Was there such a thing? Really?

"I'll have coffee," said Rachel, who had slid in next to Jake, slipped off her sandals, and now pressed cold feet against his leg.

"Water for me." Sheila sent another grin in his direction.

"Coffee," Jake nodded.

Bud dropped menus in front of them and went behind the counter, but was back in a flash with glasses of water for all and two coffees.

"I'll be back for your orders."

Rachel had no sooner withdrawn her feet when Sheila brushed the bottom of a bare foot across Jake's pant leg to get his attention. When he looked over, her gorgeous face, framed by reddish locks and highlighted with those glittering green eyes, formed a cute little sneer, and she simply said, "See."

He winked back at her while thinking she'd make a beautiful princess.

A few seconds later, Bud, the owner/cook/waiter returned, took their orders and left.

Jake was grateful for his multiple duties, since they meant there was little chance he would interrupt them. He looked at Sheila. "Does Rachel finally get a story?"

"Yeah," Rachel added. "I'm really trying to be patient, but just what did I sign on for?"

Sheila glanced first at Rachel, then her eyes fluttered back to Jake. She didn't start talking immediately, so he asked a question, hoping to get her started. "How about who you are and where were you born?"

"Sheila Wells," she answered. "Born July 4th, 1985."

Rachel's face broke into an astonished look. "Jake, isn't that the day you were born? How can she have been born on the same day you were?" Then she did a double take and looked at Sheila. "Noooo! You can't be that old."

Jake ignored Rachel. "I asked where, not when."

Sheila looked at Rachel for a few seconds, then at him. "My place of birth is recorded as St Michaels." She paused and looked down at the table. Finally, she glanced up at Jake, smiled and murmured, "Same as Jake."

That he didn't expect her to admit, although he long suspected it. He had often questioned Dad about Baltimore as his birthplace. Because of his family's history, he had thought St Michaels might be the true place, but there was no record there.

Seeing the shocked look on Rachel's face, Sheila added, "What did you think I was going to say? I came from outer space?"

Apparently mesmerized, and, from the looks of her, slightly amused by all of this, Rachel continued to stare with a slight smile. After Jake's talk of *Star Trek* and all, she thought Sheila was kidding.

"Our mother was from outer space," Sheila said with a straight face. "Same as our fathers."

The words were slow to register in Jake's mind. Was she telling Rachel, an Earthling . . . the truth?

"You're kidding, aren't you?" Rachel asked. "But you have this serious look about you. You're not joking?"

Sheila smiled and shook her head.

"Are you trying to say you and Jake are some kind of extraterrestrials? Aliens? Wait. Did Jake tell you I'd swallow just about anything? He put you up to this?"

"She's not being altogether truthful about the *where* of our births," Jake finally managed to say when he got his breath. He was worried about Rachel's reaction to being told the truth so bluntly.

Rachel punched Jake's arm. "She's telling me you're aliens, Jake, and you're latching on to where you were born?"

"That's the lie," he tried to point out. "Neither she nor I were born anywhere on the East Coast. There is no record of our births here."

"There is no *Earth* record of our births," Sheila corrected him. "But it's true. We weren't actually born in St Michaels or anywhere *on* the East Coast. We were born further east."

"Further east?" The words tumbled out of Rachel as she stared from one to the other, unbelieving. "There's nothing east but the ocean. Or maybe you mean an island? Bermuda?"

"No, we were not born on any island," Sheila said matter-of-factly.

"Then, you mean like on a ship?"

"No, like under the ocean. Specifically, in the Norfolk trench."

CHAPTER 15

ON THE BEACH

"Wow, you are scamming me," Rachel answered and smiled.

"It's a long story," Sheila said, "and our breakfast is coming."

"You lay this on me and then say you'll explain later? How can I eat now?" Rachel asked.

"Please, Rachel," Sheila pleaded. "There's no scam. I'll explain everything. Don't get so upset."

Rachel looked from Sheila to Jake and took a deep breath. One moment he thought Rachel was not taking Sheila seriously, the next he wasn't so sure.

It was all he could do to keep quiet. Jake didn't eat very much. He wanted answers for Rachel, but he suspected Sheila was going to tell her something even he didn't know. However, Rachel was quiet during the meal, and up to that moment he would have bet the farm that was an impossibility. He strongly suspected Sheila of doing more than entreating her silence.

A half hour later, they were in the car and once again moving. Sheila didn't seem to hear when he asked her to resume her narrative for Rachel. Quiet reigned in the vehicle. They were now just south of the limits of Nags Head. Quickly, they ran out of beach homes and entered an area where tall grass and sand covered the land east of the road all the way down to the beach and the Atlantic Ocean.

"Okay," Sheila said suddenly. "Stop here."

Jake pulled off the road at a convenient spot and parked. Now, away from the meager lighting of the homes in Nags Head, stars glittered above and to the east out over the ocean.

"Is anyone gonna explain to me what's really going on or tell me what the plan is? Should I call my uncle?" Rachel asked.

"Don't you want to hear the rest of our story?" Sheila asked.

"Oh yeah, your We-come-in-peace-from-outer-space-yarn. Sure." Rachel smiled.

Sheila smiled back and opened the car door. "I'd like to go sit on the beach. Would you please join me, Rachel?"

Rachel nodded eagerly and prepared to slide out behind Sheila.

"You're barefoot, Sheila," Jake pointed out.

"So? I walk everywhere this way."

Rachel took off her sandals and tossed them on the floor of the car. "Now I'm barefoot too, Jake. Is that a problem?"

"I was just concerned because there's lots of broken glass about." He held up his hands in a defensive gesture. "I'll keep it to myself." Obviously, he was now outnumbered.

They climbed over rocks and mounds of sand, through the sparse vegetation, mostly sea oats and cordgrass, all the while dodging litter like cans and bottles, and came out on the moonlit beach. Once her feet touched the beach sand, Sheila immediately took off running for the water. Rachel followed Sheila, and they waded in to their calves. In the moonlight, Jake could see that they were laughing and talking, oblivious to the waves washing in. He sat on the sand, perhaps fifty feet from the water's edge, and watched and waited.

"Sheila said it's okay if we go in the water, but we have to be very careful of fish and the like." Glimmer beamed the words into his mind as she alighted on his right shoulder. "It's still pretty dark and predator fish are out at night so, instead, we're just going to walk along the edges of the surf."

"We're then gonna feast on some of these wildflowers in this area," Ceellia added, after landing on his left shoulder. "Don't worry about us, Mr. Jake, we'll be careful and we'll be back in the car in a flash."

"You better be careful," he mentally admonished both of them. "Wait. Where is your mom, Glim?" The last he whispered aloud.

"She has to stay close to Sheila, as she's in touch with the station," Glim whispered.

"He's worried about us," Ceellia said softly. "We're doing what Sheila said was impossible."

"Huh?" he said. "What's impossible?"

"Before Sheila left yesterday," Ceellia smiled, "she told Floressa that getting through your thick skull was impossible. But we're making headway. You're worried about us." Ceellia laughed and zoomed quickly around in a circle.

"There's a big rock about twenty feet straight back of where you're sitting," Glimmer said quietly. "We're gonna leave our clothes there. When you leave, check it out. If our clothes are gone, we weren't eaten by the fishes or crabs."

"Unless you want us to strip here and you hold our clothes?" Ceellia offered her alternate plan with a wink.

"The rock is a better choice," he said. "I might not be able to control myself with you naked, Ceellia."

"Mr. Jake is not such a prude after all," Ceellia laughed, and they flew off.

Eventually, both human girls came back and settled next to him, one on each side. Rachel again punched his arm and said, "When are you going to be a little more spontaneous, lover boy? You're such a stick in the mud."

He noticed the bottom of her dress was wet and she was shivering, despite her courageous words. He wondered what they had discussed. Had Sheila brought up their heritage again?

"He's not very adventuresome, is he?" Sheila asked. "There's a reason for that. I'll tell you later, Rachel."

He glanced over at Sheila and noted her dress was wet to the waist and clung to her very shapely body. She was not shivering, and when he looked up to her face, her eyes drilled into his and gave a knowing wink. What did that mean? Like two aqua jewels, Floressa's eyes glinted from within the tumble of Sheila's flaming hair.

"My explorers," he murmured, "should learn how to dress."

Ignoring his comment, Rachel asked again, "Should I call my uncle now?"

"That won't be necessary," Sheila said, and finally released Jake's gaze. "An alternate plan has already been put into motion."

"Before we do anything," he said, "I want you to finish your story for Rachel."

Sheila looked from him to Rachel. She positioned herself closer to him, and Rachel also snuggled up for warmth. "Okay, Rachel. There is an observation post below the waters of the Atlantic Ocean, outside of Chesapeake Bay. I'm sworn to protect the secret at all costs. I will tell you just what you need to know. Is that acceptable?"

Rachel nodded. "You're awful serious in keeping up with this joke. This is all some kind of tall tale, though, isn't it? Make fun of gullible Rachel?"

Sheila kept glancing from them to the water. "You are free to believe what you want," Sheila said. "But I'm not part of any attempt to fool you."

Jake momentarily looked a little to the south along the shore and saw a tiny flash of red and yellow flitting along the beach. Inwardly, he smiled. Ceellia, he had to admit, was correct. He now did care. Very much. The two little Distans had convinced him that they were now a part of his life, and he decided then and there that he had to help protect them at any cost.

"The station was set up very long ago." Sheila's words pulled him back to her and Rachel. "Before even the explorer Columbus landed in what he thought was a New World. In fact, it was thousands of years before that event you so celebrate."

He looked over at Rachel, who hung onto every word Sheila said. Although she apparently thought they were somehow playing games with her, she appeared to find the tale compelling. A part of him had to wonder if his little princess was using some force on her to help Rachel swallow this impossible story. As he wondered, he became aware of pinpricks of yellow light behind Rachel. Ceellia. That's why she was buying this.

"It was fairly easy then to get in and out of the bay without being seen," Sheila continued. "Even in more modern times, they experienced easy access. When the bay became very busy, someone was needed who could move from the ocean and back to the bay without attracting attention. A careful study was made, and the occupants of the station decided on two of the station security workers. They were friends who had no close family members and had no desire to return to their home world. Most importantly, they knew the area of the bay well."

"In addition, they were—" he started to add.

"Let me tell the story, Jake. If you slip and tell something you shouldn't, I'll have to cover that information over in Rachel's memory," Sheila admonished him.

Rachel nodded her agreement. "Right," she laughed. "You tell him, Princess Leah."

"I'm not a princess," Sheila said with a straight face. "My name is Sheila."

"Just tell her the story," Jake said. He thought that Rachel might not really be taking this seriously, and she'd need visual proof of some kind.

Sheila continued. "In addition, it was decided to move the station out of the bay and further offshore in the Atlantic. The visitors picked a spot near the Norfolk Trench and provided the two chosen workers with a fast boat, the house in St Michaels, and enough money to live comfortably. They carried out a fishing business, to cover the operation of providing transport for the coming and going of station personnel."

Rachel shivered involuntarily, and Jake pulled her even closer. To his right, two tiny pinpricks of red and yellow flashed by. Goosebumps covered Sheila's arm, so he reached over and pulled her close, too. Grateful for his thoughtfulness, Sheila smiled up at him, glanced to the ocean, and then continued the tale of their past for Rachel, whose eyes now were riveted on his arm around Sheila.

"The two workers readily agreed to help, and things went well," Sheila continued. "The station leader at the time was Natille, a woman who desired to have a baby. The same two men had competed for her attention, and while she had an affair with one, and a female child, she didn't want the other to know. She solved that problem by convincing both, without the knowledge of the other, to donate sperm so she could be artificially inseminated. Each agreed. Unknown to them, she had two of her eggs fertilized, one with sperm from Martin Wells, who was my father, and one with sperm from Carl Foley, who was Jake's."

Rachel stiffened at that revelation while Sheila, after a glance out over the water, went on.

"Nine months later, Natille had a boy and girl, dizygotic twins, each with different fathers."

"Holy shit, Jake," Rachel said. "Sheila, are you trying to tell me you're Jake's twin sister? No. It's part of the joke right?"

"Yes, that is what I'm telling you and no, it is not a joke," Sheila said. "Our parents were not of Earth, that's why there are no birth certificates. However, Jake expressed an interest in attending the Naval Academy while in high school, and his father asked for help from the station. The certificate of birth from Baltimore was provided. I've never needed one. If anyone asks, I just say I was born in St Michaels."

There was a sudden loud sound of cascading water, and a brilliant yellowish light illuminated the beach. About three hundred yards out to sea, a circular craft at least a hundred feet in diameter had silently risen out of the ocean and now hovered above the water. It was obviously what Sheila had been waiting for.

"Look at that thing," Rachel said excitedly. "What the hell is that?"

"It's just my ride," Sheila said. "That is the change in plan. Your Navy searches only for me, not you two. We cannot take the chance that either of you will be found with me or identified as helping in my escape. I summoned one of our ships, not only to get me out of this area, but also to allow you both to leave without suspicion. And I hope this proves to you, Rachel, that Jake and I are who I said we are. I don't believe your world possesses anything like what is waiting there for me. I believe your name for it is a USO."

"That thing is huge," Rachel said softly.

"Huge?" Sheila smiled. "It's just a planet hopper. I'll have to take you up to one of our real spaceships sometime. Now, they are huge. Thanks for the ride, Jake."

"But . . ." He didn't want her to leave, but he also couldn't think of a way to make her stay.

"You have helped me a great deal by getting me out of the search zone. It is safe now for you and Rachel to go back to Annapolis. On Monday, return to St Michaels, bring Rachel, and I will answer any questions she may have."

Sheila whispered, "Take care of my brother," then embraced Rachel, who had been shocked into silence by the USO.

Wrapping her arms around Jake, she kissed him on the lips and said, "Take care, Jake. It is good that you are finally home. Your real home. I love you."

He pulled her close and hugged her.

She broke out of his arms and dashed down to the water. After wading out a short way, she started swimming toward the craft. Up above her, he could barely make out tiny twinkles of aqua light that he knew were Floressa's eyes. As Sheila swam out, the strange ship started to rotate, and then turned the spotlight off of them and directed it on Sheila in the water. It swooped in low over her and somehow extracted her up out of the water and into the craft. The ship then darted back out over deeper water and, without making a splash, disappeared under the waves.

CHAPTER 16
BACK ON THE ROAD

After the yellow rotating light had gradually disappeared from view, Rachel remained frozen in place for a few seconds, staring out over the water. Suddenly, she let out a breath and plopped herself back down on the sand.

"Holy crap, Jake. That's your sister? You're really an extraterrestrial? Was that really a USO? Why am I so freakin' calm? I'm . . ." She trailed off, and he couldn't blame her. It's not every day you find out the guy you're going with, the guy you professed to love, the one you've stuck by for years, is not who you thought he was. In fact, he might not even be the same species.

"I thought it was all some kind of joke. But that ship was real. She . . . Why have you never told me this?"

"It tends to put people off when you say you're an extraterrestrial. To Earth, an alien is a little green man with eyes like saucers, or a killer reptile hiding inside a human suit. Funny how people seeing the Star Wars movies accepted humans in that role, but in real life we're always expected to be horrible creatures that came from outer space. You know, The Thing in person. I had always assumed that a normal life for me on Earth was no longer in the cards."

He had not expected Sheila to reveal so much of who they were to Rachel so quickly. He suspected her motive had something to do with finding that Rachel had been prominent in his life at the time of the huge fight he'd had with Laura ten years ago. He'd told Laura back then that all he had ever wanted was to merely lead a normal life with someone who was in this world. The world he lived in, not the world his ancestors were from. While Laura had tried to enlist him in the station's causes by excluding Rachel, Sheila, he suspected, was trying the opposite by bringing Rachel in. Clearly, Sheila thought this strategy was the key to securing his help for the station after Laura had failed. He was just surprised that she'd use a data dump as the means of delivering the news.

However, he wondered what Rachel now thought of him. Now that she knew he was an alien.

His answer was soon clear, though, when she smiled and patted the sand. "Hey, spaceman," she said. "Sit by me."

He plunked down on the sand next to her. "I'm sorry. I didn't know how to . . ." He tried to apologize for his sister's bluntness.

"Shut up, Foley." She put her arms around him and hugged him very tightly. "It's gonna take time for me to make sense of all this. Shit, I'm in a relationship with an alien from the planet X."

He didn't know what to say. She wiped at her eyes, yet he saw no tears there.

"Things can't be all bad, though," she mumbled. "You've got the same equipment as any other Earth guy."

He couldn't help snickering. Leave it to Rachel to go there first.

"And the really good news is you can't sleep with that gorgeous red-haired creature, 'cause she's your sister. That girl is hotter than a firecracker. You can't, can you? Please don't tell me it's permissible in your society."

He shook his head. "Whether it's permissible or not, I live here on Earth and I only have one girl. That's you."

"That was all I hoped to hear. Let's go for a swim, my space invader lover. I've got to get this sand off me before we head back."

He looked at her as if she'd lost her mind. "In the midst of all this? Are you nuts? We don't even have suits. Besides, your dress has dried. Why not just brush the sand off?"

"Good idea." She proceeded to brush some off, then pulled the dress up and over her head. She began flapping the dress like a flag while looking down at her legs. "Sorry, I'm caked with sand in sensitive places. I've got to get rid of it. Come on you pansy; get your creature-from-outer-space clothes off. We can swim naked."

"You were freezing when you came out of the water. You—"

"Stop being such a wimp. The air is cool, but the water is warm. Come on before someone shows up. Get out of those clothes." With that, she tossed the sundress higher up on the beach and stood there in just her panties. A second later, she threw them after the dress and was pulling his pants down. A wind had started to kick up, and he thought of telling her to secure her clothes better, but then thought better of interfering in her mood.

"Okay, okay," he said loudly. "You are a fruitcake."

Laughing, she raced across the sand and splashed in the water. He assumed that was her method of coping with what she had just learned.

He caught up with her in the surf and she turned around, grabbed his wrist and pulled him along with her. They crashed into the waist-deep water, with her holding on to him as he recoiled from the initial shock of cold. Once immersed in the warm water, he stopped shivering and she released her hold. Instead, she entwined her hands behind his head and pulled him close. She kissed him softly on the lips, then suddenly fastened her lips firmly to his and ducked their heads underwater.

When they came up out of the water, she pulled away and giggled. "So, can you breathe underwater, Jake?"

"No, but I actually enjoyed the experience," he said.

"You don't have gills that appear when necessary?" she asked with an air of sincerity.

"No, I don't. Look, I'm physically identical to any Earth guy. I was born here, not somewhere in outer space. In fact, I've never been in outer space." As he said the words, he felt they were a lie. Had he been in space? Why was there a doubt? However, he couldn't recall many aspects of his early life, so maybe—

"So you know the answer to many of the mysteries of early Earth?" she asked.

"Actually, I don't. However, Earth was populated by our race many eons ago. There are many similar human species all over this sector of our galaxy. I don't know of any little green men or science fiction-like creatures that exist anywhere." Of course that wasn't quite true. But he couldn't tell her what danger lurked in some relatively close star systems. Dinosaurs didn't quite take here on Earth, but they and similar creatures had done fine elsewhere. And if Edgar Rice Burroughs would have set up his fictional planet Barsoom in another star system, John Carter might not be science fiction.

He wanted to explain some of the long-ago history of Earth to her, specifically what happened to the civilizations over ten thousand years ago when a comet upset the climate of Earth, but he knew that was a violation of the planetary alliance edicts when dealing with non-member planets. Better to say he didn't have any knowledge of it.

"Let's get going," he said, ready to change the subject.

They rose out of the water and walked shivering up on the beach. After they threw on what clothes they had, they walked back to the car and settled in. On the way back, he noticed the big rock was devoid of any sign the Distans had been there. Once he had the car's heater on, they both stopped shivering and Rachel became quiet.

After looking at the clock, and noting it was 6:30 a.m., Jake called Gert and told her that he would come back on Monday. Apparently, Sheila had already informed her of her returning.

Rachel silently stared out the side window. She seemed to have now settled on the rejection side of Sheila's revelations. He wondered if her teasing him in the water had been an act, hiding her real feelings.

"You okay?" he asked.

She nodded.

"Do you still want me to stay with you at your place, or would you rather I get a—"

He didn't finish, because she suddenly turned in her seat and stared at him. Her sudden reaction caught him off balance.

Then she started to cry. "Of course you're staying with me, you idiot," she wailed.

"Why are you crying?" he asked.

"Because I'm probably going to lose you again," she sobbed. "Christ, Jake, you're an alien."

"Maybe half alien," he offered. "I still look like—"

"And half asshole," she countered. "Don't you see? They probably have a plan for you. You left me once before, how is this different? That's probably why they got you to come back here. First, they spring your twin on you; then, they ask you to come with them. So it'll be stay with me or go with them, and you'll go; you did the last time you had that choice."

"I'd never go," he said. "I—" He stopped. He didn't want to tell her that he thought Sheila's plan was to lure Rachel over to their causes. He strongly suspected that Sheila thought by integrating Rachel into their lives, he would be more apt to help the station. It's what he'd have done. It's what his dad would have done. Sheila had already done it to him, using the Distans. She apparently figured that he couldn't help getting hooked on the friendship offered by the brave little creatures. Glim had already flown her way straight into his heart. Leaving would be tough.

"Don't talk stupid, Jake. You haven't heard her whole story yet. I have a bad feeling about all this, and it tells me I'm gonna lose you. Again."

"There are things I should have told you a long time ago. Ten years ago to be precise. However, I promised not to reveal any of it to anyone on Earth. Sheila has told you a little of it, that we are not exactly from your world, but there is more. Since she started telling you, I assume things have changed somewhat. How, I don't know. I'd like you to hear what she has to say first, then I'll tell you the rest. Is that acceptable?"

She nodded. "At least that would be an improvement over what I knew ten years ago."

"What do you mean?" he asked.

"You never would talk about your life before you went to the Naval Academy, Jake. Don't you remember?"

He did, but he also remembered it was because so much of that time was unclear to him. Laura used to tell him stories about the gardens and St Michaels. Maybe she could explain why she remembered it all and he didn't.

Still, he knew then this wouldn't be settled until she'd heard the remainder of the story and been introduced to the Distans. Somehow, he had to see Laura.

They had three days to wait. The stars were gone, as the sun was now climbing over the ocean, so he put the car in gear and drove north.

* * *

Rachel had started dozing the minute they crossed the bridge from the Outer Banks to the mainland. Right after she dozed off, Glim appeared and told him they were going to sleep in the trunk, where they had set up some of his clothes as a bed. When they reached Norfolk, he got on

I-64. Now, as they charged through the Hampton Roads Tunnel, Rachel's head bounced off the side window, and she snapped awake.

For a moment, he felt her eyes on him and waited for her to continue wailing about him leaving. Damned if she didn't continue to defy his attempts to classify her.

"Hey, John Carter from Mars, buy me a cup of coffee?" she murmured sexily.

He looked over to a smiling Rachel. "First chance I get, my princess."

Ten minutes later, she pointed out the window as a sign flashed by on their right. "There," she countered. "Two miles."

After they had pulled into the Pride of Virginia Coffee House and parked, and before he could open the door, Rachel's soft hand firmly gripped his arm. He turned to see what she wanted, and was blindsided by her practically vaulting out of her seat and on top of him. Her knees dug into his legs and, to avoid the steering wheel digging into her bottom, she pressed as close to him as she could get while somehow reaching down and operating the seat mechanism. The wrinkled sundress felt slick on his bare skin as she locked her arms behind him and snuggled up. When the seat hit the stops and they were where she wanted to be, she buried her lips in his and pushed her tongue roughly into his mouth. He managed to free one arm enough to reach a hand around her butt and pull her even closer. After several minutes of kissing, along with the pleasure of touching and feeling, she pulled her lips off to catch a breath.

"I feel like a slut. You never gave me time to properly dress before we left my apartment."

"I didn't rush you, I—"

"You would have left without me if I took the time to get proper underwear and different clothes. Because of you, I think some crab stole my panties on the beach," she mumbled.

"I thought I saw a seagull strutting on the beach in them," he winked.

"I kind of figured you knew. It took no time for your hand to find its way under this thin dress. Did you enjoy rubbin' my ass?"

"Your bare skin is like a magnet," he said.

In answer, she put her nose alongside his and gazed into his eyes. His view of her enchanting eyes was perfect. Their mouths were almost touching.

"Jake, you know I'm not usually like this. Most people think I'm kind of standoffish. I put people off. And here I am making out with some guy from Pluto or who knows where. You'd think I'd be more choosy, but I'm so afraid of losing you again."

He remembered how the guys at the Academy, himself included, had thought of her as Miss Icicle. That had partially explained his shock when he bowled into her that day back at the Academy and stared into those lovely eyes. He had expected a tirade of expletives—sailor girls can have potty mouths—and maybe a slap in the face, but what he got was her laughter. After that tension-breaker, they became friends and he got to see this other side of the ice princess.

"I'm not going anywhere without you." He practically mumbled the words into her mouth.

Although her entire body was crammed uncomfortably on top of him, scrunched in the driver's seat under the steering wheel, he would still never think of complaining.

"It's just my luck to fall in love with a spaceman," she remarked.

"I'm not exactly a spaceman . . ." Before he could finish, her fingers gripped his lips and held them closed.

"You didn't let me finish, Godzilla. You just like feeling me up through this paper-thin dress." She grinned and removed her hand from his lips.

"While patiently waiting for those little melons of yours to pop out," he managed to say before her hand again found his mouth.

"When we get home, big boy, when we get home. I'm hungry. Is your shirt dry yet?" she asked, and slid back into her seat.

"If not, I can wear it damp."

"Good. Get your shirt on while I fix my hair. I want that coffee." With that, she pulled the rearview mirror in her direction.

He reached into the back seat and extracted his shirt. His eyes strayed to the rear deck, and saw the two pixies huddled behind his hat. Their eyes were like little saucers, and they were grinning from ear to ear. What was this going to cost him? The shirt was still damp, but he put it on anyway. When he looked up through the windshield of the car, he saw three young waitresses from the restaurant staring out at them.

CHAPTER 17

Pride of Virginia Coffee House

Walking into the restaurant, Jake was totally embarrassed by the free show they had provided. The three waitresses stood close to the door and eyeballed them coming in. Suddenly, a little brunette with a ponytail broke free of the group and came up, grabbing two menus on her way.

Jake brushed away at sand on his exposed arms and pants as she led them to a table in back.

"Coffee?" Little Ponytail asked. They both nodded as she gave first Rachel, then Jake, appraising looks and a menu. "Looks like you two had an early morning romp on the beach somewhere."

"Can we get that coffee?" Jake asked.

Ponytail returned with two cups of coffee and asked, "You all want breakfast?" It seemed like ages ago that they had nibbled at breakfast in Nags Head while listening to Sheila's story.

"I'm starved," Rachel said, and looked up at the server. "How about you, Jake?"

"I'm starved, too."

Ponytail took their order, and when she left, Rachel leaned back in the booth and stretched. "I'm sorry I got so upset earlier, Jake. It's just that . . ." She stopped, and tears started to well up in her eyes again.

He leaned over and whispered, "I'm never going to leave you, Rachel."

"That's what I thought last time."

"Look, we've got three days until Monday. Why don't we enjoy them? If you still think I'm going to leave you on Monday, we'll revisit the topic. Let's not waste three days worrying about something we've no control over right now. You have to trust me; I'm yours if you want me." He realized now that his running from his past was history. He felt compelled to somehow and someway merge his Flammerian life with his Earth life.

* * *

For much of the remainder of the drive home, Rachel slept.

Ten minutes from Annapolis, she awoke with a start and, by the time they reached her apartment, she was bright-eyed and asking questions. Other than the stops for meals and the beach, Jake had been driving continuously for two days, including both nights. He was dead tired. Rachel was unsympathetic with his state of alertness, however, and after a string of additional questions about his activities back home, none of which he answered, she affixed her multicolor eyes on him in a condescending glare and pushed him down on the bed.

"Sleep, my big stud muffin," she declared. "I'll expect you to be ready to go tonight, though." He didn't even remember her taking his clothes off, but when he awoke, he found himself totally undressed and under the covers. Sleeping on top of him was Snow. When he stirred, Snow jumped off and once again focused on the TV above them. He'd almost forgotten about Glimmer and Ceellia, but could see their little eyes watching him.   Rolling over found him face-to-face with a grinning, wide-awake Rachel.

"Someone named Gert called," she said. "You do seem to have attracted a lot of women in your life, space boy. Gert said the Coast Guard found the boat and had contacted the Wells home. They wanted someone to come and claim it. She sounded very nice, so I told her you and I would take care of it."

"Take care of it? How? We—"

"Relax, Jake. It's already done. I have a friend, ex-classmate really, who runs a boat repair facility down that way. I figured the boat might need some work, so he's going to pick it up and check it out. It should be ready for us to pick up on Monday."

"What's today?" he asked. "How long did I sleep?"

"It's still Saturday, Jake. You only slept a few hours. It's around two."

It was only a few hours, but his biological clock was completely confused. He felt hungry and sleepy at the same time, but when he turned and saw the whole Rachel, he discovered a new hunger. She was completely naked, except for a string of pearls around her neck and a matching pearl bracelet on one wrist.

"Is this how you found your princess on Mars? I recall she had some kind of jewelry, but this is the best I could do."

"We should get ready," he implored. "Brian's party is today—"

"We don't have to get ready until four. We've plenty of time."

He mock-groaned, but it did no good at all. While desperately loving the attention from her, all he could envision was the upcoming snide remarks from Glimmer and Ceellia. Not to mention what Rachel would do if she found out she was being watched. As soon as she kissed him though, all his tiredness and concerns melted away. She always had that effect on him.

An hour later they had both showered, and as he got dressed, Jake noticed Rachel sat on the bed, still wrapped in a towel, apparently deep in thought.

"Are you tired?" he asked.

"Don't be ridiculous, Jake. You couldn't tire a grandmother. We're going to Emily's. I need just the right outfit to piss her off. Come here and do my toes while I plot some evil strategy."

He had forgotten that Rachel and Emily, Brian's wife, didn't get along. Emily had been going with Brian at the time he left ten years ago, and, out of all his then closest friends, she was the one person who had been unsupportive when he was going through the mess with April. She had believed him capable of what he was accused of doing. Of course, that had never sat well with Rachel, who back then needed little excuse to stoke Emily's fires.

He walked over, sat at the base of the bed and shook his head.

Rachel positioned her feet on the edge of the bed and handed him a small plastic box containing cotton balls, a bottle of polish remover, and the *Russian Navy* nail polish. "You do such a good job, Jake. I hated doing them myself when you disappeared. It would always bring the hurt back."

"Why didn't you just change colors?"

"Don't be stupid. It's all I had of you and I didn't want to forget you. Now, leave me be while I figure out how to really piss that bitch off. Make sure you get all the old polish off first, Jake. No quickie jobs."

"Couldn't we just forgive and forget?" he asked.

"You have no idea how that woman talked about you, do you? You're lucky I don't go to this event dressed like the princess you found on Mars. With just my string of pearls."

"Try to forgive Emily," he pleaded. "I have."

"Let's see how she treats you, first."

After first removing the old polish, he painted her toenails while she studied her open closet from afar, apparently cycling through the outfits in her mind. Then and there, he knew this was going to be trouble. Tonight, he decided, it sucked to be Emily. Rachel was devious, and he knew how her mind worked. Picking an outfit that would stir up Emily's puritanical ire would also accomplish her goal of getting him all hot and bothered. She'd win on both counts.

"Done," he announced. While she wiggled her toes in an apparent attempt to speed drying, he got ready, dressing casually in a navy blue polo and tan slacks. Finally satisfied, she jumped off the bed and glided over to her closet. She pulled out a skimpy yellow outfit and held it up to the closet mirror.

Rachel had two sides. She could be meek and demure, as she always was professionally, or she could be borderline vindictive. Of course, at the Academy most people only saw the demure Rachel. Once they connected, Jake saw both. The vindictive Rachel was not to be trifled with. Up till now, he had only known two people on that side of the fence, April and Emily. For some reason, despite his many faults—including being just a plain jackass at times—she never put him there.

April had made his princess's bad list not only for apparently trying to take Jake away, but also for the accusations that, unknown to Rachel, Jake eventually used to his advantage to escape his past. While a part of the real reason had been Laura and the station, Jake let his Earth friends believe the April affair was the cause for his disappearance. Though, to be entirely honest, April was a part of it, as he recalled.

Emily, for not supporting him to the extent that Rachel thought appropriate, was in a smaller doghouse, but nevertheless, not in Rachel's good graces. He was glad Sheila was his sister; else she'd have probably made the list just for being so damned cute.

Rachel used her body as a weapon. She had put on a pale yellow bra and panties, then slipped on a skirt that barely covered her backside, followed by a sleeveless top that embraced her figure like shrink-wrap. Again this was part of the two-sided Rachel, meek and demure at work and such, glamour girl and sexpot when she wanted to be. Poor Emily, who he recalled was no slouch in the beauty department, didn't have a chance no matter how she dressed. He was already wishing they were coming back rather than heading out . . .

Rachel shook out her hair and said, "By the way, Jake, I'm driving today. The 'Bird needs some air."

The 'bird' was her pride and joy, a 2005 Thunderbird that she had bought just before they split. She kept it in immaculate condition. He'd always thought it mirrored the two sides of Rachel, with its black interior and *Whisper White* exterior.

CHAPTER 18
BRIAN'S GET TOGETHER

Brian lived in Eastport, which was just to the south and slightly east of Annapolis. When Jake and Rachel arrived, they found that Dan, his wife, Kyra, and their kids had just beaten them there. While the kids had already departed for the backyard and its complement of playground equipment, Brian, Dan, and both wives stood by Dan's car.

As much as Emily and Rachel avoided one another, Kyra and Rachel were kindred spirits. It was as if they had collaborated on the phone. Kyra wore a very short navy skirt with an equally form-fitting white top. Jake could swear they smiled at each other conspiratorially. Apparently, Emily was not privy to their fashion statement, for she was simply dressed in a green patterned top with black shorts. Emily's eyes surreptitiously migrated from Kyra's outfit to Rachel's and back.

"Hello, Jake," Emily greeted him with an outstretched hand, as if daring him to take it.

"Hi, Em," was all he got out.

Kyra flew past her and mashed her body into Jake in a genuine display of affection. She hugged him long and hard. When she finally let go, she kissed him and said, "Damn, I missed you, Jake. How could you leave us like that?"

"Beer, Jake?" Brian mercifully interrupted, making Kyra's question seem rhetorical. Kyra snaked her arm around Jake's waist and clung to him while steering him inside. They were followed closely by Rachel, bookended by Dan and Brian, while Emily, staring at the ground, brought up the rear.

The evening went strangely. For most of it, Brian, Dan and Jake hung out outside around the grill, reliving old times and laughs. While they had kept in touch with email, both queried Jake endlessly about what he had done the last ten years and reminded him of how stupid he had been to leave Rachel. He deflected their questions as best he could, because while they were right about Rachel, he had no desire to dredge up any past misdeeds.

While they were out there, Rachel and Kyra sat inside, comparing notes on everything from fashion to their times in the Navy. Kyra had also gone to the boat school, which made her and Rachel a natural fit. Nothing tighter than two girl grads after the shared experience of enduring four years surrounded by guys and their strange habits. Academy girls were much more than the equal of the guys who went there. They had to be confidantes, fashion and dating advisors, sounding boards and, at times, moms to their male counterparts. Jake had always pitied the older guys who bragged they were at the Academy in the good times, meaning the Academy before women were allowed. If they only knew how much of a positive move it was for the academies to permit women to compete for appointments. Current male midshipmen, or mids, were so much more well-rounded for having spent their four years with the opposite sex.

At times, when he went inside to check on Rachel, go to the bathroom, or get something for Dan, Jake saw Emily linger near the two ex-Navy girls, but she always looked sad and on the outside. He knew that if he asked Rachel to let up the silent treatment, she would, but that wouldn't solve the problem of what Emily represented to her. Emily was a townie, from nearby West Annapolis, and most mid girls hated the townies. It wasn't because they were jealous of sharing their male counterparts; it was because townies seemed to despise that which they could not fathom, a girl at the Navy's school that for more than one hundred and twenty-five years had been for men only. To most townies, mid girls were freaks, someone you threw hard candy at on the midshipmen march-over to home football games, someone you made fun of at the plebe dances, called pig-pushes, someone they felt couldn't get a guy any other way but to go to a school where guys outnumbered the girls five to one. Still, he knew that despite all of that, Rachel would accept her, had she shown support for him in his difficult time years ago.

Around ten, with the kids all scattered to the bedrooms asleep, the six adults retired to the patio and pool. While the three guys stayed together, Rachel and Kyra pulled up chairs around a table in one corner, and Emily sat on the lip of the pool, her feet dangling in the water. Jake felt sorry for her. He didn't know why; she had helped make his life miserable just before he left the area. Tonight, though, she had been strangely subdued. Almost avoiding him altogether. The few times their eyes met, she would smile weakly, unsteadily. It was almost as if she was . . . sorry?

Later, Jake adjourned to the house. When he came out of the bathroom, he saw Emily, leaning against the opposite wall.

"Can I talk to you, Jake?" she asked.

He nodded.

She walked into the living room, and he followed. As she settled into the middle seat of the sofa, he chose the chair that faced her. She appeared very nervous, moving back and forth on the couch and drumming her fingers on her knees. Jake braced for the worse. Was she going to ask him to leave? Complain about Rachel?

"I'm sorry I doubted you ten years ago, Jake. I feel very guilty for the way I acted and the awful things I thought and said about you. I know you probably hate me but . . ."

He was lost. What, he wondered, had caused her apparent change of heart?

"Brian has stuck by you all these years, and I should know my husband. If he believed in you, then I should have too." While she spoke, he noticed tears well up in the corners of her eyes. "I'm sorry, please forgive me."

"There's nothing to forgive, Emily. And hate you? Please. I hold no grudges against anyone. I was stupid to leave ten years ago. I should have—"

"Is this a private confession or can we all listen in?" Rachel's voice asked.

Jake looked to the doorway, where Rachel and Kyra stood. Silently, they both went to the sofa where Emily sat, sandwiching her in. Each, in turn, quietly hugged Emily. Rachel reached over to a nearby end table and snared a box of tissues. Kyra yanked one out and used it to gently dab at the corner of Emily's eyes.

"I'm sorry I treated you like shit," Rachel stated to Emily. "None of us hates you."

"Yeah," continued Kyra. "But you didn't appear to accept Jake, and, well, Academy grads stick together, even the women."

"Truth be known," said Emily, "I was jealous of you two. When I was fifteen and stupid, I thought the only girls who chose the Academy were losers. Then I met you two. You could talk circles around me. You two could not only relate to your men, but you were gorgeous. I didn't know how I was supposed to compete with you. "

"It's not a competition," Kyra added. "Neither of us is in the Navy anymore and now, like it or not, you're one of us. We're just women. Besides, you're quite the looker, Emily."

Rachel looked over at Jake then and said, "What the hell are you still doing here, Foley? Get out with the guys. We ladies are going to talk, now."

As he got up, so did Emily. She gave him a quick hug and then sat back down.

"Everything okay in there?" Brian asked when Jake retreated to the safety of the outdoors.

He nodded. "Yeah. Thanks again, guys, both of you, for being there for me. I was stupid to run away."

"That's just fitting, Foley," Dan said. "You were always behind us in school, too."

"Yeah," Brian replied. "The only reason we hung out with you was for the chicks."

They all laughed at that. Jake recalled his older sister telling him that his brooding exterior attracted girls. Dan excused himself and went inside to use the bathroom.

When Dan left, Brian turned serious. "Speaking of chicks," he said. "Ever think of her?"

"Who are we talking about?" Jake asked.

"April Elliot," he replied.

Jake looked down, and then back at him. "I'd be lying if I said I didn't. But that part of my life is closed, not to be revisited," he answered.

"I think you might want to reconsider that, Jake. She's with a VFA squadron in Oceana."

"Yeah," Jake interrupted. "Rachel told me. She thought that's why I came back. But I had no way of knowing that and, to tell the truth, it's been ten years. I doubt she even remembers me." Even as he said it, he knew it wasn't true. And, he had begun to suspect that April was part of the reason he was drawn back here. "I always thought she'd make one hot-ass fighter jock, though."

"Not remember you? Boy, you are naive. You guys doing anything tomorrow?" Brian's voice broke his recall.

Jake shook his head.

"If I set it up, will you go to Oceana? Talk to April? There are things you should know, Jake. Only April can tell you."

He was about to say no dice, he had to resist seeing her, but hesitated. He knew there was no way Brian could know the actual truth of what happened ten years ago, but what did he think he knew?

"What do you mean? How do you know she'd even talk to me? What can April tell me?"

At first, Brian was quiet. Then finally, he spoke.

"Some things happened after you left, Jake. I only found out 'cause of my job. I don't know the fine details of what occurred back then when you left, just what you told me and what was in the Academy report. The actual records of the formal proceedings are sealed. My instruction, a note from April actually, should you ever surface, was to simply contact April. So I talked to her yesterday, and she explained to me the broad facts, but insisted that to no one, except you, would she ever tell certain things and she had to be the one to tell you. She requested that I ask you to please come down to Virginia Beach and meet with her. That's all I know. Honest."

That started all kinds of things whirling around in Jake's head. What the hell had happened after he left? Had April . . . no, she wouldn't. What was he going to tell Rachel about all of this? But he needed to know what the heck April was supposed to relay to him. Maybe she wanted to discuss their pact. Maybe she could shed light on what was going on.

Because he was beginning to suspect there was more to his visit here than he realized.

In the end, he nodded to Brian. "Set it up."

He realized he had made the decision not to come clean with Rachel and tell her he needed to see April. He hated to lie again, but kept telling himself it was for the best. He did not want to chance blowing their tenuous relationship.

The next morning came all too quickly. When Jake awoke, he kind of remembered Rachel had stayed sober at the party, and they had left around two a.m., but for him the night had definitely ended in a beer-induced haze. He struggled to see the clock, but it was too blurry. Then Snow appeared from nowhere and bumped his shoulder. He rolled over to face Rachel. She did not look happy.

"Well, look who's up, Snow. Were you planning on sleeping all day, spaceman?"

He shook his head. "What time is it?"

"Seven, lover boy, and I use the term loosely."

He struggled into a sitting position and gazed around. Snow had picked a spot next to him and sat, primly licking a silver paw. "I think I need a shower to wake me up."

"I think you need more than that, but first, what are we doing today?" Rachel's eyes bore into him. Could she already be suspicious? "I've already showered. So, while you're doing that, I can get dressed. I just need to know for what."

"How about the beach?" He hoped that sounded casual.

"Sure, Eastern Shore? Want to go to Ocean City?"

He shook his head. "I was thinking more like Virginia Beach."

"You want to go all the way down to Virginia Beach? Why? We won't get there till late."

"I thought we could walk the beach this afternoon, get a hotel room down there, stay the night and in the morning, hit the waves and then drive up to St Michaels to meet Sheila."

"Okay, Jake, if that's what you want."

He thought that was a little fast in the agreement department, but he let it go.

Before they had left last night, Brian made the call to April and then took Jake aside and instructed him to drive down to Virginia Beach and park along the ocean, south of 25th Street. From there, he was to walk north along the beach. The meeting, Brian assured him, would look accidental. Of course, April would probably not want to talk with Rachel there, but that was his problem. He just hoped that Rachel would buy that the meeting was accidental, and that she wouldn't go ballistic on him when he tried to talk to April alone.

He quickly showered and dressed, and by 7:30 a.m. they were at Buddy's Crabs and Ribs, in Annapolis, for brunch. By 8:45 a.m., they were on the Interstate down to Virginia Beach. It was a good five-to-six-hour drive to the beach area, so he let Rachel take her T-Bird. She drove the first couple of hours while he napped. When they stopped for gas down around Richmond, he took over.

As soon as he got behind the wheel he checked the rearview mirror. Tiny eyes stared back at him from behind his ball cap, which told him his little companions had successfully kept up. If Rachel deduced anything odd about him bringing the ball cap everywhere, but not wearing it, she didn't vocalize her notions. At times she stared out the front windshield, at other moments he felt her eyes on him. He had thought that she would want to nap, but that was not to be. It was like she had guard duty, and he really began to wonder what she knew and didn't know. Did she suspect where they were going? Was this a test to see if he'd tell? He felt so goddamn guilty. Finally, just south of Williamsburg, he took the next exit and pulled to the side of the road.

"Why did you pull off, Jake? Is there something wrong with my car?"

"No," he said. "We need to go back. I can't do this."

"What? Don't you want to talk to *her*?"

She knew. Damn that Brian and his big mouth.

"I'm sorry to deceive you. I . . ."

"Do you think I'm dumb, Jake? Why else would you drive over two hundred and fifty miles to go to a particular beach? A beach that just happens to be close to where she is stationed. I just don't understand why you took me along. How were you gonna get away from me? How did you plan to get on the base anyway?"

He sat quietly, amazed at her powers of deductive reasoning, and mentally apologizing to Brian for thinking he told her. He was unsure how he should tell her the rest.

"Oh my God. Is she meeting you somewhere? Did you make some arrangement with her? Did you call her?"

"Stop it, Rachel. No. I didn't talk to her. But yes, I was to meet her. Brian arranged it. It wasn't my idea." He explained how there was something she could tell only him, and he assumed it had to do with things that happened ten years ago.

"You know what's saving your ass here, my little Buck Rogers? You've never really had time away from me to make a phone call. I actually believe you didn't set this up yourself. Of course, knowing how political the Academy is makes this whole 'secret' thing plausible. But I'm sure you want to know how I knew, don't you?"

He nodded.

"Emily and I are now best buds. That tell you anything?"

He should have guessed that.

"So what now, spaceman?"

"I'm sorry to drag you this far only to come to my senses at the last minute. Let's head back."

"Are you crazy, Jake? You told me the truth. On your own. That's the only important thing here."

She stared across at him. It was true, he realized. He had finally put her first.

"You've got to find out what this is, Jake. Besides, I'm wearing my new bikini and I want to show it off." She opened her blouse and showed him a bright red top that he swore seared his eyeballs. If this girl wasn't the hottest thing. "Keep the meeting, Jake. Maybe I'll get lucky and pick up some normal guy from Earth on the beach. Get our asses back on 64."

He did.

CHAPTER 19
APRIL ELLIOT

Walking north along the beach, Jake was relieved to have told Rachel the relative truth, but knew that she might not be that happy if she heard the whole story. Heck, April wouldn't exactly be happy to revisit the past either. Everyone seemed to think the 'affair' with April was why he left ten years ago, but that was simply coincidental to his problem with Laura, the station and, to a lesser extent, his pact with April. Was he now headed down the same road? Only with Sheila instead of Laura?

Rachel had volunteered to walk off into the surf and let him talk with April alone. She had a blind faith in him, which he couldn't help but feel he had done nothing to deserve. And of course, after she had stripped down to the postage stamp-sized red bikini, he was hesitant to let her out of his sight. As they walked, she ignored the zillions of beach-goers' eyes focused on her, choosing to instead remind him that he was her choice by periodically using her bare feet to kick sand on him and giggle.

When they got in the area near 27th Street, he began to pay close attention to girls, especially those with light blonde hair. Brian had said she would meet him somewhere in that area. Suddenly, Rachel stiffened and squeezed his hand. When he looked over at her, she was staring off to the west. Looking in that direction, he saw a large umbrella planted in the sand shading two beach chairs. One was empty; the other was occupied by a girl in sunglasses and an orange bikini, waving at them. Seeing them stop, she threw her no longer short, but now curly, much longer, pale yellow hair back and smiled, then bounded up out of the chair and ran down to where they stood.

A huge smile on her face, April Elliott flipped her sunglasses up onto her head and looked from Jake to Rachel. For several long seconds, no one spoke.

Then April broke the tension by putting her arms around Jake and hugging him. He had thought she was hot when they first met at eighteen, more so at twenty-two, when she was at the Academy. Now, at thirty-two, she was sizzling. He didn't know what to do. She solved his dilemma by pulling away, but continued to smile up at him.

"How are you, sir?" she purred.

"You no longer need to call me that," he said. "I've been out of the Navy for a long time."

Rachel and April looked at one another with neither disdain nor any perceptible emotion. Jake stood silent, weak in the knees at the sight of the girl who almost made him forget Rachel.

"I'm sorry, Rachel." April was the first to speak. "You probably hate my guts, and I can live with that, as long as you make him happy."

"I'll let you two *talk*," Rachel replied a little icily and turned away from the surf.

"Wait!" April said. "There's some Sam Adams in my cooler. Please help yourself. I'll make it as brief as I can. If possible, I do want us to be friends, Rachel."

"No need to hurry." Rachel's icy glare thawed slightly as it shifted from April to Jake. "I think Jake is in his glory. Orange is his second favorite color." Rachel then smiled at April. "Red wins though, honey."

As Rachel headed toward the cooler, April focused all of her attention on him. "You're looking well, sir."

"Sir?" he replied. "You outrank me now, April. Plus, I told you I'm out of the Navy."

"You're still the finest officer I've ever met. Heck, you know how I feel about you. You were always a premium person." She gave him a silent wink as if they were co-conspirators, which in fact, they were. "You were always there for me when I needed someone, Jake. You fell on your sword for me; don't think I've ever forgotten it. Not for one day in these last ten years."

By now, Rachel had made her way over to April's little oasis in the sand, and Jake watched as she opened the cooler and pulled out a beer. Her eyes, though, never left them.

"Rachel is even prettier than I remembered from that picture on your desk. You've done well, Jake."

"I don't deserve her," he said. "Let's cut the bullshit. What's this all about, April? I thought we were finished."

"Oooo, you're all business. That's so like you. Don't worry, I've kept our secrets. Were you wondering about that when Commander Hurst said I needed to see you?"

"No, April. I knew you were an honorable person. Not many of us around. I trusted you implicitly. I assumed it was something else."

"Yeah, you're right. This has nothing to do with our pact. The four guys confessed, Jake. Right after you left. They went to the Commandant and told him the truth, how they lured me out into town, got me drunk and left me on a bench by the Dock. See the effect you have on people? They exonerated you. Told the 'Dant that you were the best of the best and wanted you brought back. But you were already gone." April pulled on the straps of her top. "The 'Dant brought them up on charges, but I convinced him that he'd already lost one fine officer to this sordid affair, why lose an additional four future officers? I told him I didn't want to press charges; I just wanted you reinstated." Her eyes seemed to get misty and her voice lowered.

"Since so few people knew what really happened, he thought that the best solution was to let things lie. He said he knew you were thinking of retiring anyway, and he wanted to avoid adverse publicity for the Academy. Heaven knows you and I were dragged through the local papers enough. I don't see how they thought what might have happened was so inappropriate anyway. Just cause you were my company officer shouldn't have mattered. I even called the paper to tell them I was a consenting adult."

"Yeah," he said. "I didn't think they'd play up all those smutty angles. However, you were a student, so what they thought we did was wrong. Remember they said we were meeting in town and stuff. Even though it wasn't true, many people believed it. And look at you. You're a vision. If I remember correctly, probably every guy in your class hit on you at one time or another. Why should me doing it have been so unbelievable?"

"Pooh on that. I think some of my classmates invented shit back then just to get even with me. Finally, after a lot of tears, I agreed with the 'Dant. After all, I knew you would, and there was no way you were coming back. I knew it fit into our plan. He then brought the four guys and me in his office and told them what essentially were my wishes.

"He also said he found it a bitter pill to swallow that they would get off unpunished. His ruling was that none of us were allowed to ever speak about it again. They were restricted to the Yard for the remainder of the year but allowed to graduate. After he dismissed them, he told me that the only person I was allowed to speak to about any of this was you, should I ever meet with you. He wanted you to know what happened. Although he had no right to say that, I agreed. Hence the note I left asking that I be notified if you ever showed up. I never expected it to come true. I was lucky one of your buddies was at the Academy. For what it's worth, I'm sorry, Jake. It's my fault your career got cut short. I know that was the plan, but . . ." She wiped at the tears running down her cheeks.

"No problem, April. All I wanted was to see you get your chance. Plus I needed to get away from that Flammerian bullshit, which you knew. I don't know how we got talked into— " By now they had stopped walking and stood a few yards from the water, probably a hundred yards up the beach from where Rachel sat. But now, she was not alone. A tanned, middle-aged guy in a navy blue swimsuit was sitting in the other chair and talking to her. April grabbed his arm.

"Commander Bill Evans, Jake. A friend. Well, actually, we're dating." She blushed. "Uh, he's also the squadron CO."

"What?" he exclaimed. "Haven't you learned anything since the Academy? You can't fraternize with your commanding officer."

Her fingers dug into his bicep. "It's a complicated situation. Please don't say anything. It's my problem, and I'll solve it."

While he was furious with her apparent lack of common sense, he also knew he was no longer her advisor and she was well past the age of reason. "Okay," he said. "You need not apologize for ten years ago, April. There are things you don't know either, but now is not the time. I had other reasons for bolting, and they didn't have anything to do with you. Seeing you, what you've become, makes our pact all the more worthwhile. But be careful with that guy."

"I will. You know, Rachel was one of my other reasons for getting you down here. I actually tried to see her back then, explain what you did, but in the end I felt bound by the promise I'd made to you."

"It's a good thing you didn't. You might have slipped and told her too much."

"Hey, you forget who you're talking to. Do you think I'd be foolish and tell her about that day on the beach? I'm a Flammerian. Anyway, I even went to her apartment several times but just couldn't ring the bell. I think she should know the truth of what happened in relation to the four guys, why . . . Anyway, she's a grad; I think she can keep our secret."

Jake's eyes narrowed in disagreement.

"Not our pact or . . . origins, Jake, the Academy secret. What you did for me."

"Are you sure?"

She nodded. "Yep. Can I tell her? Over dinner? Will you guys join me?"

"Just you?"

She nodded eagerly. "Just the three of us."

"Okay. But you're not going to tell her everything, are you?"

"Of course not. Don't worry, our secrets, including the pact, will remain safe." Her grin was instantaneous, and her blue eyes flashed with excitement. He could finally see what April Elliott looked like when she was happy. This was not the nervous girl he knew from the Academy. She threw her arms around him and hugged him tightly.

"Thanks, Jake. I'd like to kiss you, but I don't want to push my luck and get you in trouble. I think we'll both be better able to cope if your future partner knew the truth."

He pulled away. "Hey, how do you know she's my future partner? I never—"

"Please, Jake. A girl knows these things. And, besides being the best fighter pilot you ever met, I'm still a woman."

"Best fighter pilot? You're so full of yourself."

"You made me so," she laughed. This was a first. He had rarely seen this girl laugh, nor had he ever seen her cry. "All I am today I owe to you."

"You owe me nothing."

"I saw the way you look at her." April's blue eyes sparkled in the sun as she talked. "I have to admit, you have good taste."

"She's an Earthie. You hardly know her."

"Yeah, I think I do. I ran into this helo pilot on the Nimitz that was a classmate of hers. She said Rachel had a reputation as some kind of ice princess at the Academy. Guys couldn't even get to first base with her. Except for one guy. I heard he knocked her over at a basketball game while she was cheering." She grinned, bent down to the water, and splashed her face to remove the traces of tears.

"Yeah, but I was stupid then," he said to her bent figure. "At the time, I never followed up on that."

She popped up and fixed sparkling blue eyes on him. "You never followed up on me, either."

CHAPTER 20
APRIL'S REVELATIONS

"I could never keep up with a girl who uses JP5 for deodorant," he said matter-of-factly, but was she actually interested in him? He'd thought the affair after meeting on the beach was the extent of their relationship.

"Jet fuel?" April sniffed her arm. "Are you saying I smell like the carrier?"

"No," he said. "I was being funny. Trying, anyway."

"Yeah, well, this girl has confidence. If Rachel wasn't sitting there watching us, I'd have you eating out of my hand."

He glanced at that orange bikini as discreetly as possible with Rachel watching. Little did April know that was very close to the truth.

"Anyway, you came back to Maryland. Why else, but for her?"

He was about to say, "No, I came back on family business," but caught himself. He decided he wasn't ready to revisit their pact, and if he was to close this chapter, it was best to let her think what she wanted. If there was another assignment that had drawn him back here, April was obviously not aware of it. Yet.

She linked her arm in his and they walked back to the spot where Rachel sat with April's friend. As they got close, Jake could see that although Rachel was pretending to listen to CDR Evans's sea stories, her eyes kept shifting from April's arm entwined with his to her figure in the tiny orange bikini.

After April introduced Bill to him, they made some small talk. She only gave Jake's first name and said he was one of her old instructors from the Academy. Obviously, he knew nothing of their history, but it was all Jake could do to avoid punching him in the mouth. CDR Evans, more than anyone, should have been aware of the Navy regulation against fraternizing with his staff officers.

Rachel smiled and nodded pleasantly, and Jake assumed that she had said nothing about why April and he were talking while she and Bill had been by themselves. As wild as Rachel could be when they were alone, in public she was stoic. That's what had earned her the ice woman tag at the Academy.

"Sorry, I've got to get going," Bill said. "Duty calls."

After Bill left, April asked, "How about the three of us do dinner?"

Rachel's dual-colored eyes flashed to Jake's blue-grays, hung there for a second, then returned to April's blue ones. "I'd like that," she said softly.

* * *

April had suggested the Bluefish, an upscale seafood restaurant to the south of Virginia Beach. Jake remembered it from his time in Norfolk. Luckily, as she got in her car for the ride over, she called and got them a reservation, saving a twenty-minute wait.

Rachel and Jake drove themselves. She was understandably quiet.

"We okay?" he asked.

"Was holding her hand necessary? The news that good?"

"Come on, Rachel. I meant nothing by it. Besides, she slipped her arm into mine."

"I know. That's the only thing saving your ass, lover boy."

When he had a chance to look back in the rearview mirror, the two Distans pointed at him and pretended to laugh heartily.

* * *

After an enjoyable seafood dinner, they ordered some wine.

Inevitably, the conversation switched over to the Yard and that past incident. Rachel started asking discreet little questions regarding April's shared experience with Jake.

"Look, I know you're fishing for what the status of our relationship was back then," April announced suddenly, looking over at Rachel. "That's perfectly understandable. Despite what you might think, at the Academy it was strictly platonic. You need to hear what I have to say. Events did not happen the way you or others may think. Simply put, Jake stepped in and saved my Naval career."

Rachel shot a quick look at Jake, then picked up her wine and sipped.

Clearly, April had her attention.

"I didn't get along with my classmates." April looked directly at Rachel. "They didn't like me because I treated them like the juveniles I thought they were. Jake tried to convince me to join in their little games, if only to make friends. So I thought I'd try it. Four guys from my company took me out one night, I thought in the spirit of camaraderie. You know . . . shipmates. Instead they got me drunk and left me on a bench by the Dock area. When I was found by the Annapolis Police, they took me back to the Academy where I was brought up on charges. I wasn't underage, but I was out after liberty and, according to them, publicly drunk and disorderly. Yeah, I slapped one of them. I thought he was a little overzealous in a touchy-feely way.

"As you know, Jake was my Company Officer. When he came to get me, I told him what happened, and he brought the four guys into his office and confronted them. They all denied doing anything to me. They admitted going out with me, but said I ditched them and went off on my own. They intimated that I met up with some other guy; that I was the one covering things up. Jake tried, but could not break their alibi and story. Everyone in my company but Jake thought I was guilty."

Rachel's fingers twirled her empty wine glass as she listened.

"Jake appealed to the four as future officers to tell the truth. They insisted they were doing just that. I thought I was doomed. I knew the 'Dant would have no choice but to have me kicked out. Jake knew that all my life I wanted nothing else but to fly for the Navy. He watched as I started to crumble. My dream had turned into a nightmare."

As April talked, Jake's mind went back to those days, because at the same time he had been personally going through the ugly business with Laura. He had seen both incidents as his chance to escape from both that situation and his heritage, so he'd suddenly bolted from Annapolis and never looked back. Back then he'd thought they could think what they wanted, but now he didn't really want that. Now he had to set the record straight. At least with Rachel.

"Then, Jake took me aside and told me he had a plan." April continued to relate what had happened. "He instructed me to tell the 'Dant that he'd also met me that night, and he was the one who got me drunk and left me at the dock."

Rachel gasped and dropped her glass, which rolled towards the end of the table. Jake caught it just before it went over the side.

April had started to cry. "I didn't want to do it," she mumbled between tears. "Jake was my rock; he believed in me when no one else did. He was what I considered the ideal naval officer, and here he was asking me to betray him. For the longest time, I continued to refuse. I just couldn't. He insisted. Said he was getting out of the Navy anyway. I knew he had a girlfriend, and I asked him about what you would think. He said . . ." April looked over at him.

She was doing great, he thought, and nodded for her to continue.

". . . He said he believed your relationship was headed south anyway, and that this would give him an excuse to leave."

Rachel's head dropped.

April wiped at her eyes and looked back at Jake.

"He finally convinced me it was for the best. So I did it. Told everyone we were having an affair even though Jake never touched me. He never showed any emotion toward me. I hated to, but it settled the matter immediately. Jake resigned, I was exonerated for extenuating circumstances, and I went on to graduate. However, Jake left the Navy and dropped, I thought, off the end of the earth. Until now. You have no idea how happy I was to hear he was back."

April picked up her small purse and pulled out a tissue. After wiping her eyes and blowing her nose, she continued.

"It's so good to have the record set straight, at least with you, Rachel. By the way, I forgot to say this is for your ears only. Jake and I just agreed on the beach to let you in on the secret."

"You did that?" Rachel asked, staring over at him. "Took the fall to give her a career?"

Jake nodded. There was more to it than that, but he was not ready to go there.

Suddenly, April stood up. "I should go. I think you both would like some privacy. I'll be on the beach tomorrow morning, same spot. If you guys have the time, join me before you head back."

Rachel got up and hugged April. Then April was gone. Rachel began twirling her wine glass again and looked up at Jake.

"Sorry," he said. "After all that happened ten years ago, I thought it best to leave the area. April and I had sworn to each other never to tell a soul what really happened."

"You two haven't seen each other since?"

With a shake of his head, he said, "I imagined that April ended up graduating the following year and went on to flight school. However, when I left, that was the last I ever heard of her. Until today. At the time, I thought you and I were on the verge of splitting, so . . ." Even now he was hesitant to tell Rachel that it was family and mission problems that had ultimately caused his exodus. He was also glad April had prefaced her story of their relationship with 'at the Academy.'

"Forget ten years ago, Jake. She had you come down so that you'd agree to let her tell me?"

"No. That came up while she told me why she really wanted to see me. She had an update for me on what happened after I left." He paused.

Rachel fidgeted, waiting for an explanation. He poured her more wine.

"After I left, the four guys confessed up to being the real villains in all that mess. I was exonerated, but the Academy wanted to keep from dredging up more negative publicity in all of this, so, since I had already gone, everyone was sworn to secrecy and life went on."

"Life went on?" Rachel said. "How could they not want to—?"

"April tried to get me reinstated, but the 'Dant told her that was not possible, that in fact she was lucky he was keeping her. After all, April and I had both lied about what had happened, and you know the Navy never likes to acknowledge they made a mistake. However, the 'Dant knew April had him over a barrel, and in exchange for her silence he allowed her to continue at the Academy. He told her if she ever found me again, she could tell me. Now I'm telling you. I thought you should know. For the record, I agree with all that was done. It's over. Obviously Brian knows, though. I'm sure that's why Emily felt so bad."

"Wasn't this something that only April and you were supposed to know?"

He nodded.

She kissed him on the cheek. "Wow, first I find you're actually from someplace out where Orion lost his belt, and now I find you're like the ultimate friend. If you did that for her, I can only imagine what you'd do for me to keep me safe. I knew it was right to trust you. Let's go to the hotel."

They say be careful what you wish for, and it was evidently true in this situation. Jake had hoped that Rachel would still be around after she heard all of the secrets inside him, and here she was. Well, not quite all of them. Ten years ago, he ran away because he thought he could never mix his personal life with his off-world heritage. Now it looked possible.

Of course, new things, like the Distans, had surfaced. Wasn't that life? Now all he could think about was Rachel hearing the rest of Sheila's revelations and introducing her to his tiny female companions. And Laura. Could he go so far as to tell her the whole truth about April?

Rachel seemed particularly happy that he did not suggest they meet April the next morning, and she was quick to show him how she felt. Over and over. He was never as sore as when they started for St Michaels the next day.

Started is about all they did. They hadn't driven five miles when Sheila broke into his head.

"Jake, is it possible for you and Rachel to pick up the boat and drive it to St Michaels for me? I'll take you back tomorrow to pick up your car. It's important, or I wouldn't ask. It's been serviced and is parked at the public dock in Poquoson."

He looked to Rachel, who smiled and nodded. He envisioned Glimmer and Ceellia transmitting their unspoken agreement.

"Thanks, both of you. There's just one more thing, Jake."

"What's that, Sheila?" Like a fool, he said it aloud.

"The Coast Guard is holding it. Please don't tell them anything."

* * *

171

They arrived at Poquoson, just south of the wildlife refuge, a few hours later. He parked the Bird in a secure space, and after Rachel caught up with her classmate, they walked over to where Sheila's craft bobbed on the water. A Coast Guard UTL boat blocked it from leaving. There was also a black speedboat parked next to it. Two guys in suits waited on the dock for them. They accompanied Jake and Rachel on the cruiser and immediately started asking questions.

"Can you tell us your relationship to the owner of this boat?" Suit Number One asked.

"My dad was a good friend of the owner, who died this past week," Jake answered. "I came out to pay our respects, and the wife asked me to pick up the boat for her. Apparently, some fine citizen took advantage of her grief to steal her late husband's boat. But I'm sure you know all that, don't you? Do you need my ID?" He reached into a back pocket.

"That's not necessary, Mr. Foley. Do you have any idea who might have stolen the boat?" Suit Number Two asked.

Surprise, surprise, Jake thought, he knew my name. "I flew in a couple of days ago from Chicago. I have no idea."

Both looked at Rachel.

"I don't even know the family," Rachel said.

The men looked to each other, and Suit Number Two nodded.

"Have a safe trip back," Suit Number One said. They both then hopped into their little black boat and drove it away. The Coast Guard Utility boat followed them.

"Are you worried about your car?" he asked.

"No, I told you, the owner and I were classmates. He'll watch it for me until we get back to pick it up."

Several hours later, they had put a few miles behind them and were now roughly in the middle of the bay, headed north. The old cruiser skimmed along as if it were still new. He had to wonder if it was one hundred percent Earth manufactured.

When Rachel retired below to make some coffee, he took the time to get an update from Glimmer and Ceellia, who had slipped aboard during the transfer.

"She almost saw me, Mr. Jake," Glimmer said. "You were supposed to get the stuff out of the back seat, not her."

"In case the two of you haven't noticed," he whispered, "it's a little hard to tell her what to do. Now, what is Sheila's plan?"

Glimmer had transmitted Sheila's voice into his head, which confirmed his suspicions. The boat had been modified and was only serviced by the yard in Poquoson. By chance, Rachel had made arrangements with the correct boat shop. Sheila also confirmed something else he had suspected. No Earth spy device could function within the confines of the boat. The Suits' bugging devices were useless. They knew that now; it would explain the helicopter that shadowed them just on the southern horizon.

As Glimmer facilitated their communication, Rachel came into the pilot compartment unnoticed. On her face was a look of absolute astonishment.

"What's going on, Jake? What are those things? Are they drones or are they . . . alive?"

"Drones?" Ceellia sputtered. "Did she just call me a drone?"

CHAPTER 21
DISTANS REVEALED

"Ceellia, you were supposed to be watching," Glimmer said.

"I was listening to Mr. Jake," Ceellia replied, a little sheepishly. "Glim, she called us drones."

Jake couldn't get mad at them, because the damage was done. "Uh . . . you need to sit down, Rache," he said. "There's something, err . . . someone, you don't know about. Well, that's really not true, because you did ask who Glim was."

"Are you crazy? You told me there were no little green men. So are you going to say they're red and yellow? And that they're only six inches tall and have wings? Are you hiding behind semantics?"

"We're not men," Glimmer spoke. "We're Distan women, and so what if we're all different colors? Our species does have men, though. Would you like to meet one?"

Rachel ignored her. "What's next? Is your pet sea monster gonna swim up and take a bite out of my ass?"

"Mr. Jake has a pet sea monster?" Ceellia said to no one in particular.

"Look, Rache, you're overreacting. Let me explain who they are."

"I don't care if you come from Baltimore or Betelgeuse, you're not going to get me to accept some giant mosquitoes as life forms." Rachel was clearly at the end of her rope.

"Mosquitoes?" Ceellia was in Rachel's face immediately. "We are not mosquitoes. Or drones. I don't think I want to be your Distan anymore." Ceellia turned quickly, whipping her long blonde hair across Rachel's nose. She flew over to Jake and hovered near his shoulder. On her face was the angriest expression he'd seen on the normally cordial Distans.

Jake knew he should have explained things to Rachel earlier; now he had to try to nullify the damage done. Sheila had told him the boat had an automatic pilot that could steer the boat as well as detect anything in their path, so he flipped the switch, as she had instructed him, and pulled Rachel out of the cabin and onto the bow, where she stared at him with a gloomy expression on her face. He slipped his hands around her waist and she turned into his embrace. Her multicolored eyes looked deep into his while her arms came up and positioned themselves on his chest as if in a defensive manner, obviously prepared to push him away.

"Look, Jake. I don't think this is going to work," she said. "Ten years ago, you were the absolute love of my life. Around you I would act completely out of character. I basically threw myself at you. But even back then I saw the looks you gave other girls, so I lied and told you maybe we should move on. Did I really want to? No, not for one second. I was ecstatic when you came back into my life. I even accepted that you may not have origins on this planet. But I'm getting constant vibes that I can't trust you. Why are you keeping all this shit a secret from me? Are you out to see if I can accept any strange life form? How many of these things are there? Is that what you are? One of those shape-shifters?"

"No! I'm just as human as you. Moonglimmer and Ceellia are Distans and their species is in danger. My people shield them from those who would enslave them." He wanted to tell her that he had kept silent out of respect for Sheila and Laura, but decided it was time to start taking the blame himself.

"Come on, Jake. I think my original prediction when I first found out about this alien stuff was correct. They'll ask you to go with them, and you will. You'll find yourself a girl from your own world, take your little . . . sparrows . . . in there and leave." She whirled around, looked toward the south horizon, and then stopped and snarled. "By the way, aren't you concerned that chopper is going to discover your little friends?"

He tried to shake his head, then gave up. "No," he croaked. "I know they won't."

The boat suddenly lurched and slowed. It was as if a giant hand had gripped and held it.

"What was that? Did we hit something?" Rachel asked. "Your sea monster buddy?"

"I don't think we hit anything and I don't have any sea monster relations. The automatic pilot should have detected anything in our path. That felt like we might have run up on a shoal or sandbar."

"But we're still moving," she answered. "Maybe there was some damage the yard didn't notice. I'll check out the stern of the boat." About halfway there, she was surprised by Sheila, dressed in a dark gray, metallic jumpsuit. She climbed aboard on the side of the boat out of view of the helicopter. Shaking the water out of her hair, Sheila smiled and motioned them both toward the cabin.

"What . . . how . . . ?" Rachel stammered. She was completely taken aback by Sheila's sudden appearance. "Where did you come from?" she finally got out. "We're in the middle of the Bay."

"I was going to try to be funny," Sheila chuckled. "Tell you my pet sea monster brought me, but you might take me seriously. Actually, my skimmer, that's what we call our small underwater ships, brought me. It's right under this boat. I believe you on Earth also call our skimmers USOs. Jake doesn't care how they work, but I know you would. If you like, Rachel, later I'll have someone explain it to you. I'm not a technical person. Now, as you noticed, you're being watched by that helicopter, so let's get inside."

"That's the feds, and they're pretty sophisticated," Rachel said. "They can probably pick up this conversation."

"Sophisticated? Please, Rachel. You underestimate me and my toys." Sheila looked to Jake. "The entire boat functions as a scatterer."

He nodded as she practically pushed them through the hatch into the boat. The two little Distans sat up on the instrument panel and watched them enter. When Rachel appeared to shy away from them, Ceellia got visibly agitated.

"Boo!" Ceellia said as she flew up close to Rachel, who backed away even further from her.

"Ceellia!" Sheila said. "Rachel is a guest."

Ceellia turned to Sheila. "You said she was warrior class. I don't see it. She called us drones. I want to be reassigned back to—"

"That's enough, Ceellia," Floressa's voice came from behind Sheila, where she was hidden in Sheila's hair.

"We'll talk later, Ceellia," Sheila added.

Having heard Floressa, Rachel looked around for the source of the strange voice.

"Glimmer, you and Ceellia know what I want you to do," Sheila said.

The two Distans immediately flew through the open hatch to the outside.

"My apologies, Rachel. Ceellia has a lot of sass," Sheila said, while Rachel stared at the strange, metallic suit. "This suit absorbs radar and sonar signals," Sheila continued as she shook out of it, exposing a one-piece, metallic green swimsuit.

"Won't they detect those . . . little creatures outside?" Rachel asked, and looked at the open hatch.

"Distans know how to evade detection," Sheila smiled. "After all, they've been with you whenever you were with Jake, and they didn't let you notice them until I told them to."

"You mean they saw . . .?" Rachel's eyes got big as she looked to Jake. "How long have they been with you?" she asked him.

"Apparently since the first time we re-met at the Dragon Pub," he confessed. Rachel buried her face in her hands. "I was unaware then that they were assigned to me. There's a reason they are with me, but that's Sheila's call to explain." He glanced back at Sheila. "*You* told them to let Rachel see them? Now you've gotten her all upset."

"Yes, I instructed them to make it look accidental. Despite what just happened, I think you misjudge Rachel," Sheila announced. "Besides, I have a missing Distan and I needed Glim and Ceellia to continue that search while I'm talking to you."

"Glim? Is that the Glim who . . ." Rachel suddenly put one and one together.

"Yeah, that's what I was trying to tell you," Jake replied. "A missing Distan?" he repeated to Sheila.

"I'll tell you about that later. First I need to qualm Rachel's fears or else she'll let her mind run in the wrong direction."

Rachel shook her head and replied, "Despite all these surprises, you misjudge me, Sheila. My mind won't go off in crazy directions. I do believe your intentions are honorable and that you're not thinking of taking over my planet. However, those creatures—"

"Taking over your planet?" Sheila said. "Why would you even imagine that? We've been here continually for ten thousand Earth years. If we wanted it, which we don't, we'd have taken it long ago. Those little creatures you've now seen are very fragile, and need a world that's stable and perfectly suited to them. Earth is such a world. When their planet became part of a galactic dispute and war, we transported them here. And have guarded them ever since. They are not why I came here today, though. With your FBI watching the house, I thought I'd just meet you out here and finish the story, as well as bring you up to date. While you may think I favor Jake's side in this, Rachel, I wanted desperately to be your friend. It's okay if you reject me. However, I trust you to keep our secret. So, if that's okay, I'd like to offer you a little tour of our research station. After that you're free to go, but I hope you'll accept the Distans and believe me when I say, I'm not here to take my brother from you. I merely want him to help me on a single mission, maybe two. In fact, I might need you too."

That brought a mixture of smile and frown to Rachel. "I think I angered that little bird," Rachel pointed out. Her smile told Jake she thought it was merely a slight, but he recalled how hurt Ceellia had been when he called her a flying Barbie.

"Yes, you did, and that presents me with another problem," Sheila said with a shake of red curls. "I'm afraid Ceellia will now never consent to what I hoped would be her role in this."

"Her role?" Rachel asked, wide-eyed.

"Yes, you see, the Distans facilitate thought transmission between humans. I have a Distan that allows me to talk to Jake from afar. Floressa, come out here."

From behind Sheila, Floressa silently appeared. "Floressa is my Distan and Glimmer's mother. When Jake was a company officer at the Naval Academy, Floressa was his Distan, although Jake didn't know it."

"Are you saying that . . .?" Rachel started.

"Yes," Floressa smiled. "I was with Jake. Always."

CHAPTER 22
SHEILA'S TALE

"Oh my," Rachel said, with a glance at Jake. "Is there video too?"

Floressa laughed and flew off Sheila's shoulder to land on Rachel's. "You were always my favorite out of all Jake's girlfriends," Floressa said. "And no, there is no video."

"I meant no harm when I called Ceellia . . ."

"If you stay with Jake, I'll find another Distan for you." Floressa smiled and flew back to Sheila.

"Jake has Moonglimmer to receive my communication to him and transmit back his reply," Sheila continued. "When you heard me talking to Jake that night in your apartment, it was because Ceellia, who I hoped to be your Distan, made that possible."

That confirmed what Jake had already figured out.

"You mean Ceellia was sending the words to me?" Rachel was struggling with all this. Her manner, usually unflappable, was excited, but she seemed to be accepting of everything that happened.

"Exactly," Sheila said with a smile. "She would then transmit your thoughts and actions back to me."

Jake could see Rachel's face as she started to realize just how much Ceellia and Glimmer had seen. "We have an agreement," he said. "They didn't tell Sheila everything that they heard and saw. Our privacy was respected."

"Glim has told me that when you and Jake were intimate, she and Ceellia would not look," Floressa added.

Rachel instantly relaxed. "I didn't know all of that. Ceellia is kind of cute. Can I apologize to her?"

"No, sadly it's not that simple." Sheila's face turned into a frown. "When you offend a Distan, it's very difficult to undo. Ceellia is an especially free spirit and cannot stand to be called anything but by her name. I think you called her by several non-flattering ones."

Rachel looked crestfallen.

"But I called her a flying Barbie and she seemed to forgive me for that," he pointed out.

"But there's a difference, Jake," Sheila replied quietly.

"A difference?" Rachel asked before he could.

"Yes. What I don't think Jake has yet discovered is that Moonglimmer and Ceellia are very much in love with him. They'll forgive him just about anything."

"In love with him?" Rachel said. She got to her feet with a quizzical look. "But . . ."

"Not what you're probably thinking, Rachel," Sheila said. "This is a love born of loyalty and admiration. The reality of the Distans has been kept a secret on Earth for thousands of years. Very few male humans have ever known of their existence. Most, like Jake's father and mine, were first told of them when they were much older. Jake is the very first young male taken into confidence. Partly because of the Distans' own decision that this be so. In fact, they consider him sort of an idol, a celebrity. The honor of being his Distan is one that is very coveted. That's why Ceellia instantly forgave him."

Of course, he had come to love the little girls just as much. They were very loyal and adept at knowing the right thing to do in any situation. Now he wondered what would happen to Ceellia, who had so looked forward to staying with Moonglimmer.

Sheila continued, "I've slowed the boat down to just a few knots, so we have plenty of time. Your authorities have no idea I've come aboard. This cabin is impervious to any spying methods. We're invisible to them in here. Anything on deck sends them spurious signals. If we made that completely stealth, they'd get suspicious."

"I do want to accept your offer of a tour and go with you. Do I get to ask some questions like you promised?" Rachel asked.

"Absolutely, and I'll answer anything," Sheila explained.

"Can I try to tell Ceellia I'm sorry?"

"It really won't do any good," Sheila replied. "Besides, Glimmer and Ceellia are skimming over the waters of the bay toward home right now. The two of you don't need them for thought transmission, and they can help in the search for Reena. Floressa is with me if the house needs to contact us."

"Reena?" Jake asked. "Little Reena is the one missing?"

"Yes," Sheila replied. "Has been since the morning you left."

Before he could press Sheila for details, Rachel said, "Okay, but before we do the tour, could you please finish the explanation of what you started telling us on the beach in Nags Head?"

Rachel sat down at the small table while Jake sat in one of the long seats. Sheila paced up and down the cabin, obviously trying to think something through.

Jake was feeling guilty. Did he have anything to do with Reena's disappearance? He tried to remember their conversation, but couldn't. Was it a coincidence? Finally, Sheila sat in the pilot's seat and rotated the chair to face them.

"Are we going to stay on autopilot?" Rachel asked.

"In a way. My ship below is still attached to us, and the pilot has matched the normal speed of this boat. He will take care of our movement. We should be undisturbed. Questions?"

"First of all," Rachel said. "I've been drawn into this adventure, so I should at least know whose side I'm on. Where are your ancestors from exactly?"

Sheila was confused by Jake's lack of attention. Something seemed to be bothering him. Hoping to regain his focus, she put a hand on Jake's cheek and turned him further toward her while addressing Rachel. "Flammeria. It's a planet of the star known to Earth as Alpha Centauri B."

"You started to tell me that." Rachel looked to Jake. "I thought it was bullcrap."

"No bullcrap," Sheila said. "In case you're not up on your astronomy, Alpha Centauri B is part of a three-star system in the southern constellation, Centaurus. It is also the closest star grouping to your solar system. However, Jake and I are actually descendants of an Earth race called the Lemurians. Their civilization here on Earth was destroyed when a comet's fragments broke off and plunged into the Southern Pacific Ocean about twelve thousand years ago. Lemuria was swamped, broke apart and submerged while most of the citizens were killed. They were an advanced civilization, and their astronomers had warned of the possible danger from the erratic comet. Many took to boats and eventually landed on different shores after the cataclysm ended. Many reached the western Americas."

"You okay, Jake?" Sheila asked as he continued to stare at a bulkhead.

"Yeah, sorry," he said, "go on." While Jake was concerned primarily about Reena, Sheila's words should spark memories in him. They did not and he couldn't understand why.

"Twelve thousand years ago?" Rachel interrupted. "I thought civilization here started in 6000 BC, with the Sumerians."

"That's what your world would prefer to believe. They ignore things that appear older to advance their own agendas. Trust me, Jake and I are actual descendants of Lemurians that were rescued and taken to Flammeria, and eventually our parents migrated back here."

"Then you're not totally aliens?" Rachel asked.

"Let me explain further," Sheila said. "There actually is such a thing as what you on Earth liken to a Federation of Planets, and they gave the blessing to a rescue attempt proposed by Flammeria. A large group of survivors on one of the remaining pieces of Lemuria was picked up by several Flammerian ships."

"How many survivors?" Rachel asked.

"I think the number was five thousand, seven hundred and fifty-six," Sheila answered. "They were taken to Flammeria and indoctrinated into their way of life. Some were deemed unsuitable and went to other planets. A few were eventually returned to live out their lives back on Earth. Several groups asked to go elsewhere, and they were accommodated."

"Indoctrinated?" Rachel again interrupted.

"That may be too strong a word. Flammeria is a very peaceful world with no weapons. It is mainly a world of explorers and world monitors, and they do not make war on other planets. Most Lemurians fit right in, as it too was a fairly peaceful civilization. Flammeria had to make sure they were not allowing individuals into their home world that did not embrace the concepts they held so dear. The ancestors of Jake and I were among those people. I'm sure Jake has told you that we are no different from the humans who consider themselves native to this planet; after all, we have a common origin. So you're free to interpret our planet of origin anyway you wish."

"Actual Flammerians are . . . Human?" Rachel asked.

"Most intelligent races on other planets, but not all, are human. That's because of the seeders who originally populated the worlds. I can't tell you more than that."

"Why did Jake leave this area to go to Illinois over thirty years ago, and you remained here? If you're siblings, why were you raised apart?" Rachel asked.

"Believe it or not, it started with a love affair between Jake's father and our shared mother. Forty years ago they had an affair out of which Jake's sister, Laura, was born."

"Holy crap," Rachel said loudly, and looked at Jake. "How many sisters do you have?"

"Just two," he said. "Sheila and Laura, at least that's all I know about."

"I already relayed to you what happened afterward and how Jake and I came to be," Sheila continued.

"I'm a little fuzzy on all that. Can you explain that again?" Rachel asked.

"Sure. Sorry, I was intent on watching for my ride, so I probably glossed over things. Jake's dad, Carl, liked his women—kind of like someone you know? He was especially sweet on the station leader, Natille. However, so was Martin. To avoid upsetting Martin, Carl and Natille conducted their affair secretly. Martin liked his privacy, and spent a lot of time at his house in St Michaels. Natille lived primarily on the station, so Martin never really saw her and Carl together. When Laura was born, Carl covered up Martin's questions about who was her mother by saying she was an Earthling and couldn't know about the existence of the station. So Natille was never seen around Martin's house. Of course, she had reiterated to Carl that was necessary.

"Martin was also interested in Natille, so she came up with that plan where she had her eggs fertilized by each of them. The result of that was Jake and me. About that same time, right after Jake and I were born, it was determined that, for several reasons, some of the residents should live away from the station. The primary reason was that other, more warlike planetary systems might try to interfere in Earth's development and, if so, they might immediately attempt to nullify our station. So, it was decided having people outside of the station might be advantageous. Carl and Natille volunteered to be one of the 'families' to move. Just before, Martin had found out about their relationship, so Carl and Natille took Laura and Jake and moved to Illinois."

"But she was your mother too," Rachel pointed out.

"That was very difficult for my mother, Natille. However, Martin was adamant that one of the twins was his. Jantine, one of the station workers, had told him of the whole plot. Carl thought the male baby, Jake, would in the future best serve the station, so I was left behind. At the time, Jake and I were year-old infants, and soon after they left, Martin partnered with Jantine, who became my mother. Natille visited us often, and I remember thinking she doted on me a lot, but I didn't know the true story of who I was until Laura told me just ten years ago."

At that, Jake winced. So that was why Sheila had attempted to contact him while all the other crap was going on in his life. And he had ignored her communications. He had thought it had something to do with some Flammerian mission. At the time, he was trying to avoid entanglements. Now, hearing Sheila's biography of their lives, he was starting to wonder how she knew more about his early life than he did.

And with that thought he saw two tiny aqua eyes peek out from Sheila's hair, and a tiny hand motioned him to come. Unseen by Rachel, he moved closer to Sheila. Floressa's head popped out and she whispered, "Laura knows everything."

Now what did that mean?

"So Carl and Natille had Laura the normal way, and you and Jake were like some kind of test tube babies?" Rachel asked, pulling Jake back to their conversation as he returned to his former position.

"You could look at it that way. Make no mistake though, I do not feel like Jake somehow got the better deal. My brother has had a much tougher road in life. I was not deprived, though except for the Distans,

I had few friends." Rachel glanced thoughtfully at Jake while Sheila paused.

"I grew up always knowing I was different, that my ancestors were not of this planet," Sheila continued. "Even though I was homeschooled by one of the station workers, and had very few Earth friends, I couldn't help but notice I had abilities others did not. Besides being able to somehow read minds, I could carry on thought conversations with certain individuals. My teacher brought these talents to the forefront. Of course, I didn't know then that all these powers were coming from my Distan at the time.

"Living in the house in St Michaels kept me out of the politics of the Station. I wasn't aware that I was being groomed for a high position within the observatory staff. Unbeknownst to me, Jake's sister, Laura, was to be the next station commander, while I was to assume responsibility for the Distans in St Michaels. Fifteen years ago, when Laura took command of the station, she and I became fast friends, and together we have made many changes. Unlike those who lived on the station, by living in St Michaels I had a life in your world. I could come and go between the house in St Michaels and the observatory in the Atlantic Ocean. My mental abilities, honed through the Distans, allowed me to take on many roles for the station, but my primary focus has been on protecting the Distans, and now I'm searching for a new home world for them."

Rachel appeared stricken. "Were you like a spy?"

"No, I prefer to think of my role as an observer. I never caused Earth any problems, never stole any secrets. What's to steal? War plans? We had no need of them. Besides, Earth doesn't even know its own history. They consider Lemuria and Atlantis as myths. They think the Egyptians built the pyramids."

CHAPTER 23
CHESAPEAKE BAY

Jake's attention began to waver as Sheila continued her explanation for Rachel. "Anyway, Laura and I assumed the leadership roles in the missions of Flammeria. About ten years ago, the Zantites, a race from another star system, became interested in your world and wanted to set up an observatory like ours. That's when I found out about who I really was, that Laura was actually my sister and I had a brother. While ours was strictly a peaceful observation station, Laura told me the Zantites harbored aspirations to someday take over this world. Five years later, they sent their first ship here. To us, Earth is a mission that has few rewards, and frankly, we'd sooner leave and let them fight it out. But more importantly to us, they were a known threat to the Distans."

Something clicked for Jake. "Five years ago is when my dad told me he started seeing the heads on the wall," he noted out loud. However, he couldn't shake the thought his returning was due to more than the Zantite threat.

"Very good, Jake. Yes, as a native Flammerian, your father had abilities beyond those of most humans. He was the one who first alerted the station to the presence of the Zantites. The station urged him to track them, but cover his abilities as much as possible."

Jake tried to pinpoint Dad's first mention of the "heads on the wall," but five years blurs many things. He had long ago decided it was silliness and a product of old age. Now, he found himself impressed at his father's wiliness. He had gone about his investigation right in front of Jake by making it appear to be some type of dementia. And Jake had gone along with it.

It was how Mack got him to come here in the first place. While it seemed like a long time ago, the conversation with him was just a couple of weeks previously…

* * *

"I saw Martin Wells on my wall last night," Mack called over from his kitchen.

When Jake didn't immediately acknowledge his proclamation, Dad biffed him on the side of the head. He looked up from his newspaper.

"Your old partner? If this is to get me involved in some mission, I'm not falling for that, Mack." Jake had gotten into the habit at an early age of calling his dad Mack, and his dad liked it.

For the last five years, Jake's seventy-seven-year-old, silver-haired father had told him that people came to visit him by materializing on his kitchen wall. They entered through the closed windows as black spots, moved up to where the walls and ceiling met and took the shape of a person's head. Mack didn't claim to see the actual faces of his visitors, but said he could tell who each one was by their silhouette. That's right, no details, just a profile. When a new spot appeared, he kept guessing people's names until the shape bounced up and down. That, according to Mack, indicated he was correct.

He was consistent in his experiences, and Jake wasn't sure if he was making it up. The catch was he'd only seen people who had died . . . at least those were all the ones Jake knew about. And there was one more thing Jake considered regarding the plausibility of his dad's ability; while one might chalk it up to plain old senility, it more likely had something to do with the fact he wasn't born here on Earth. Mack and Mom were actual extraterrestrials, aliens, born on the planet Flammeria, in another star system.

That morning, with his usual scowl, Mack returned to the stove and stirred his breakfast potatoes, turned the sausage and, of course, ignored Jake's statement. Jake continued to shuffle through his Chicago Sunday newspaper, looking for the movie listings.

"He won't be in the paper," Mack mumbled in his direction.

"Why? Oh wait, that's right. Maybe Earth doesn't know yet. Probably a better chance to find the obit if this was the Flammerian Gazette, right?"

"Don't you be a smart ass, Jake."

"I wasn't being a smart ass, Mack. Maybe he just died and came directly here to visit with you." He could tell by Mack's firm stare he thought he was being made fun of, so Jake returned to his still unanswered question. "Does your telling me this have anything to do with the Flammerian station? I'm not doing any 'jobs' for you, Laura, or the Man in the Moon."

Mack ignored him, turned the burners on the stove off and shuffled off somewhere, so Jake thought that had ended the discussion.

He looked up from nursing his coffee when Dad came back into the kitchen and thrust a piece of paper under his nose. "Here," he bit off the word. "Call Jantine and ask her about Martin."

"Jantine? In St Michaels?" Jake asked. He had thought this nonsense was over, so he was determined not to make this easy for Mack.

"Yes, Jantine. Martin's wife, you smart little shit. Call her. Right now."

Jake took the paper and saw, written in his dad's shaky scrawl, the name Martin and a phone number with the Maryland area code 410. So Jake called, talked to Gert, and now here he was.

* * *

"Who are these Zantites?" Rachel's question pulled Jake's mind back into the boat.

"They are from a planet called Zant," Sheila replied. "It's a world in the Gamma Cephei system. They are always looking to expand their empire, but they don't really like to fight. They prefer peaceful takeovers. Like us, they know that there is little of value here on Earth. We believe their only reason for considering Earth for conquest is they suspect that there are Distans here."

"I don't understand why you think it's necessary to operate your station here on Earth?" Rachel pointed out. "If our planet is worthless, just why are you here?"

"To protect the Distans, of course. Earth is still a very unstable world," Sheila replied. "You have lots of earthquakes, and at times in the past they've caused titanic destruction. The comet that came close to your world in the past, and was responsible for the demise of Lemuria, caused much seismic activity. The comet's fragments then destroyed another civilization in the Atlantic Ocean, the one you call Atlantis."

"Atlantis was real too?" Rachel asked.

"See," Sheila smiled. "You on Earth have no idea of your own history. Of course Atlantis was, and still is, real. Only now you call it Antarctica. What's left of the civilization that wasn't destroyed by the comet's passing is now buried under miles of ice."

Jake interjected to Rachel, "The Flammerians monitor this world for signs of another disaster like the one that destroyed prior civilizations." As long as Sheila was in the revelation department, he thought to share some of the history that Laura had told him.

"I'll explain more of that later, because we're short on time," Sheila interrupted. "Laura has recently detected signs that Earth's climate is deteriorating, and we've decided to move the Distans to another, safer world."

"You're leaving Earth?" Jake said quietly.

Sheila gave a quick bob of her head in agreement. "Eventually, but not soon."

At the sound of noises from below, both Rachel and Jake looked down as if someone would ascend through the wooden deck.

"There's a twofold reason for giving you a tour of the station, Rachel," Sheila said, while looking at Jake.

"Laura?" Jake asked.

"She wishes to see you."

He nodded, secretly thrilled at the possibility of seeing her. "Is she coming here?" he asked.

"She is not coming to us; we're going to her," Sheila replied. "The ship below us has reattached itself to a special hatch installed in the bottom of the boat. It is how I usually come aboard and is well hidden. The shipyard in Poquoson is unaware of it, and even the government search failed to find it. We will exit through it to my skimmer, and a replacement crew will take over for you and get the boat to St Michaels. They will stay aboard until you return and take their place. No one will realize you even left."

"Wait a minute. What about Rachel?" he asked.

"Why, she's going with us, of course. I promised Rachel a tour."

The boat's engine quit unexpectedly, but it kept moving as if nothing had happened. The old craft lurched slightly, and there were more noises from below. Metal clanking sounds and scrapings punctuated the air.

In response to Rachel's alarmed look, Sheila cautioned, "No cause for fear. Two people are preparing to come aboard to take your places. As I mentioned, while the inside of this boat is safe from snoopers, we cannot adequately protect the outside without causing suspicion. If neither of you were to come out of this cabin for the entire trip up to

St Michaels, it might raise their alarms, and they could possibly attempt to board it. So, we have chosen two of our people who closely resemble you in size and general appearance to take your places while you are gone. They know not to look directly to the south where their faces could be seen."

Sheila handed them clothes so the replacement couple could don theirs and assume the roles. Jake and Rachel quickly changed in the small sleeping quarters of the boat, and minutes later a man and woman entered the cabin from below. Sheila nodded to them and then led Jake and Rachel down. Entering the engine compartment, Jake was amazed to see the engine was tilted on its side, revealing a hidden hatch below it.

"One of our modifications," Sheila said. "When the watertight hatch seamlessly closes, the engine rotates back into place and automatically reattaches to the propeller shaft. This allows us to come and go from this boat without anyone being seen. Our ship below simply takes control and propels this boat along as if it was crewed. Anyone observing would not suspect anything."

Jake went down the hatch first, with Rachel following and then Sheila.

"This craft will take us to the station and return us to this area," Sheila said. "As you both know, the bay is very shallow, so we designed this craft to traverse through the deeper parts and get us out to the ocean and back. It merely holds the pilot, Cragin, and has room for just three other people. Right now that is us."

Cragin looked to be about Rachel's height, with sandy-colored hair and a slim build—your everyday guy on the street. He smiled in greeting and, at a signal from their replacements that they'd resumed control of the boat, he pressed a button. The circular craft suddenly disengaged from the boat above, turned around, and began to move south through the bay at a high rate of speed.

"Isn't there some sort of wake visible above, on the surface of the water?" Rachel asked the obvious question.

"Like the big craft you saw when I left you on the beach in the Outer Banks, this one leaves no wake, nor does it create a splash when it enters the water," Sheila explained.

"How does it do that?" Rachel asked.

"Through a specially designed magnetohydrodynamics system," Sheila smiled at Rachel.

"MHD?" Rachel asked. "We're working on such a system at NG, but I didn't know it would be so invisible, and allow vessels to enter and exit the water with no splashes."

"Yours can't," Sheila simply said. "By the way, I don't think I need to explain that all you see and hear is not to be relayed to anyone else."

"I thought you'd just wipe my memory clean," Rachel said.

"Please, Rachel," Sheila chuckled. "You read too many science fiction books."

"You mean you can't do that?" Rachel asked, with a surprised look on her face.

"I didn't say that," Sheila smiled. "Besides, why give you a tour if you cannot remember it afterwards?"

As the craft moved through the water, Jake glanced over the inside. While he knew of their existence, he had never been in one of these crafts. It was circular, with the pilot's seat in the middle surrounded by equipment. A semi-circular seating area about six feet wide held just room enough for three people. Sheila had deposited herself in the middle, with Rachel on her right and Jake on the left. However, the Ocean Engineering degree in Rachel would not let her sit down. She spent the entire thirty-five-minute trip standing and leaning over into Cragin's space. He calmly answered her endless questions about different instruments and what they did. When her questions returned to the propulsion system, Cragin paused and looked down at Sheila.

Sheila simply nodded her affirmation he should answer. Then, she turned to Jake and smiled. "Maybe we will have to do that memory wipe in Rachel's case," she joked.

"Rachel is intensely interested in the sea and propulsion systems," he explained.

"Yes, something we hope to be able to make use of in the future," Sheila said and sighed. "Listen, Jake. Your father advised us to move quickly as the threat becomes more ominous."

"Are we talking the Zantite threat to the Distans, or does Laura now include humans in her fears for Earth? Or, is it something else?"

"Distans threat only. Earth should be safe for humans for quite some time yet. I'm sorry I'm the one who has to thrust this all upon you. I know the last time Laura entreated you to do something for the station, you fled. Ten years ago, she had hoped you'd somehow diffuse the desires of the Zantites to come here. If you had, we'd not be in this situation now."

"Just a minute, Sis. I'm sure you know she wanted more than that. She wanted me to go, not only to Zant, but to Aldebaran to arrange some future mission. I don't do outer space errands." He suspected that Sheila, like him, was still in the dark about the real reason for his return.

"What if I asked you to?"

"Are you?"

"At this moment, no. However, let me remind you, you said you'd do anything for me." She paused, and for a moment stared over at Rachel being instructed by Cragin in the workings of the craft. When Sheila looked back at him, Jake thought she was on the verge of tears.

"What?" he asked. "Look, for you I might consider it."

She immediately put her hand to his cheek, a gesture he found oddly soothing. Her eyes flitted to Rachel and Cragin, and that told him she did not want them to hear. She leaned over and whispered, "I want Rachel's visit to be a positive one. I will tell you more when we are alone."

With that she relaxed and settled back in her seat, pulling Jake closely to her. When he leaned back in the seat, she lay her head on his shoulder and sighed, "Please don't let this erupt into another fight with Laura. Remember, you are now dealing with me in relation to requests for your assistance. The time to go to Zant and talk to them is past, and Laura went to Aldebaran herself and did the planning for that future mission, so you can relax. Any requests will come only from me. However, step one is you are to apologize to our sister for your vulgar behavior ten years ago."

He simply nodded at Sheila, but inwardly was excited at the prospect of seeing Laura. There was no need to apologize, though. According to Floressa, Laura knew everything.

CHAPTER 24

LAURA

With that, Jake's thoughts centered on Laura.

She had always been a protective older sister. When he was in high school, she'd insisted on meeting his dates. Even to this day, he judged all women to a standard set by his big sister, but few had even come close to that criterion.

But, as he thought on it, he realized he couldn't remember any of his high school dates—or hers either. Who were his friends? Did she have any?

His mind switched to the shock of seeing her that day, ten years ago, when she came to his apartment in Annapolis. She hardly ever left the Flammerian station, so he knew something was up.

At the door, she pushed past him and said, "Look at my nose, Jake. I shouldn't be out in the sun. Are the freckles already coming up?"

She seemed to think the mere act of going out into the sun caused freckles to appear. When he grabbed her by the shoulders and turned her around, that beautiful reddish hair tumbled over his hands. "You look your best with freckles on that cute little nose, Sis. But, forget the freckles; I can't believe it's you. Here, in my apartment."

She knocked his hands away from her shoulders, pulled him close and gave him a big smooch. "You are so full of shit, little brother. How have you been? Still fighting the girls off?"

"I've got a steady girl," he said. "How about you? How are you doin' in the love department?"

She brushed off his question. "Screw love. Look, we need your help, Jake. I need the two of you to go to Zant and deliver a message."

"You know neither of us embraces the 'it's my heritage' bullshit, Laur. Get one of your lackeys to do it."

"This is important, Jake, and I don't have lackeys. The Zantites are thinking of mounting an expedition here to Earth. We can't have them getting a foothold; they might find there's more here than they thought. Anyway, it's about time the two of you started thinking of your people."

"What the hell does 'more than they thought' even mean?"

"That's not my immediate problem," she replied. "I also need you to go to Aldebaran and arrange for an Eternals mission in the future."

"Eternals mission? Why do you need to get involved with Eternals?"

"Come on, Jake. You know what I'm getting at. A mission involving Eternals needs the approval of the highest level, and that takes time. Plus, I want a specific team that recently resurfaced. This mission will be in conjunction with another, and—"

"No! You know I hate even the thought of going into space. I know the after-effects. My system gets screwed up for weeks. Besides, I have my own fish to fry, Laura. Get someone else."

At the time, he was having other problems on two fronts, and didn't appreciate Laura bringing up the question of his home planet loyalty. And why should he even consider it his home planet? He wasn't actually born there.

"I have no one else to send, Jake. If you don't go, I'll have to go myself."

"Bye."

"Come on, Jake. You recall what I told you about the house when we were growing up, and the secret it holds. I really can't afford to be away. We can't have the Zants finding out about it."

"You were never specific about that bullshit, but isn't that the Wellses' problem anyway?"

"No, it's partly my problem," she said. "I'm responsible for everything on this planet, including you. But speaking of the Wells, why haven't you acknowledged Sheila's requests for you to visit? She has important things to tell you—"

"Stop, Laura!" Even today he regretted having to raise his voice to her and turning the conversation into a confrontation. "I'm an Earthling, not some alien. I was born on Earth, and I fit into Earth very well, thank you. I never met Sheila, and I don't think I want to if she espouses the same Flammerian bullshit that you do. Will both of you just leave me the hell alone?"

It had hurt to scold her. He had never raised his voice to Laura, and even back then he had wanted to immediately apologize. But he didn't. Instead of grabbing her and saying he was sorry, he let her turn and silently walk out the door.

Afterward, she tried to contact him several times, but he had to pretend that he was such an ass that he ignored her requests and left her out of his life entirely. He hadn't seen her since. Truth be known, he missed his sibling terribly.

A week later, Laura went to meet with the other future mission co-leader, and Jake left for Illinois with his 'family.' He promptly 'forgot' about the mission and thought he was living his life. However, that morning with Mack started the plan in motion. And, here he was.

* * *

After about thirty minutes, the craft slowed and finally stopped its forward motion. It seemed to gently rock on its horizontal axis. Sheila, he noticed, had been listening to Rachel's questioning of Cragin while he had mentally relived that last encounter with his big sister and realized it was connected to the as yet unknown mission.

Suddenly, the overhead hatch opened, and a brighter light filtered down a long ladder. It reminded him of the precarious ladder on the Navy destroyer he'd served on in the Navy years ago. The ladder, barely wide enough for a person, descended several decks into the ship's magazine. Sheila smiled, jumped on the ladder and led the way. He helped Rachel and she ascended after Sheila. When she reached the top, she stopped with a gasp, then stepped out, clearing the way for him. He had climbed to within six inches of the top when a female hand reached down and gripped his. It was not Rachel's or Sheila's, but it was familiar. The hand helped pull him up to the top, and he looked into the eyes of Laura, the sister unseen in ten years.

He was a little uneasy and hesitant to move any further, but she tugged on his hand and he stepped up and out of the small craft. Laura immediately wrapped him in a bear hug. He could not believe she was actually that glad to see him.

"How are you, little brother?" she asked, and tousled his hair.

He returned her hug, savoring the sweet smell of her. The ten years had not changed her in appearance at all. She was still a striking beauty, with ginger hair that might have been slightly shorter now, and those dazzling green eyes. While she still kidded him and talked the same, her air was that of royalty. And, royalty she actually was.

Laura smiled in response to his lack of speech. "Hey, don't worry, I'm not asking you ever again to do anything *for the station*. That's Sheila's job now. I've learned to delegate. I just wanted to see you and find out how you've been. Dad said you've been wasting your life."

Her emphasis on the words 'for the station' was not lost on him. He already suspected her upcoming mission had nothing to do with Earth. "Well, I had thought it was my life to waste, but now I realize I was an ass ten years ago," he answered, suddenly feeling very repentant.

To say he was overcome with emotion at seeing Laura would be putting it mildly. He pulled her to him again. "I'm so sorry, Laura."

Laura smiled wryly. "It's okay, Jake . . . it was probably for the best. We both know now it was meant to be. However, I'm glad Sheila didn't freak you out. She and I have been close sisters a long time, and I really wanted you to know that I wasn't the only female relation left in your life."

"No," he said. "Now, I want to know everything."

"Later," she said with a wink. "Now is not the time."

"I promised Rachel a tour of this station," Sheila said to Laura, "but you know it so much better than I do. Besides, she asks very technical questions. Would you mind?"

"Love to," Laura said, and grabbed Rachel's hand. "I've been so looking forward to meeting the girl who brought my brother to his knees. Jake is my only brother, and I love him more than anything."

Rachel turned to him. "Jake, you never told me your sister was so beautiful."

"I know," he said. "However, when you grow up with her and know her a little . . ."

"Jake," cautioned Laura.

"Anyway," he said. "She gets freckles on her nose when she's out in the sun. And be leery of that smile."

"You always told me you loved the freckles," Laura pointed out. "Come on, Rachel," she continued. "Ignore anything about me that ass says. I'm ready for your questions."

After they walked over to a bank of instruments, Sheila leaned in close to his ear and said in a heavy whisper, "I'm not privy to what's going on between you and Laura, but the time is right to bring Mattik's daughter in on our plans, and this time, I'm the one asking you to contact her. You and I will talk more of this later."

He became aware that Rachel and Laura had returned, and Rachel was trying to listen to Sheila.

Laura laughed to cover their conversation and asked, "Did you think we were going to take Jake away from you, Rachel?"

Rachel glanced at him, looked down and nodded.

"Jake is much more valuable to us in Earth's world. We may ask him to do things from time to time, but short of kidnapping him, we could never make him leave your world. That is, not unless he wants to. He is a pseudo-earthling through and through."

"What's going to happen to me now that I know all of this?" Rachel asked.

"I don't understand your concern," Laura smiled.

"Aren't you afraid I'll tell someone?" Rachel asked.

Laura looked to Rachel and laughed. "Do you plan on telling anyone about this?"

"Are you kidding? I barely believe it myself. Besides, I'd never do anything to betray Jake, no matter what I've seen or what he did to me."

"There's your answer. You're one of us now. I'm aware that you're an ocean engineer. Would you like to know more about the station?" Laura asked Rachel.

She nodded eagerly.

As Laura drew Rachel over to a large instrument of some kind, Sheila pulled at Jake's arm and led him down a short corridor. He was reminded, by the gentle curvature of the floor and outside walls, that they were in a circular structure.

The station was not that large, and consisted of three concentric work areas interspersed with concentric ring corridors. The Outer Concentric Ring, or OCR, closest to the water outside, consisted of work and laboratory areas, Laura's combination office and living quarters, an ocean viewing station, and several visitors' cabins. The outer concentric ring corridor separated those areas from the Mid-Concentric Ring, or MCR, which consisted of about twenty-one workers' living quarters. Finally, the inner concentric ring corridor separated those spaces from the Engineering and Propulsion spaces.

Where they had entered the station was an area that contained, besides the entry and exit shaft, two small conference rooms that looked out on the deep ocean. Sheila had directed him into one of them that was empty except for a few tables and chairs. He was immediately drawn to a large window that faced into the sea. The water, deep blue to black at this depth, caused him to feel like he was in some strange aquarium. Sheila pulled out a chair close to the window and motioned him to do the same. As he did so, she put her bare feet up on a ledge that ran along under the window and rocked back on her chair. At that point she looked very unassuming, reminding him of any of the everyday girls he'd met since his days at the Academy.

She smiled over, cocked her head, and asked, "I've got to know. A few days ago, when you came to the garden and found out I was your sister, did you think me strange?"

"Strange? Don't you know my reaction from reading my mind that day?"

"I don't read minds, Floressa does. Do you think I have her just read people's minds as I'm walking down the street? I didn't want Floressa to invade your privacy and get that personal with you, so I had her stay away from your inner thoughts. It might be hard for you to understand, but I try not to use her in that way and abuse my powers. Besides, Floressa has grown up since your Academy days. She's very discreet now, and it's rubbing off on her daughter."

"At first, when I met you, I thought you were aloof," he said. "That was before I knew you were my sister."

"So, my being your sister countered my apparent standoffishness?"

She had him there. He knew she was teasing, and coming from her, it was welcomed.

"Come on, Jake. What did you really think of me when we first met?" she continued.

"I thought you were one of the most beautiful girls I'd ever seen." He had to admit that to her because she was striking and deserved the compliment, and especially because she was his sister. He hoped that no one ever asked which sister he thought was more beautiful, as he never wanted to go there.

To that she wrinkled her nose and waved a hand at him in dismissal. "I'm nowhere near as pretty as Laura. Besides, I wasn't fishing for compliments." Then, she laughed out loud. "It was fun watching your expression when you first found me. Do you remember?"

He nodded. "How could I forget?"

"Of course, I knew all about you and who you were," she continued. "Remember, I'd seen you in the flesh when I took Floressa, and later Roseena, on trips to your school. However, it was gratifying to finally meet and talk to my brother in person."

Slightly embarrassed at her revelations, he looked out the window and watched small lights winking on and off in the ocean—the bioluminescence of deep-sea fish. Sheila poked his thigh with the toes of a bare foot to regain his attention.

When he turned back to her, he saw her expression had turned somber.

"What?" he asked.

"There are things I must tell you, Jake."

Here it comes, he thought. Her real reason for wanting him here. No, wait. It wasn't Sheila. Since he'd reconnected with Laura, he'd had a premonition that it was Laura who had drawn him back for . . . something.

"Let's set a few things straight, though." Sheila shook her head as she spoke. "Ten years ago, Laura appealed to you to interrupt your Earth life and do some work for the station. That plea ended badly; we now know that back then you were not prepared to make that sacrifice. In the ten years since, my father and our shared mother have passed on. Jantine is too old to be of any help to us now, and your father, despite his uncanny abilities to track the invaders without need of a Distan, is not here at the station, so he can't help us. Our former station commander, Mattik, returned to Flammeria, and like you his . . . daughter still refuses to cooperate. I know it's because you two made some kind of a pact. We have no military, so Mattik has tried to get our home world to send us some off-world freelance military types, but thus far has been unsuccessful.

"Now, enter the Zantites. Those of us at the station are in no danger unless we choose to interfere with the invaders' plans. Our home world abhors wars and can't be counted on to help. However, I'm not yet ready to move the Distans, so to protect them we must get involved. It would be up to us—Laura, you and me, and maybe Mattik's daughter, if she can be so convinced, to lead the fight. While Rachel would probably help if you asked her, it's unfair and unwise to appeal to her at this time."

His eyes drifted back out to the ocean depths in front of them. He realized that Sheila and he had been manipulated all along. Everything that had happened was—

Laura's voice sounded in his head. "Okay, it's time you came to my office. We need to talk."

CHAPTER 25

CHANDELLE'S REVELATION

"There has been no manipulation," Laura's voice cut into Jake's thoughts. *"Let's call what you and Sheila are experiencing an awakening. Chandelle, my Distan, is communicating this to you because I don't wish Rachel or Sheila to hear. I've got to dump Rachel off on Sheila so we can discuss something."*

He turned and saw that Laura and Rachel had moved in behind them, but out of range of their conversation. A small, bronze-haired Distan, presumably Chandelle, hovered just behind Laura. Obviously, Laura could mentally communicate too.

"The Eternals don't control everything," Laura's voice continued. *"Your reestablishing relations with Rachel and your friends was not influenced by them. Wasn't that part of the reason you came? It is good that you have pursued that, though, and have put your previous friendship situation to rest. However, I must straighten out one other misconception that Chandelle told me you harbor. When I gave you that statue of Moonglimmer with Sheila's face, I did not say she was the missing love of your life. I said she was the lost woman in your life, simply meaning your twin sister. It was also meant to introduce you to the Distans. I'm not a fortuneteller, Jake. I have no idea who the love of your life was, is or will be. And keep all of this to yourself for now. It's too early to talk with Sheila about our mission. It's only being stirred in you."*

Her comment about the Moonglimmer figure reiterated what Sheila had implied. The statue was no accident. It was meant to signal him that Sheila was destined to be in his life. In thinking back and analyzing the situation, the statue had done its job. He might have written her off as a kook had it not been for that connection. And it had definitely aided in his quick acceptance of Moonglimmer.

Laura, with Rachel trailing, came over, and Sheila grabbed Rachel's hand.

"How about some coffee?" Sheila asked. The two of them went down the corridor while Laura steered him into her office.

"How about a nice squeezy hug, Jake?"

He was more than willing to comply with her request. After they parted, Laura sat in a small love seat she had for visitors. She indicated that he should sit by her.

"I had to get that in before I laid a bombshell on you. After I reveal things and awaken some memories, you might not wish to be around me."

"I'd never not want—"

"I may not be your sister," she interrupted.

He felt faint momentarily. Not only from her shocker of an announcement, but also because his mind began to fill with things long kept hidden from him. His past. Where were Laura's childhood memories? His?

"You're joking, right?"

"I don't joke, Jake. We may not be related. Let me start from the beginning."

"What are you saying? I can see you as a young girl . . ."

"Can you? Or do you have a snapshot-like memory of me then?"

She was correct. His memory was based on a photo-like image. All of his younger memories were based on still scenes.

"The Distans may be far more intelligent than we thought, Jake. Chandelle has always told me my memories of youth were strange, like photos, she said. She's always said the same thing to me about Sheila's.

I didn't think much about it. But it puzzled her, and when you came aboard, she immediately looked at your recollections."

"She what?"

"Just listen. I think she made a startling discovery. Let me have her tell it. Chandelle, please come out here."

"Are you upset, Mr. Jake?" A melodious voice came from Laura's hair.

"Of course not," Jake said.

The small bronze-haired Distan carefully parted Laura's hair and peeked at Jake.

"Mr. Jake won't hurt you, Chandelle." Laura gave Jake a smug look. "Chandelle is a very faint soul, Jake. You've got to give her time to get used to you."

When she finally ventured out, Jake realized she was the smallest full grown Distan he had seen. He estimated she was barely more than six inches tall.

"Can I sit on your shoulder, Mr. Jake?" she asked.

"I'd be pleased if you did, Chandelle."

With a big smile, she stepped out of her slippers and flew up to Jake's shoulder. She immediately planted her bare feet next to his neck, sat down, and faced the side of his face. It was plain she had accepted him on the word of Laura.

"Wow," Laura observed. "I think she likes you, Jake."

Immediately, Chandelle began to relay what she had discovered in her scan of Jake's mind. "Your real memories were overlaid with false ones, Mr. Jake. I've discussed this with the other Distans that have been assigned to you, especially Floressa. They told me they always knew you were someone else."

"Wait," Laura said. "How come no one ever told Sheila or me this?"

"It's kind of involved," Chandelle explained. "There's a little note in your covered up memories warning not to share the information. Mr. Jake has the note, too, but I got a mental message to tell you, Laura, when Mr. Jake came."

Chandelle, apparently completely at ease with Jake now, looked at him. "Did you know that Floressa was in love with you, Mr. Jake? She's always wished she was a grown human so she could be your girlfriend. Don't tell her I told you."

Clearly embarrassed by that, Jake changed the subject, "You can drop the mister. So, do Moonglimmer and Ceellia know too? About my memories?" he asked.

"No," Chandelle replied. "They are a little too young. They will develop this ability to discern memories when they get about nineteen. Laura's memories are true from the time she took command of the station on. Sheila's real ones begin with her and the Distans. Yours, Jake, began just before you started at the Naval Academy."

"This is unbelievable. Well then, who the hell are we?"

"Will you just listen to Chandelle?" Laura insisted.

"I'm not sure yet," Chandelle explained. "I was able to get into yours further than I have with Sheila or Laura. I found memories of you in Germany in a uniform and also here in this country working on a railroad. On the railroad you were with a young man, helping him. You also had a different girl than Rachel, but she looked similar—"

"What about Rachel?"

"She's human, but you, Laura and Sheila are not," Chandelle revealed.

"What? We sure look human," Jake said.

"Think, Jake," Laura said. "Who looks human but aren't?"

"Eternals? Chandelle, are you saying we're Eternals?"

"Yes," Chandelle replied.

"I doubt that," Jake insisted. "I think—"

"What do you think?" Laura interrupted. "She says that's the real reason we can so easily mentally communicate."

"But Eternals remember past lives and can manipulate their births."

"Unless they've been tampered with," Chandelle observed.

"Tampered?"

Chandelle slowly nodded her tiny head and stretched out, placing her feet further up on Jake's neck. "Your memories have been tampered with, Jake. I discovered you were last born in 1887."

"1887? That would make me over a hundred—"

Laura smiled. "Eternals can also live very long lives, Jake."

"But why all this subterfuge? Who the hell are we, then?"

"I'm sure time will tell," Laura replied. "Let's see where it all goes. Chandelle and I haven't mentioned any of this to Sheila, and I think you and I should not discuss it again after we leave the room. I'm sure that whoever is responsible for this has a plan in mind and will clue us in at the right time."

"If what Chandelle says is all true . . ." Jake said.

"What's that?"

Jake put his arms around Laura and pulled her into a close hug. "I mean if we're not brother and sister," he whispered in her ear.

Laura pushed him away. "Ewww, Jake! Let's treat it as a theory for now. Besides, you have Rachel. You were right, Chandelle, he can be such a pervert. Let's do what we discussed and suspend his memory of our little talk."

"Okay," Chandelle replied. "But Jake can't really help who he is. He's always liked women, and they are attracted to him. Floressa was in love with him, and I'm starting to feel . . ."

"Chandelle?" Laura warned.

"Okay, but in Germany he had—"

"Just suspend his memory."

Seconds later, Jake found himself following her out of her office. Why had he been in there?

"At the right time, you'll remember what we just discussed," Laura's voice came into his head.

Sheila and Rachel waited inside the small observation room. Laura pushed Jake over by Sheila and told him, "I'll let Sheila finish her plea." Laura then guided Rachel away from the room.

"Sit by me, Jake," Sheila said softly.

After sitting next to her, he could sense by how tightly her feet pressed against the railing that this was difficult for her. He put an arm around her shoulders and pulled her close.

Tension seemed to ooze from her. "I'm so scared," she said quietly, and looked over at him. "I can't believe I'm asking you to put yourself in such a situation." Shakiness was not only in her voice; her body trembled.

"What's the problem? Relax, Sis, you can tell me anything."

"You say that now . . ." She momentarily got taut, but then the shivers seemed to return. "My wish was that your reunion with Laura, and the first meeting between you and I, would be carefree. I envisioned sharing my, I should say our, world with you in an unhurried way."

"Hasn't that happened?" he asked.

"Yes, but the next step is not going to be easy. I'm basically an honest person, so I can't ask you to do this mission without Rachel's knowledge, and that might cause you to lose Rachel."

"Just tell me, Sheila."

"A Zantite scout ship has entered Earth's oceans. It is probing to see if there is any possibility Earth can detect and engage them."

"Is that all?" He couldn't see why this had caused her to get so anxious. "So the Zants think Earth is an easy conquest because this planet knows nothing about other worlds and they suspect we harbor the Distans?" he asked.

"Remember how, fifty years ago, one of their ships came down in the New Mexico desert? The USA, like the Germans who recovered one in 1922, reverse-engineered the wrecks, and they advanced their technology by leaps and bounds. Back then, the higher levels of Earth's governments took steps to show the Zants that they were aware of them and would not stand idly by if they became a threat. Now, present day governments seem to have forgotten that, and the Zants are once again stepping up their probes. Our high-placed diplomats in various Earth governments, particularly the USA and the Russian Confederation, have failed to convince the countries that there is a menace in the skies of Earth. Besides, Earth doesn't know a friendly extraterrestrial from a bad one, and our own ships could be attacked.

"The Zants know Earth's warlike tendencies, and would move on and look elsewhere if Earth showed resistance of any kind. Earth just doesn't have that much to offer, and we think the mere suspicion there are Distans here is not enough for them to risk any kind of long-distance war. Laura and your dad think that you and Mattik's daughter would be the best persons to foil their plans to construct a permanent station here on Earth. The resistance must appear to come from Earth, not us. I told you already how our world could not get involved, and there is no one on our station with the experience or resources to counter the invaders anyway. Once again, all hope lies with the two of you, Jake." With that, her shivers ended and she was silent. He could still sense the high state of anxiety in her body by how hard her feet pressed the railing.

"Is that all?" he joked to get her to relax. "You merely want the two of us to save the Earth and the Distans?"

In answer, she looked over at him and nodded. "However, up until you showed up, I was lonely but able to cope. Now that you're here, I want to make up for the time we were forced to live apart. We're twins, but don't know one another. Our parents separated us and stole our childhood. I understand that having some of our people live elsewhere was decided long ago as a possible defensive move in case someone attacked our station, but now that we're together, I want to be with you always. I don't want you sent on some mission for Earth where you could possibly be killed." With that, she deflated to tears and looked away.

"Rachel might not like that," he chuckled in an attempt to break her apprehension.

"My only close friend is Laura, but she's my sister. Rachel and I could be close friends, something I've never had. I'm physically no different from Earth women, yet I have none as friends. Her knowing you are the brother I've been deprived of by fate all of my life might make her willing to share your presence."

"You seem to trust Rachel an awful lot. How do you know she won't tell someone your secrets?"

"Rachel has been under scrutiny for a long time. Despite her choice of schooling, she hasn't a military bone in her body. She's a lover, not a fighter, except where you're concerned. If she really was a warrior, we might not need Mattik's daughter."

"But she went to the Academy . . ."

"So did you, and so did Mattik's daughter. However, Rachel went to learn engineering, not to be a soldier."

"Okay, first of all, let's stop calling April Mattik's daughter."

She nodded slightly. "Laura and I know about your pact. April currently does not have a Distan, so we've tried electronically contacting her. However, all she'll reply is, 'Talk to Jake.'"

As we'd agreed she'd do, he thought. "Let's continue with first things first. What is it you expect April and me to do to counter this invasion?"

"Your father has a plan."

"My father? He's—"

"A very great actor," Sheila interrupted. "Just listen."

He felt more of the tension drain from her as she turned to face the ocean view and loosened her feet on the railing. She brought his attention back to the task at hand by continuing.

"We must go to see your father in person, because the invaders could pick up information transmitted to our station. This station, my boat and the specific locations back in St Michaels equipped with scatterers are the only places that are safe from their listening devices. Like you, they have no idea of your father's involvement. All of his information came to us carefully coded by email. Here, all of our planning and decision-making is done in this room. There isn't time to communicate with him through coded messages and it might be dangerous to bring him here, so I thought that we, that's you, Rachel and I, could visit him under the guise of Rachel meeting the family. He will outline the plan for us."

"Scatterers," he said out loud, suddenly remembering talking to Reena. Her mention of the word reminded him . . . Had he stood on a scatterer? "Uh . . . I think I screwed up, Sis. I talked to Reena the morning I left to meet Rachel," he said.

"What?" Sheila asked excitedly. "Why didn't you tell me? When and where did you see her?"

"Reena buzzed up and talked to me as I was walking to the car."

"Jake. Were you standing on a scatterer?" Sheila said in an exasperated voice.

"No. I forgot that part of my instruction." He squeezed his eyes shut and dropped his head.

* * *

Two hours later, the tour cut short after Jake's revelation, he and Rachel were back on the boat headed for St Michaels. Sheila had departed immediately after he revealed to her how he had fouled up. The plan was for Sheila to go to Poquoson and retrieve Rachel's T-Bird and drive it back. To avoid suspicion, Rachel and Jake had to bring Sheila's boat back. Cragin took them back in the small shuttle craft.

It was the first time Rachel and Jake had been alone since they left the boat to go to the station. She immediately told him that, based on what she had seen and heard, she once again believed that somehow he would choose to return to 'his people,' as she put it, and indicated she needed to think about things. With the inklings of the important mission beginning to surface, he decided not to try to dissuade her.

After that she lapsed into quiet for the remainder of the trip.

* * *

Quiet was fine with him, for he had to once again think about April and her possible involvement. He had hoped their meeting yesterday was a final one and he would not be drawn into the spell that girl could weave. Now, as Rachel sat quietly staring into space, he recalled that first meeting, on the beach at Nags Head. It was before the fateful meeting with Laura ten years ago in which he severed their relationship. Previously, Laura had called him and asked him to do her a favor.

* * *

"Is this a station thing?" he asked.

"Well, yeah, but it involves a pretty girl and it's not like some dangerous mission."

"You know I have a pretty girl and—"

"Come on, Jake. I just need for you to convince this one she's Flammerian, that's all. I don't want you to get involved with her in any way . . . at least not now."

"Okay, Laur. I'll do you this one favor."

Laura told him the girl would be on the beach in Ocean City. She described her and warned him to be very careful. Her dad had tried to tell her, but she'd laughed at him and was suspicious of strangers. But, she stressed, she's a Flammerian and not to be taken for granted. He scoffed at her concern. "Come on, Laur, it's a girl."

The following Saturday he made some excuse to Rachel and drove to the beach alone. Of course, he was ill prepared for the seductress awaiting him.

When he found her, she wore a skimpy black bikini and was sitting on a rock by herself. Thinking her naive, he approached her with one of his lines.

"Wow, that bikini really sets off your blond hair," he said.

"What about my blue eyes?" she replied. "Aren't you going to mention them?"

"Uh . . ." She caught him off guard with her directness.

"You're supposed to be Flammerian? Do you know my dad?" she asked. "Did he put you up to this? You going to tell me I'm an extraterrestrial with some mission?"

He took a step back. Laura had not adequately warned him of the girl's capabilities.

"Well," she said as she looked him over, "at least you're cute. Come on, give me your spiel. My name's April. What's your name?"

"My name's Jake," he tried to counter her directness. "I—"

"What do you do when you're not hassling supposedly Flammerian girls on the beach, Jake?"

"I'm a Naval officer."

"My dad said Flammeria doesn't have a fuckin' Navy." Less interested, her eyes looked past him out to sea.

"It doesn't. I'm in the United States Navy."

That seemed to reinvigorate her curiosity and she jumped to her feet. "Are you a pilot?"

"No, I drive ships."

"Did you go to Annapolis?"

"Yes."

"I just got an appointment," she boasted. "Shipmates!" She held up her hand for a high five.

She shocked him with those words. Why hadn't Laura told him that? Maybe she thought that was his in. He held up his hand to hers, and she slapped it.

"You know you're going to lose those long blonde tresses," he said.

"They'll grow back. Besides, I think I'll look cute with short hair, don't you think?"

Her blue eyes bore into his, and he suddenly realized he no longer was the pursuer, but—

"Okay, Jake, let's go." April linked her arm into his.

"Go?" he said. "Where?"

"My apartment. You're successful, you picked me up. Wasn't that your real goal? I've got lots of questions about the Academy. I need answers. That's my price for listening to your spiel."

CHAPTER 26
SEARCH FOR REENA

"But . . ." Jake was confused.

"Look, if you're cooperative, I'll pay attention to your Flammeria bullshit. Otherwise . . . well, you won't like otherwise. Come on, let's go."

He smiled as he recalled she did listen to his Flammeria 'bullshit.' In fact, she actually believed him. Her main goal in life had been going to the Naval Academy, and she told him that having met him dispelled those doubts. Following their tryst, they became very close friends. Jake became her mentor.

That friendship came to a head when, unbelievably, by chance she was assigned to his company the following year. By that time, he was enamored of Rachel and found it awkward to have April so close by. However, he recalled that after April saw Rachel's picture on his desk, without a word, she let him off the hook.

* * *

A sudden clanging of the escape hatch told Jake they had reached the cabin cruiser. Rachel quietly followed him up the ladder and they took over Sheila's craft. When they got to the Miles River and up to St Michaels, he anchored the boat in the location just south of the house where Sheila had instructed. There was a buoy in the river at the spot, and attached to it was a small speedboat which he used to get them to the beach. When they got to the house, both Rachel and he were surprised to see the T-Bird already in the driveway. Despite her sheltered life, he realized his newfound sister had somehow learned to drive fast. After arrangements were made to pick her up for the flight to Chicago in three days, Rachel left. He had decided to broach Rachel's misgivings when they went to see Mack.

"Shouldn't we get to searching for Reena?" he asked Sheila.

"Reena's not up here," Sheila replied. "At least not alive, I fear. If she was, the Distans would have found her. We need to look for clues as to how the Zantites got her . . . or find her remains."

* * *

Two hours later, after searching the flowerbeds and general area in silence, Sheila sat on the rock by the riverbank, her feet planted on the scatterer, while Jake stared across the channel. Darkness closed in on them.

"I don't understand," Sheila announced, breaking the silence between them. "We should have found some clue. The Zantites are not that good at being stealthy."

He glanced up into the tree branches swaying above them. A lone bird was perched on a branch a few feet above their heads. When Jake looked at it, the flyer let out a loud chirp. Sheila's head snapped up, and she tried to imitate the little bird's call.

"You don't usually hear birds chirping at night," Jake said, gazing at the fearless little avian. "I wonder. What's the possibility that some insect like a spider, or even a bird, attacked Reena?"

Sheila shook her head. "I would doubt that Reena was attacked by any creature. Distans are one with most of the life forms around us. They can even win over cats or other bigger carnivores. While there are some creatures that pose a threat, Reena knows how to take care of herself. I'd say the possibility of her encountering some harmful creature in the gardens is very low."

He again looked up at the bird, a male cardinal, and it flew to a lower branch, even closer to them. Then it chirped once again. It was almost like it wanted to talk.

"Did Reena associate with bugs and birds?" he asked.

Sheila looked over. "Wait a minute. Reena had a close friend who was a bird," she said. "I'd almost forgotten." When Sheila looked at the bright red avian, it chirped at her and strutted on the branch.

"Can the Distans communicate with the birds?" Jake asked.

Sheila nodded.

"Come on," he said. "We need a Distan."

Under the moon's shining aura, they silently made way to the house.

Once down in the Keep, he was immediately approached by Glimmer. He was thankful for her light coating of fur, because it was immediately apparent, except for what appeared to be satin undergarments—red of course—she was not dressed.

"I need your help," he told her.

"I was getting ready for bed, Mr. Jake."

"This is about Reena," he said.

She instantly flew onto his shoulder. "I'll do anything you ask."

"Can you put on some clothes?" he smiled. "We're going outside."

"Sure, Mr. Jake," she said. She turned to fly off, then stopped as Ceellia, in a similar state of undress, but in yellow, flew over. "Ceellia, duty calls. Mr. Jake needs us. You need to be dressed, though. Remember, Mr. Jake is a prude."

With a smile, Glim turned and looked at him. The smile got even bigger when he winked. Then she flew off into one of the little homes and returned seconds later wearing jeans and a red top. She landed on his shoulder and looked questioningly at him. Soon after, Ceellia landed as well, dressed in cut-off denim shorts and a yellow top.

"They need to be extra careful in the dark, Jake," Sheila said. "You two go in Jake's shirt pocket. It would be easier if you helped them,

Jake. Just pick each one up and hold their wings close in back. Then slide them, feet first, into your pocket."

"Just watch where you put your fingers," Glimmer giggled. "I'm ticklish."

He did as Sheila suggested, and Glimmer smiled up at him as she held on to the material that formed the front of the pocket. When he attempted to pick up Ceellia, she stopped him with the admonishment, "Be careful of my girl parts. I'm very excitable." He laughed at her and put her in next to Moonglimmer. He was grateful that both had not bothered with their spiky shoes.

As they mounted up the basement steps, Sheila said, "I contacted Laura. Other than the ocean exploration craft, there are no other Zantite ships anywhere near Earth. There haven't been any for weeks. They could have deposited a land-based team, though. If so, that's good. We might be able to locate them."

"What do the Zantites want with the Distans?" he asked.

"Their unique communication abilities, of course. They have been searching for them for a long time. They've long suspected that we're the ones who are harboring them on some world, but have never found proof. If they've captured Reena, they have the proof they need, and their council could authorize an invasion of Earth to get our colony."

* * *

Once outside, they hurried down to the water and the tree. Sheila quickly slid up on the rock and nodded that it was safe to speak. Jake looked up and saw the cardinal still perched there. The winds stirred again, and to the west flashes of lightning indicated that storms were brewing.

"Girls," he said to his pocket. "Can you speak to this bird? It seems to be trying to tell us something." He first helped Glimmer out of the pocket, and she looked up at the bird while standing on his hand.

"That's Peree," Glimmer said. She flew up to the branch, alighting next to the bird who strutted excitedly in apparent recognition of the little Distan.

"Me too," Ceellia squealed. As soon as he lifted her out, she swatted his hand away and joined Glimmer and the striking scarlet bird.

For a few seconds the three traded chirps and whistling sounds. Glimmer then returned to him, again landing on his outstretched hand. Ceellia remained on the branch next to the bird. When a gust of wind threatened to blow her off, Glim jumped to his shoulder, holding on to his shirt collar to counter the wind's effects.

He put a finger up for her to grab. Glim clutched it and said, "Peree said that she and Reena flew across the river after you left her. They got caught in a sudden storm, and Reena landed in some sort of a container and was captured by a small human."

Sheila gripped his shoulder. "Zantites are smaller than Earth humans, Jake. They have different features, but in the dark they could be mistaken for human."

Glimmer continued, "Peree said other birds tried to help by diving to scare the human, but it chased them away and took Reena. She said only a big, stronger human can rescue her. But Peree doesn't know where she is now or if she's still alive."

"If?" he asked.

"She said that some humans kill birds and it's been a day since she saw Reena. Birds are afraid to fly near the river in the dark. Owls hunt the river and foxes the shore. She fears either could have gotten Reena. Distans are not close friends with larger wild predator birds or mammals."

"Jake," Sheila said. "We must do something. Maybe if I got the boat . . ."

"That may be too late. I'll swim across and see if I can find her. Get the boat and come over when you can. We can use it to get her back." He looked at Moonglimmer. "Did she tell you about where this happened?"

"She told me exactly where it happened," Glimmer replied. "I'm going with you. Ceellia will guide Sheila over when she's ready."

"You can't come," Jake said to Glimmer. "It's too dangerous. Tell me how to find it."

"We have a deal and you're wasting valuable time," Glimmer said, slightly perturbed that he would dare to even consider leaving her behind. "I'll ride over by standing on your head while you swim. If you need to go under or rotate, I'll hover."

"You cannot argue with a Distan," Sheila said. "Do as she says."

Against his better judgment, Jake gave in and dove into the water, wincing at the cold, and began to swim. As he settled into a crawl stroke, he felt Glimmer's little feet on his head.

"Hurry," she urged.

* * *

Within minutes, he reached the other side, came out of the water and looked around.

"Through the bushes on the right," Glimmer's voice told him.

He followed her instructions, and soon they came upon a fallen tree, but there was no sign of Reena. Glimmer and Jake searched everywhere, softly calling her name and leaving no leaf unturned. After a while, Sheila and Ceellia joined them, but found no Reena or remains. Jake decided it was just too dark.

* * *

He was crestfallen when they returned to the house after rowing back in the rain. Glimmer and Ceellia hid in his pocket, but did not stir. He knew they were very distraught that they had been unable to find

Reena. When they got to the house, the four dried and warmed themselves by the fireplace. Jake promised them they would go across the following morning to resume the search, but received no reply.

Sheila took both girls down to the Keep by herself. Jake could not face the little fairies with such grim news. He felt like a coward, but Sheila assured him it was perfectly okay. Gert found him in the kitchen and made some coffee. After an hour, Sheila returned and joined them.

"I feel it's my fault," he said. "I should have made sure that—"

"Don't talk like an ass, Jake," Sheila cut in. "Reena knew the rules. No going over to the other side without telling your mother and taking a partner. She told no one, and I guess she thought that cardinal was a suitable partner."

"Wait. Can't we try to communicate with her by thought?" he asked.

"Distans are relays," Sheila said. "They normally don't put their own thoughts into a communication unless they've been trained like Ceellia and Glimmer. They pick up your conscious message and the names, and picturing the parties, pass it on. Unless trained, they cannot receive messages directed at them and answer back. No, we have to find her without trying to communicate mentally. Reena's too young to have been trained. We'll just have to wait until daybreak to resume looking."

Later, Jake collapsed on the bed. He briefly struggled in an attempt to analyze where Reena could have gone, but quickly fell into an exhausted sleep. The next thing he knew, he was being awakened by a ticklish feeling on his nose.

When he opened his eyes, Glimmer was sitting on his nose and Ceellia was standing on his bare chest. Both were wearing matching two-piece outfits: a striped top and denim shorts. Glimmer's was red, of course, and Ceellia's was bright yellow. Glimmer saw his eyes lingering on their outfits and smiled.

"We're both wearing a halter top and panties underneath," Glimmer said. "Just like last night."

"See?" Ceellia said as she turned down the front of her shorts, revealing her bright yellow panties.

"Ceellia, what did Sheila say not to do?" Glimmer asked.

"Oops," Ceellia said. "We're not supposed to tantalize you with our nubile bodies. Those were Sheila's exact words."

"Come on, Mr. Jake," Glimmer said. "Get dressed. It's dawn. We came to help you continue the search."

Ceellia, he noticed, suddenly gripped her miniature nose with a tiny thumb and one finger. "I think you need a shower, Mr. Jake." Ceellia frowned.

"Scat, get out of here," he replied. "Wait a minute. Where's Sheila?"

"Sheila?" Glimmer repeated.

He nodded.

"Sheila is getting dressed in her room," Glimmer said. "It's the one connected to yours."

"Will you two go and tell Gert I'll be right down? Tell her I'd like some coffee if possible."

"Don't you want us to help you in the shower?" Ceellia asked. "Sheila says I'm a very good hair washer and Glimmer can—"

"NO!" he said a little too loudly. "I don't need help bathing." He shooed them out and shut the door, hearing them giggle as they flew away.

CHAPTER 27
NORA AND KARA

After the Distans left, Jake was able to enjoy a peaceful, solitary shower. He had been too tired the night before, and even though today he was going to repeat the task of swimming across the channel, he needed the shower's relaxing hot water to soothe his aches. After getting dressed, he stopped in Sheila's room before going down.

"I'm almost done here, Jake," Sheila said. "Did you sleep okay?"

He nodded yes even though he actually didn't. "No need for you to hurry, I just wanted to tell you I'll go across the river with Glimmer and Ceellia to see if we can find any trace of Reena. I'll leave the boat for you in case we find something and you need to cross."

"Thanks. A swim in that yucky river was not on my list of to-dos," Sheila said. "Oh, by the way, I think you'll be accompanied by a flock of birds. Glimmer already enlisted their aid. They'll be waiting by the river. It's actually a good idea. They can cover a lot of territory by air."

* * *

An hour later, standing at the shore of the Miles, Jake was pleased to note that, as annoying as Glimmer and Ceellia could be with their teasing innuendos, once the search for Reena resumed, they were all business. It was difficult to adjust to their complete turnaround. The morning, however, had broken clear and bright, and he was thankful for that.

"Ceellia and I will fly over to the other side with the birds and start to search for any sign of Reena or her captors," Glimmer said. "We'll keep you in sight once you swim over."

Both flew off across the Miles along with more than a dozen birds of several species. Jake stepped into the cold river and slowly swam across. Once on the opposite shore, he slipped through the bushes as he had the evening before and, surprisingly, found himself in the backyard of an older home. In the dark last night he had not realized they were on someone's property. The rearmost section of the yard, where they had searched, was covered in long grass, shrubs, and weeds. But now, in the morning light, he could see there was a middle section, land that contained more organized planting and far fewer weeds. It gradually gave way to a green lawn leading up for maybe a hundred feet to the house. A little girl of perhaps eight sat on a small child-sized picnic bench behind the home.

Jake walked to where the lawn started and noticed the little girl wore cut-off jeans and a purple top. The shirt had a design of yellow ants crawling across her chest, over her shoulder and presumably down her back. Her dark hair was pulled back in a ponytail, and she wore an old pair of sneakers. She stared intently at him, and he pictured her at any moment screaming for Mom.

Realizing he would find nothing without the aid of the Distans and birds, and not relishing the idea of explaining what he was doing in this family's backyard, he turned around and walked back to the beach, where he sat down to wait. After a few minutes, there was rustling in the bushes and the little girl came out of the shrubbery.

"Are you lost?" she asked.

"No," he said. "I'm sorry if I disturbed you."

"You're all wet," she informed him.

"I swim for exercise."

"You swam across the river?"

He nodded while scanning the skies for any sign of the Distans.

"That's a long way. I'm not supposed to play by the river," she said. "Or talk to strangers," she added.

"Good rules you should obey. I won't tell if you don't," he replied, anxious for her to be gone before Glimmer or Ceellia returned.

But instead she walked up and plopped herself on the shore next to him. "Are you resting before swimming back?" she asked.

He smiled and nodded, unsure how to get her to go back home and not knowing how to get away from her without being obvious. He didn't want her to see the Distans, and wasn't sure what Glimmer or Ceellia would do if they came back with news and found him sitting here talking to this little girl.

"My name is Nora," she informed him. "I don't have very many friends."

He knew the best course was to shoo her away, but how can you do that to someone who just looked up at you with her big dark eyes and informed you that she hasn't any friends?

"Hi, Nora," he said. "My name is Jake. Would your mom want you to talk to me?"

"No, but I think it's okay. She's real busy and told me to stay out of the house. Her friend is over, and she doesn't like me to come in when he's there. I might mess things up." With that she sighed and looked out across the water.

Of course, he didn't know what to say. People can be cruel to their kids without knowing it.

"Are you from there?" She pointed with a small finger toward the gardens across the river.

"Yeah," he said. "That's my place." The phrase rang in his ears. My place. He had never owned a place before.

"Are you married to the girl with the red hair?" Nora asked.

"No," he said. "She's my sister. Her name is Sheila."

"I wish someone would marry my mom," she said. "My dad went away and never came back."

"Where did your dad go?" he asked.

"I don't know," she said. "Mom doesn't like to talk about it. Maybe you could marry my mom?"

"Things don't usually work out that way," he said.

For a moment they were both quiet and stared over the river at the gardens. He could barely make out a couple of the Distans flitting about. Then it dawned on him. Nora might have seen someone in their yard. The Zantites weren't invisible.

"Did you see any strange men around your backyard the last few days, Nora?"

She looked up at him, shielding her eyes from the rising sun. "Nope. No one ever comes in our yard. Except you."

That was that. He needed to somehow get away from her without her thinking he was abandoning her like everyone else.

"And the fairies," Nora added.

"Fairies?" His heart skipped a beat.

"Yep. You have them in your backyard. If you squint you can see them. Mom says they're just dragonflies. But I've seen them up close. They're like Barbies, only they have wings. I looked them up in a book I got from the library. It says they're called fairies. There's one that comes in my yard and plays a lot with the birds."

His heart raced at this news. Sheila thought the Distans were safe from prying eyes . . . yet this little girl knew of their existence. Of course, Reena may never be coming in her yard again, unless they could get her back from the Zantites.

"I want her to be my friend," Nora said. "But she's sad."

That got Nora his full attention. "What do you mean?"

"I trapped her."

"You have Ree . . . you have her?"

"Yep. She's in our old fish tank in the shed. Mom says I can't keep pets. She doesn't know about my fairy. You won't tell her will you, Jake?"

"No, Nora, I wouldn't snitch on you. Can you take me to see the fairy?"

Nora scrunched up her face in deep thought. "I guess it's okay. But we have to be careful and not make too much noise. If she hears us, Mom will get mad."

Nora led him back through the bushes and into her backyard. The shed was located where the lawn ended and the planned planting began. Nora quietly went to the door, which she pushed open. On a shelf, just a foot off the floor, was the fish tank with a glass lid held in place by a large flat stone. Even without the stone, it looked like there was barely enough shelf clearance to open the tank lid. Sitting dejectedly in the middle of the tank was Reena.

"Don't let her out, Jake. She'll fly away," Nora said.

At the sound of Nora's voice, Reena looked up and saw Jake. He put his index finger to his lips. Reena looked from him to Nora, her cute little face in a pout.

"If she wants to get away, Nora, shouldn't you let her?"

"But I need a friend."

"Maybe if you let her go, she'll be your friend. Maybe she wants you to be her friend just as much as you want her to be yours. You know, she's probably hungry."

As Nora scrunched her face up in thought, he glanced at Reena. She nodded her understanding and agreement.

"Do you really think so?" Nora asked.

"I'm positive. You trust me, don't you?"

"I guess. But how do I know she'll play with me?"

"If you let her out, I'll ask her."

"You can't talk to a fairy. Even I know that," Nora frowned.

"Reena is a special fairy, you said so yourself."

"How do you know her name is Reena?"

"She and I are friends. Will you let her out?"

Nora's eyes grew wide, and despite being obviously stunned at the news that a grown man and the fairy were friends, she slid the stone off the tank and took the glass cover off.

Reena flew out and landed on his shoulder. She gripped his cheek in her little hands and kissed him. "Thanks for saving me, Mr. Jake," she chirped.

Nora's eyes opened even wider.

"Hi, Nora," Reena said. "Of course I'll be your friend if Mr. Jake says it's okay, but you can't tell anyone, and you can't ever lock me up like that again."

"She talks," Nora beamed. "She knows my name."

"Come on, let's take her back to the river," Jake said. "She needs to fly home and tell her mom she's okay. Everyone was worried about her."

"You have a mom?" Nora asked.

Reena bobbed her head up and down. "Her name's Roseena."

They walked down to the river's bank, Reena sitting on Nora's shoulder.

"Okay, Reena, you fly back and tell your mom you're okay," Jake instructed her. "Tell Sheila I'll be back in a little while. I have to talk to Nora."

"Bye, Nora," Reena said. "I'll be back to play with you when I can. I promise."

"Bye, Reena," Nora said quietly.

Nora and Jake sat in silence for a few minutes after Reena had crossed and was out of sight. He was trying to think of how to get Nora to promise not to tell anyone what she had just witnessed. After a few moments, he looked up and saw a flock of birds headed across the river. Glimmer and Ceellia were with them. News traveled fast.

"What are you doing with my daughter?"

Startled by the voice behind him, Jake jumped and turned. Hands on her hips, dressed similarly to Nora in cut-off jeans and an *Adventure in Canada* T-shirt, was an attractive young woman. Obviously, she was Nora's mom.

"This is Jake, Mom," Nora said. "He swims the river."

"Nora, what did I tell you about talking to strangers?" The woman brushed reddish brown curls, similar to Sheila's, from her eyes and eyed him suspiciously.

"Jake's not a stranger, Mom. He lives in that house across the river with all the gardens and those big dragonflies."

"Is that true?" She locked her brown eyes on his. They appeared to have flecks of gold in them.

He nodded and held out his hand. "I'm Jake."

She looked at his hand, then Nora. Finally she looked back and gripped his hand. "I'm Kara. Just what did she tell you about me?"

"Uh," he stammered, thrown off by her directness.

"Oh boy," Nora said. "I'm in trouble now."

"I'm sorry, I'm confused," he said.

"She tell you her father abandoned us?" Kara asked. "That I was with some guy in the house?"

"I'm sorry, Mom," Nora said.

"What did I tell you about that movie, Nora?" Kara turned to him. "Look . . . Jake," Kara said. "My daughter watches too many grown-up movies. I'm a single mom. I've never been married. There's no guy in my house, and the nuts and bolts of why I have Nora are none of your business, okay?"

Wow, he thought. But he could understand a mom's fears for her daughter's safety with a stranger, even when the stranger was him. He nodded and said, "You don't have to explain anything to me." He had gotten the picture. Nora obviously shopped for a dad whenever she could. She was willing to ignore the *Don't talk to strangers* rule if it meant she got a father.

Kara's chin came up and she crossed her arms. "I'm not interested in any guy, either," she said.

"Jake's gotta sister," Nora interjected.

Kara looked over at him. "Oh. The little redhead who sits on the rock all the time?"

"My sister, Sheila," he acknowledged.

"I heard Mr. Wells died," Kara said. "Sorry about that. I didn't know he had a son too. Prodigal returns?"

"Nope," he said and smiled. "None of your business, okay?"

Kara finally smiled. "Touché, Jake."

"I'd better get back," he said. Nora smiled and winked at him. A signal he trusted meant she would not tell her mom about Reena. "Nice to have met you, Nora," he said, trying to exit the delicate situation he found himself in.

"Bye, Jake," Nora replied.

"Kara," he nodded, unsure what to say.

"Can Jake come over for lunch some time?" Nora asked her mom.

"Naw," he said. "It's okay. I'm sorry to have interfered in your mom's rules. How about if maybe my sister comes and gets you in her boat and you can come visit us?"

"No, I think it might be better if you and your sister called on us sometime first," Kara replied and smiled again. "Bye, Jake."

CHAPTER 28
MACK

Twenty-four hours later, Rachel and Jake sat about twenty rows back from the front of a plane as it prepared to leave BWI airport for Chicago. Sheila, excited to see Jake's dad, sat across the aisle in a window seat. Several passengers separated her from Rachel and Jake. While they were at the underwater station, Sheila and Laura had encouraged Rachel to come along as it would aid them in this ruse to fool the Zantites and learn his dad's plans.

Jake found Rachel was subdued when they picked her up, and now she brushed aside his attempts to talk with some comments about having worked a lot the last couple of days and being tired. With that, she turned and put her head against the window and closed her eyes. Jake was heartened, though, that Rachel had not gone back on her promise to unwittingly help them in covering up the real purpose for their trip. After all, it was a strange request.

His mind raced. Why had he not revealed more of his strange family to her earlier, instead of dropping it on her at once? Even now, he couldn't come up with the right thing to say to her. Going over the events that had happened between them since that night he burst back on the scene at the Dragon Pub, it was obvious that she had been pulled emotionally in several directions. He wouldn't be surprised if she wished he had just stayed away and never returned. His appearance had complicated her life.

Why did his life have to be such a complex affair?

As he sorted these thoughts out in his head, he glanced past the passengers that separated him from Sheila. His eyes met the emerald ones of his twin. For a moment, they held each other's eyes, then she smiled and winked. Did she know what he was thinking, three seats over from where she sat? As there were no Distans with them, no mental communication was possible.

For the entire flight, Jake tried to think of a way to get Rachel to accept him for who he was. When they landed at Chicago's Midway Airport, they quietly gathered their meager baggage and endured a silent cab ride to his apartment on the city's near north side.

There, they collected his car, and twenty minutes later, the three of them cruised south down the Kennedy Expressway. Sheila sat by Jake in the front seat while Rachel sat alone in the back. He tried pointing out landmarks in an effort to get Rachel to speak, but all he got was nods of the head or just plain silence.

She responded to any questions that Sheila asked, but it was apparent she did not want to talk to him. He wanted to say something meaningful to Rachel, but didn't know what.

He finally sighed and glanced over at Sheila. She was staring intently at him.

"What?" he asked.

"You are clearly troubled, my brother. Would you want my assistance?"

He was tempted to dump the problem on her; maybe she would know how to intercede on his behalf with Rachel, but something told him that was not the right thing to do. He shook his head, having decided he needed to fix this on his own, but first they needed to do what they had come there for.

* * *

"Are you okay, Mack?" Jake asked after his dad finally poked his head out of the side door of the ranch house in a far southwest suburb of the city. They had pounded on the windows and doors for several minutes. He knew Mack was a little hard of hearing, but that was ridiculous.

"Of course I'm okay. Why wouldn't I be? I was napping." Mack quickly glanced to Sheila, and she came forward and gave him a big hug.

"At long last," she said. "I finally get to see you again. I've always thought of you as a second father."

"I'm amazed I have such a beautiful daughter and hardly ever get to see her."

"You remember Sheila, Dad?" Jake said.

"I know its Sheila!" Mack turned and practically yelled it at Jake. "Who is this other gorgeous creature?"

"I'm Rachel Anne Paney, Mr. Foley. I'm a friend of Sheila and Jake." Her characterizing him as a *friend,* and putting his name after Sheila's, was not lost on Jake.

Something appeared to click in Mack's head though, as he quickly glanced back at Jake. Somewhere along the way, Jake had probably mentioned Rachel to him, and he had mentally just put two and two together.

* * *

On the day before he left for St Michaels, Jake recalled glancing around Mack's little ranch house. He had traced the odor that permeated the air to the dirty dishes in the sink and the greasy frying pan still sitting on the stove. He noted the floors hadn't seen a broom or vacuum in weeks, and Jake was afraid to go into his bathroom. Outside, his garden had been overgrown with weeds. Suffice it to say, the whole place was messy and smelled old, like him. Jake knew that if he pulled out the vacuum and tried to clean things up, Mack'd have a fit and start yelling at him. Sometimes helping out wasn't worth the aggravation.

Additionally, Jake recalled that before he went to Maryland, his dad had developed into quite the hermit, and not one who was necessarily concerned with neatness. Whenever Jake had come over, it had been up to him to wash the myriad dishes piled high by the sink and on the table, as well as vacuum the floors, take out the garbage, and, well, you get the picture.

* * *

"Call me Carl, both of you," Dad told them, bringing Jake back to the present. After a final evil eye look at Jake, Mack led them all inside.

Now, once inside, Jake was flabbergasted. He could see that Mack's housekeeping skills had apparently returned. Everything was neat and orderly, in its rightful place.

"Is this the Rachel you left when you fled Annapolis?" he asked Jake.

He nodded, surprised he remembered. Jake tried to recall if he had actually told him that.

"Idiot," Mack said with a shake of his head. "Were you surprised to meet your twin sister?" he added with a smirk. In fact, Jake could see Mack knew a lot more than he had given him credit for. Jake quickly realized that phase of dad's life, following his mother's death and Laura's departure, had all been an act.

"Uhh, Rachel knows who we are, Mack," Jake tried to point out.

"I know that," he replied. "I talk to Laura. You think you know a lot, but you know nothing."

Mack momentarily looked at Sheila, who gave a minute shake of her head. He then returned his attention back to Jake. "Sorry, Jake, but we had to deceive you. The Zantites knew I had once been part of the station and had moved here. For a while they had me under observation, and I needed to convince them that I was not a threat. So, I became feeble-minded. We all felt it was best you didn't know until it was time. Now is that time."

Jake thought himself an outsider compared to what Sheila and Dad shared.

Apparently, his thoughts were painted on his face, because Sheila's small hand reached over, took his, and gave it a light squeeze. "Don't be upset, Jake."

Jake glanced from Sheila to Dad and then at Rachel, who stood across the room and looked at all of them while apparently trying to figure out what was going on. The urge to just get up and walk out was strong in Jake, but he knew he was done walking away from problems. There had to be a better way to say no.

After a few silent moments, he asked, "How do I fit into this War of the Worlds? Just what is it you all are expecting me to do?"

"Watch what you say, Jake!" Sheila said, and looked from him to Mack, who nodded almost imperceptibly. "While they know your dad's not a threat, I'm here, and we're not sure if they'll find that suspicious. They have very sophisticated methods of eavesdropping. Do you think Earth's drones are highly developed? Try all of that technology in a lifelike mosquito. As for what we expect you to do, I told you before, we need you to bring this incident to a close," Sheila whispered.

"Is someone going to tell me what's going on, Sheila? I thought that's why we came here."

"Your dad and I decided it's best to wait until we get back in case they are monitoring this location."

"I thought it best that Sheila explain it to you later, Jake," Dad added. "It might cost you, though." He stole a glance at Rachel, who was watching them carefully. "More than you know."

Jake liked neither his inference nor his foreboding tone, but kept silent.

* * *

The next day after breakfast, Sheila grabbed Jake's hand and tugged him outside, down the long, crushed stone driveway and toward the forest preserve.

"I'm sorry if your Dad and I've been secretive." She began what he hoped would be an explanation for all the cloak and dagger. "There's something you don't know yet, and I wanted to be sure your dad was in agreement with what I'm going to tell Rachel."

"What does this have to do with Rachel?"

"You have to go to enlist April in our plans."

"April?"

"Did I not tell you that you were followed everywhere by a Distan when you were in Annapolis? So was April. Even when April was eighteen and not conscious of her destiny, she had a Distan. When the two of you met at the beach that day, Roseena was with you and April had Sentelle, Ceellia's mother, as her Distan. At the time, both reported directly to Laura, so the Keep never heard about the two of you spending the weekend in her apartment.

"Laura knew, when you yelled at her that day you left, it was about April, not her. Roseena and Sentelle told her about your pact. You'd resign your commission in the Navy and take off, which would leave April free to pursue her dream of being a Naval Aviator and forget all about Flammeria. Laura was so disappointed with you, she convinced your Dad and me to forget you. I tried to contact you, to hear your side of the story, but you ignored me."

"I . . . I'm sorry, I—"

"I'm not interested in what happened back then. I think I understand your motivation. You were in love with April, and didn't understand that she . . . Well, that's up to her to own up to. My concern is that you are loyal to me now. I've waited twenty years. I hope it was not in vain."

Thoughts of another vanishing act flew out of his mind. He would honor his commitment to Sheila. "I'm with you, Sheila. What was done is the past. I won't disappoint you."

"Do you remember I said there were two of you that will have to do something about the Zantite threat?'" Her voice had dropped to a whisper. "Well, it's you and April, same as ten years ago. We have no one else. I'll explain all of this to you in detail when we get back and are in the safety of a scatterer. It should be safe here out in the open, but your dad thought there's no reason to tempt fate by telling you now.

"I just wanted you to know that it's not in my makeup to lie to friends. And I want Rachel to be my friend very badly, therefore I must tell her what I'm having you do. If you ever hope to gain Rachel's love and respect back, you too must be honest with her. That includes telling her of your affair with April."

CHAPTER 29
JAKE'S CONFESSION

Sheila told Rachel she was asking Jake to do the mission that required the assistance of April the morning they left Mack's, on the car ride back to Jake's apartment. In the dark as to what the mission entailed specifically, Rachel assumed that Jake would leave her soon after, and hardly talked to him. Eight hours later, the three landed back at BWI. On the return flight they had all sat together, but in relative silence. Now, as they exited BWI, Jake realized he had no place to stay. Rachel had professed to him a need for time to think things through, so he was sure she wouldn't want him to hang with her, and Sheila had not offered him an extended place to lodge. Should he have just remained home with Dad?

"Can we give you a ride to Annapolis, Rachel?" Sheila asked. When Jake looked at Sheila, she smiled back at him. "You're staying with us in St Michaels, are you not, Jake?"

Although confused, he was grateful for that and nodded.

"I have a great idea," Sheila announced. "Why don't you come and stay a few days too?" she asked Rachel. "I'd like to be friends."

Rachel looked up, surprising Jake with her response. "Sure, sounds like fun, you and I getting better acquainted. Oh, but I have my cat—"

"We'll stop at your place; you can pack some stuff and pick up your cat. Snow is welcome at our house in St Michaels."

Rachel looked from Sheila to Jake. "What about the Distans? Would Snow be a threat to them?"

"I assure you that the Distans are very friendly to cats," Sheila pointed out. "Your Snow has already bonded with Ceellia and Glimmer."

"Sounds like a plan," Rachel smiled. "I'd like that very much."

After Jake had dropped off Sheila and Rachel, who needed to pick up her things, Snow and car, he drove to St Michaels alone. Maybe Sheila's time with Rachel would help ease her fears that he was going to disappear again.

* * *

When Jake arrived at the house in St. Michaels, he was welcomed by a smiling Gert. An hour later, as she and Jake sipped a cup of coffee and talked, the front door swung open and Rachel and Sheila came in, carrying several bags and Snow. Gert jumped up as Sheila introduced her to Rachel and Snow.

"What a beautiful cat," Gert said.

"Rachel is an old friend of Jake's," Sheila added. "She needed a few days off, so I invited her to spend a couple of days here. She knows who we really are. In fact, she knows everything. Is that okay with you, Gert?"

"Splendid," Gert cooed.

Jake drained his coffee and put the cup in the sink before announcing he was taking a walk. He was sure no one cared and, not waiting for a reply, he burst out of the front door and headed straight for the Miles. When he reached the river, he stood on the bank for several minutes, trying to make sense of all that had happened. As he contemplated his options, Glimmer and Ceellia flew up.

"Hi, Mr. Jake," Ceellia greeted him.

"Good to see you are back," Glimmer added. "All of you."

"I didn't think you'd be glad to see Rachel," he said.

"I'm not," Ceellia pouted.

"That'll all work out in time," Sheila's voice, from behind them, added. When Jake twisted around, he saw her perched on the rock as she had been when he first met her. "I'm sorry you're confused and upset, Jake. Believe me, there's a reason for all of this. Right now, I can't say any more." Both Distans flew around Sheila in greeting, then a single pointed finger from her sent them winging off toward the center of the garden.

"Walk with me, Jake." With that she slipped off the rock and headed toward the house. He shrugged and followed her all the way to the base of the stairs, where she had stopped and was looking into the wisteria garden that was circled by the long driveway. When he put an arm around her shoulders, she looked up.

Her jade eyes glistened with tears, and she gripped his hand and pulled at him, reversing her course and leading the way back down to the Miles. She was quiet as they slipped through the beautiful gardens, although she stopped once at one of the ponds and watched several small turtles swimming among the lily pads. As before, Glim and Ceellia tracked toward them, but Sheila again raised a hand and made a motion to them that indicated she and Jake were not to be disturbed, and the Distans reversed course. Sheila and Jake ended up at the rock they had left moments ago, and she effortlessly scooted back up, flipped off her sandals and trained her eyes on him.

"I hated the idea of asking you to do this, Jake. In fact, I was going to chicken out. That's why my strange meandering." She paused and looked out at the river as a small boat drifted by. "What I hated even more was telling Rachel that in order to help Flammeria, it was necessary for you to team up with April. I feel like I've driven a spike into your relationship. I'm hoping I can convince her you're not making a conscious choice to leave her for April, but are doing something important for Earth and Flammeria. Now, I need for you to tell Rachel the truth of your relationship with April."

"Did you reveal to her that April is a Flammerian?" he replied.

"No, I thought you should be the one to do that."

"I think you're right about that. And that it's time I was honest with Rachel. I need to talk to her before I leave."

"That's good. Remember, you've already agreed to do this mission, but when it's done, as far as I know, you're free to go. Right now you must come completely clean with Rachel and tell her about your tête-à-tête with April ten years ago, and then stress to her you're going back to see her in conjunction with this mission. You can't have a serious relationship with Rachel based on some lies. Please, Jake, trust me. I've already told you how I hate to ask you to do this mission."

"What am I supposed to tell April? What's your big plan?"

"Please convince her that the two of you should abandon your pact. I have to confess to you though, your father and I had no real positive ideas about how we should oppose the Zants. You know we have no weapons, and there are just the two of you. I was hoping that you spending a couple of days with April would lead to some plan."

"You want me to stay with her for a few *days*?"

"Just how did you envision doing this?" Sheila's voice rose. "Walk in, tell her you changed your mind about things and run? Come on, Jake, even you are not that dense. Damn, this is hard enough without your lackadaisical attitude. Get this into your head. I need you to convince April to help us. After all, despite what you both think privately, you're both . . . Flammerians, and I need your aid in this fight. Screw your pact. Believe me when I say, she is the key to everything."

"Is that all?" he said a little sarcastically. "Our pact is not about us fighting Zants. And why me? Why doesn't Mattik convince her? He's her father. Why do you all think she would listen to me?"

"Mattik tried." Sheila took in a deep breath, struggling for words. "Mattik said he attempted telling her once she might be asked to defend the station or Earth, and she laughed at him, said she'd already sworn an oath to defend America, but only when ordered to do so against their enemies. Last she heard, the Zantites were not on that list. It's a trait of those of Atlantis heritage to be mistrustful, unlike us from Lemuria. However, April knows you. She trusts you. Because of your shared past, we think she would sooner follow you, but it might take you some time to convince her. That's why it needs to be days. Do it gradually, not a garbage dump like we did to Rachel. I have straightened that out, by the way. She now even accepts that many Earthlings can be traced back to either Atlantis or Lemuria."

At first he was silent, still having a hard time wrapping his mind around the fact that the pact he and April had made had been known all along to his sisters.

"Moonglimmer told me you wanted to talk to me." Rachel came up behind Jake.

"Yes, it's about time I was telling you the truth about everything."

"I'd certainly welcome that," Rachel said.

"Why don't you join me up here?" Sheila moved over to make room on the rock.

Rachel scooted up, then faced Jake.

"April and I have more of a history than you thought," Jake started. "We met before she came to the Academy, and had an affair. This was about the same time that you and I were getting reacquainted. Before I even knew she would be assigned to my company. I had nothing to do with that, pure coincidence."

Jake paused for a moment, then said, "You might have guessed this, but I wanted to be sure you know. April is a Flammerian, like Sheila and I."

"I should have known. She's just as beautiful as your sisters," Rachel agreed.

"April has always been a very focused individual. Kind of a daredevil, if you will. Laura knew when she was in high school that her taking over the station, the role originally planned for her, would be a difficult fit. At one point, Mattik, her father, insisted they should just let her be, never even tell her of her lineage to another world; just let her grow up thinking she was an Earthling."

"How is it that she was even allowed to go to the Academy?" Rachel asked.

"Thirty years ago, our station leaders had decided that it would be helpful if some of the offspring were trained to fight. That led to my parents leaving the station. Even back then, they envisioned it would eventually come to this. I was the first selected. It seemed perfect, as my father had decided to move us away, and secrecy in my upbringing was paramount because the projected enemies of Earth were always listening to our messaging. It was decided that when I reached ten years of age, my father would urge me toward a military career. Since the station is underwater, Mattik, who took over for my mother as station leader until Laura was ready to assume command, suggested my desires be channeled toward the Naval Academy. It was close to the station and provided the most overall training.

"Several years later, Mattik decided a second individual with military training might be needed, preferably one who would mesh well with me. Mattik felt it was too much to ask of any other station inhabitant, so he offered April, his own newborn daughter. Mattik gave up command of the station and moved April to Wyoming."

"So first you, then April was selected years later?" Rachel asked.

"Yes, the station needed us both shielded from any other race that harbored plans to come to Earth. First, my parents moved to Illinois and seemingly abandoned their birthright, then, years later, April's parents moved to Wyoming. They arranged birth certificates from Baltimore for us both.

"It proved prophetic, as it was about that time that the Zantites first began their probes into this world. They were unaware of me and April, since we were never at the station and they kept no records of either of us. They never contacted us, so we both lived in obscurity. Our fathers felt that someday they would need our services. That day has come. However, I wish it hadn't come to this. Sheila feels we need April involved, so she's asking me to convince her."

"You can't get cold feet on us now, Jake," Sheila urged. "Come up with any story you think appropriate for why you've sought April out again; you never have any trouble with women. And this one you've already slept with."

"Easy, Sheila. I'm not getting any desires to abandon you or the station. Rachel needs to hear everything. I'm not done yet."

"So what is it April's supposed to help you do?" Rachel asked. "And how are you to do it?"

"I'll tell you both that when we figure it out. Now, let me finish bringing you up to date."

Jake smiled over at Rachel. "Okay so far?"

She nodded.

"Okay, our pact. April and I brought you up to date on the happenings at the Academy that contributed to my getting lost ten years ago. There was more. April was extremely upset over my being a scapegoat in what happened. Despite wanting to fly more than anything, she wanted to just give it up rather than face a similar decision years later. She felt as long as our Flammerian birthright hung over us, someday she'd face similar circumstances. First she wanted to just run away with me. We'd hit the road together and never look back. We seriously considered it. Finally, we realized we had a sense of duty. We had sworn to defend the country of our birth, plus we shouldn't completely close the door on the world of our parents. So we went our separate ways with the promise that we'd shield each other from the station. Neither of us would answer to any requests for help. April got her career, and I was free of responsibility."

"So you abandoned me too, without a word. How did that work out for you?" Rachel asked.

"Terrible. I thought of you for ten years. When my dad asked me to return, I said no, then thought of you. So I came hoping to see you, then . . ."

"Then what?" Rachel pressed.

"Then I couldn't leave. Seeing you and meeting Sheila made me realize what a terrible decision I made ten years ago. Now I've got to go to April and convince her we erred."

"Are you still in love with her?" Rachel asked.

"I was never . . ." Jake looked out over the James River. "I don't know."

"Over those ten years, who did you think about more?" Rachel asked. "Her or me?"

"You. Most definitely you. But, I . . . slept with her."

"That one time?"

He nodded.

"SOL, Jake. Remember what we said when we re-met years ago at the Academy?"

"SOL?"

"Yeah, Statutes of Limitations. Anything in the past was in the past. April and I are friends now. I'm trusting you."

"Furthermore, Jake . . ." Sheila said.

"What?" he asked.

"You must be completely truthful with April, just as you've been with Rachel. It's the proper way of the Flammerians. Besides, she, like I, can detect untruths. You will be taking Glimmer and Ceellia with you, and Ceellia has been reassigned as April's Distan. Once she is with Ceellia, April will discover the Distans can read minds. She'll at first believe it's more of her own intuition, but she'll develop very quickly. But you must be careful, because April could easily fall back in love with you."

"Back?"

"Come on, Jake, even you're not that naive. You must know that she was very much in love with you at the Academy. Glimmer told me she is entangled in a hopeless relationship now, and so I think she is vulnerable to grasping onto one she thinks might work. You can't lie to her. You were, and will be again, very drawn to April."

"I think I can handle myself," he huffed. "I'll see you back here on Monday."

CHAPTER 30
TO APRIL

An hour later, Jake and the two Distans were already through Easton and driving south down U. S. Highway 50.

"Why aren't we taking the Interstate, Mr. Jake?" Ceellia asked.

"I chose to take the roads on the eastern shore of Maryland and Virginia because it would waste too much time for me to go back to Annapolis and then have to drive west to get back to Interstate 95."

"But don't you wish to drive those faster roads?" Glimmer asked. Both of them were lying on the dash of the car, their little bare feet pressed up against the windshield.

"We're not in any hurry. We have three days to kill. No sense spending them stuck bumper-to-bumper on 95 in the Washington DC area." He imagined any driver who glanced over and noticed the Distans would think him some kind of deviant, with what looked like two Barbie dolls planted on the car's dash. However, they were having a great adventure, and he could not bring himself to have them hide somewhere.

Picking up US Highway 13 around Salisbury, they headed further south, eventually entering Virginia. After getting their fill of the sparse scenery on the back roads, both little 'girls' dozed atop a small rug on the back seat.

Jake realized that even after his reveal, it was not really his seeing April that bothered Rachel, but the thought that he might once again pick up and leave her. Hopefully his admissions had blunted that. While he hated revealing to Rachel his history with April, she seemed to realize that they had not been seriously together when that happened.

Could Rachel somehow fit into the Flammerian mission? He could not leave her again. Those thoughts swirled around in his head until he hit the Virginia border.

From there it was an uneventful ride through small towns to the Chesapeake Bay Bridge-Tunnel. Both Distans were enamored of the twenty-mile-long bridge with its two-mile-long tunnels that connected Virginia with the Delmarva Peninsula. Once through that, Jake picked his way past Norfolk on the beltway to Greenbrier Parkway, an exit for the city of Chesapeake. Getting close and into a more populated area, he rousted the Distans and asked them to make sure they made themselves scarce until he could introduce them to April. Since Ceellia had been assigned to April, she seemed overjoyed at the prospect of meeting her.

From the exit, it was a short drive to April's apartment building. But before he could get out of the car, Sheila's voice, through Glimmer of course, broke into his head.

"Be careful. April might try to seduce you again, Jake. I just know it. She'll make it appear to be your fault. Resist her, but don't forget that April Elliott is one of us. She's Mattik's daughter, so don't hurt her feelings."

"I know a little more about our relationship than you, Sheila."

"Relationships with a female Flammerian are complex. You don't . . ."

"Bye, Sis."

After he mentally disconnected from Sheila, he sat in the car and revisited his conversation with April when she'd first arrived at the Naval Academy almost twelve years ago.

* * *

He was sitting at his desk, doing Company Officer paperwork as usual, when a female voice had nervously called out.

"Request permission to come aboard, SIR!"

The "SIR" part rang loudly in his ears. He had looked up to see April in loose-fitting whites, the standard issue white uniform for midshipmen, standing in his doorway, her bright blue eyes in the boat—that is, staring straight ahead. Even then, in that thoroughly unflattering uniform, her short blonde hair sticking out in all directions from under her cover (Dixie hat), he couldn't help thinking that she was one beautiful girl. She was Laura in blonde hair. He had already seen his list of assigned midshipman with her name on it. Since he was now dating Rachel, he sensed April might mean trouble ahead. He had briefly considered going to the Dean and getting her transferred, but thought he, being a Flammerian also, would be a better fit for her. He just had to keep her away from Rachel.

"Granted," he had answered, and she stepped into his office. "Have a seat and relax, Miss Elliott. Welcome to the United States Naval Academy."

After having fumbled uneasily with the chair, she sat on the edge of it, ready to spring into action.

"I said relax, Miss Elliott."

Untensing slightly, she moved her body back into the chair.

"I wasn't sure how to act around you," she said.

He chuckled inwardly as he noted that his plebe detailers had already managed to embed in her a fear of officers, even though she knew him well.

However, he also knew that in the close confines of Bancroft Hall the walls had ears, so he needed to pretend he had not known her in the past. Already, several of his upper-class mids loitered just outside his door, probably anxious to know something about this beautiful girl. He recalled glancing down at her record and noticing her place of birth. "You were born in Baltimore?" He said the words loudly so they would hear.

She nodded with a questioning look, but he had meant it as a rhetorical question. They knew each other's past.

"Just play along," he mouthed, then continued in his normal voice. "So was I. Don't ask me anything about it, though, as my folks moved us to Illinois when I was in diapers."

"Likewise, sir." Still confused, she loosened up slightly, and even winked at him. "Actually, that's such a coincidence, sir. My folks moved me to Casper, Wyoming, right after I was born." She leaned forward a little. "But you already know that, Jake," she whispered.

Afraid that those outside might hear something they shouldn't, Jake got up and went to the door.

"I suggest you have better things to do," he said to the midshipmen gathered in the hall, and they scurried off.

"I suggest you forget that we previously met, *Miss Elliott*," he said icily as he sat back down. "We need to be discreet, understood?"

"Yes, sir. Sorry, sir."

"Forget our past association. You can expect to be treated like any other midshipman. Understood?"

"Yes, sir," she rang out. Their previous meeting was never mentioned again, until they met just before Jake left the area and came up with the pact.

* * *

As he mulled over that time in the past, a white Mustang convertible parked alongside his rental car and pulled him back into the present. When he glanced over at the car, he first saw her bright blue eyes, then her curly blonde locks, blown about by the wind. Her huge grin looked back at him.

"Damn," he heard Sheila mutter in his mind. *"Please do what I asked of you and get the Hades out of there as soon as you can."*

"Bye, Sheila!" He turned slightly so April could not see his face and looked back at Glimmer. *"Stop telling Sheila everything that happens,"* he mentally demanded of her.

"But she told me . . ." came back to him.

"Who is your responsibility?" he hissed the words back at her.

"You, Mr. Jake. But, April is beautiful—"

"Then do what I say, Glim."

Glimmer and Ceellia had positioned themselves by the rear window and raised their heads just enough to peer out at April without being seen.

"I don't know why Sheila is so concerned," he sent to both Distans. *"I can do this . . . I have willpower."*

"She's even prettier than I remembered her," Ceellia sent back to him. "You're doomed, Mr. Jake."

A moment later, April was out of her car and standing by the driver's side of Jake's. She rapped on the window and pointed down. He lowered the window.

"What a tremendous surprise it was to hear your voice, Jake. But why did you want to see me? Just what are you doing here?"

"It's a long story. Why am I here? Mid girls always gave good advice. Besides, I don't know many people around the east coast, and I thought—" He knew the excuses had to sound lame, but what was he going to say? I'm helping fight an alien invasion and thought you might want to lend a hand?

"Say no more." She reached into his car, grasped a forearm and gave it a yank. "Come on. Get out of your car and into mine. You can buy me dinner while I listen to your tale of woe. Okay?"

He nodded and she released his arm. He watched as she strutted back around her car. Her clothes, a pair of jean shorts and a red and white checkered top, looked like they were painted onto her body. Okay, so it wasn't going to be easy.

"Ready, girls?" he turned and mentally asked.

"Don't worry about us, Mr. Jake. Just leave the window open a little bit," Glim beamed back. *"Come on, Ceellia, we get to ride in a convertible."*

"Uh, does Mr. Jake know that—" Ceellia began.

"Come on, Ceellia," Glim repeated.

After briefly wondering what that was all about, he lowered both his window and the rear window behind him about five inches before he got out and into April's car. She slipped back into the driver's seat and asked, "Seafood okay?"

"None better," he said as she restarted the car.

"Where were you thinking of staying tonight?" she asked as she pulled out onto the street. "Surely you're not driving all the way back?"

"No, I have a couple of days to kill. I thought of going down to the Outer Banks later and finding something."

"Like hell. You're staying with me," she purred, her blue eyes flashing his way momentarily.

He shook his head. "No, I don't want to prey on our friendship. I'll stop at a motel somewhere."

"No!" she said, rather emphatically, then continued talking while they were stopped at a stop sign. "That wasn't a suggestion, it was an order. Besides, we have history. My price for advice just went up. You're staying with me those couple of days. There is no compromise on that." She banged on the steering wheel for emphasis.

"I can't do that. What would Bill think?"

"Are you seriously comparing yourself to Bill? I told you before, he'll soon be part of my past. Furthermore, he's deployed on the Nimitz this week. I was supposed to go too, but my bird went down for a bad radio. Now I'm hypothetically flying out on Saturday. Come on, you know how shipmates treat each other. And you definitely were... shit, you still are my shipmate. Damn, you've been my bunkmate." She took her eyes off the road and glanced over at him. "Anyway, it's none of his fuckin' business who I see. There, it's settled. You're in my spare bedroom."

She pulled the Mustang into a parking space in front of a small restaurant that was located mere blocks away from the apartment.

Over dinner, Jake wanted to keep secret his problems with Rachel. But, Sheila's insistence on the truth caused him to tell April that he didn't know how to convince Rachel that he was back to stay. That part was true.

He had to wait a few seconds for an answer as April pushed at a piece of her salmon in its mango sauce while she stared at the plate. Then her head shot up. "Excuse my French, Jake, but you sure know how to fuck things up. What the hell's the matter with you? I can't believe that you don't know how to convince a woman you love her."

"Hey, I didn't say anything about—"

"We're not talking about sex, Jake," she interrupted. "I'm talking about love. I'm sure you know how to screw her. That's the voice of experience speaking. You just don't know how to talk to her . . . to love her. You didn't know how to talk to me either."

There was an element of truth in what she said. Why hadn't he seen that all along? Things had been different when Rachel and he had been together ten years ago. Now that he had returned, he had let his family origins get in the way of his relationship with her. He should have . . .

"Let's go, Jake," April said.

As they walked out of the restaurant, he thought about explaining to April about the Distans, Sheila, and how—

"Why did you even agree to stay with her? You're messing everything up," Sheila's voice hissed in his head as they got to the car. He glanced back to where Glimmer and Ceellia hid in the back.

"Should I remind you this was your idea?" he mentally sent to Sheila.

"I thought you'd have sense enough to get a room in a motel or someplace," she replied.

"Leave me alone, Sheila," he replied mentally. *"You don't know everything."*

"I know you're making an enormous mistake."

April walked around to the driver's side while he waited for her to unlock the car. Having glimpsed Glim in the back seat, he took the time to send an additional urgent message to Sheila by thinking about it. *"You promised to stay out of my head, Sis. So do it. Now! Glimmer, you stop forwarding her messages to me."*

"It's your funeral, Jake." And she was gone.

"Why are you standing out there, Jake? Get in the car," April said. Mentally sparring with Sheila had prevented him from noticing she had unlocked the car and now sat in the driver's seat.

"Sorry," he said and got in. "I'm trying to think of how to make this right."

"Lucky you," she said, lightly brushing the fingertips of her hand across his cheek. "That's why you bought me dinner tonight. It's earned you a place to stay and my expert advice."

She accelerated out of the restaurant parking area, and moments later pulled back into the space next to his rental car. He grabbed a bag out of his car, and April, all smiles, came around to stand next to him.

"Come on, clueless," she teased. "You've got some lessons coming." With that she grabbed his free hand in hers and pulled him toward the building entrance like they were teenagers navigating down a high school hallway.

CHAPTER 31

April's Apartment

For the entire elevator ride up to the fifth floor, during which Jake was preoccupied with whether Glim and Ceellia had been able to follow them, April held his hand. He relaxed somewhat when, almost in answer to part of his mental wrangling, he felt the tiny fingers of four little hands caress the back of his neck. He was beginning to think the little creatures could write a book on stealth. No matter where they went, when he needed Glimmer, she was there. Now the main source of his concern was his hand held in a tight grip by April.

They took a left out of the elevator and April pulled him down the hall to the last apartment. He relaxed somewhat when she finally let go of his hand to fish her keys out of a small pocket in her jean shorts and open the door. In one smooth motion, she shoved him inside, flicked the light switch and flipped off her sandals. He found himself standing in her living room. A flat-screen TV hung on a wall facing the seating area.

"Bill's idea," she explained, after seeing him eyeball the TV. "Like most males of Earth, he can't seem to do without sports. I hardly watch the damn thing."

Using her toes as pointers, April indicated a door off the kitchen and said, "Your room." Her foot moved on, aiming toward the next closed door. "Bathroom." Lastly she trained a light blue-painted big toe on the door to the far left. "My room. Stay out unless you're invited in. I want to be friends with Rachel. Both bedrooms have a door into the bathroom, so you might want to knock first if you're going in there. Unless you're feeling daring," she ended with a smile. "I'm opening a bottle of wine, Jake. You have any requests?"

267

"I'm drinking what you're drinking," he announced. *I can do this,* he thought but he felt his resolve began to waver.

April walked into the small kitchen, reached under the divider that shielded it from the living room, and pulled out a bottle. When she held the merlot up for him with a questioning look, he nodded, then walked over to her and took the bottle from her hand.

"Opener?" he asked.

She turned, opened a drawer, and pulled out a corkscrew. Her tongue flashed out across ruby red lips as she laid it in his hand. Her follow up coy smile should have told him he was making a huge mistake. Jake quickly realized that when they were at the Academy, he'd had his sense of duty to protect him from the feelings she stirred in him. Now, in her apartment, he was totally disarmed.

"Relax, my pet," she smirked. "I'm not going to rape you or anything. I've grown up, and I know how to control . . . my . . . urges. Geez, Jake. You look terrorized. There'll be no funny business like that first time we met. Shit, I was just eighteen then. Look, I'll listen to your shit, and in return you're going to keep me company. Deal?"

Realizing this might have been a mistake, he nodded dumbly. Had he really thought he could come down here and resist the attraction he'd always felt for this beautiful creature? The shy and nervous girl he remembered from the Academy had been replaced by this self-assured woman. She moved through her apartment like a stalking cat.

"Have a seat." She purred the words. He took a seat in the middle of the larger couch. She pulled out two glasses, poured the wine and slithered over. He took the glass her hand held out for him.

She slipped over to the loveseat, sat on one side and set her wine on the cocktail table in front of her. "Get your ass over here," she said while patting the seat next to her. "I'm not going to shout, and there is no reason for you to be afraid of a little girl. Remember, you came to me."

Where was Sheila when he needed her? Of course, he had ordered her to stay out of his head and business. He could have sworn, though, he heard her voice say one word: *"Idiot,"* followed by giggling from Glimmer. By now, he assumed, Glim and Ceellia were probably hiding in his designated bedroom.

What the hell was he afraid of? She was just a girl. Feeling braver, he picked up the glass and went over and sat down next to April. After all, she was just going to talk to him and give him some pointers. He took a sip, probably more like a gulp, of the dark liquid, set the glass down next to hers, and looked over at her.

"Kiss me, Jake," she purred.

"What?" he asked, shocked.

"I said kiss me, Jake. How do you think I'm going to help you if I don't see what you've been doing? Or, more correctly, not doing." She moved in closer to him and licked her lips expectantly. "Don't forget, I want you to put a little desire in it. Make me feel the lust."

Forgetting Sheila's warnings and drawn in by those ruby lips, he quickly warmed up to the idea and leaned over to kiss her.

"I warned you, Jake. Flammerian girls almost unconsciously go after male or female conquests. April is reveling in finally getting her desires met. You, my dear brother, are a goner." Sheila's words, courtesy of Glimmer, shot into his head like a thunderclap.

He was determined to wrestle control of the situation. However, curiosity about something else Sheila said vexed him. Flammerian girls liked female conquests?

"I hope it's clear that this is me helping, 'cause—" April's words brought his full attention back to her.

"Crystal," he said, and cut her off with a finger over her lips. Then he kissed her, intending to just peck her on the lips. But when he got close to her, he couldn't help himself. He first lightly massaged those bright red lips with his, then touched them with the tip of his tongue. After their initial fling years ago, he had wanted to relive the magic in those lips many times back at the Academy, and now it was like finally getting a chance to experience a fantasy. Once his tongue touched them . . . Sheila was right, April seized control.

Her reaction was instantaneous. Her lips parted and, accompanied by an excited moaning from deep within, her tongue shot into his mouth. She vaulted off the seat and was on top of him in a second. Wrapping her arms around him, she ground her body into his. His reaction to that was also immediate. Rising to the occasion, he slipped his hands under her red and white checkered top. At that instant, April pulled her tongue out of his mouth, loosened her grip, and finally shoved him away. She dropped back onto her side of the loveseat, breathing heavily. His hands were still partially under her sleeveless top.

"Wow, Jake," she finally spoke. "Is that how you kiss Rachel?"

"I'm sorry. I don't know what came over me. I was going to barely kiss you, and then . . . I don't know." Of course, as they both sought to catch their breath, he knew. What could have been with April was the unfulfilled fantasy in his life. And now he had found the attraction was not only mutual, but magnetic.

"Lesson's over," she said. "It took everything I had to break us up. I might not be able to do it again. Okay, I've had my fun. What the hell did you really come here for?"

"I have a problem. Rachel is . . ."

"That's bullshit and we both know it. Your sisters could have helped you with that far better than me. Come on, Jake. The truth. Is this about our pact? You want me to do one of their f'ing missions with you?"

Her cell phone rang, and she padded on bare feet over to the kitchen counter, where it was lying. She glanced at the screen. "It's Bill, Jake. The bird farm must be close enough to shore to get a call out. I'm going to take this in my room. Make yourself at home but don't forget, I'm expecting a confession when I return."

He took a small slug of wine and moved over to a chair in one corner. That loveseat, he figured, was off limits now.

He looked up as April walked out of the bedroom with a scowl on her face. "Fuck," she said, and threw her phone at the loveseat where it bounced off the back cushion and wound up in the shag carpet.

"Look, I didn't mean to cause you any trouble. I'm terribly sorry," Jake said.

"What the fuck are you talking about?" Her blue eyes sparkled like gemstones. "My being upset has nothing to do with you. I needed to do some practice landings this weekend, you know, touch-and-goes on the carrier to requalify. I should have flown off with the group two days ago, and I'd be done. Now there's something wrong with the ship's arresting system, so I can't fly out until it's fixed. In fact, half the squadron is returning tomorrow. Bill's staying, though." She then appeared to settle down and eyeballed him. "Regardless, you're not going anywhere. I promised to put you up, and that's what I'm doing. Besides, you've got squealing to do, so why don't you start? Why are you here?"

"Okay, but first what can I do to cheer you up?"

"For now you can fill my wine glass and yours, Jake. Then I need you to massage the knots out of my shoulders. Then you will stop your stalling and tell me why you came to see me."

He nodded, then got up and went into the kitchen for the bottle and filled their glasses. Returning, he sat on one end of the sofa, then motioned April to sit in the middle. She did, but facing him. "Turn around," he said.

"I love a man giving me orders," she said as she complied. "But you're the only one I'll take them from when I'm not on duty. Talk to me."

"Give me a minute."

He proceeded to massage her shoulders. Even touching her stirred him up, but he kept his hands in the appropriate places. She turned around and smiled. "Your sister, Laura, came to see me once."

"I forgot to warn you about that, Jake. More importantly, watch yourself. It's instinct for Flammerian girls to capture the heart of those they love. She simply cannot help herself. For April, it's doing what is natural." Sheila's voice had a hint of humor in it. Whose side was she on?

"Laura came to my graduation with my dad. My mother never liked the idea of me going to the Academy, and hated that my father urged me along. So she refused to come. However, you remember, I'm sure, that it was my decision to go there. Flying is my life. I'd fly a bathtub if it had wings. Anyway, that's when my dad tried to get me to do some kind of mission for Laura."

"Probably the one I said no to," he interrupted.

"Yeah, something about going to Aldebaran to meet with some explorers."

"Do you know what it was for?"

"Nope. She ended up going herself. I assumed it had something to do with the station, but she never told me what it was for," Jake shrugged.

"She knew about our pact, but she said she wanted to appeal to my loyalty." April snickered. "I told her my loyalty was to you, not Flammeria. She seemed to accept that. Even clued me in about the scent."

"Scent?"

"Yeah. I never realized Flammerian women gave off this scent that . . . uh . . . inspires men. Not Flammerian men, but others. Some kind of musk, I guess. Hey, that's probably why I became so popular after you left the Academy. And I thought it was just because I became a cheerleader. Anyway, Laura taught me how to control it. But I occasionally used it to tempt guys or get even. Always gets me in trouble. That's how Bill got in the picture. But, I digress. Confession, Jake. Admit it; you are here to get me to help you with something, right?"

He nodded.

"Look, Jake, I went along with your pact shit because you wanted me to. As long as I did what you wanted, you did what I wanted. However, I never thought you'd actually leave and never come back."

"But I told you I was going to leave Rachel and—"

". . . Go do your own thing. I thought you were bullshitting that part. How could you leave me? I loved you. Then."

"How come you didn't tell me . . . then?" he asked.

"You were going with Rachel. I didn't want to interfere. You said you were going to break up with her . . ."

"To leave and live my own life," he repeated.

"I really did think you said all that because you were going to come back to me."

"What made you think that? Did you know that I had feelings for you when you were at the Academy?"

She stiffened when he said that, and turned around so fast that wine splashed out of her glass onto her jean shorts. "You did? You had feelings for me? Why didn't you tell me then?"

"Wasn't being a plebe at the Naval Academy enough trouble for you to deal with at the time? What difference would it have made anyway?"

"A lot, actually. Damn. Didn't you realize that back then I was completely and madly in love with you?" she said. "You are one dumb son of a bitch. I can't believe you didn't know that. I gave you enough fuckin' clues. Did you think my constantly coming to your office was just about the way I was being treated by my classmates? Damn, Jake, none of that shit really mattered to me." She paused and looked out the window.

Jake stopped rubbing her shoulders, and she pulled back. They stared at each other.

"Do you know you have a sailor's mouth?" he asked.

"I am a fuckin' sailor, you dumb ass. Shit . . . this is not good. Fate should not have tossed us together like this." She looked down at the dark spot on her shorts. "I spilled wine on my shorts. I'm soaking these and getting into something more comfortable."

She went into her room, and he heard water running in the bathroom. A few moments later she returned wearing a robe. After sitting down next to him, the bottom of the robe parted to reveal her shapely legs as she put her bare feet up on the cocktail table.

"I was going to suggest you get back to your reason for coming, Jake. Our time to love one another is past. However, you know what? I'm tired now, so I no longer give a shit why you came," she said, standing suddenly. "I'm going to bed."

CHAPTER 32
NIGHT HAPPENINGS

Jake simply nodded.

From outside came the distant rumble of thunder, followed by a weak flash of lightning.

"Is it supposed to storm tonight?" There was a bit of tension in April's voice.

"Yeah, I think I heard that on the radio coming down," Jake replied. "No biggie though, nothing severe and you're not flying tonight."

"No, it's just . . . I . . . nevermind. Night." She turned and hurried into her room.

Jake finished his wine while making a plan. Why couldn't she stay awake a few more minutes so he could have explained his reason for being here? First thing tomorrow, he vowed to tell April the news. Like him, she'd been ducking out on her home world, and it wasn't right.

There was a rumble of thunder that sounded much nearer, and the lightning flash this time lit up the apartment. He thought he heard a sound from April's room.

"You okay?" he called out. She didn't answer, so he assumed she was asleep and maybe had just cried out or something. After putting the wine glasses in the sink, he grabbed his bag that was still lying by the entrance and went into his room. Hearing no answer to his soft knock on the bathroom door, he entered and brushed his teeth. Returning to his room, he saw no sign of the Distans as he undressed and crawled into bed. Another flash of lightning and a loud crack of thunder sounded nearby. This time he swore there was a yelp of some kind from April. Hearing nothing further, he dismissed it and went to sleep.

* * *

The next morning, Jake awoke with a distinct memory of being kicked a lot during the night. When he rolled over and faced the other side of the bed, he saw the reason. April was sleeping next to him. He took comfort in the knowledge that should he ever appear on a quiz show, he could respond to the question, *What does April Elliot wear to bed?* with the answer: *Nothing at all.*

He was unable to think of a tactful way to wake her, so he shook her gently. "Hey, April. Wake up. What the hell are you doing here?"

Her eyes flew open as she gasped out, "Oh my God! Fuck." She quickly scooped up the sheet around her.

"Sorry," she finally said, looking a little confused. "Must have been the storm. I'm afraid of thunderstorms, Jake."

"Really?" he laughed. "I thought they only did that wrap yourself in the sheet thing in the movies. A little late for modesty. Hey, anyone ever tell you that you kick while you sleep?"

She stuck her tongue out at him, then studied his face for a minute. "I'm so glad you came down, Jake. It seems like every time I need a friend, there you are. You showed up at my door yesterday just like you did on that beach years ago." She dropped down on her elbow and propped her head with her hand, pulling the covers around her. Her nose was inches from his as she continued to hold his eyes. "I always thought there was something different about you, Jake. You're not like other guys. There's some kind of a connection with you that I can't quite explain. Must be our Flammerian birthright. Even if you make up with Rachel, will you stay in my life? As a friend? The gods know I need one."

"As a friend, I'll always be there for you, April." At that moment, he so wanted to tell her that they needed to end our 'let's turn our backs on Flammeria' pact, but he knew that lying in bed together was not the right time.

April got up to go to the bathroom, and Jake let his mind wander. He couldn't believe the changes that had occurred in his life over the last few days. Sheila was his sister. He had recovered, at least temporarily, Rachel, the girl he now was convinced was his true love. He had not only put the ugly incident of ten years ago to rest with Laura, but had also recovered his friendship with April. But was he in love with April too? That question was one with no easy answer. However, there was one thing he did know. He would willingly give his life for her.

"You're not yet done, Jake," came into his head from Sheila. *"You still haven't told April why you're really there. Be careful, though. Remember, she is still in the Navy, and we don't know the extent of her loyalty there. And one more thing, Jake. You might want to rein in your little partners."*

"What do you mean, rein them in?" But she was no longer there. Shit, he wondered. Just what did those two little schemers do now?

The bathroom door flew open and April, freshly showered and dressed simply in a mint green bra and panties, walked in while toweling her hair.

"Your turn in the shower, Jake." She grinned and, after patting his butt cheek, walked out.

Damn, he was in serious relationship trouble.

* * *

April, dressed in very short, black, denim cut-offs and a bright green sleeveless top, drove to a small restaurant a few miles from the apartment. Jake wore jeans and a short-sleeve, light green cotton shirt that April had found in his bag. It had caused her to scream in delight,

"Jake, I have this color, we'll match!" Yep, he thought, my hot, macho fighter pilot was just . . . a girl. She seemed pleased they sat them in a booth in the rear of the restaurant, even though it was practically empty.

After they ordered, April stared at him while she sipped her coffee.

"What?" he asked.

"I have a confession to make, Jake."

"What?" he repeated.

"I'm afraid you're gonna get mad."

He first gave her a big sigh, then said, "I won't get mad."

She stared at him.

"Honest," he said. "Cross my heart and hope to die."

After affixing a shy little smile on him, the tip of her tongue came out, and she slid it from one corner of her mouth to the other. "I'm not afraid of thunderstorms."

"What?" he said, a little too loudly.

"You promised that you wouldn't get mad. You said, 'cross my heart and hope to die.' By the way, that was so juvenile," she grinned. "Really? Cross your heart and hope to die?"

"Then what was last night all about?"

"My intentions were simply to let out little squeals, like I was afraid, and you'd come rescue me. I wanted to give you some payback."

"Payback? For what, goddammit?"

"For two years of sexual misery at the Academy. You said you had a thing for me, yet you never told me. We could have been screwing like rabbits, and I wouldn't have been so damn miserable if I had had you for a lover back then. You never let on. So, last night I was hoping to get even."

He stared at her, waiting.

"The thing is, Jake, it apparently didn't work out the way I planned. You never came to me, and somehow I crawled in bed with you. I don't know how that happened. Must have been after I had the dream."

CHAPTER 33
THE PACT

April shook her head. "I guess I must have just gotten up and wandered into your room, then fallen asleep there in your bed. Maybe I'm a sleepwalker."

"You are one strange girl," Jake said. "What dream, though?"

"I dreamt I was visited by some little fairy-like creature. At least, that's what I thought at first."

"What?"

"In my dream I woke up and found the fairy was sitting on my chest looking at me. She reminded me of me."

"Don't tell me. She had your color hair, but very curly, and like you she was well proportioned, except she was about seven inches tall with wings."

"How the hell did you guess that?" April stared at him with a slight smile. "Anyway, the fairy said to follow her, and I remember getting out of bed in the dream, but nothing afterwards. You know something about this?"

Jake immediately realized that was what Sheila meant by reining them in. He heard Ceellia chuckling in his head. "Later, April," he said. "I'll tell you later."

"Well, now that we got that settled, what do you want to do today?" April purred, seeming strangely willing to let the subject go. "I'm all yours. I'm not even reporting in until tomorrow."

"Something tells me you already have something in mind," he replied. "You know you're going to get your way, so just tell me."

She nodded. "How about we just go down to the Outer Banks and kick off our shoes, walk the beach, and you finally tell me why you came down here to see me?"

Jake nodded, although he knew he was putting himself in a vulnerable position. He was confident however, that he could weather the storm, so to speak. April needed a friend, and he needed to tell her the truth about his mission in visiting her. And explain to her what really happened last night.

Again he heard what sounded like a girl giggling in his head, and assumed this time it was Sheila having a laugh at his expense. "Can't I just tell you here?" he asked.

"No. You said it was my choice. I've chosen."

An hour later they were on their way, retracing the route to the Outer Banks he had taken with Sheila and Rachel, when they fled from the authorities. He tried to formulate a way that he could break the news to April and convince her that she, like him, was needed to fight the menace that threatened Earth. This whole thing seemed crazy, though. What could just two people with no weapons do?

April had put the top down on her Mustang, so the wind noise made it hard to hold any kind of a serious conversation with her while she drove. Jake assumed the Distans were able to cope with that. After all, they seemed excited to ride in a convertible. In the end, he decided to just wait until the two were walking the beach to broach the pact subject.

Soon they were over the bridge and turned onto US 12, the main road that traversed the stretch of North Carolina Barrier Islands.

"Where do you want to stop?" she asked.

"Let's continue on past South Nags Head. Stop when we run out of houses," he said.

* * *

As soon as April cleared the commercial end of Nags Head, the ocean side yielded to scrub grasses, beach and a scattering of large homes built on stilts. After the houses ended, April drove a little farther, then pulled off the road and parked. For a moment they both just stared out the windshield at the grasses and vegetation that grew along both sides of the road. Further south, rising out of the vegetation, Jake could see the Bodie Island lighthouse.

He got out of the car, went around to the other side, and opened the door for April.

"I love this place," April said. "I wish I could stay here forever." While she breathed in the sea air, he took a quick peek into the back seat area where he saw Ceellia running fingers through her windblown hair.

April and Jake then made their way through the bushes and grasses until they came out on a sandy beach. There were small breakers rolling up onto the shore, and various seabirds were everywhere. Some strutted on the beach and pecked at things in the sand, while others flew over the water. The birds eyed the two beach visitors to see if they had brought something good to eat. Ghost crabs scurried out of their way as they finally reached the area where waves broke gently onto the sand. Jake was nervous as hell about what was to come.

"I brought this bag for our shoes and whatever," April said as she held the canvas tote bag up for him to see. She slipped off her sandals and deposited them in the bag. Jake felt unprepared as he sat down on the sand to remove shoes and socks. She was right when she called him a tourist. After he dropped them into the bag, she handed it to him. "Would you carry it, Jake? I like to look for stuff on the beach."

"Sure," he said. "But first, can we just sit on those rocks for a few minutes and watch the waves?"

"Of course," she said. "One of my favorite things."

After they sat, all kinds of ways to start the conversation bounced around in Jake's head. Finally, he just said, "You remember our agreement?"

Her head twisted around towards him a little too fast, he thought.

"I thought that's what this was all about," she said. "Having second thoughts? Is that all that's made you so nervous?" She watched a brown pelican scoop something out of the water and wing to the south. "You want to renegotiate it, don't you? I knew that."

"You knew?" he asked.

"Of course I know. Everything. Laura and Sheila ought to have known I can read minds."

"How?" he blurted. "You need a Distan."

"She has one," Ceellia's voice came into his head. Seconds later, two little yellow eyes peered out at him through April's yellow locks. "If she needs one. She seems to do fine on her own, though."

"Oh my," Sheila's voice came into Jake's head.

"You two are so busted," April laughed. "I didn't tell you all that little fairy told me last night, *Mr. Jake.* So now you want to change our pact. But you forget something very important."

"What?" he asked.

"It was your pact. Your freakin' idea. I went along with whatever my hero wanted. Remember? I was just a barely-out-of-her-teens naive little girl. You said we should do this, and I said yes."

"Jake, is that true?" Sheila's voice came into his head again.

* * *

In his mind, the scene flashed back to his office at the Academy and April sitting there. Jake had suggested to April that they agree to ignore any requests from the Flammerian base to assist in any missions. He'd go his way and she'd go hers, and both would claim no knowledge of the other's whereabouts.

"Whatever you say, Sir. You know best."

* * *

"Remember now?" April asked.

Jake nodded. "Wait a minute," he said. "That means you were conscious of coming to my bed last night?"

"Of course. It was get even time. I was naked and what did you do? Nothing. I think I embarrassed you. Last night was part of the price you're gonna pay for my cooperation in whatever Sheila wants us to do. *Hi, Sheila! This is gonna cost you too.*"

"*Hello, April,*" Sheila's voice seemed to echo between them. "*What is it gonna cost me?*"

"I think you know, Sheila. I know a lot about you and your desires. Ceellia is very informative."

"*Whatever it is, I'll pay it. I'll contact you both later.*"

"It's time you had a history lesson, Jake." April shook his hand free of hers. "My family traces its history back to Atlantis. They survived that calamity and were taken to Flammeria, then returned when the earthquakes and volcanic devastation subsided."

"I know Atlantis was real," Jake interrupted. "My family goes back to Lemuria, the advanced civilization in the southern Pacific Ocean. Our story is similar. Flammerian history says that Earth started wobbling when a huge comet passed close to us about twelve thousand years ago. It set off a cataclysmic chain reaction that ended in tidal waves, earthquakes and volcanic devastation. Both Atlantis and Lemuria were destroyed, but the planet Flammeria rescued many survivors. Flammeria instigated a planet watch of Earth by constructing the station under the Atlantic in the Norfolk trench. Ancestors of both our families returned, and since have been part of that station's history. That includes you and me."

"Are you fuckin' through?" she smiled. "I wasn't thinking about any of that shit. Besides, there are things you don't know, but it's not my place to tell you. What I was leading up to was a lesson in Flammerian women. Women from Lemuria are different from women who originated in Atlantis. All the women you knew were from Lemuria. Except me. I'm an Atlantean. I have my own . . . hang-ups."

CHAPTER 34

Beach at Nags Head

For a moment they just stared at each other.

He tried to catch a glimpse of Glim, since Ceellia was close by.

April pointed to her head, then his. "Ceellia just told me that you were thinking about Glim?" Ceellia popped out of April's hair and sat on her shoulder.

"I want to be your closest friend and partner, Miss April."

"You're so damn cute," April gushed. "You're already my closest friend, Ceellia. And who are you?" April's voice cut into his consciousness.

He looked up to see that Glimmer now sat on April's other shoulder.

"My name is Moonglimmer, but everyone calls me Glim or Glimmer, Miss April. I'm Mr. Jake's Distan. I'm the one who has been transferring Sheila's voice to Jake."

"Look at those long red curls on you," April smiled. "I know grown-up girls, human and otherwise, who'd kill for hair like that." April then smiled over at Ceellia. "But you and I will stick to being blond, right, Ceel? Is it okay if I shorten Ceellia sometimes?"

A big smile broke over Ceellia's face. "You bet, Miss April. I'm gonna love working with you."

"Huh?" Jake muttered as April's previous words became clearer. "Wait a damn minute. You knew everything?"

"Not only that, but Atlantean women can make you do things," April laughed. "It's not even a challenge."

"You brought me out here knowing everything I was going to tell you?" he asked.

"I brought you out here to show you why I don't want to get involved. I love this place and I don't want anything to interfere in that."

Jake looked from her to the two Distans on her shoulders.

"Lucky you, Jake, with all the gorgeous girls in your life," April said. "You know that shortly after I was born, my dad supposedly got a transfer to Casper, where we lived for two years. Then he was transferred back, and we settled in Virginia Beach, just south of Oceana. That's where I grew up, watching the planes fly in and out of the air station. I knew every model and type."

She paused a few seconds. "Once I was able to drive, I came down here to the Outer Banks every weekend. It's an idyllic place. My idea of heaven." She lapsed quiet.

Jake tried to help by explaining to April what little he knew of her dad. "My older sister, Laura, told me Mattik longed to return to Flammeria, and one day decided to do so. She took over the station after him, and I suppose you're next in line."

"Dad said something about that. But Sheila's your twin sister. What about her?"

"She has a different mission."

For a moment April was quiet. "This is insane, Jake. I don't want that. What am I supposed to do? End my Earth life and . . ." She stopped as tears began to roll down her cheek and struggled to get to her feet. "I want to go walk the beach, Jake."

"Glimmer and I will wait here," Ceellia said. "It is best we not take too many chances of being seen, plus the big seabirds might think we're prey."

"Of course," April smiled.

Jake helped her up and they walked in silence down the sandy expanse. Every now and then she stopped to squish the sand between her toes. After walking a few minutes down the beach, she led them into a tidal pool. In the middle of the ankle-deep water, she stopped and said, "I want to talk. Let's sit, Jake."

He looked around, but they were not near any rocks. "You mean in this water?" he asked.

She rolled her eyes and tilted her head. "What's a little water? You were in the Navy. You're quite the spontaneous one, aren't you?" With that, she knelt down in the shallow water and looked up at him. "Sit your ass down!"

What was he to do? He felt compelled to join her. He tried to balance himself without getting wet, but with an exasperated look, April put a hand on his shoulder and pushed him off balance, causing him to sit in the water.

"You are a fruitcake," he told her.

She ignored him, her head staring low into the water.

"Are you okay?" he asked.

She looked out over the water before answering. "I love flying, but I'm fighting a losing battle." He sensed her drifting toward melancholy.

"Look, they're not asking you to quit and take over the station right now. My sister didn't appear ready to give it up, anyway. Sheila only talked of a single mission."

"I don't want to talk about Flammerian bullshit right now, you idiot." She lifted both feet out of the water and brought them down hard, spraying water and wet sand on him. "Listen to me. First they retired the Tomcat, which was the plane I joined the Navy to fly, and now I'm always stuck on shore when I should be on the ship. There's always an excuse, like with the ejection seats. There was cause for concern that smaller women could be hurt or killed when they fired. So it was, 'Wait until we get the ejection seat firing modified. If you have to eject you might get killed.' They'll only let me fly so long anyway, you know, and then I'll have to yield to the young kids. You know how the Navy works: commission officers, train them and put them into a reserve for 'someday.' The cycle keeps repeating. And . . . now this."

She shook her head. "It's hard for me, because while it's easy to control you, I cannot control my career. I want to see my parents, and how do I do that? Is there a local rocket ship to Mars or wherever the hell they retired to?"

"Flammeria," he said. "It's in the Alpha Centauri system."

"That was rhetorical, you ass. I know where Flammeria is. However, I'll probably never get the chance to go there." She wiped her bare arm across her nose.

Suddenly, Jake jumped up, pulled her to her feet and scooped her up again to carry her.

"Whooo, do I get a free ride to my car for a tissue?" she grinned.

"Nope," he said, while carrying her further out into the surf.

"What the hell are you doing? Put me down, Jake."

He was now standing in water that reached his thighs. "Put you down? Sure." He unceremoniously dropped her.

"Jake!" she managed to wail before she submerged in the warm water. She came up wiping at her face. "You son of a bitch!" she yelled, and swung at him, striking his shoulder a glancing blow. "Why'd you do that?" she asked.

"I did it because I'm your friend, you bawl baby," he said. "The water's up to your waist and you're acting like you're drowning. You're a fuckin' sailor, and the toughest girl I've ever met, so start acting like it. Now that our pact is ended, Flammeria wants us to do a mission and I agreed. You in?"

She blew her nose into her hand, then rinsed it in the water and was quiet for a few seconds. "Okay, I guess I needed that. Thanks. Yeah, unlike you, I was always in. Let's go back to the car and you can explain the details to me."

* * *

"You're kidding, right? You and me against a Zantite ship?" April slammed her hand on the steering wheel in frustration. "And you agreed to that shit?"

"Maybe I was a little quick in the agreement department," Jake admitted.

"Ya think?" April smirked.

* * *

That evening, Jake knew he should have just left and driven back to St Michaels. They had not come up with any way they could repel a Zantite ship. April had apparently always known what he had been tasked to tell her, and he knew that no good would come from the two of them being together with time on their hands. But she appealed to him as her friend to stay at least one more night. He had tried to call Rachel, but she still would not pick up.

He agreed to stay not because she made no attempt to force him, but he thought that maybe, just maybe, an idea might pop up. Besides, he couldn't resist her charm, so he finally capitulated.

While he once again vainly attempted to contact Rachel, April had tried several times to call Bill to see what the chances were for her to take off for the ship tomorrow. He had not answered, and she assumed they were out of range. Her call to the base had confirmed a COD (carrier on-board delivery) aircraft had departed that afternoon with requested parts to repair the arresting gear.

Of course, all of this negativity in her Navy life had added up to put her in a foul mood. Although it was not aimed at the two Distans and Jake, they still tried to keep out of her way as she moped around and cursed nonstop.

"Jake?" she called from the loveseat as, having finally decided it was best to leave, he had started to throw stuff together in his room.

"What?" He stopped what he was doing and walked to the door.

"Can you come and talk to me? I need cheering up. Aren't you my friend? Isn't that your job? And where is Ceellia?"

"Stop with all the questions," he said and walked over to her. "She's probably hiding. None of us wanted to get in your way," he mumbled.

"Get in my way? Come on, Jake. I'm glad you're here. I need you to offset the crap happening in my life." Her phone rang in her room and she jumped up. "Hold that thought. Be right back."

As soon as she disappeared into her room, Jake sent a mental flash to Sheila. Her voice came right back into his head.

"Is everything okay down there? Jake, why have you . . ."

"How's Rachel doing?" he interrupted. *"I've tried calling her several times but she doesn't pick up."*

"Why aren't you on your way back by now?"

"Will you just answer my question? How is Rachel?"

"It might be bad news, Jake. I don't know what to make of this."

"Will you get to the point, Sheila?" He was afraid April would return any minute.

"Rachel has returned to her apartment in Annapolis. She said she needs to think things through. I tried to get to you sooner, but you have Glimmer blocking my communications with you unless they are considered significant. Really, Jake? You're letting a Distan decide what is important? Anyway, Rachel refused to wait and talk to you. On top of the fact that she thinks you've left, like you did ten years ago, I think she has talked herself

into believing you went willingly to be with April. I'm afraid she's even more adamant you're not the guy for her. I'm so sorry . . ."

Not wanting to hear any more, he willed Sheila gone. Crap, what else could go wrong?

Almost as if in answer, April stormed out of her room, closed the door with a resounding crash and threw the phone at the shag carpet where it bounced noiselessly on the rug. She immediately came over and dropped into the seat next to him.

Now what?

"That was Bill. He said I can't come out till Monday. He ignored my questions, told me to just suck it up. Bastard." She stopped and looked at him. "What's wrong with you?'

"Rachel couldn't accept my staying with you. I'm doomed."

"How do you know . . .?"

He pointed to his head.

"Oh, Sheila. Shit. Sorry, Jake. It's all my fault." Tears welled up in her eyes.

"Look, it's not your fault. I'm sorry about Bill and you not being able to get requalified."

For several moments they were quiet, staring ahead and lost in their individual woes.

Then, moments later, Sheila's voice echoed in their heads. *"April, Jake, I need for both of you to come to St Michaels. Now."*

CHAPTER 35
APRIL AND SHEILA

Sheila had briefed Jake before he left that, if she needed him, she would only say those words because she might be monitored. He was to take them to heart and come immediately. That she included April in her appeal was a surprise.

As they prepared to leave, April's phone rang, and she went back into her room to talk.

"Did you look in the fuckin' head?" While she ranted at some poor person on the phone, she walked into Jake's room and watched him gathering up his stuff. Suddenly, she said loudly into the phone, "Shit . . . no, it's okay, I just had an idea. Hang loose, I'll call you right back." She put her cell phone down and looked at Jake. "Jake, I need a favor."

"What do I have to do?" he said warily.

"I need a back-seater for a flight tomorrow. I can't take the hop alone. My guy disappeared, probably down at the beach. We weren't supposed to fly anyway, so I can't blame Todd for not answering their page. We'll just make a quick hop out to the ship, deliver a part and then come back. Have you ever flown in a back seat of a fighter?"

"Yeah, I flew in an F4 a couple of times. I never operated any equipment though."

"I never said you'd operate . . . hang on." She picked the phone up, pressed a number to call and put the silver rectangle back to her ear. "PO2 Marsh? . . . Good, you're still there. Listen, I got a replacement . . . yeah . . . we'll be there tomorrow afternoon." She closed her cell phone and looked at Jake. "Now all the enlisted will think I'm shacking up with some stud."

"Woo Wee! I get to fly in a Hornet?"

"It's not just a run of the mill Hornet, you ignorant ship driver, it's an F/A-18F."

"Oh, pardon me, a Super Hornet."

"We call it a Rhino. It's a two-seat fighter-bomber. The back-seater is a weapons officer. However, I don't think we'll run into any bogies on the way. To answer your direct question though, nothing. You do absolutely nothing. You touch anything back there, I'll eject your ass out over the Atlantic and solve all of Rachel's problems. Hey, come to think of it, that would solve some of mine too." Her bright blue eyes twinkled at the thought, and he guessed she was only half-joking.

* * *

It was mid-afternoon when they finally rolled into St Michaels. "Rachel?" Jake asked Sheila, who met them on the driveway.

"No, Jake. This isn't about her. Come with me, quickly." She grabbed his hand, he grabbed April's, and with Glimmer and Ceellia flying beside them, Sheila proceeded to drag them to the rock where it was safe to talk. He had warned April on the drive up that this was the expected forum for communication. After Sheila perched herself on the boulder, she took April's hand.

"Slip your tongs off and come up by me, April," Sheila whispered. April did and sat next to his sister, who hugged her closely. "I've so looked forward to meeting you," Sheila said. "Other than Laura, you're as close to a sister as I'll ever have."

"Even though I helped screw up your brother's love life?" April said. "I love your brother, but I never intended to mess him up with Rachel. I'm sorry about that."

"We're Flammerians, and your stock originated in Atlantis. From what I know about Atlanteans, you had no choice. Besides, you didn't mess up Jake's life. That had nothing to do with you," Sheila said. "Rachel's leaving because you were with Jake was just an excuse. She's an Earthling, and they have untrusting emotions, unlike you and me who . . ." Sheila looked over at Jake. "Well, we use charm. Besides, it's a problem Jake must solve himself."

Sheila noticed Ceellia, hovering by April. "I see the two of you became friends quickly."

"Ceellia and I will be great friends," April smiled. With that, Ceellia landed on April's shoulder and Glimmer came to Jake's.

"Now I know why Ceellia was not answering my requests for what was going on down there. I could understand Glimmer protecting Jake, but I thought I could depend on Ceellia. Well, you and I have always been destined to be close friends too," Sheila said. "You do realize that with Ceellia's help, your powers are kicking in now?"

"My powers kicked in a long time ago. Ceellia and I've been practicing reading minds using Jake," April replied. "But he's getting better at hiding things."

"I have?" he replied. He had not consciously done any such thing.

"That's Glimmer," Sheila nodded. "She knows to do that to protect him. Both of your Distans are breaking the mold and doing things others have not done. And what do I owe you, April, for agreeing to our mission? Remember, I said I'd do anything."

"I'm counting on that," April said. "This is for starters." With that, April leaned over to Sheila and kissed her passionately.

When they parted, Sheila said, "I didn't expect a reward."

"I'm confused . . ." Jake started to say, but stopped when Sheila raised her hand.

"It's okay, Jake." While Sheila talked to Jake, her eyes were on April.

"Laura told me," April said to her, then looked at Jake. "Stop with the shocked look. In case you haven't noticed, your sister is the Queen Vixen of the foxes."

"Jake is easy to shock," Sheila said. "But listen. Both of you." Sheila got serious. "I need to tell you both why I had you come up here. There is a Zantite ship in the area. Did you come up with any way to repulse them?"

"Sure," April smiled. "I suggested shooting fireworks at them. Maybe we'll get lucky and start a fire."

Sheila stared back, apparently not realizing April was joking.

"Seriously," April said. "What do you expect Jake and me to do? We need weapons."

"Wait a minute," Jake interrupted. "Shoot fireworks at them. That's a great idea."

"That was sarcasm, Jake. You can't hurt them with fireworks."

"But we can disrupt them with missiles and bullets," Jake pointed out.

"What?" April and Sheila said at the same time.

"How about you and I steal one of your fighter jets and use it to shoot up a spaceship?"

CHAPTER 36

Oceana Naval Air Station

"You want to do what?" April asked, her tone incredulous.

"Use one of your fighter jets to shoot up a Zantite explorer craft," Jake explained. "At least fire on it to show them Earth's not afraid of them. It's perfect. You're scheduled to take that hop tomorrow. We'll just change the mission."

"Steal a Navy jet? Shoot at some spaceship? Are you friggin' nuts?" April asked.

"Will that work, April? If so, it's probably the only way to end this," Sheila finally said.

Still in a shocked state by Jake's suggestion, April nodded.

"Look, I'm not ignorant of the consequences, you two. I know what you're proposing to do is very dangerous, and you both could easily be killed. If you say no, April, I'll understand. However, before you decide, I want you to know I just contacted Glimmer and Ceellia, as they must go with you and could be killed also. They too have a huge stake in this operation. Both immediately volunteered to go where you go."

Jake looked over at April, but her reaction was unreadable as she listened to Sheila.

Then April asked a question, her voice calm and collected. "Let me get this straight, Jake. You're suggesting Ceellia, Glimmer, you, and me steal an F18, find this spaceship and then shoot at it?"

"Yes," Jake answered.

"I don't want to kill anyone," April whispered.

"That's not going to happen," Jake said. "I do know something about spaceships. They're built to withstand being hit by stuff in space. The power plants are designed to just suck up things that penetrate it. We'll blast away at the back of it while all the crew are in the front. It'll disrupt their flight but not harm anyone. Except, they can shoot back if they get too angry."

"We can't assist," Sheila said, "except we'll lead you to the Zantite ship and monitor the entire affair, help if we can. The station possesses no weapons though; we can only assist in a rescue or provide a diversion."

"Tell me again, why are we doing this?" April asked.

Sheila explained the plight of the Distans and her hope that this would end the Zantites' threat. She ended by saying, "If it helps your decision process, April, I believe the Zantites are told not to engage Earth ships or aircraft under any circumstances. They are supposed to run away."

Jake added with the observation that they were going out to the ship tomorrow, and that would be the perfect time to attack the Zantite craft, as it was in the area.

April glanced out of the corner of her eye at Ceellia and looked back to Sheila. "Okay, we'll probably get the craft that will defy orders and stand and fight, but I'm in. Are you sure, Jake?"

That April would agree so readily surprised the hell out of Jake. He nodded with a low-voiced, "Of course."

* * *

Jake, April and the Distans returned to April's apartment in relative silence that evening and went to their own rooms. That lasted until April called out, about an hour later, that she and Ceellia wanted Glimmer and Jake to come and sleep in the same room with them.

"This may be our last night alive," April said. "No sense spending it alone." She and Jake slept close together in her bed, but there were no carryings on. They simply held each other, and tried not to think of the upcoming mission.

The next day, for most of the drive to the air station, April was quiet. Both Glimmer and Ceellia sensed her mood and also kept quiet. After they were waved through the Tomcat Avenue gate, April drove right up to the flight line and parked.

"You know we can't just walk up to a Hornet, hop in and take off. Wait here until I check on some things," she said and, not even waiting for a reply, slipped out of the car.

"Hey," Jake said, before she could walk away. "How exactly are we gonna pull this off? Do you have a plan or are you making it up as we go?"

She whirled around, and he could see that she was close to tears. "Look, you ignorant ex-tin can sailor. I should just have gone on with life and stopped wishing for that second chance with you. Now take a peek at where it's gotten me. I'm about to steal an airplane and use it to shoot at people I don't even know. Hell, I don't even know if they're people or some kind of reptiles or . . ."

"I don't really know," he offered. "I never asked. Never saw one."

She sighed and repositioned her folded arms on the door of the Mustang. "Do you have any bright ideas, boy? Maybe you and I should just run away from all this and go bumming around the country until the inevitable invasion. You know, reinstate our pact? How about it, Ceellia? Glimmer? Would you two come with us?"

Ceellia stood and crossed her legs. Jake could tell she was completely befuddled by the situation. "I . . . I only eat certain foods . . ." Ceellia was clearly at a loss for words. "Besides, I can't desert my people."

"Relax, Ceellia," April said. "My inclusion of you and Glimmer in that scenario was sarcasm. But would you, Jake? Run away with me?"

"I've done the running away scene before, remember? And what has it gotten me? I can't blame you, though, if you choose to haul ass out of here and go on with life rather than the alternative. Let's not forget that I've moved on to Rachel. If I was going to retreat, it would be with her."

To that she pursed her lips in a mock kiss and said, "I wasn't serious about running away with you. I'm just looking for your opinion. What would you do in my place?"

"I'm the guy that ran away before, remember? Do you really want my point of view?" he said.

"Yeah, Jake. Dazzle me with your bullshit."

"We said we'd do this, and we need to. It's our turn to take some responsibility. Right now we—" he nodded to Glimmer and Ceellia, "—want to go flying with you," he grinned. "Can you arrange it?"

"Our turn . . .? Okay," she smiled. "You three wait here while I go map out our destiny."

"Yeah. Go. Get the hell out of here and clear it so the four of us can go flying." He watched her walk down the flight line, and knew at that moment he loved her as much as any other woman he'd ever known. It wasn't a physical kind of love, though, and he relished in the knowledge that April and he could now truly be the very closest of friends. That is, if they survived this approaching experience.

* * *

"Let's go, Mr. Jake," April called out as she came back to the car. "We'll get you a flight suit and get this show on the road. You girls will need to stay close to us, because we don't have flight gear in your size. But you really don't need it, 'cause we won't be flying high or doing any G maneuvers. I hope. By the way, Jake, if anyone asks, your name is Peter Piezynski, but everyone calls you Peter Pie."

Jake stopped in the midst of getting out of the car. "My name is Peter Pie? What the hell, April. What's going on?" Both Glimmer and Ceellia flew up onto the dash.

"Did you honestly think I could take just anyone in one of those aircraft? Wake up, Jake."

"I thought you went to clear me—"

"Only the skipper can do that, and he's on the ship. I went to see who was off on holiday. Peter is, so you are *PETER*, and you agreed to go with me as the Weapons Officer. I signed off the yellow sheet with you as my back-seater. So, *PETER*, let's cut the crap and move, shall we? You two," she indicated Glimmer and Ceellia. "Wait here in the car until I mentally buzz you. Then haul ass to the plane you see us get in."

"Yes, ma'am," Ceellia saluted.

"Are they really necessary?" Jake asked, hoping to save the Distans at least from what he perceived could end up being a suicide mission.

"Sheila said we could go," Glimmer said. "We must do this to save our homes. Besides, if we're not with you, you won't be able to communicate with her. We have a deal; we share all your adventures."

"Look you two. No matter what Sheila fed you, this is dangerous," April said. "We could end up not coming back. You should make your own conscious decision to go, not blindly follow someone else's orders. Orders that might make you fish food."

"We know, April," Glimmer replied. "No one gave us orders. We did make the decision ourselves. Ceellia and I have talked. We both want to go wherever you and Mr. Jake go. Including now."

It was not lost on Jake that his Distan had dropped the Miss and called her April.

"So you little guys have guts too," April replied. "Okay, but both of you stay in the rear seat with Jake. I have enough shit to worry about."

"No!" Ceellia said loudly. "I go where you go. You can't communicate without me. I won't cause you any worries. I can figure things out for myself. We're a team."

"Okay, toots. You get in my part of the cockpit, then, but you're on your own, agreed?"

"Agreed," Ceellia smiled.

Rather than wait in the car, Ceellia and Glimmer convinced April and Jake to let them hide in his shirt pocket. As they walked into the squadron ready room, Jake noted it was empty. April commented that it was Saturday, and after they had all flown back yesterday, they had immediately left for the weekend. Except for Bill, who had remained aboard the carrier.

"I picked Peter because you're about the same size and he is pretty quiet," April offered. "Any enlisted we come across will not expect you to yak it up with them. His locker is on the end. Get his flight suit and equipment; I'll try to explain all of this to him later. That is, if I'm still among the living."

"What about weapons?" Jake asked. "How are you going to get them to arm the plane?"

"No problem. Ever since Nine-Eleven we fly with Sidewinders and a fully loaded cannon. Never know when we might be called on to intercept some wayward aircraft. It would be nice to have some radar-guided birds, but they might get suspicious if I asked for them. Besides, we don't even know if the Zantite ship will send back an echo. What we have will have to do the deed."

After getting ready, April gave Jake some last minute instructions and they made their way out to the flight line. As Jake walked, April elbowed him in the ribs. "Keep those sunglasses on, put your helmet on and keep the visor down. The plane captain will strap you in; he'll be calling you Lieutenant Commander or Mr. Pie. Don't blow this. Mumble or something. Don't make him suspicious. No unnecessary talking. That goes double for you little mosquitoes," she said as she tapped his shirt pocket.

They walked toward an aircraft with an enlisted sailor standing next to a huffer cart that was used to start the engines. On the nose of the aircraft, and also high up on the tail, was the number 740. Missiles that Jake recognized as heat-seeking sidewinders were on matching launchers on both wingtips.

Jake stopped and grabbed April's arm.

April shook the hand off her arm. "Watch the fraternization, Jake. You never know who is watching. Act professional."

Jake nodded. "By the way," April added. "Your call sign is Baker."

The enlisted sailor looked up at them and waved. "Morning ma'am, sir" he called out.

"Morning, Briggs," April answered, while Jake just waved.

Briggs, her plane captain, walked out and met them at the nose of the craft.

"Thanks for checking her out, Briggs," April smiled. "Is that part aboard?"

"Stowed in the nose wheel well, ma'am, like you asked. You won't even have to get out of the bird aboard ship."

"Great, let's you and I pre-flight all of the ordnance. Baker will do the external checks."

April had instructed Jake in the ready room on where to check for dripping fluids, and he was smart enough to look inside the engine intakes for foreign objects. His short stint on the carrier Nimitz helped him to look like he knew what he was doing. In addition, he had been around older aircraft, like the F4 Phantom, and knew what to check for on a preflight. By the time he was finished, so were Briggs and April.

While he waited for them to walk over, Glimmer poked him and pointed up. Stenciled on the outside of the cockpit, just below the pilot's seat, was LCDR APRIL ELLIOTT. Right above it, in ice blue lettering, was the word ICICLE. How apropos, he thought. Her call sign is Icicle. She and Rachel were not all that different. He pushed Glimmer back down in his pocket as April and Briggs started his way.

"I checked the fluid levels, Mr. Pie; they're all fine," Briggs said to Jake.

He nodded and grunted.

"Mr. Pie didn't appreciate me dragging him out of bed, Briggs," April covered for his silence. "Just ignore his sullenness."

"No problem, ma'am, sir," Briggs smiled and nodded back.

After they climbed a ladder into the cockpit, Jake tried to quickly figure out all the equipment while April and Briggs performed the cockpit pre-flight. She had told him they needed to check all the circuit breakers, the electrical system and ejection seat. While they went over things on her checklist and talked, Jake checked the same things in the back seat.

When they all finished, Jake started to secure himself in the aircraft as April had instructed him in the ready room. Briggs appeared outside his cockpit and began silently hooking up Jake's leg restraints and fittings to those matching in the aircraft. Lastly, he gripped the helmet fitting and attached that to the aircraft.

"All ready, sir," he said with a tap on Jake's helmet.

Jake mumbled thanks and Briggs climbed down off the aircraft. As soon as he left, Glimmer and Ceellia came out from Jake's pocket, and Ceellia immediately dove into April's compartment. Jake watched as the canopy lowered into place. Glimmer crawled in his lap and shimmied under the safety harness.

In the forward part of the cockpit, Ceellia did the same with April. With Briggs operating the huffer cart, April started the engines, which quickly settled into a low whine. Briggs continued to communicate with her through an intercom connection on the side of the aircraft. Finally he disconnected, pushed back the huffer cart and manned a fire extinguisher in case of an emergency. Jake waited in silence as April called the tower with a radio check, and they gave her permission to taxi.

The engine began to scream louder as April ran up the power setting in a final test; then it settled in at a higher pitch and loud whine. Jake was suddenly slapped back in the seat as she released the brakes. The nose of the plane dived initially, then came back up. April pulled straight out of the flight line, then turned down a taxiway that led to the main runway.

"Baker, switch channels like I told you." April's voice came over Jake's headset.

He dialed the frequency as she had instructed him earlier. "Can you hear me, Icicle?"

"Didn't take you long to find that out, did it? We don't pick our call signs, you know that. I got it in training. I wouldn't go out with any of them so they immediately put that moniker on me. I kind of like it, though. I'm the queen bitch, no one fucks with me.

"Remember, though, this aircraft costs quite a few doubloons. And more importantly, I don't want to get my hair wet today, swimming in the Atlantic. So don't touch anything unless I tell you to, okay? If you do, I swear I'll fire that ejection seat of yours and you can swim back. Got it? Another thing—someone could be monitoring this channel. Watch what you say. I'm switching back to the tower frequency. You can monitor, but don't talk except mentally through the Distans. I'll come back on this frequency when we're clear of the field and feet wet."

The Hornet's nose swung around, and they were facing down the long, main runway. Almost immediately, Jake could hear and feel the deafening roar of the twin turbofan engines as April kicked in the afterburners, and they shot down the runway for a few microseconds, before lifting up in an almost vertical climb. At the same instant, he could hear the wheels retract back into the bird. It climbed up at astonishing speed and, when Jake thought to look down, all he saw was the blue of the Atlantic. They were already feet wet, Navy slang for over water.

CHAPTER 37

Over the Atlantic Ocean

"Wow," Glimmer said excitedly from where she hovered near the top of the canopy and looked out. When Jake glanced forward, he realized that Ceellia had also left the safety of April's seat belt and now floated near Glim. Equally excited, her long hair billowed out like a yellow cloud. It dawned on him that, while they could fly, they had probably never flown this high or fast. For them, he imagined, it was a high time in their lives.

Per the instructions from Sheila, April angled the jet slightly north so that they would overfly the undersea Flammerian base instead of their scheduled rendezvous with the carrier. It only took a few minutes to get to the position, and April descended to an altitude of two thousand feet to get a better look. Joined by the Distans, four sets of eyes gazed out expectantly, but saw nothing except a calm sea. Without a word, April started a climb to return back up to ten thousand feet. Jake could tell she shared his confusion. Sheila had not told them specifically what to look for, and he thought maybe they did something wrong. Was this all for nothing?

"Cupid01, come back on course," a voice from the carrier instructed.

"Glim," Jake mentally asked, "can you pick up any mental transmissions?"

"No, Jake," she replied. "But I detect a strange sound coming up from the water."

At that moment, something exited the sea a few miles north of their position. A huge, cylindrical craft climbed to about half the F18's altitude and turned to the south.

"Cupid01, switch frequencies to Nimitz Strike," the voice from the carrier instructed. Obviously, they had also picked up the intruder on their radar.

"Hang on, Glimmer, Ceellia," Jake transmitted on the mental net. *"Here we go . . . moment of truth."*

"Cupid01, Going to Strike." April acknowledged the CDC's order. "Strike, Cupid01"

"Cupid01, Eyes has an unidentified heading your way at Angels five, speed one point two, no IFF," a calm male voice informed her. "Eyes said it appeared to come out of the sea. Please identify."

"Cupid01, I have him, huge target on collision course. Will intercept."

She made a high speed turn to starboard and went into a shallow dive.

"Explain what's happening to us, Jake," Glim requested. *"Who is eyes?"*

"Eyes is an E-2C Hawkeye, an Airborne Early Warning Aircraft which electronically monitors all air traffic around the carrier. Angels five tells April that the target's at five thousand feet—"

"How high are we?" Ceellia interrupted his explanation.

"We were passing ten thousand when we got the call," Jake said. *"But now we're diving down. Speed one point two indicates it was traveling at Mach one point two, which was just over the speed of sound, about seven hundred and sixty-eight miles per hour. Finally, all friendly aircraft have a transmitter, called IFF, Identification Friend or Foe, that broadcasts a constant signal to indicate it is a known friendly aircraft. This one did not. We know why."*

"Wow," Ceellia's voice came over their private mental net. *"Mr. Jake's smarter than I thought."*

At a closing speed approaching fifteen hundred miles an hour, April was on the unidentified object in seconds. Upon closing in on the giant spacecraft, April best summed up the feelings in the aircraft.

"What the fuck?" she said aloud. "How are we going to stop that?"

CHAPTER 38
ZANTITE CRAFT ENGAGED

The unidentified cigar-shaped craft was huge, approximately three hundred feet long. It appeared to be the width of a large, sea-going ship. Its silvery metallic surface was mostly smooth, with few protuberances. It made no noise.

"April, you must engage the craft immediately." Sheila's words, beamed to her and Jake by Glimmer and Ceellia, seemed to echo in the cockpit as if Sheila were sitting with them.

"Engage?" April said aloud to no one in particular.

"Fire your missiles at it from the rear. Quickly," Sheila pleaded.

"Cupid01, do you have a visual?" the carrier's Strike Operator asked.

April was sure that by now her radar blip had merged on the carrier's monitor screens with the large radar return from the unknown craft.

"Cupid01," April said calmly. "Intruder in sight. It's simply gigantic. I don't know what it is but it can't be friendly. Permission to engage."

After a short delay, the Strike Operator responded. "Cupid 01, Negative. Shadow him. Help is on the way."

"You must strike now," Sheila's voice said again. *"Before it gets away."*

April had asked for permission to fire in the hopes that it would be approved and she wouldn't have to attack the strange craft without authorization. But the Strike Operator's refusal had left her with little choice. Inwardly she agreed with Sheila. She did not want the ship to get away; all they had done would have been for naught. Moving into a position behind the craft, she matched its speed. The titanic ship began a shallow dive, taking it and April back closer to the water. An almost blinding sun reflected off its smooth, metallic surface.

"Jake?" April asked.

"Your finger is on the trigger, doll. The rest of us are along for the ride."

"April, listen to Sheila. Fire your weapons immediately," urged a voice Jake didn't recognize.

"Daddy?" April asked, both audibly and mentally. *"I thought . . ."*

"Fire," Mattik repeated. *"That craft is the enemy of Earth's people. This is your only chance to discourage their thoughts of conquest. If you don't, all of our maneuvering will have been for naught. Do it. Don't question. Shoot!"*

Her father's words appeared to be all April needed. Jake watched as her radar painted the target on her HUD, and she aligned the craft in her crosshairs. There was a flash on the port wing as the sidewinder's rocket motor fired, and after a second or two it reached a velocity that allowed it to break free of the launcher and tear off across the sky at the alien craft. By now they were only a few hundred feet off the surface of the Atlantic.

"Did it even have a heat signature?" Jake mentally asked. The Sidewinder was an infrared homing missile, and it homed in on the target that emitted the largest amount of infrared radiation.

"It's surely warmer than the surrounding sky or the ocean," April said, while continuing to track the huge target. *"Besides,"* she continued. *"I had tone."*

Already she could hear the electronic squawking noise of the second missile's infrared detector, a signal that told her it had acquired the target. April pressed the trigger button, and after a flash on the starboard wing, that missile too was away, leaving the launcher rail just as the first missile exploded on the back end of the UFO. It did not appear to damage the craft. After another ten seconds or so, the second missile impacted with similar results.

"*Shit,*" April lamented. "*That did a lot of good.*"

"*April, do you see a cross-hatched pattern at the rear of the craft?*" Mattik's voice filled the cockpit.

"*Yes, I do.*"

"*Fire your cannon at that area. It will disrupt their power system, at least temporarily. They may, however, take defensive action against you. Be prepared and be careful, April,*" Mattik advised.

"*Jake?*" April asked. "*You with me?*"

"*You bet. No one lives forever.*"

"Ceellia?" April said softly.

"Glimmer and I are prepared for our fate . . ." Ceellia's tiny voice answered.

April accelerated and brought the F18 close behind the craft, which now appeared to slow slightly. Her small finger engaged the firing trigger of her M61 20MM Vulcan cannon. Mounted just above the radar screen in the Hornet's nose, the gun, with its rotating barrels to prevent overheating, spit out all of the five hundred and forty rounds of ammunition at its disposal.

The gigantic craft that dwarfed her fighter slowed down at an alarming rate. April banked the F18 to port and drew her ship alongside the alien craft.

"*Shit, Jake, all I've got left is spit. Unless we can figure out a way to hit him with an air-to-ground missile. Maybe I can fly above it and drop one on him.*"

Suddenly, a narrow beam of light shot out of the huge craft and all of the F18's electronics went dead as the engines shut down. The unknown ship faltered and then hit the water, sending a huge spray in all directions. April banked the powerless Hornet further to port to keep away from the spacecraft and settled into a shallow dive.

"At this altitude and with that thing still in one piece, I don't trust blowing us out, Jake. I'm going to ditch. You okay with that?"

"We can't bail out even if you wanted to. We have the Distans inside," he replied.

The Hornet skipped once on the waves, then struck the surface a final time and settled on the water. It started to sink almost immediately. Looking to her west, April saw the alien craft, about a mile from them, silently lift out of the water.

April popped open the canopy and shouted back at Jake, "Get out before it sinks and takes us with it." Glimmer tried to assist Jake with the helmet fittings while Ceellia flitted about April's head, unsure how she could help. They had all survived the impact, but were far out in the Atlantic.

When Jake looked in the direction of the alien craft, he saw that it was gaining altitude fast. April's cannon had slowed it down, but apparently not seriously damaged it. Inwardly he cursed this whole exercise in futility. They had sacrificed April's aircraft and probably themselves for nothing.

"Hurry," came Sheila's voice. *"You must get out of your craft and into ours before the helicopter arrives and sees us."* Surprised at her words, Jake looked around. He then realized they were sitting on an island, a huge metallic, circular island. The Flammerian saucer-shaped craft had surfaced right under them, preventing them from sinking.

By now he was free of the cockpit, and followed April as she slid down onto the nose strake and then off onto the circular disk below. April skidded on the surface of the undersea craft and fell. Jake quickly bent down, scooped her up and headed for the opening from which the upper half of Sheila's body protruded, while from the northeast came the unmistakable *Whoop, Whoop* sound of a helicopter's blades biting the air.

The two Distans continued to circle around them, obviously anxious to help in any way they could. Jake waved them toward Sheila, but they refused to leave until he and April reached the open hatch. In moments they were through it, and Sheila hesitated for another few seconds as the Distans fluttered in before she closed the hatch door and dropped down beside them in a small passageway. Wordlessly, she embraced April, then spoke.

"Thank you, April. You don't know how instrumental you just were in . . ." Sheila paused, looking behind her at Glimmer and Ceellia. "Anyway, all four of you are safe. All they will see is your craft settle under the waves. The depth here is three thousand fathoms; I doubt they will even attempt to recover your aircraft."

"What about Jake and me?" April asked.

"No one knows Jake was on that flight. We can put him ashore, and he can go on as if nothing happened. I'm afraid you'll be considered lost."

"How can I be lost? What about my job?"

"If you went back, how would you explain this incident? Who, they'll want to know, rescued you? Who was the person you described as Peter Pie and where is he? This craft has now docked at our station. Come, we'll transfer to it and listen in on the search. Everything has been worked out and will be explained in time."

April looked stricken as the consequences of their action hit her. Like a true warrior, she had given her all to uphold the oath she had taken when she entered the Navy. Only she had done it against her Navy's orders.

They followed Sheila as she led the way out of the huge spacecraft and to the station's safe room, where their conversations could not be heard by any intruders. Once they entered the station, the two Distans flew off down a corridor. Jake assumed they were seeking some dry clothes. In the small room, Laura was listening to a ceiling-mounted speaker that was tuned to the Navy search and rescue operation being conducted for April.

When Laura saw Jake, she hurried over and silently embraced him, squeezing tighter than he thought possible. When she finally let go, she whispered in his ear, "Thank you, Jake. Now our real task can begin." When they parted, Jake saw April staring at him.

"Just how many damn girls do you have, Jake?" she asked.

"Girls? Well," he replied. "Let's see. There's Rachel who seems to have abandoned me, my twin half-sister Sheila who just saved our asses, my two little protective Distans, Glim and Ceellia, and this—" He paused to put an arm around Laura's shoulders. "We've talked about this one, and I believe you've met her. My one and only full-blooded sister, Laura. You know she's in charge of this station. Oh, and of course, there's you."

"You don't have two Distans," April smirked. "Ceellia is mine."

". . . it just took off out of the ocean and went out of sight. It was immense," a voice that Jake assumed was the helicopter pilot reported from the speaker.

"Rescue1, what about Cupid01? Any sign of life down there?"

"Negative, Mother. We got here just in time to see the plane go under. Apparently the UFO either collided with our guys or somehow knocked them out of the sky. It doesn't look like either of them made it out. The water was pretty agitated under them, though. Not sure what caused that. I thought I saw something under the bird. It seemed to be in the shape of a huge disk."

"Rescue1, say again... Are you reporting a USO in addition to the UFO?"

"Negative, Mother. I don't want to report one of those things. Let's leave it at my eyes were playing tricks on me."

"Rescue1, what about the strange craft? Any markings? Can you estimate its size?"

"I'd say it was easily three hundred feet long. It was cylindrical, looked like a cigar, metallic for sure. It seemed to come out of the water or was floating on it. I saw no markings. When it got to a certain altitude, it took off south at an astonishing rate of speed. I don't think any nation on Earth has something like that . . ."

"Rescue1, one of the DDGs is on its way over to conduct a search. Orbit until he arrives. Did you pick up any communication from Cupid01?"

"Negative. I picked up no SOS from Cupid01. I'll hover over this spot until the ship arrives on station."

Once it was determined that the rescue helicopter had not clearly seen the USO under the F-18, Laura relaxed. "Come with me, April. Jake and Sheila have things to discuss, and so do you and I," Laura said as she led April from the room, leaving Jake alone with Sheila.

The small room had little furniture, just two tables each surrounded by four chairs. The huge panoramic window presented a spectacular view of the under-ocean. Obviously, others thought the same thing, as there were also several small chairs that fronted it for someone to sit and admire the dark undersea and all of its life. Sheila gave him a nervous smile and tentatively reached out a small hand for his. He took it, and she pulled him to the chairs by the window.

"Sit," she pointed, and he did. She pulled a chair up close to his, looked from one chair to the other, and then asked, "Do you have room for me on your chair?"

He scooted back, leaving enough room in front for her to squeeze in.

She responded by sitting in his lap, and leaned back into his chest. "I steeled myself in case I lost you," she said, "and now I celebrate your return."

"Now that the threat is over, are you going to explain to me what happens next?" Jake asked. "What's going to happen to April?"

Sheila turned to him, her curly hair whisking past his nose. She looked at him with a puzzled expression. "Does it really appear that we don't understand? April did not seem happy with her present assignment. I think she chose to throw that life away. Hopefully, with what Laura has planned for her, she will be more than compensated. I'm sorry if you felt manipulated. I told you before; they sent you both to the Naval Academy with a purpose in mind. Now you have completed that objective, but the threat is far from over." Sheila turned away and momentarily stared into the inky sea.

"What will happen to April?" he insisted.

"April will return with Laura shortly, and she will explain. Till then I wish to be close to you," Sheila said. "Let me, in my own way, enjoy the fact that you came back." With that she turned away, staring out at the black water and falling silent.

A few minutes later, Laura and April reentered the room.

"Can I have some time with April alone?" Jake asked.

"Of course," Laura agreed, and looked to April. "I trust you know it is not yet time." Then both she and Sheila left the room.

"You okay?" he asked. "I'm sorry. We should have let the pact stand. What did she mean, 'It's not yet time?'"

He could tell April was close to tears again.

"Forget what she said and the hell with the pact. We did the right thing, but I'm dead to Earth, Jake. Your sister is very understanding, but she doesn't seem to comprehend that. She just keeps saying it was for the best. I know I didn't have many friends, but I liked my cozy apartment, eating out at restaurants, walking the damn beach . . .

flying. Now I'm supposed to be dead. What am I supposed to do? Live somewhere in a hole?"

"They seem to have more plans for us," he said. "You and Laura know something—"

"Actually, I know about as much as you do. I think we've all been brought together for some mission, but only Laura has an inkling of what it is."

"So it's Laura, Sheila, you and I?"

"I don't know, Jake. She wasn't specific, just said it's all of us."

Jake chose to ignore that and asked, "That was your dad's voice on the radio. Is Mattik here?"

"No, he watched it all back on Flammeria on some kind of feed from this ship, and his voice was relayed to us in the cockpit by a series of Distans, including my Ceellia."

With that, April's inner strength was again breached by an onslaught of sniffles and tears. Jake slid his chair right up next to hers and put an arm around her shoulders.

About ten minutes later, Laura and Sheila returned. He was momentarily stunned to silence at the sight of his sisters side-by-side. They had the definite appearance of siblings. They shared the green eyes, but while Sheila's hair was a more common, but no less striking, mixture of deep brown and red, Laura's was that very rare ginger color. It was shorter now; he recalled it had been long in high school. Of course, they shared the same mother, so why shouldn't they look alike?

"Are we okay? Need more time?" Laura asked.

Jake looked to April and she nodded. He pointed a finger at Laura and said, "Okay, Sis. We're ready. Dazzle us with your bullshit."

"There seems to be something going on that I'm not privy to, but let me review what I know for April," Sheila said. "The Zantites counted on no resistance from the residents of Earth. They do not have the facilities to wage a war with Earth, so they hoped to quietly set up a station and gradually build up a base of power. From that point, their main objective was to locate the Distans. All of their plans counted on secrecy, with no resistance from the residents of Earth. We hoped your attack on their craft would change their minds about this planet."

"Did it work?" Jake asked.

"We won't know for a while," Laura said. "We need to see if they come back, and in the meantime, our spies have already intercepted communications in which they classify this world as warlike. We are trying to find out what reaction this encounter has caused in the invaders' government."

April massaged her temples. "Let me get this straight," April said. "The price of driving off the alien invaders was fucking up the futures of Jake, Rachel, and myself. Is that about correct?"

"Well, I wouldn't use those words, but all things did not go as I'd hoped," Laura said. "At least with Rachel. I was hoping that she would understand things. However, she didn't leave because of you. She's just lost faith in her having a future with my brother. Who knows, maybe she'll still come around."

"I don't think so," Jake muttered. "So, it was okay to mess up April's and my life?"

"You call hanging out in Chicago and pretending your home world wasn't yours a life?" Laura then turned to April. "And you, April. You were not that happy in your chosen career, I believe. I think we can offer you a better one."

CHAPTER 39
APRIL'S NEW MISSION

Both April and Jake gave Laura their full attention. "What do you mean?" April asked. "They may have treated me like shit, but at least I got to fly. Plus when I knew Flammeria's fucking peaceful mission was in danger, I came back."

"I like your colorful language," Laura smiled. "Listen, Blondie. We need a new pilot for our ship, the one that makes the runs from Earth to Flammeria. You know, the fucking craft that just rescued you. Would you be interested? I guarantee you no one will treat you like . . . shit."

April's eyes were huge. "You want me to fly a spaceship?"

"Yes," Laura said. "I thought that might appeal to you. But you should know that in your case, I'm thinking of a different route than just Earth to Flammeria."

"Wow." A smile spread slowly across April's face, and Jake smiled and winked at her. April said to Laura, "Okay, I think I'd like that . . . I'd fly that thing to wherever."

"That's about where we'll be going."

"Just a minute," Jake said. "April liked a lot about living on Earth. The Outer Banks and its beaches, shopping... Is there some way we can salvage some of that?"

"Those arrangements are being made as we speak," Laura said. "We can present April with a complete disguise to use when she is here on Earth. However, we understand she might like to look herself, as she exists now, to certain people like you, Jake. She will still have that option." Laura looked back at April. "We are setting you up in a house in Avon on the Outer Banks. I think that is your favorite place. Am I right?"

"I love Hatteras Island. I go down there to walk the beaches all the time. That's my dream spot," April smiled.

"Well, you'll have a big house very close to the ocean to live in when you're back on Earth. Meanwhile, the ship returns to Flammeria in two days. You'll start your training then, and you'll get to see your parents and meet some friends that you'll be transporting to . . . wherever. Would you like a tour of this station?"

"Do you even have to ask?" April bounced out of her seat and joined Laura.

After they left, Sheila gripped Jake's arm. "Are those arrangements satisfactory, Jake? I feel you are the big loser here, since April and you might not be together very often. Not to mention, you've lost Rachel."

"If they satisfy April, they satisfy me. April and I are friends, but that's it. I'm still hoping somehow to reconnect with Rachel."

"I'm terribly sorry about Rachel, Jake. I thought sure she'd give you a chance to explain, a hearing at least. Maybe . . ."

He stopped her with an upraised hand. "Let's not go there. My life and my problem. I, more than anyone here, understand the need to sacrifice. I went to a college where it was expected. What are my options now, Sis?"

"Well, you've heard Laura hinting about some kind of mission, but I'm in the dark. As far as I'm concerned, your life's kinda your own, Jake. However, if you choose, you can stay with the station. Returning to your former Earth life is also an option, but one I do not recommend. My mother is returning to Flammeria. She's thought of leaving the house in St Michaels to you and your father."

Jake considered his present editing job and few friends in the Chicago area. It seemed like all of his real friends and relatives were here.

"Come," she said, and pulled him back over to the chairs that faced a view of the dark sea. For a moment she watched an anglerfish attempting to lure prey into its range. Suddenly, she turned and faced Jake.

After a few seconds' pause, she added, "Or . . . there's always the choice of doing something different."

He suspected that was a hint, so he bit. "What do you mean, different?"

For a brief moment, their attention was focused on the unsuccessful anglerfish, which swerved and wobbled away. Then she turned back to him. "You'll recall I mentioned moving the Distans elsewhere."

He nodded. "Is that the mission Laura keeps hinting at? Is that why I came here?"

"I don't know. I've discussed moving the Distans with her, but she keeps telling me, 'All in good time.' It seems that all of us seem to be gravitating toward something, but I don't know what. I guess Laura will tell us when the time is right. Regardless, we need to move the Distans, but for right now I'm still working out the details."

* * *

Two days later, April returned from checking out her new home in Avon. Brimming with excitement about operating the spacecraft and visiting her parents, she left with Ceellia on her inaugural flight to Flammeria. Jake was impressed with how quickly she'd been able to adjust to the idea of her new life. Before she left, he promised to come to her house when she returned.

Later that morning, the shallow water bay craft took Sheila and Jake to St Michaels. Sheila had spent much of the past two days urging Jake to go to Annapolis and try once more to convince Rachel that he had not abandoned her. However, he refused to try anymore, telling himself instead that maybe it was not meant to be and time would heal the disappointment. Yep, he was back to running away from problems.

Then there was the matter of Mrs. Wells. April would return with the interplanetary ship in about two weeks. At that time, after a short vacation, she would transport Mrs. Wells back to Flammeria. Jake had much to do in that timeframe. He made a quick visit to Mack to make arrangements to move them both to St Michaels, but Dad surprised him by vetoing the move. He told Jake he was also considering a return to Flammeria. Jake stayed with him a week, and then headed back to his apartment to pack up his meager belongings and move to St Michaels permanently.

The morning following his return, Sheila met him at the kitchen table. "Let's walk."

As soon as they were outside, Sheila kicked off her shoes at the driveway and pulled him along through the gardens.

"What's this all about, Sis?"

She shook her head for silence and didn't speak or stop until they reached the rock by the river. After quickly climbing up, she put her bare feet on the rock below and finally spoke.

"We have a couple of problems. Gert said your friend, Brian, called while you were away. He probably needs to tell you that April was lost at sea. You need to act like you know nothing about it. There was nothing of the event in the papers, on TV or on the internet. I'm sure the military is playing this one close to the vest. Remember, they know little of her parents or family; they don't have to worry about relatives asking questions. They can keep the incident hush-hush."

"Okay, I'll call him and pretend I don't know anything. What else?"

"Mother is selling the boat to get rid of suspicion surrounding our house. It's been arranged that another secret station offspring, who knows our dilemma, will purchase it and see that it gets lost at sea. The boat is no longer needed anyway. Also, I need to find a replacement person to occasionally visit the station."

"You mean you're not going to be the go-between Earth, the Distans and the station any longer?"

"No. I will continue to have responsibility for the Distans. Until they can be . . . moved. I already told you that. But therein lies the other problem. Before I say anything else, I think you need to talk to Laura."

"When are you and the Distans leaving?"

"Talk to Laura. I'm sure, like I, she's given you inklings of another mission. She's in charge. All she'll tell me is, 'everyone is not yet in place,' whatever that means."

"Tell me what I'm supposed to do, Sheila."

"I promise to tell you after you to talk to Laura. However, your first order of business is seeing your friend in Annapolis, so contact him and get that straightened out. I'll leave you to do that while I go visit the Distans this morning."

He held her hand as she stepped down off the rock, then watched as she ran up toward the house. Walking down to the riverbank, he pulled out his cell and called Brian.

"We need to talk, Jake," Brian said. "Can you meet me tonight at the Dragon?"

"Sure," Jake said. "Dan too?"

"Uh . . . I'll see if he's available. See you at seven," Brian replied and hung up.

Brian had sounded more official than friendly, but Jake wrote that off as his being worried about giving Jake the 'news' about April. There were a million things swirling through his mind too, not the least of which was what he should do next. Yellow flower petals blew past him as sudden winds whipped up. He recalled the forecast tonight was for storms.

After checking in with Sheila to make sure he was not needed that evening, Jake and Glimmer drove to Annapolis to meet Brian. Glim was quiet; he knew she missed Ceellia terribly. Jake had no idea how to solve that problem. He missed Rachel too, and was equally clueless on what to do about that. As usual, he had planned to arrive a little early, hoping that maybe Brian would too, and he'd be able to get back to St Michaels early. Jake had not been to Annapolis since Rachel and he had separated.

A thunderstorm caught him just north of Easton, forcing him to slow down and lose time. Parking was difficult as per usual in Annapolis, and Jake was forced to park in a garage off West Street. One of his first orders of business, after returning from the station, had been to buy a jacket with a large front pocket positioned high up. He had found the perfect one in Easton, navy blue and bulky, so that Glimmer could go with him everywhere. All he needed now was to find some way to spark the life back into his little partner, as she was still despondent over her and Ceellia's parting. With April flying the spaceship, they'd see little of each other.

The rain had just about ended as the storm moved further east, and Glim quickly took her position in his pocket as they left the garage. Jake hurried over to the Dragon Pub, and was pleased to see that Brian was already there. With the storm, searching for parking and walking, he was twenty minutes behind his schedule, but he was still ten minutes early for the meeting. Brian stood up and waved. He seemed tense.

"Hi, Jake," Brian said. "Dan had to go out of town today. I asked Dan about calling Rachel too, but he said the two of you broke up or something. Sorry, I didn't know."

"Yeah," Jake said. "I'm nowhere on her radar any longer. I'm not ready to talk about that, though, okay?"

"Sure, I've only got a short time anyway. Sorry for dragging you back here and then bailing. The Supe called a meeting for tonight that I didn't get the word on."

"That'll work out okay," Jake said. "I'm real busy back in St Michaels anyway."

Brian looked up as Ellie approached and asked what they wanted. Both ordered a draft. Jake sensed Brian was nervous.

"What's up?" Jake asked.

"I'm not sure how to say this, so I'm just going to throw it all out there. April disappeared—by the way, that's classified. She was supposed to fly a spare part out to the carrier, but their radar and others picked her up deviating off course. She ran into some UFO and actually engaged it."

"Engaged it? A UFO? Did she check with the ship's CIC first?"

"Nope, she just started launching missiles, then emptied her cannon."

Jake recalled April asking permission to engage. As usual, he thought, they were covering that up.

"What about a back-seater?" Jake asked. "Isn't that a two-person aircraft?"

"That was supposed to be Lieutenant Peter Piezynski, but we found out he's very much alive and was not on that flight."

"So what happened to April?"

"Not sure, but she ended up in the drink and the plane sank before they could get a rescue underway. She apparently went down with it. I'm sorry to have to tell you all this, Jake."

"If this Lieutenant wasn't her back-seater, who was? Or did she actually go alone?"

"The plane captain who helped her insisted it was the Lieutenant. At least he was the same general build. He didn't talk much."

"Maybe she was giving her boyfriend a ride?"

"Her squadron says that was not like her. The skipper said she didn't have a boyfriend."

"Wow, that's a shame," Jake said.

"Funny this happened right after you went down to see her, Jake. Did you pick up anything that would give us a clue?"

"Nope, we just talked about what happened ten years ago. I got out of there quickly before Rachel got jealous. Can't help you, Brian."

For a few seconds, Brian just stared over at Jake and said nothing. Then he got up.

"Sorry to have bothered you, Jake. I have that meeting tonight, so I have to go. I'd like to talk more. Can you meet me tomorrow at the house? Say oh seven hundred?"

Jake agreed and they shook hands, then Brian left. Ten seconds later, as Jake sat deep in thought, Ellie arrived with their beers.

"Sorry," Jake said. "Commander Hurst had to leave."

"No problem," she said. "Do you want me to leave both of them?"

His phone suddenly erupted with the words of *River of Time,* and he watched a hand, fingernails painted in a familiar shade, reach out and pick up one of the beers.

"I'll take one of those brewskies, if it's alright," Rachel said.

CHAPTER 40

RACHEL

Standing next to the booth, Rachel turned off her phone. The unorthodox ring tone on Jake's phone stopped.

"Sit," he said.

She smiled and slipped across from him. "Cheers." She lifted the mug toward Jake and then took a swig. "Surprised to see me?"

"Surprised, but thrilled," he said. "You're a sight for sore eyes."

"I saw Dan this afternoon before he left for Baltimore. He told me you were coming in to see Brian, and I gave him the business for interfering. Doesn't take a space alien to figure out he was matchmaking again. He insisted I was wrong in my thinking that you were planning to skedaddle again from this area. Before he left, he reminded me that you were an asshole, but a lovable asshole. I thought about that and finally came to the conclusion you do have some redeeming qualities. Most important was you're still here. You really never intended to leave me, did you?"

"I want to be with you for eternity."

"The corker was I got a phone call from April. We had a heart-to-heart. She was funny, said she had to run but we'd talk when she returned. She said something about leaving Earth."

"She now pilots that ship you saw come out of the water in Nags Head," Jake replied. "Please don't talk to anyone else about her call. She's supposed to be dead to Earth."

"Dead?"

"Long story. I'll tell you sometime."

"You mean she wasn't joking?"

He shook his head.

"How about you and her?"

"April is probably my best friend," he said. "Emphasis on friend." Jake felt a pinching on his chest that could have only come from Glim poking him with her little high heels. "Along with Glim," he added.

"That's what she told me. She said you two shared a bond, but it wasn't about love. She said you were one special guy, and I would be stupid to not forgive you. I've decided she's right." Rachel smiled and put her hand on his arm. "How about we drain a few brewskies then head back to my place? My toenails need to be repainted and my cat misses you."

"What about Snow's owner?" Jake asked. "Does she miss me?"

* * *

Two hours later, Jake was once again in Rachel's bed, interlocked with her so tightly he thought it might take dynamite to separate them.

"I'm sorry I was so damn scared you'd leave me, Jake," she muttered after temporarily lifting her lips off his. "I need you. I so missed you. And you're sure you're not with April now?"

"Other than the times I've told you about, I was never *with* April," he said. "If I was with April, would I be here? April and I are very close friends. That's all. Can you accept that?"

"Of course." She kissed him all the harder. "Will you take me back?" she asked.

"You were never gone," he said.

"Jake! Where are you?" Sheila's voice sounded exasperated as it echoed in his head.

"I'm in the arms of my true love."

"You're with Rachel?"

"Is there any other?"

"So that's why Glimmer ignored my initial mental transmissions. I swear both her and Ceellia need retraining after being with you. Look, that's great you're back together, but I need you here. We have to talk. Will you be back tomorrow?"

"I have to meet Brian early tomorrow morning. Is after that okay?"

"No problem. If possible, please bring Rachel and Snow with you."

* * *

Jake awoke to Snow lying next to him with Glimmer perched on her head. Just behind them was Rachel. She had apparently been talking to Glim.

"So Ceellia is now with April?" Rachel asked.

"Yep," Glim answered. "But don't worry. If you require a Distan, Sheila will find someone for you."

Moonglimmer, seeing Jake's eyes open, turned to him. "Jake, will it be a problem for you and Miss Rachel?"

"Will what be a problem?" he asked and yawned awake. "What time is it, Rache?"

"Us spending time with April so I can see Ceellia," Glim said.

"It's five," Rachel said, then looked to him for an answer to Glim's question, he assumed.

Jake's mind whirred as he considered the implications. Finally, he looked at Rachel, and then answered Glimmer. "I think Miss Rachel would not have a problem with us seeing Ceellia . . . and April."

Rachel smiled. "No, I don't. I hope April and I can be friends. I called in for a couple of days of vacation, Jake. Is that okay?"

"Great," he said. "Let's go visit Brian and then head to St Michaels. Oh, and everything you hear at Brian's is not to be repeated. Ever. Please, no mention of April. I'll explain on the way."

"You're the boss," Rachel replied. "Shower?"

* * *

Emily greeted them at the door in her robe. She apologized profusely for not being dressed and gave Jake the business for not telling her that Rachel would be with him. This time Rachel was casually dressed in a plain white shirt and a short, navy blue skirt. Emily got them both filled coffee mugs and told them she was going to get dressed.

"Can I go with you?" Rachel asked.

"Sure," Emily said.

Rachel retrieved her coffee cup and followed.

Jake watched as Emily started down the hall, then stopped when Rachel put a hand on her shoulder.

"Great to see you again, Em," Rachel said.

Emily turned and embraced Rachel, causing her to almost spill her coffee. "Thanks for coming, Rache. I've a lot to tell you, if that's okay?"

Rachel nodded and actually buzzed Emily's cheek with a girl-to-girl kiss.

They then continued down the hallway, passing Brian, who greeted Rachel and then joined Jake at the kitchen table. "You're back together," Brian said. "Great."

"What did you want to talk about, Brian?" Jake asked.

"Come on, Jake. What's going on? April did all of this after you went down to see her."

"I don't know what to tell you, Brian. I'm here talking to you, and April's apparently on the bottom of the Atlantic. Look, if she flew out with some guy in the back seat, wouldn't someone else have seen him?"

"That's what I reasoned. I even talked to her plane captain. He said he assumed it was Lieutenant Piezynski, but said he didn't talk much. However, that is the Lieutenant's style. Doesn't associate much with the enlisted. Turns out he was visiting his parents in Wilmington at the time, though, and he's very much alive. The Navy assumes she was giving some friend of hers a joyride for the carrier landing, but it's puzzling that she defied orders and engaged a UFO with him in the back seat. "

"It is puzzling she engaged a UFO without clearance. Not the girl I remembered. Is that how she crashed?" Jake asked innocently.

"Yeah, but that's kind of on the QT. I shouldn't have told you about the UFO. Please forget that part."

"What do you mean?"

"I misspoke yesterday. April offered to engage it, but the ship told her to stand by and they were going to send a couple of Hornets to check it all out. For some reason April fired at it and ended up in the drink. Helo pilot claimed initially that there was something under her Hornet when he was approaching. He also swore the canopy was open and there was no one in the plane. Just before he arrived on scene, he said it seemed like there was a swirl on the surface, like something big was diving down under the plane. And then there was a kind of whirlpool and the Hornet was sucked under. When he overflew the spot, he thought he saw a huge, metallic USO under the plane, but it disappeared below. Nothing could plunge under that fast, though. Something that size would displace an enormous amount of water, create huge swells, don't you think?"

"Hey," Jake said, wary of where Brian was taking this. He knew the admission of the UFO was no accident on Brian's part; he wanted to see Jake's reaction. "I'm curious as to why the helo jockey was just watching instead of trying to rescue her. Besides, I'm not a sub guy. What do I know of displacement and all that shit? Do you have a point to all of this, Brian?"

Brian looked at him and drummed his fingers silently on the table. "No, I guess not. Let me know if you think of anything you forgot to tell me, Jake. And, I think the helo pilot would have rescued someone if he saw them. I'm sorry about April, Jake. I know you were some kind of friends. Let's you, I and Dan get together real soon, okay? Not wait ten goddamn years."

"Sure. I'll be in St Michaels for a while, so I'll call you next time I'm up this way."

"Great. I have an early meeting, so gotta run." Brian got up. "Hope you and Rachel work things out. By the way, thanks to you and Rachel for the other night. Ever since the little party we had, Em's been like a new person, like a great load was lifted off of her. She told me that she's finally made friends with Rachel and Kyra. It meant a lot to her. She's really happy now."

* * *

Three hours later, they were in St Michaels. Glimmer took off out the window the moment they pulled in, eager to see her friends and get some flowers to eat. Gert greeted Rachel warmly and took Snow into the house.

Sheila also met them at the car and excitedly greeted Rachel with a hug and kiss, then put a finger to Jake's lips.

"Can I borrow Jake for a few minutes?" she asked Rachel.

"Sure, I'll join Gert in a cup of coffee."

Sheila waited until Rachel disappeared inside the house, then led Jake to the rock by the lake's shore.

Once she was in contact with her rock, she spoke. "Great to see you back with Rachel. Is this for good?"

"I hope so," he answered. "So, do I get the whole mission briefing now?"

Sheila smiled briefly, and then went on. "Yeah, Laura couldn't leave the station, so I get to tell you. I've already told you Laura and I thought this was a great area for the Distans, but it's just too dangerous. The Distans in Europe have managed to remain undetected by the Zantites, but we think the Zantites somehow suspect the existence of a group in this area and may someday try again. We have no choice but to close it down."

"Where will you move them?" Jake asked. "Back to England?"

"England? No, that's too dangerous. The Zantites might be watching this area. We don't want to tip them off to the larger group in England."

"So, is this the mission Laura and you have mentioned?" he asked.

She nodded. "It's my mission, and you're to help me, but I don't know what Laura told you. I'm not in on anything else she's planning."

"Tell me about moving the Distans. You sound like you're tasked to go to Mars or somewhere. Where to? Some little island?"

"I'm not contemplating a move to Mars—that's much too close. We need to move them much further than that."

"Further? And, you assume I'm going? What about Rachel?"

"She's included, of course. You and Rachel are to leave Earth with us and move to an untamed planet."

CHAPTER 41
MISSION REVEALED

"Before you say anything, Jake, let me finish. Our people have kept hidden the location of a pristine world unknown to the Zantites or any other warlike system. The planet is conducive to the Distans' special needs."

"Where the hell is this place? An astronomer I am not."

"A long way away," Sheila answered. "There's no Earth name for it. Even its star system is unknown to Earth. The star is directly behind a larger one that blocks its light from Earth. One planet there is suitable, and it's been decided by the Council of Flammeria that I and a few others will take about half of the Distans and go there. If the Distans agree, we'll build a new Keep and the rest will follow a short time later."

"You want me to . . ."

"Listen! The Distans have made their selections," Sheila continued, and her tone of admonishment caused him to keep quiet. "And I've made mine. I want you and Rachel to come with me, along with my pilot and the twenty Distans who have been initially chosen to go. That includes Moonglimmer and most of the younger ones."

"Does Rachel get a choice?"

"Of course. I only imagined she'd go where you go. You know she's more than welcome. I assumed you'd handle that."

"What about this place? Gert, Laura and all?" Jake asked.

"Therein lie some of the problems. It would be very suspicious if we all left Earth at the same time. Gert will stay here with the house for now. I had hoped your father would come to the house and live here, but I do see his point regarding returning to his home world. As far as Laura, she is stuck at the station until she can find a replacement for herself, and someone to take care of the house until we return. However, that was the funny thing. I didn't think she was even coming, but she hopes to join us a few months after we depart. However, it's very difficult getting Flammerians to come here to a backward, warlike planet."

Jake's mind shifted into overtime. "Well, with so much to be done, maybe it's time we trusted some true Earthlings to assist us, speed things along. You've seen how Rachel fit in and has kept the secret."

"You have someone else in mind?"

"Maybe. First, tell me more about the Distan move and new planet. What do any of us know about shaping some new world and building the Keep?"

"We don't need to go in with that knowledge. Remember that mission that Laura wanted you to undertake, and she ended up doing herself?"

"The one with Eternals?"

"Yes. She has contracted with them in the Aldebaran System. They specialize in tasks like setting up new worlds. In fact, they did this one. Several times. The leader, his name is Alex, and his crew will be in charge of the total expedition while we work with the Distans. The Distans asked to name the new world since they'd be living on it, but it was already named: Io27. I don't know very much about it, but Laura chuckled, 'It's every little Earth boy's dream world.'"

"How's that?"

"What Earth calls dinosaurs seem to thrive there."

"Isn't that dangerous?"

"No, every world has their hazards. Alex and his crew scoffed at the idea of lizards being a threat. After all, they faced a few here when he originally did Earth."

"What kind of bullshit are you feeding me, Sis? How could he have done Earth? That would make him a gazillion years old."

"He is. Eternal, remember? There's a lot about life and the universe you still need to learn, Jake. Now's not the time. However, regarding Io27's dinosaurs, there are two very large land masses there, and the large reptiles live on one while the Distans will be on the other. And, might I remind you, something as big as a dinosaur would not be looking to eat something as small as a Distan."

"We're not the size of Distans," Jake smirked.

"Well, I doubt we'll ever see one. We'll only be on the continent with the Distans from how Laura talked. How about for now, you talk to Rachel. I'm hoping she'll come with us."

As Jake tried to wrap his mind around all that, his eyes strayed across the river, and he saw Nora sitting dejectedly on the opposite shore. Curious, he looked to Sheila and said, "Something seems to be troubling little Nora."

Sheila glanced across the expanse of river and replied, "Yes, Reena told me her mother lost her job and they have to move. Reena'll miss playing with Nora and her mother."

"Nora's mother knows about the Distans?"

"Yeah, it turns out she knew all along. You might be right in saying we should trust more Earthlings. You just gave me a great idea. Let's take the boat over there."

It took them just a few minutes to scoot across the river in the motorboat. Sheila shut down the outboard and guided the boat to a gliding stop on the sandy shore.

"Hi, Nora," Jake said as he stepped out of the boat.

"We have to move, Jake," Nora confessed. "Just when I was getting to be good friends with Reena."

"I'm very sorry to hear that, Nora. I brought my sister, Sheila," he said.

Dressed in a green top that featured a dragonfly, and jean shorts, Nora surprised them both by doing a sort of curtsy to Sheila. "I'm very glad to meet you at last," Nora said. "Thanks for letting Reena play with me."

"Reena didn't need my permission to play with you," Sheila replied. "She's able to choose her own friends. She just needed to follow the rules. I'm glad to meet you though. I came to find out if I could help you and your mom in some way. Is she home?"

"I heard voices, Nora. Who are you talking with?" Kara asked as she slipped through the brush behind their home and onto the beach. "Oh," she exclaimed on seeing Jake. "You again."

"I brought my sister. This is Sheila." He then turned the introduction around, "Sheila, Kara."

Kara held out an open hand to shake, but Sheila ignored it, choosing to first embrace Kara, then Nora. "I'm very happy to at long last meet my neighbors," Sheila smiled.

"Not for long," Kara said. "I lost my job, so I have to give up this house. I imagine Reena already told you that."

"Yes, she did, and I wanted to thank you for keeping our secret. But maybe you won't have to move very far," Sheila said. "What is it you do?"

"You mean my job?" Kara replied.

Sheila nodded.

"I'm a… that is, I was an interior decorator."

"My brother and I are leaving on a long trip. I'm looking for someone to housesit and take care of the gardens. Many of the Distans are going with, including Reena, but about half will remain here, so Nora would still have some playmates. We might be gone for up to a year. Maybe longer. We were hoping you might be interested, and perhaps you could even give some design tips. There would be some additional duties, too. Are you busy tomorrow evening?" Sheila asked.

"No," Kara answered.

"Can you come over to our house then? I'll tell you what I expect and you can see the house and decide for yourself. Think about it, and we'll look forward to seeing you at five."

Kara smiled and nodded, still looking a bit surprised at the sudden offer, while Nora did a little dance on the beach.

With that, Sheila climbed into the boat and Jake followed. They both waved, and then Sheila started the motor and drove back to the opposite shore.

"Are you sure about this?" Jake asked.

"You said I should trust people more, so that's what I will do. You thought them trustworthy to keep Reena a secret didn't you?"

"I thought only Nora knew of Reena, not Kara."

"I found that doubtful," Sheila said. "That's why I had Floressa scan Kara. She and I are a lot alike . . . In a number of ways. But even if it were true that only Nora knew, I'd be willing to guess like daughter, like mother."

By this time the two were by the scatterer. Sheila hopped on it and pressed her feet to its surface. When Jake glanced toward the house, he saw Rachel hurrying toward them.

"Glimmer said you wish to speak to me," Rachel said when she reached the rock.

"Are you comfortable with things now?" Sheila asked.

"Yeah, I was an ass to think Jake would abandon me. I bonded with Glimmer last night while Jake slept. I wish she was my Distan. I am sorry that Ceellia was to be mine, but now she's April's."

"That turned out to be a match made in heaven," Sheila laughed. "Those two little blondes belong together. I think April longed to have someone to lavish with her love. Because she traveled a lot, she couldn't have a pet. Ceellia is a terrible tease and flirt, but fiercely loyal. The two of them bonded quickly, and now I'd say they're inseparable. But don't worry, if need be, I think I have just the Distan for you. She's in training right now, but will be ready to accompany you in a week or two."

"Hi, Mr. Jake," came a voice from directly behind them.

"Hello, Reena," he answered. Reena looked at Rachel. Jake had thought that she would be the perfect one for Rachel. Their hair color was similar, and Reena was not as outgoing and mischievous as Glimmer or Ceellia.

"Hello, Miss Rachel," Reena said tentatively, and smiled at Rachel. Jake could tell from the look on Rachel's face that she knew Reena was the one.

"Are we going to be together?" Rachel asked.

"Yes," Reena nodded. "Is that okay? I know I'm kind of small but . . ."

"You're perfect," Rachel said. "Absolutely perfect."

"Scarce, Reena," Sheila said, and the little Distan flew off toward the center of the garden. "We have things to discuss," Sheila added. "Slip your shoes off, Rachel, and come up on this rock. You're one of us now. You remember how I told you to . . ."

"Keep my feet in contact with the rock," Rachel said. "Yes, I know."

When Rachel was in position, Sheila looked over at Jake. "Okay, Jake, you take over. I've got a zillion problems to solve before the move."

"Move? Where are you moving?" Rachel asked.

"Jake will explain. I'll leave you two to talk," Sheila answered, and slid off the rock. "Remember, feet in contact, Rachel."

Jake had been wondering how he was expected to break the news to Rachel, and it was now obvious that Sheila was aware of his indecisiveness. So she had set this up. "Your thought that the Distans would be the reason for me leaving was not far from the truth," he said.

Rachel's multicolored eyes fastened on his blue-grays. "What are you saying, Jake? You're leaving me?"

"No. What neither of us realized was there was a simple solution to that—you can leave too. At least I hope you will. I want you to go with . . . us . . . me."

"You want us to go where?" Rachel seemed barely able to get the words out.

"Sheila wants us to help her move the Distan colony. It's no longer safe for them here."

"Move them where?"

"To a planet in another star system." Jake said it with trepidation. Again, he expected a reaction where Rachel would break down in tears and beg him not to go. But, he was wrong again.

"Of course I'll go with you. When do we leave? Will we ever come back? Who else is going?"

"We don't leave for a while yet, and we should return in about a year or so if all goes well. You don't visit your relatives that often, so it'll be perfect. Sheila already has a cover story where you take a job on some small, difficult-to-get-to island, so no one would plan to just drop in on you. It'll just be the four of us, the Distans, and an exploration group from another star system. My sister Laura will join us later, I think."

"Four? Who's the fourth?" Rachel asked.

"That would be me." They both looked over in the direction of the voice. Walking toward them from behind the trees was April, with Ceellia perched on her shoulder. "I fly the ship."

"We," Ceellia interrupted. "We fly the ship."

"That's what I meant," April said, with a can-you-believe-this expression.

"Come up here and sit by me, April," Rachel commanded.

Eyeing Rachel, April at first hesitated to do what she suggested.

Sheila's voice, directed by Ceellia, rang in their heads. *"April is now my pilot. She needs to come with us, as she'll be the one to transport the remaining Distans as well as bring us supplies. April has no interest in pursuing any kind of romantic relationship with Jake. However, I need no distractions on this voyage. Rachel, you need to accept April and cast painful memories aside. Otherwise I need to rethink my crew. April, however, is not negotiable."*

"I'm sure she meant to include me as a pilot," Ceellia added.

"Shush, my pet," April replied. "Do you remember what I said about being a snob?"

Ceellia bowed her head and crossed her tiny legs. Sparkling yellow eyes peered through her hair. "Yes, ma'am. I'm sorry, but you said I was your co-pilot."

"Silent co-pilot," April laughed.

For a moment all was quiet, then Rachel reached one hand down and pulled April to her, enfolding her in a tight embrace. "I always knew that we were going to be great friends."

Epilogue

Irene

Sheila puttered around the outside table that Gert had loaded with enough snacks to feed Patton's Fifth Army and then some. Besides cookies, cakes, several dishes of candy, and bowls of fruit and veggies, there were pitchers of iced tea, lemonade, hot water for tea and freshly brewed coffee.

"Don't forget," Gert whispered loudly to Sheila. "You can offer them wine or beer."

"Beer?" Sheila asked. "Since when do we have beer?"

"I bought it," Rachel said. "It was mainly for Jake and me. Is that okay? Anyone can have some."

"And you call me a prude, Sis," Jake said.

In answer, Sheila stuck her tongue out at him and went into the house.

A white Subaru Forester pulled into the drive, drove up to the wisteria turn-around, and Kara and Nora exited the vehicle and walked over. The sun had just faded behind the Miles, and lightning bugs dotted the gardens with pinpricks of light.

Jake introduced the prospective house sitters to Rachel and Gert.

They all looked up when the door opened and Sheila walked out. Carrying a bottle of wine, she came down to the table and then walked straight over to Kara.

"Hi, Kara," she said. "I forgot to mention to you yesterday that I am 'the redhead who sits on the rock.'"

Kara looked over at Jake. "You told her I said that? Do you have any common sense?"

"I see we agree," Sheila said. "My brother is sans decorum. I'd give him to you, but Rachel here already has a claim on him."

"It's tenuous at best," Rachel laughed. "I'm entertaining offers."

"Well, I'll pass on the big lug," Kara laughed. Kara glanced over at Sheila, then continued. "He's not my type. I'd rather have . . . some of that wine!"

Sheila took to Kara quickly. Jake soon saw they were alike in many ways. While Gert plied Nora with cookies and juice, Sheila kicked off her shoes and poured wine for Kara and herself.

"Sheila needs a close girl pal," Rachel said as she hopped into Jake's lap and wrapped her arms around him. "For so many years she's had to carry on alone. She was quite lonely, you know."

"How do you know all of that? Are you saying she needs a guy?" Jake asked.

"Not quite, clueless. We talked a lot while you were out saving the world with April. Besides, Sheila told me she could never take an Earth guy into her trust. Too much is at stake. Thanks to you, she met me, and now feels that Earth women are trustworthy. Her meeting Kara yesterday was enough to convince her that she and Nora would hold the secret."

Jake ignored her 'clueless' comment.

Twenty feet from them, Kara and Sheila giggled together over some joke. Probably at Jake's expense. Kara brushed her brown curls off one eye at the precise moment that Sheila pushed away her reddish-brown ones and, noticing themselves, they chuckled over the timing.

Kara was in many ways similar in appearance to Sheila. Both were small, attractive women. Their hair was curly and shoulder length. When they talked, their eyes seemed to glitter. Jake looked down, under the table where they sat and saw Kara, like Sheila, had abandoned her shoes. When he looked back up, Sheila's eyes were on him. With a flip of her hair, she motioned him over.

"Duty calls," he whispered in Rachel's ear.

"That's okay," she said. "I wanted to talk to April anyway. She's still inside getting dressed."

When Jake got to their table, Kara pushed out a chair with her bare foot. He sat down and looked to Sheila.

"Okay, Jake," she said. "I want both you and Kara to hear this." Sheila shifted her attention to Kara. "Jake did me a big favor when he met you and your daughter."

"He did us a favor, too," Kara added. "Especially me." Her eyes remained on Sheila.

"I told you yesterday that Jake and I will be leaving soon, and we might be gone for a long time."

"Yes, I've been thinking about that and your offer. Just what am I getting into here?" Kara asked. "This is on the up and up, isn't it?"

"Of course," Jake said.

"We need to move this party down by the river," Sheila said.

Both Sheila and Kara took their glasses of wine, and Sheila led the way to the river. Once they were down by the rock, Sheila scooted up and left a spot on the side of her.

"I need you up here, Kara," she said. "There's something you need to know concerning Jake and me."

While Jake stood at the base of the rock, Kara crawled up beside Sheila. Sheila put her arm around Kara's shoulders and drew her up close. After Sheila instructed her to keep her feet in contact with the stone, the two of them scooted even closer to each other. Sheila explained the off-world origins of her and Jake. Having knowledge of the Distans, Kara was easy to convince. As he listened, Jake was suddenly taken aback by a mental message from . . . Rachel!

"Jake," she said. *"Isn't it great? April has invited us to vacation with her at her new house in Avon."*

That "vacation" would last three months, during which time Glimmer and Ceellia, along with Reena, would enjoy a carefree time on the beach, while April and Rachel bonded. Sheila and Floressa, when Sheila wasn't helping Kara at the house, also spent time with them. Frequently, Kara and Nora visited too. Sheila introduced Nora to Shalleena, who was to be her new playmate, since Reena was going with Rachel.

This lax period was interrupted when, the day before the scheduled departure, Laura came and told Jake and Sheila to "Come walk with me." When they were maybe a hundred yards down the beach, Laura stopped and looked to Sheila and Jake.

"I'm afraid I haven't been entirely honest with you both about our past," Laura explained. "Before we leave tomorrow, you must know the whole truth."

"Does this concern some dreams I've been having?" Jake asked.

"This is scary, Jake," said Sheila. "I've had weird dreams too. It's like I was living a life not my own."

"What could be so—" He stopped when Laura held up her hand.

"We are not who we've always thought we were," Laura explained. "Most of my current memories returned weeks ago, but you two still have a block on your memories that will be removed soon. Chandelle told you some of it, Jake, when you were at the station. You should be recalling that now."

That memory of the little Distan's revelation in Laura's office returned to Jake. He was working for the railroad and had met an Eternal. At the time, Jake was already working with other Eternals, and one was his . . . *girlfriend*. And Jake was to be their . . . leader.

Chandelle appeared out of Laura's hair, and her tiny voice interrupted his thoughts. "Yes, you are in charge of part of the quest to find Zeus. The Eternal you found, Oceanus, is leading this quest we are to undertake. It'll start after you help complete the Distans' move."

Laura looked to Sheila. "When you brought Jake out to the station, Chandelle confessed to me that the Distans had much more in the way of skills than we ever thought possible. She told me that the three of us all had hidden memories of other existences, and we had all been brought together for a reason. Later, when April was aboard the ship, she found that April, too, was part of the plan.

"Actually, the four of us are Eternals," Laura continued to Sheila. "Both of you, me and… April. All of us were shielded from our true selves so that we could be brought together secretly to aid in this long-ago planned mission."

"Who exactly am I, then?" Sheila asked. "Don't Eternals remember past lives? And what about Rachel?"

"We'll all discover our Eternal names and recall our past existences when the block that was imposed for secrecy is removed," Laura said. "Rachel is who you think she is, a normal human. As are Kara and her daughter. Their role in our plan has not changed, although they are considering having Kara and Nora join us as caretakers for the Distans in the future. After the Distans are settled, the four of us have additional roles to perform in a quest planned many eons ago. We, and possibly Rachel, will assist the other group of Eternals. It will all be explained later when we reach Io27."

"Is that why my childhood memories seem incomplete?" Jake asked.

"Yes, Chandelle explained this all to you… you'll remember that soon. All of our current childhood memories are planted ones to fit their needs. That's why they appear only as still images. Your memories, from the time you entered the Naval Academy on, are real. As are yours, Sheila, from the time you took over the care of the Distans."

"Wait. You and Sheila. Is it true that we're really not actually related?" He could barely get the words out.

"Yes, it is. Neither Sheila or I are real sisters to you, Jake," said Laura. "Doesn't change my feelings for you, though, and I think I speak for Sheila."

"Hell," Sheila said loudly. "Sheila speaks for Sheila, and she agrees."

"So don't get any amorous ideas, Jake. I still think making out with you would be akin to doing so with a brother."

"Ditto, Jake," Sheila added. "Don't ruin things with Rachel. Besides, I think you know that my preferences are different. "

"I was told," Laura continued, "one of the other crew was once your sister in a previous life. She will reveal that to you at the right time."

"How did you—" he stammered.

"Find this out?" Laura interrupted. "The mission you refused to go on . . . to Aldebaran? If you had gone, you would have known, since you're to be initially in charge of our part of this. Part of the plan was explained to me then by Alex, who is the leader. It was covered over in my memories until two days ago when I met with him and Heike, who is one of Alex's crew. I won't tell you who she is. I think she should do that if she wishes."

"This is crazy. I've always said Eternals are a strange lot," Jake replied. "Now Chandelle's saying I am one."

"Yes. Anyway, that meeting with them brought the memory of who we were to the forefront. I told April yesterday, and now you. However, after our walk, when we return to the house, you will temporarily forget this until you meet Irene, the hopper pilot, tomorrow. Meeting her will bring the memory of who you are back, but you will speak of it to no one until we are on our way to Io27. At that time, you may reveal to Rachel who we really are."

"Irene? Why does that name sound familiar?" Jake said aloud.

Laura was quiet.

"And April?" asked Jake. "Does she know who she actually is?"

"April will recall who she is at the right time. She'll be assisting the pilot of the planet hopper when we all get picked up tomorrow. The planet hopper will take us first to one of the moons of Mars, where you'll wait for the other crew. When they come, we'll all be taken to the *Flammerian Dawn*, your ship which is currently orbiting on the far side of Mars. After you leave, I, of course, will return here."

"By the way, Jake." Sheila smiled at him. "My returning memories tell me none of the other crew or us really need Distans to communicate mentally. However, Rachel will need hers to talk to us over a distance. There are no phones in more advanced places."

* * *

The next morning, after a flurry of goodbyes to Gert, Nora and Kara, Jake, Sheila, Rachel and April, along with Laura and the first group of Distans, boarded a saucer-shaped craft that was being flown by a girl that Laura introduced to Jake as Irene.

Something about Irene filled him with déjà vu, but he couldn't quite place that beautiful face.

Laura, sensing Jake's intense interest in Irene, poked him. "Irene's an Eternal, Jake. I don't think she appreciates that you're staring at her."

"No, it's okay," said Irene. "Jake and I probably met in another life. He'll recall his previous lives when his memories are restored."

"No, we did more than just casually meet in some long-ago existence," said Jake. "I don't need to wait for old memories to resurface. You are . . . we were—"

"Strangers. I think you have me confused with someone," Irene interrupted with a glance to Rachel. "Maybe you once dreamt of someone that looks like me."

"No. I'm sure we've met—"

"Leave the girl be, Jake," Laura interrupted. "She's an off-worlder. How could you know her?"

"We need to get him off the subject of me," Irene mentally sent to Laura. *"I told Alex this was a bad idea. It's too fresh."*

"I don't understand," Laura sent back. *"What's too—?"*

"Earlier in this life of ours, Jake and I were living together for many years. In fact, we've lived many lives together. He's always been able to sense my presence, and I his."

Hearing an intake of breath from April, and stunned herself by this news, Laura turned to April to deflect her questions. "You're co-pilot on this shuttle," she informed her. "After you drop us off on Mars's moon, Phobos, you have another pickup to make. Irene will fill you in."

Irene seemed to realize that she had upset them both with her revelation. She turned to April and said, "Hey, April. That was another life. But, I should tell you that the other group also has an April in their crew. One of you might have to go by another name. Maybe Merope, your Eternal one. That's the name I knew you by. Whoops, I probably shouldn't have told you that. Belay that. You and she can talk about that on the flight after we pick her up."

"Merope? That's my Eternal name?" said April. "It just seemed a natural fit when you said that. You know, Irene, since you seem to know what is going on, lately I've been having this reoccurring dream where I have lots of sisters, except . . ."

"Except what?"

"We all have light blue skin."

354

"That makes sense. You're a Pleiad. All of you have blue skin," Irene replied.

"Pleiad? What's a Pleiad?"

"Someone who originated in one of the worlds in the Pleiades, of course."

"Am I . . . I'm not from Atlantis?" April asked.

"I didn't say that." Irene smiled. "Look, I wasn't supposed to tell you or the others your Eternal name, so until you are on your way to Io27, please forget it."

"You seem to know all of our Eternal names," said Laura. "Who is Sheila?"

Irene shrugged, then shook her head, giving in to the questions. "Okay, what the hell. She's my Eternal sister, Clotho. Don't tell Alex I told you. No more though."

Irene looked out over the group. "April and I will drop you off at the Phobos base, then fly the Distans to the ship orbiting the other side of the planet. Tomorrow April and I will return to Earth early to pick up the other group. After we have them, we'll return for you and fly you all out to the ship later tomorrow."

"What about me?" asked Rachel. "I feel like I don't belong."

"You stick with your man, Rachel. Don't let all this Eternal talk upset you. You are very much a part of this group. Laura, I know you're not going to Io27 yet, but want to make the trip to the Phobos base. I'll pick you up after I take them to the ship tomorrow and fly you back to Earth."

"Thank you, Irene, that's so sweet of you," Laura replied.

"What happens after we get to the big ship?" Sheila asked.

"Why, then April is flying you, the other crew and the Distans to Io27. Good luck in your journey."

Michael Kott

The Temporary End

Acknowledgments & Author Notes

Thanks to Zora Knauf for doing her usual incredible job of formatting both printed and E-Book. My appreciation to Fiona Jayde of Fiona Jayde Media for her inspired cover ideas and design.

My profound gratitude to Moonglimmer's beta readers, Lesley-Ann Smith, Tricia Hayner Zora Knauf, and Zola Copeland-Monehen. They all gave fantastic feedback, pointing out the myriad of things that I needed to fix. Zola even read it twice, the second time to compare it against LifeShift. No one deserves more praise than my hardworking editor, Calee Allen, without who this would have never have reached a finished stage and been integrated with LifeShift. Calee was untiring in her advice and in cleaning up my missives.

The events of Moonglimmer, like LifeShift, are a work of fiction. Names, characters, places and incidents are the products of the author's imagination or are used fictitiously and are not to be construed as real. Any resemblance to actual events, locales, organizations, or persons, living or dead, is entirely coincidental.

Like it's forerunner, LifeShift, this novel has undergone many changes from the original that was started back in the very early 2000's. The two were gradually integrated together and will culminate in currently being written, Io 27.

While this is a work of fiction and uses characters of various mythologies, it also incorporates known world mysteries. Many Native Americans, when asked where they originally came from, pointed to the Pleiades. Many other cultures and civilizations have claimed their ancestors came from up there, while pointing to the stars.

While I believe that we evolve to some degree I do not buy into spontaneous life. How incredibly arrogant we are to think that this small world is where life actually started.

Underwater submerged objects (USO's), like unidentified flying objects (UFO's) are a known phenomenon and are constantly being reported. While the existence of Lemuria is denied by so called experts, all civilizations in that area speak of its prior existence in the period described in this novel.

Hopefully, someday, the truth of all these mysteries will be known.

Io 27

A SEQUEL TO *LIFESHIFT* AND *MOONGLIMMER.* COMING SOON...

A little background:

The formation of Alex and his team of Eternals was covered in the first novel, *LifeShift*. A secret second team, led by Jake, was uncovered in the novel *Moonglimmer*. *Io 27* will bring both teams together in the search for Zeus and the conclusion of this series. It may be one or two novels. The ending of the novels *LifeShift* and *Moonglimmer* both culminated in the year 2025 with the groups being transported to the ship that would take them to the huge world, *Io 27*. The giant, Earth-like planet consists of two main continents, Atlantis and Lemuria, connected by a land bridge named Hyperborea and surrounded by deep oceans.

Following the meeting of the two groups of Eternals, *Io 27* describes their introduction to some of the lifeforms of the new world and the location for the site of the new Keep. A lifeform identical physically to the Distans, Tremblemites, are quickly discovered, and the two species decide to live together. The Eternals, after enlarging the Tremblemites living area to accommodate the Distans, then proceeded with their own agenda, the search for some trace of Zeus. When an underground room near, what is now known as the Keep, is accidently discovered, the Eternals divide into two groups, one led by Circe and the other by Celaeno, with Alex in overall command. Circe's team is to explore the underground discovery while Celaeno leads her team to the huge unexplored land area to the north.

The novel is written from multiple points of view, but mainly from Ceellia and Moonglimmer's, the Distans who accompany each exploratory *group with the responsibility of recording their findings. Ceellia and Moonglimmer were fairy-like Distans that had been transported to Io 27 from the planet Earth to set up a new home. Upon arrival on Io 27, they had quickly discovered that what appeared to be long-lost cousins already lived there. They were known as Tremblemites.*

Both species stood about six to seven inches tall, and had human-like bodies. The females, who had hair, skin color and a light coating of fur, each in different shades of the rainbow, possessed the unique ability to send mental communications across great distances. Due to the planet's huge size, Tremblemites had evolved with the ability to send mental messages across much greater distances than the Distans could. In case long range backup communications were needed, Lennore was attached to Circe's team and Sissel to Celaeno's. Circe and Nona, who was Alex's assistant, had expressed the opinion that Tremblemites and Distans were actually of the same species. The unknown was how had the Tremblemites gotten to Io 27?

At this point in the novel, Circe has discovered that Alex was in possession of some sort of map that he had kept a secret. Below is an excerpt from Io 27.

THE MAPS
CEELLIA

Underground Atlantis Group Mission Recorder

Still rattled by the exchange of words between Alex and Circe, Ceellia flitted about the meeting area. Circe, who had left the room, was obviously gone to mentally communicate with Celaeno. Now, Ceellia reasoned, *the cat's out of the bag.* That's what Circe was fond of saying when she exposed Alex's faults. One of the reasons Ceellia liked Circe so much was she, like Jake, had adopted so many of the quaint Earth people's sayings. Ceellia didn't need Glim to tell her that Celaeno would be furious that Alex did not share knowledge of the old map with their group. Circe's admonishment had indicated that Celaeno's group might have use for that map, if they could figure out what it represented.

Circe returned to the meeting area, so Ceellia pretended to restart the mission recorder.

"Switch on," she said softly.

"Look, I didn't even know if the map was accurate," Alex pleaded to Circe, drawing Ceellia's attention back to their argument. "It's just a layout of blocks, what look like rooms or something."

As the two Eternals resumed their arguing, Ceellia wondered what she and Lennore were supposed to do now. Maybe she should contact Glim.

* * *

At that moment, Glimmer was near the end of Ceellia's range, Lennore would soon have to take over group communications on their end, while Sissel, the Tremblemite who was with Glimmer and Celaeno's party, handled theirs. Distans provided short-range messaging between the Earth humans, up to five thousand miles, while Tremblemites provided planet-wide long-range communications.

It frightened Ceellia that she would no longer be able to mentally communicate with Glim directly. However, before they started this exploration of the planet, the Distans and Tremblemites had their own meeting and pledged solidarity. The Tremblemites vowed to assist the Distans in learning to increase their range.

* * *

"But you said it accurately showed the Tremblemites hill which is now the Keep." Circe fired the words at Alex, once again pulling Ceellia's attention to their conversation. "Plus the Eirenians have verified everything south of the Eirene Mountains was depicted accurately. Where did you expect to find the inaccuracy?"

"The Eirenians only verified the shape of the planetary map. They had no idea of what the squares represented or what all those additional detail-like maps are. Besides, I'm in charge and I made the decision," Alex said loudly. "Cope with it."

Oh, boy, Ceellia thought, *that bellowing won't sit well with Circe or Celaeno.*

"Celaeno is completely in her rights now to go it alone, you . . . bozo!" Circe jabbed a finger in his direction as she yelled at Alex, then noticed Ceellia fluttering about and frowned. "Are you recording this, Ceellia?"

She nodded, afraid to speak, but thought, *What am I to do?*

"You are?" Circe chuckled, which calmed Ceellia somewhat. Circe's eyes flashed showing Ceellia the stunning, Eternal ice blue shade she rarely shared with anyone. "And why do you have that deer-caught-in-the-headlights look?"

Deer in the headlights? Ceellia hadn't heard that one before, but guessed it was because of her blank stare. Ceellia adored both Circe and Alex, so she was petrified of offending either of them.

"I didn't hear you say, 'switch on,' like I told you so the recorder picks it up." Circe blinked as she said it, flashing those ice blue beauties like beacons, so Ceellia relaxed. Circe always knew when Ceellia needed TLC, and used her Eternal eyes to show she was joking with her. Silently, Circe sent a mental message to the little Distan, *"Remember, Alex doesn't know the recorder is always on."*

"Oh, yeah," Ceellia admitted. *"But I did say it. Kind of softly."*

"Let's hear it," Circe chuckled.

"Switch on," Ceellia said loudly.

Circe shook her head and laughed at the little Distan. Then she moved closer and whispered, "On my shoulder, Blondie. Let's go over in that corner."

"Did I do something wrong?" Ceellia asked "Do you think it didn't record? I can summarize what just happened. Then we'll be sure it's all on the recorder." While Ceellia feigned being upset, she knew that in actuality the recorder worked all the time.

"No, squirt." Circe then whispered close to her ear. "It's all recorded. You don't really have to say, 'switch on,' It's for show. You know that Alex would have a cow if he knew I rigged the recorder to always record. When you say 'switch on', it zeroes in on whatever you look at. If someone talks, the recorder automagically zeroes in on them."

"Does Glimmer know that too?" She asked it but Ceellia already knew the answer. Unknown to the Eternals, she and Glimmer could work the recorder to start, stop, or play back. They could also erase things. Neither Circe, nor the other Eternals, of course, had any inkling the Distans had these abilities.

"Jake and Sheila know, so I'm sure they'll pass it on to your little girl pal. Other than you two, no one knows that only Eternals can play back or edit. And only Alex, Celaeno and I can stop it. Don't tell anyone that, though."

"Thanks, Circe. You always make me feel better." Ceellia smiled and thought to herself, *If you only knew. . .*

"Alex told me to start the dictation with a description of who we all are, but I never got around to it. Can you & that little redhead dictate who we are and what our mission is?"

"You mean about our teams being composed of all different species? Eternals, Flammerian and Earth Humans, Distans, Tremblemites and Eirenians?"

"Start with who you Distans are. You do know that the Flammerians are really Eternals, don't you?" Circe asked.

Ceellia nodded.

"Do yours now while we're getting ready to start. You don't need to get all this detail of me setting Alex straight. When you pass recording to Celaeno's team tell Moonglimmer to do the same thing."

Circe then advanced toward Alex, yelling, "I told you to respect the Eternal creed. Share everything you know or else risk failure!"

* * *

"Switch on," Ceellia repeated for show as Circe left.

Then, heeding Circe's suggestion, Ceellia beamed her background into the recorder.

"My name is Ceellia, and I'm a teenaged Distan. To be exact, I'm seventeen years old and humanoid in shape, except I'm only seven inches tall. A thin coat of soft yellow fur covers all of me except for my face, hands and feet. Well, maybe a few other kind of private places too. The color of my fur—Circe calls it peach fuzz—matches my long, yellow hair and my yellow eyes. That's yellow, not blonde. And, I have wings and can fly. Very fast. Plus I can read human thoughts and transmit what they say to another Distan, Tremblemite or a nearby human that's been trained to receive my mental communications. That's why I'm part of the team. I transmit for the non-Eternals, or the non-trained—that's Jake and Sheila on the other team, and the Eternal that's untrained. Her name is April and she's the one I'm actually assigned to.

"April drives the spaceship we came here on. Right now, April and the Earth girl, Miss Rachel, are not with us, having returned to Aldebaran for supplies. I don't like Miss Rachel, who is Jake's girlfriend, but she's Glimmer's responsibility. Jake says Miss Rachel and I just 'got off on the wrong foot,' whatever that means. However, I'll probably never accept her. Jake could do better, and while he denies it, I saw him flirting with the Eternal named Irene who took us from Earth to the huge ship that brought us here. Circe told me she's her sister, and Jake and Irene had history, but would not elaborate. I liked Irene a lot even though I never spoke directly to her. Circe says she may return with April. I hope so.

"April loaned me to Circe. Circe, Iris, and Celaeno, along with Miss Nona and Miss Apate, who arrived just before we left and stayed at the home base with Iris, are all goddesses. I mean, actual goddesses. The other Eternals I know on this mission are April and Jake's sisters, Laura and Sheila. Miss Rachel is human, and even though I don't like Miss Rachel, I tolerate her for Jake. Laura is to join us later. Perhaps she'll return with April."

Ceellia frowned and stopped recording. *Oh my, maybe Sheila's right, I am a Gossip Gertie. I shouldn't have put all that in the log about Miss Rachel and Irene. What if Jake finds out I said that?* Ceellia then went back and erased everything from she didn't like Miss Rachel on to where she had ended it.

When Circe gestured for Ceellia to join her, Ceellia dictated, *"Circe just gave me the 'Come here,' signal, so I'll fly close to her and continue the background stuff later."*

"Switch on," Ceellia said with a wink at Circe.

"Okay, squirt, wrap it up. Once we drop into the underground, we might lose communications with the surface. We go in about ten minutes. While we may not be able to send messages from underground, the recorder will be working".

Ceellia fretted over that news for about two minutes then began an urgent mental appeal for Moonglimmer.

Surface Atlantis Group Mission Recorder

Five thousand miles to the north, at the extreme limit of Ceellia's range, Moonglimmer had just reboarded the shuttle which had landed in a forest clearing at the base of the Mountains. They were eventually bound for the Hyperborea land bridge, but were right now awaiting Celaeno's orders.

She instantly answered Ceellia's call, knowing by her voice she was distressed.

"Why do humans seem to relish keeping secrets from each other, Glim? We're headed underground and now I don't know if I can do this. I wish you were here with me." Ceellia's thoughts radiated out in all directions across the surface of the planet and into the space above it.

"What's happening, Ceel? Why are you sad?" the small Distan asked in a return mental message.

"Arguments make me uneasy, Glim. This time the trouble started, as I knew it would, when that Mr. Alex admitted to Circe he had an old planetary map."

"He has a map? This is all on the mission recorder, right?" Moonglimmer asked. "I can just replay it so you don't have to relive it by telling me."

"Yes, just go back one hour. Remember, don't let any of the Eternals know we can play it back. They don't know—"

"The change. I know. Sissel told me she doubts you'll be able to reach us from underground but contact me when you can. And stop fretting, you'll do fine. You always do."

"Thanks, Glim. Oh, and Circe wants you to dictate backgrounds of your team members. Mine's already in there. I didn't get a chance to do the rest of my team. You be careful."

"I will, you too. Good luck," Moonglimmer then nudged the recorder to play back from one hour ago.

"*Alex, how could you be so ignorant?*" Circe's voice came into Glimmer's head.

Glimmer listened as Circe continued to loudly scold Alex, the overall mission leader.

"*Why didn't you share the map with Celaeno and her team?*" Circe practically screamed it at him. "*What's so damn secret?*"

As she listened, Glimmer could tell by Circe's voice that the normally calm Eternal was livid. Her anger must mean this map was important, but how did it affect their search?

Celaeno, Glimmer's team leader, was a close friend of Circe, so Glimmer surmised that Circe would send Celaeno a mentalgram regarding this 'map' development before they left. Circe and Celaeno were not only the team leaders, but also Eternals. So they didn't need Distans or Tremblemites to pick up and transmit their thoughts.

Glim paused the recorder and looked over to where Celaeno sat in the pilot's seat and, sure enough, saw anger building on her face. Circe had apparently wasted no time filling her in, as both female Eternals resented Alex's penchant for secrecy.

Having heard all she needed to, Glimmer stopped the playback and mentally nudged Ceellia.

* * *

"Glim," Ceellia's voice rang in her brain as the recording ended. "Maybe you should tell Jake. Oh, what to do?"

"Settle, Ceel." Glimmer's voice came back. "Circe just told Celaeno so let's see how this plays out. I reset the recorder back to where you left off. Restart it whenever you need to. Act like nothing is amiss."